THE
WALL OF
WINNIPEG
and Me

THE
WALL OF
WINNIPEG
and Me

a novel

MARIANA ZAPATA

AVON

An Imprint of HarperCollinsPublishers

THE WALL OF WINNIPEG AND ME. Copyright © 2016 by Mariana Zapata. Bonus Epilogue Copyright © 2023 by Mariana Zapata. All rights reserved. Printed in the United States of America. No part of this book may be used or reproduced in any manner whatsoever without written permission except in the case of brief quotations embodied in critical articles and reviews. For information, address HarperCollins Publishers, 195 Broadway, New York, NY 10007.

HarperCollins books may be purchased for educational, business, or sales promotional use. For information, please email the Special Markets Department at SPsales@harpercollins.com.

Originally published as *The Wall of Winnipeg and Me* in USA in 2016 by Mariana Zapata.

Designed by Renata DiBiase

Library of Congress Cataloging-in-Publication Data has been applied for.

ISBN 978-0-06-332585-2

24 25 26 27 28 LBC 6 5 4 3 2

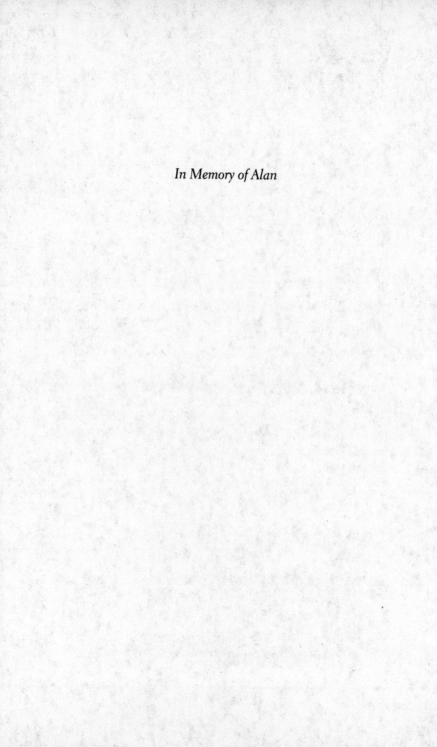

In Memory of Alan

ONE

I was going to murder his ass.

One day.

One day long after I quit, so no one would suspect me.

"Aiden," I grumbled, even though I knew better. Grumbling only got me the look—that infamous, condescending expression that had gotten Aiden into more than one fight in the past. Or so I'd been told. When the edges of his mouth turned down, got tight, and his brown eyes went heavy lidded, all it made me want to do was stick my finger up his nose. It's what my mom used to do to us when we were little and would pout.

The man in question, who was on the verge of either a bloody, imaginary death or a carefully crafted one that involved dish soap, his food, and a long period of time, made a noise from behind the bowl of quinoa salad in front of him, which was big enough to feed a family of four. "You heard me. Cancel it," he repeated, as if I'd gone deaf the first time he'd said it.

Oh, I'd heard him. Loud and clear. That was why I wanted to kill him.

Which basically showed how amazing the human mind was; how you could care about someone but want to slit his or her throat at the same time. Like having a sister who you wanted to punch right in the ovaries. You still loved her, you just wanted to sock her right in the baby-maker to teach her a lesson—not that I knew from experience or anything.

The fact that I didn't immediately respond probably made him add, with that same facial expression aimed right at me, "I don't care what you have to tell them. Get it done."

Pushing my glasses up the bridge of my nose with my left index finger, I lowered my right hand so that the cabinet could hide the middle finger I aimed right at Aiden. If his facial expression wasn't bad enough, the tone he was using annoyed me even more. It was the voice he used to warn me it was pointless to argue with him; he wasn't going to change his mind right then, or ever, and I needed to deal with it.

I *always* needed to deal with it.

When I'd first started working for the three-time National Football Organization's Defensive Player of the Year, there had only been a few things I wasn't a fan of doing: haggling with people, telling them no, and sticking my hand into the garbage disposal, because I was both the cook and the cleaning lady of the house.

But if there was something I hated doing—and I mean really, *really* hated doing—it was canceling on people last-minute. It got on my nerves and went against my moral code. I mean, a promise was a promise, wasn't it? Then again, this wasn't me letting his fans down, technically. It was Aiden.

Freaking Aiden, who was busy inhaling his second lunch of the day without a care in the world, was oblivious to the frustrations he was going to make me face when I called his agent. After all the trouble we'd gone to schedule it, I was going to have to break the news that Aiden *wasn't* going to be signing anything at the sporting goods store in San Antonio. Yippee.

I sighed, guilt niggling my belly and conscience, and reached down to rub my stiff knee with the hand that wasn't busy expressing my frustrations. "You already promised them—"

"I don't care, Vanessa." He shot me that look again. My middle finger twitched. "Have Rob cancel it," he insisted, as his giant forearm went up so he could shovel what looked like eight ounces of food into his mouth at once. The fork he was holding hovered in the air a moment as he flicked that dark, stubborn gaze to meet mine. "Is that a problem?"

Vanessa-this. Vanessa-that.

Cancel it. Have Rob cancel it.

Boo.

As if I loved calling his asshole agent to begin with, much less so he could cancel an appearance two days before it was supposed to take place. He was going to lose his mind, and then direct his frustrations at me as if I had some kind of pull over Aiden "The Wall of Winnipeg" Graves. The truth was, the closest I'd ever come to helping him make any kind of decision had been when I recommended a camera for him to buy, and that was only because he "had better things to do than camera research" and because "that's what I pay you for."

He had a point of course. Between what he paid me and what Zac chipped in from time to time, I could manage to put a smile on my face—even if it was a forced one—and do what was asked of me. Every once in a while, I even did a little curtsy, which Aiden pretended not to witness.

I didn't think he really appreciated the amount of patience I had exercised when dealing with him for the last two years. Someone else would have already stabbed him in his sleep for sure. At least when I went through plans for how I'd do it, it was usually in a painless way.

Usually.

Since he'd ruptured his Achilles tendon barely a month into the season last year, he'd turned into something else. I tried not to blame him; I really did. Missing nearly three months of the entire regular season and being blamed for your team not making it to the postseason was hard to deal with. On top of that, some people had thought he wasn't going to make a full comeback after having to take six months off to recover and rehab. The kind of injury he'd sustained was no joke.

But this was Aiden. Some athletes took even longer than that amount of time to get back on their feet, if they ever did. He hadn't. But dealing with him on crutches, and driving him to and from rehab and appointments, had taken a toll on my patience more than once.

There was only so much cranky little bitch you could handle in a day, even if it was called for. Aiden loved what he did, and I had to imagine he was scared he wouldn't be able to play again, or that he would come back and not play up to the same level he'd been used to, not that he would ever voice any fears out loud. That was all understandable to me. I couldn't imagine how I would feel if something happened to my hands and there was a chance I might not ever be able to draw again.

Regardless, his crankiness had hit a level not previously documented in the history of the universe. That was saying something, considering I'd grown up with three older sisters who all had periods at the same time. Because of them, most things—most people—didn't bother me. I knew what it was like to be bullied, and Aiden never crossed the line into being unnecessarily mean. He was just a jackass sometimes.

He was lucky I had a tiny, itty-bitty crush on him; otherwise, he would have gotten the shank years ago. Then again, just about everyone with eyes who happened to also like men had some kind of a thing for Aiden Graves.

When he raised his eyebrows and looked at me from beneath those curly black eyelashes, flashing me rich brown eyes set deep into a face that I'd only seen smile in the presence of dogs, I swallowed and shook my head slowly as I gritted my teeth and took him in. The size of a small building, he should have had these big, uneven features that made him look like a caveman, but of course he didn't. Apparently, he liked to defy every stereotype he'd ever been assigned in his life. He was smart, fast, coordinated, and—as far as I knew—had never seen a game of hockey. He had only said "eh" in front of me twice, and he didn't consume animal protein. The man didn't eat bacon. He was the last person I would have ever considered polite, and he never apologized. Ever.

Basically, he was an anomaly: a Canadian football-playing, plant-based-lifestyle—he didn't like calling himself a vegan—anomaly that was strangely proportional all over and so handsome I might have thanked God for giving me eyes on a couple of occasions.

"Whatever you want, big guy," I said with a fake smile and a flutter of my eyelashes, even as I still flipped him off.

"They'll get over it," Aiden said casually, ignoring his nickname, rolling back two immensely muscular shoulders. I swear they were wide enough for a small person to drape across comfortably. "It isn't a big deal."

It wasn't a big deal? The promoters wouldn't feel that way, much less his agent, but then Aiden was used to getting his way. No one ever told him no. They told me no, and then I'd have to figure things out.

Despite what some people thought, the defensive end of the Three Hundreds, Dallas's professional football team, wasn't really an asshole or hard to work with. For all his faces and grumbling, he never cussed and hardly ever lost his temper without good reason. He was demanding; he knew exactly what he wanted and how he liked every single thing in his life. It was honestly an admirable quality, I thought, but it was my job to make those requests come true, regardless of whether I agreed with his decisions or not.

Only for a little bit longer though, I reminded myself. I was so close to quitting, I could feel it. The thought made my soul rejoice a bit.

Two months ago, my bank account had finally hit a comfortable number through sheer willpower, penny-pinching, and working long hours when I wasn't Aiden's assistant/housekeeper/cook. I'd hit my goal: save up a year's salary. Finally. Halle-freaking-lujah. I could practically smell freedom in the air.

But the keyword there was "practically."

I just hadn't gotten around to telling Aiden I was quitting yet.

"Why are you making that face?" he asked suddenly.

I blinked up at him, caught off guard. I raised my eyebrows, trying to play dumb. "What face?"

It didn't work.

With a fork hanging out of his mouth, he narrowed his dark eyes just the slightest bit. "That one." He gestured toward me with his chin.

I shrugged in an "I don't know what you're talking about" expression.

"Is there something you want to say?"

There were a hundred things I wanted to tell him on a regular basis, but I knew him too well. He didn't really care if there was something I wanted to say or not. He didn't care if my opinion was different from his or if I thought he should do something differently. He was just reminding me who the boss was.

Aka not me.

Asswipe.

"Me?" I blinked. "Nope."

He gave me a lazy glare before his eyes lowered to focus on the hand I had hidden on the other side of the kitchen island. "Then quit flipping me off. I'm not changing my mind about the signing," he said in a deceptively casual voice.

I pressed my lips together as I dropped my hand. He was a goddamn witch. I swear on my life, he was a freaking witch. A wizard. An oracle. A person with a third eye. Every single time I had ever flipped him off, he'd been aware of it. I didn't think I was that obvious about it either.

It wasn't like I gave people the middle finger for fun, but it genuinely bothered me that he was canceling an appearance without a legitimate reason. Backing out because he changed his mind and didn't want to take an afternoon off from training didn't seem like one. But what did I know?

"All right," I muttered under my breath.

Aiden, who I was pretty sure had no idea how old I'd turned this year, much less what month my birthday was, made a face for a split second. Those thick, dark eyebrows knit together and his full mouth pinched back at the corners. Then he shrugged, like he'd suddenly stopped caring about what I'd been doing.

What was funny was, if someone had told me five years ago that I'd be doing someone else's dirty work, I would have laughed. I couldn't remember ever not having goals or some sort of a plan for the future. I had always wanted something to look forward to, and being my own boss was one of those things I strived for.

I'd known since I was sixteen at my first summer job, getting yelled at for not putting enough ice into a medium-sized cup at the movie theater I'd worked at, that I would one day want to work for myself. I didn't like getting told what to do. I never had. I was stubborn and hardheaded—at least that's what my foster dad said was my greatest and worst personality trait.

I wasn't shooting for the stars or aiming to become a billionaire. I didn't want to be a celebrity or anything close to that. I just wanted my own small business doing graphic design work that could pay my bills, keep me fed, and still have a little extra left over for other things. I didn't want to have to rely on someone else's charity or whim. I'd had to do that for as long as I could remember, hoping my mom would come home sober, hoping my sisters would make me food when our mom wasn't around, and then hoping the lady with social services could at least keep me and my little brother together. . . . Why was I even thinking about that?

For the most part, I'd always known what I wanted to do with my life, so I'd naively thought half the battle was in the bag. Making it work should have been easy.

What no one tells you is that the road to accomplishing your goals isn't a straight line; it looks more like a corn maze. You stopped, you went, you backed up, and took a few wrong turns along the way, but the important thing you had to remember was that there was an exit. Somewhere.

You just couldn't give up looking for it, even when you really wanted to.

And especially not when it was easier and less scary to go with the flow than actually strike out on your own and make your path.

Scooting the stool he was sitting on back, Aiden got to his feet with his empty glass in hand. His Hulk-sized frame seemed to dwarf the not-exactly-small kitchen every time he was in there . . . which was always. Big surprise. He consumed at least 7,000 calories a day. During the regular football season, he bumped it up to 10,000. Of course, he was in the kitchen all day. So was I—making his meals.

"Did you buy pears?" he asked, already pushing our conversation and the middle finger incident aside as he filled his glass with water from the refrigerator's filter.

I didn't feel guilty at all about getting caught flipping him off. The first time it had happened, I thought I was going to die of embarrassment and then get fired, but now I knew Aiden. He didn't care if I did it, or at least that was the impression I got since I still had a job. I'd seen people come up to him and try goading him, calling him all sorts of names and insults that made *me* reel back. But what did he do when people did that kind of stuff? He didn't even twitch; he just pretended not to hear them.

Honestly, it was a little impressive to have that kind of backbone. I couldn't keep it together when someone honked at me while I was driving.

But as impressive as Aiden was, as much as his perfect butt made women double-take, and as dumb as most people would think I was for resigning from a job with a man who starred in commercials for an athletic apparel company, I still wanted to quit. The urge got stronger and stronger each day.

I'd busted my butt. No one else had done the work for me. This was what I wanted, what I had always wanted. I'd kept my eye on the prize for years for the opportunity to be my own boss. Having to call assholes who made it seem like I was an inconvenience, or folding underwear that clung to the most spectacular ass in the country, wasn't it.

Tell him, tell him, tell him right now you're planning on quitting, my brain egged on almost desperately.

But that nagging little voice of indecision and self-doubt that liked to hang out in the space where my nonexistent spine should have been reminded me, *What's the rush?*

THE FIRST TIME I met the Wall of Winnipeg, the second thing he said to me was, "Can you cook?"

He hadn't shaken my hand, asked me to sit down, or anything like that. In retrospect, that should have warned me of how things would be between us.

Aiden had asked me my name when he first let me in the front door and led me straight into a beautiful, open kitchen that looked like something straight out of a home renovation show. Then he'd gone straight for questioning my cooking skills.

Before that day, his manager had already interviewed me twice. The position was in the income range I'd been aiming for, and that was all that had mattered to me back then. The employment agency I'd signed up with had already called me into their offices on three separate occasions to make sure I'd be a good fit for "a celebrity," as they called him.

A bachelor's degree; a wide range of jobs I'd worked at that varied from being a divorce lawyer's secretary for three years while I went to college to summers spent doing photography for anyone who would hire me; a pretty successful side business selling makeup and stuff from a catalog; and excellent references had gotten me a callback.

I was pretty sure that wasn't what really got me the job though; it was my ignorance when it came to football. If there was a game on TV, chances were I wasn't paying attention to it. I'd never even seen Aiden Graves before my first day. I didn't exactly walk around telling people the only games I ever watched were the ones I'd been to in person during high school.

So when his manager had mentioned the name of my potential employer, I had stared at him blankly. I would more than likely never know for sure if it was my lack of excitement that scored me the position, but I had a feeling it was.

Even after Aiden's manager offered me the job, I hadn't bothered looking him up. What was the point? It wasn't like anything the internet said about him could change my mind about becoming his assistant. Really, nothing could have. I wasn't ashamed to say he could have been a serial killer and I would have taken the job if the pay were right.

In the end though, I thought it was a good thing that I hadn't done a search on him. As I would later learn when I was busy sending out promotional pictures to fans, photographs didn't do him any justice.

At six-foot-four, just a quarter-inch shy of six-five, sometimes weighing up to 280 pounds in the middle of the off-season, and with a presence that made him seem closer to some mythological hero than an average mortal, Aiden was a beast even fully clothed. He didn't have cosmetic muscles. He was just plain massive. Everywhere. I wouldn't be surprised if X-rays showed his bones were more dense than normal. His muscles had been honed and crafted for the specific purpose of as-effectively-as-possible blocking passes and tackling opposing quarterbacks.

An extra-extra-large T-shirt that morning of our first meeting didn't hide the massive bulk of his trapezius, pectorals, deltoids, or much less his biceps and triceps. The guy was *ripped*. His thighs strained the seams of the sweatpants he'd been wearing. I remembered noticing his fists reminded me of bricks, and the wrists that held them to the rest of his body were bigger than I'd ever seen.

Then there was the face I would be looking at for the next chunk of my life. Where his features might have been bluntly shaped, like so many big guys' were, Aiden was handsome in a way that wasn't aesthetically beautiful. His cheeks were lean, the bones above them high, and his jaw lantern shaped. The deep set of his eyes highlighted thick, black brows. Short, trimmed facial hair that always resembled a five-o'clock shadow, even after he'd immediately shaved, covered the lower half of his face.

A white scar along his hairline, from his temple to below his ear, was the only thing the short bristles couldn't hide. Then there was that mouth that would have seemed pouty on any other man who might have been smaller and who didn't glare half as much as Aiden did. He was brown-haired and olive-skinned. A hint of a thin, gold chain had peeked out from the collar of his shirt, but I'd been so distracted by everything else that was Aiden Graves, it wasn't until months later that I learned it was a medallion of St. Luke he never went anywhere without.

Just his size alone had been intimidating enough for me initially. His piercing brown-eyed gaze only added to the massive amount of intimidation he seemed to bleed out of his pores.

Regardless of that though, my first thought had been, *Holy shit*. Then I had shoved it away, because I couldn't be thinking things like that about my brand-new boss.

That day of our first meeting, all I had managed to do was nod at him. I'd gone in convinced I'd do whatever was needed to keep the job. His manager and the agency had made sure during the interview process that I knew cooking was part of the job requirement, which wasn't a big deal. When I was a kid, I'd learned the hard way that if I wanted to eat, I was going to have to do something about it, because my older sisters weren't going to trouble themselves, and I never knew what kind of mood my mom would be in. During college, I'd mastered the art of cooking on a contraband hotplate in my dorm room.

Aiden had simply stared at me in response before laying the bomb on me that no one had prepared me for. "I don't eat any animal products. Will that be a problem?"

Did I know how to make anything without eggs, meat, or cheese in it? Not that I could think of. No one had even mentioned that stipulation beforehand—and ignorantly, it wasn't as if he looked like most vegans I'd met in my life—but there was no way in hell I was going back to working three jobs if I absolutely didn't have to. So, I'd bullshitted. "No, sir."

He'd stood there in the kitchen, looking down at me in my navy khakis, cap-sleeved, white eyelet blouse, and brown heels. I'd been so nervous, I even had my hands clasped in front of me. The agency had suggested business casual attire for the job, and that's what I'd gone with. "Are you sure?" he'd asked.

I had nodded, already planning to search for recipes on my phone.

His eyes had narrowed a bit, but he didn't call me out on what was obviously a lie, and that was more than I could have hoped for. "I don't enjoy cooking or going out to eat. I usually eat four times a day and have two big smoothies too. You'll be in charge of meals, and I'll handle anything I eat in between," he said as he crossed his arms over what seemed like a three-foot-wide chest.

"The desktop computer upstairs has all of my passwords saved. Read and respond to all my emails; my PO box needs to be checked a few times a week, and you're in charge of that too. The key is in the drawer by the refrigerator. I'll write down the post office it's at and box number later. When I come back, you can go make a copy of my house key. My social sites need to be updated daily; I don't care what you post as long as you use some common sense."

He'd definitely made sure to meet my eyes when he added that, but I hadn't taken it personally.

"Laundry, scheduling . . ." he went off to include more tasks that I filed into the mental vault. "I have a roommate. We talked about it, and if you're up for the task, he might want you to make him food too sometimes. He'll pay you extra if you decide to do it."

Extra money? I never said no to extra money. Unless it required a blowjob.

"Do you have any questions?" my new boss had asked.

All I had managed to do was shake my head. Everything he said was common for the position I was taking, and I might have been too busy gaping at him to say much else. I'd never seen a pro football player in person, though I'd been friends with someone in college who played for our school. Back then, I hadn't thought people could be built on such a large scale, and I might have been trying to figure out how much Aiden had to eat to get in the amount of calories he needed in his diet.

His brown gaze had swept over my face and shoulders before returning to my eyes. That hard, unrelenting face stared right at me. "You don't talk much, do you?"

I smiled at him, a little one, and lifted a shoulder. I wasn't a big talker, but nobody could say I was shy or quiet either. Plus, I didn't want to mess this up until I figured out what he wanted and needed from me as an assistant.

Looking back on it, I wasn't sure if that was the greatest first impression, but tough shit. It wasn't like I could take it back and do it over again.

All Aiden, my new boss at the time did, was tip his chin down in what I'd later find out was his form of a nod. "Good."

NOT MUCH HAD changed over the last two years.

Our work relationship had progressed past me calling Aiden "sir" and using more than two words at a time when I talked to him.

I knew everything I could about Aiden, considering how pulling personal information out of him was like yanking teeth. I could tell you how old he was, how much money he had in his bank account, what spices made him cringe, and what brand of underwear he preferred. I knew his favorite meals, what size shoe he wore, what colors he refused to wear, and even what kind of porn he watched. I knew the first thing he wanted when he had more time on his hands was a dog—not a family. He wanted a dog.

But that was all something a stalker could learn, or someone really observant. He held on to the details of his life with both of his dinner-plate-sized hands. I had a feeling the number of things I didn't know about him could keep me busy for the rest of my life, if I were to try to pry them out of him.

I'd tried being friendly once I realized he wasn't going to go Incredible Hulk on me for asking questions, but it had all been in vain. For the last two years, my smiles were never returned, my every single "How are you?" went unanswered, and other than that infamous look that made my imaginary hackles rise, there was that tone, that almost smug tone, he took sometimes that just asked for an ass whooping . . . from someone much bigger than me.

Our boss and employee roles became more and more pronounced each day. I cared about him as much as I could care for someone who I saw a minimum of five days a week, who I basically took care of for a living, but who treated me like the friend of a pesky little sister he would rather not have. For two years, it had been fine doing duties I wasn't a huge fan of, but the cooking, the emails, and all things related to his fans were my favorite things about being his assistant.

And that was half the reason why I kept talking myself out of putting in my notice. Because I'd check his Facebook account or go on his Twitter and see something one of his fans posted that made me laugh. I'd gotten to know some of them over the years through online interactions, and it was easy to remember that working for him wasn't so bad.

It wasn't the worst job in the world—not even close to it. My pay was more than fair, my hours pretty good too . . . and in the words of almost every woman who had ever found out who I worked for, I "had the sexiest boss in the entire world." So there was that. If I was stuck looking at someone, it might as well be someone with a body and a face that put the models I put on other people's book covers to shame.

But there were things in life you couldn't do unless you stepped out of your comfort zone and took a risk, and working for myself was one of them.

That was why I hadn't actually gone through with it and told Aiden *"Sayonara, big boy"* on the eighty different occasions my brain had told me to.

I was nervous. Quitting a well-paying job—a steady one, at least while Aiden had a career—was scary. But that excuse was getting older and older.

Aiden and I weren't BFFs, much less confidants. Then again, why would we be? This was a man who didn't have more than possibly three people he spent time with when he managed to tear himself away from training and games. Vacations? He didn't take them. I didn't even think he knew what they were.

He didn't have pictures of family or friends anywhere in the house. His entire life revolved around football. It was the center of his universe.

In the grand scheme of Aiden Graves's life, I was no one really. We just sort of put up with each other. Obviously. He needed an assistant and I needed a job. He told me what he wanted done and I did it, whether I agreed with it or not. Every once in a while, I tried futilely to change his mind, but in the back of my head, I never forgot how pointless my opinion was to him.

You could only try for so long to be friendly with someone and have them shut you down with their indifference before you gave up. This was a job—nothing more, nothing less. It was why I had worked so hard to get to the point where I could be my own boss, so that I could deal with people who appreciated my hard work.

Yet here I was, doing the things that drove me nuts and putting my dreams off for another day, and another day, and another day . . .

What the hell was I doing?

"The only person you're screwing over is yourself," Diana had told me the last time we'd talked. She'd asked if I'd finally told Aiden I was quitting, and I'd told her the truth: no.

Guilt had pounded my belly at her comment. The only person I was hurting *was* myself. I knew I needed to tell Aiden. No one was going to do it for me; I was well aware of that. But . . .

Okay, there was no *but*. What if I crashed and burned once I was on my own?

I had planned it out and built up my business so that wouldn't be the case, I reminded myself as I sat there watching Aiden eat. I knew what I was doing. I had money squirreled away. I was good at what I did, and I loved doing it.

I'd be fine.

I'd be fine.

What was I waiting for? Every time I'd thought about telling Aiden before, it just hadn't seemed like the perfect moment. He had just gotten cleared to start practicing again after his injury, and it didn't feel right laying that on him then. I felt like I'd be abandoning him when he'd barely gotten back on his feet once more. Then, we'd immediately left for Colorado for him to train in peace and quiet. On another occasion, it hadn't been a Friday. Or he'd had a bad day. Or . . . whatever. There was always something. Always.

I wasn't staying on because I was in love with him or anything like that. Maybe at some point, right after I'd begun working for him, I might have had a giant crush on him, but his cool attitude had never let my heart get any crazier than that. It wasn't like I'd ever had any expectations of Aiden suddenly looking at me and thinking I was the most amazing person in his life. I didn't have time for that unrealistic crap. If anything, my goal had always been to do what I needed to do for him, and maybe make the man who never smiled, smile. I'd only succeeded at one of those things.

Over the years, my attraction to him had dwindled so that the only thing I really mooned over—correction: *appreciated* in a healthy, normal way—was his work ethic.

And his face.

And his body.

But there were plenty of guys with amazing bodies and faces in the world. I should know. I looked at models almost every day.

And none of those physical traits helped me in any way. Hot guys weren't going to make my dreams come true.

I swallowed and clenched my fingers.

Do it, my brain said.

What was the worst that would happen? I'd have to find another job if my customer base dried up? How horrifying. I wouldn't know what would happen until I tried.

Life was a risk. This was what I'd always wanted.

So I took a breath, carefully watched the man who had been my boss for two years, and I said it. "Aiden, I have something I need to talk to you about."

Because really, what was he going to do? Tell me I couldn't quit?

TWO

"You can't."

"I am," I insisted calmly as I watched the man on my laptop screen. "Aiden told me to let you know."

Trevor gave me a look that said he didn't even remotely believe me, and I found myself not really giving much of a crap what he thought. While it took a lot for me to dislike someone, Aiden's manager was one of those people I avoided like the plague whenever possible. Something about him just made me want to abort mission each time we had to interact. At one point, I really tried figuring out what it was about him I didn't like, and it always came back to the same reasons: he was snobby, but mainly he just gave off massive amounts of asshole-ish vibes.

Leaning forward, Trevor planted his elbows on what I could assume was his desk. He tented his hands and hid his mouth behind them. He exhaled. Then he inhaled.

Maybe, just maybe, he was thinking about all the times he'd been a jerk to me and was regretting it; like all the times he'd chewed me out or yelled at me because Aiden wanted something done that frustrated him. That had been pretty much every week since I'd gotten hired.

But knowing him, that wasn't the case. To regret something would mean you would have had to care about it at some point to begin with, and Trevor . . . the only thing he cared about was his paycheck. His body language, and the way he'd spoken to me even back when he'd first interviewed me, made it abundantly clear I didn't rank very high on his list of priorities.

Me quitting was going to make his life slightly more difficult for a little while, and *that* he wasn't a fan of.

Apparently, he was bothered a lot more than Aiden had been the night before when I sucked it up and told him the deep, dark secret I'd been withholding. "I want to thank you for everything you've done for me"—in hindsight, that had been pretty suck-up of me to say; he hadn't actually done anything besides pay me, but oh well—"but I'd like for you to find someone to replace me."

While I'd always known and accepted that we weren't friends, I guess a small part of me had been foolish enough to think I meant just a little, tiny, microscopic something to him. I'd done a lot for Aiden over the course of the time we'd worked together. I knew I would more than likely miss the familiarity of working for him at least a little bit. Wouldn't he feel the same way?

The answer to that had been a big fat *nope*.

Aiden hadn't even bothered looking at me after my admission. Instead, his attention had been focused on his bowl when he replied easily, "Let Trevor know."

And that was that.

Two years. I'd given him two years of my life. Hours and hours. Months at a time away from my loved ones. I'd cared for him on the rare occasions he got sick. I was the one who had stayed with him at the hospital after his injury. I was the person who had picked him up after his surgery and read up on inflammation and what I could feed him that would help him heal faster.

When he lost a game, I always tried to make his favorite breakfast the next morning. I'd bought him a birthday present—that I may or may not have left on his bed, because I didn't want to make it awkward. You didn't remember someone's birthday and not get him a gift, even if he never thanked you.

What had he given me? On my last birthday, I spent it in the rain at a park in Colorado, because he'd been filming a commercial and wanted me to tag along. I'd eaten dinner by myself in my hotel room. What did I expect from him now?

There had been no begging me to stay—not that I would have anyway—or even an "I'm sorry to hear that," which I'd heard when I'd left every other job before this one.

Nothing. He'd given me nothing. Not even a damn shrug.

It had stung more than it should have. A lot more. On the other hand, I recognized that we weren't soul mates, but it became even more apparent after that.

It was with that thought, that slight amount of bitterness in my throat at being so dispensable, that I swallowed and focused on my video chat.

"Vanessa, think about what you're doing," the manager argued through the camera.

"I have. Look, I'm not even giving you a two-week notice. Just find someone sooner than later. I'll train them, and then I'm out."

Trevor tipped his chin up and just stared forward at and through the computer's camera, the hard glint of the hair product he used catching in the sunlight in his office. "Is this an April Fools' joke?"

"It's June," I said carefully. Idiot. "I don't want to do this anymore."

His forehead furrowed at the same time his shoulders tensed, as if what I said was finally really sinking in. One eye peeked at me from over his fingers. "Do you want more money?" he had the nerve to ask.

Of course I wanted more money. Who didn't? I just didn't want it from Aiden. "No."

"Tell me what you need."

"Nothing."

"I'm trying to work with you here."

"There's nothing to work with. There isn't anything you can offer me that will get me to stay." That was how dead set I was on not getting wrangled back into the world of the Wall of Winnipeg. Trevor got paid for making things happen, and I knew if I gave him an inch, he would attempt to take a mile. It would probably be easier for him to convince me to stay instead of finding someone else. But I knew his tricks, and I wasn't going to fall for his shit.

Picking up the glass of water sitting on the kitchen counter next to my tablet, I took a sip and studied him over the top of it. I could do this, damn it. I would do it. I wasn't going to keep my job just because he was giving me the closest thing to puppy eyes pure evil was capable of.

"What can I do to get you to stay?" Trevor finally asked as he dropped his hands away from his face.

"Nothing." If a slight bit of loyalty to Aiden and genuine worry had gotten me to stay since I realized I could afford to quit, the night before had cemented my leaving.

I didn't want to waste any more time than I already had.

Another pained expression took over Trevor's features. When we'd first met two years ago, he'd only had a couple of gray hairs scattered throughout his head. Now there were more than a couple, and it suddenly made so much sense. If I considered myself a fairy godmother, Trevor must have been seen as a god; a god who needed to make miracles happen out of the most dire of places.

And I wasn't helping by quitting on who I was sure was one of the most difficult of his clients.

"Did he say something?" he asked suddenly. "Do something?"

I shook my head, not fooled at all by his act. He didn't care. Before I'd asked him to call me—and he'd insisted we do a video chat instead—I had asked myself whether to tell him why I was quitting or not. It hadn't even taken a second to decide. Nah, he didn't need to know. "There are other things in my life I want to pursue. That's all."

"You know he's stressed out about coming back after surgery. If he's a little on edge, it's normal. Ignore him," Trevor added.

Normal? There were different standards for what "normal" could be considered when dealing with professional athletes, especially athletes like Aiden, who breathed and lived for his sport. He took everything personally. He wasn't some burnout who played because he didn't have anything else to do, and wanted to make money. Maybe I understood that better than Trevor.

Plus, if either of us had more firsthand experience with the way Aiden had been since his Achilles tendon rupture, it was me. I'd witnessed it all up close and personal; I also knew how he usually got right before training camp started, and that was right around the corner too, adding on to the things he worried about. Trevor had worked for him longer, but he lived in New York and only visited a few times a year. Aiden only talked to him directly on the phone once a month, if that, since I was his scapegoat.

"I'm sure there's at least a hundred other people who would love to work for Aiden. I really don't think you will have a problem finding someone to replace me. Everything will be fine," I told him smoothly.

Were there at least a thousand other people in the world who would love to work for Aiden Graves? Yes. Minimum.

Would Trevor have a problem finding a new assistant for Aiden? No.

The issue would be finding someone to stay who could deal with the long hours and his prickly personality.

"This isn't going to be easy," Trevor had said to me after the workforce agency had sent me his way. *"Athletes are demanding. It's basically part of the job requirement. Will you be able to handle it?"*

Back then, I'd been working three jobs, sharing a tiny house with Diana and Rodrigo, and unable to sleep some nights, because all I could dream about was the massive student loan debt I was swimming in. I would have done just about anything to get out of that situation, even if it meant dealing with someone who may or may not be a psycho by the way others portrayed him.

While Trevor hadn't been lying—Aiden wasn't *that* bad once you figured out what made him tick—at least he'd given me a warning of what I'd be facing.

A demanding, cranky, perfectionist, workaholic, arrogant, aloof, clean freak of a boss.

No biggie.

Aiden Graves needed an assistant, and I had been lucky enough to get the job.

At that point, I had a plan that worried me to death, and student loans that were giving me an ulcer. I'd thought it over a million times and concluded that working for him, while keeping my own business on the side and trying to grow it at the same time, was the best way to move forward in my life, at least for a little while.

The rest was history.

Saving money and working seventy hours a week had all finally paid off. I saved enough to keep me afloat in case my business slowed down, and I had my goals to guide me. When things were tough, it was my aspirations and the hope they brought me that kept me going.

So even on the days when Aiden had me standing behind him envisioning myself stabbing him in the back, because he wanted me to do something ridiculous, like rewash his sheets because I'd left them in the washer for too long, I always did what he needed. All I had to do was remember my student loans and my plans, and I persevered.

Until now.

"You're killing me, Vanessa. You're fucking killing me here," Trevor literally moaned. *Moaned.* He usually just bitched and complained.

"It'll be fine. He doesn't care that I'm leaving. He probably won't even notice," I said, trying to be as understanding as I could and at the same time not really giving much of a crap that he was sweating bullets.

The grimace on his face quickly dropped, a total act, and got replaced by a glare, making him look more like the manager I'd been forced to get to know than the one who was attempting to backtrack and be nice after so long. He sniped, "I highly doubt that."

I understood why I was a good fit for Aiden. I was pretty patient, and I didn't hold his callous, picky nature against him. I knew how to handle crazy in all its forms, thanks to my family, but maybe I'd just been expecting so much worse from him, and he'd never gone straight into anger-management zone. He was way too controlled for that.

Realistically though, especially after yesterday, I wasn't going to hold my breath. Maybe I'd feel worse about quitting if Aiden was my friend or if Trevor had actually been nice to me, but neither one of them would remember me two months from now. I knew who cared about me and who meant something to me, and neither one of them were on my list . . . and sure, that made me feel a little bad. But survival of the fittest and all that crap, right?

Both Aiden and Trevor would have dumped me like a hot potato if our roles had been reversed. I'd let my misguided sense of loyalty, paranoia, and self-doubt keep me shackled to my not-so-bad cell.

All Aiden needed was someone who could do what he wanted. Cook, clean, wash, fold, answer emails, call Trevor or Rob when he wanted things out of my jurisdiction, and post things on Facebook, Twitter, and Instagram. Then there were the things I had to do when he traveled. It wasn't anything crazy.

Anyone with a little bit of patience could do it.

But from the look Trevor pierced me with, he didn't feel the same way. Mostly, I thought he was just being lazy. He blew out a breath and started massaging his temples as the chat buffered and his image blurred for a moment. "Are you positive you want to do this? I can talk to him about reducing your hours . . ." His voice carried over the speaker even as the screen froze.

I only just barely managed not to ask him to let me think about it. "No." I couldn't. I wasn't going to half-ass this opportunity in my life to go solo. I didn't want to invite failure in the door by being hesitant.

"Vanessa . . ." he groaned. "You're really doing this?"

This was exactly what I'd been working toward from the moment I finished school with my undergrad in graphic design. Graduating had been an uphill battle that sometimes felt like plain torture, and I'd done terrible, awful things to get my schooling done. It was why I had worked multiple jobs at once, why I now technically only had two, and why I had been sleeping four hours a night for the last four years and lived off the bare minimum. I took almost any and every job that hit my inbox and jobs that didn't: book covers, web banners, posters, bookmarks, business cards, postcards, logos, T-shirt designs, commissioned pieces, tattoo designs. Everything.

"I'm positive." I had to fight the urge to smile at how confident and determined I sounded, even though I definitely didn't feel that way.

Back at massaging his temples, Trevor sighed. "If that's how you're going to be, I'll start looking for a replacement."

I nodded and let a sense of hesitant victory tickle my throat. I wasn't going to let that smart-ass comment at the beginning bother me. This was exactly how I was going to be.

He waved a hand in front of the screen. "I'll let you know once I find someone."

Without another comment, he logged off the chat like a rude jerk. He reminded me of someone else I knew with his lack of manners. If it wasn't for Zac and some of the other Three Hundreds he'd introduced me to over the years, I would have figured everyone in their industry was self-absorbed. But no, it was only a few people, specifically the ones I had to surround myself with. Go figure.

It wasn't going to be my problem anymore though, was it?

"Vanessa!" a familiar voice bellowed from somewhere upstairs.

"Yes?" I yelled back, exiting the app on my tablet and wondering if he'd overheard my conversation with Trevor or not. I mean, he was the one who told me to call him in the first place, wasn't he?

"Did you wash the sheets?" Aiden hollered from where I could only assume was his bedroom.

I washed his sheets Mondays, Wednesdays, and Fridays, and I had every week since getting hired. For someone who worked out almost every day of his life, and sweating had become as natural as breathing, he was religious about having ultraclean sheets. I learned from the very beginning how important it was that his damn sheets were clean, so I never missed doing them. Ever. "Yes."

"Today?"

"Yes." Why the hell was he asking? I always . . . *oh*. I always left a piece of the chocolate peppermint patties he liked on his pillow—because it made me laugh—and I hadn't put one on there this afternoon. The store had been out of them. I guess I couldn't blame him for being uncertain, but I could blame myself for spoiling him. He'd never acknowledged my little gift, or told me to stop leaving them, so I hadn't figured he cared. Now I knew better.

Aiden didn't immediately respond, and I could already envision him humming to himself with uncertainty before sniffing the sheets to make sure I was telling the truth. When there wasn't a response, I figured he confirmed I wasn't lying. But then he started yelling again. "Did you pick up my clothes from the dry cleaner?"

"Yes. They're in your closet already." I didn't flinch, roll my eyes, or have an annoyed tone. I had the self-control of a samurai sometimes. A samurai who wanted to go *ronin*.

I'd barely managed to put my tablet back into my purse when he hollered again. "Where are my orange runners?"

That time, I couldn't help but cross my eyes. Dealing with him reminded me of being a little kid and asking my mom to help me find something after I'd looked about a total of five seconds. They were where he'd left them. "In your bathroom."

I could hear movement upstairs. Zac hadn't made his way back to Dallas yet, so it could only be the big guy looking for his tennis shoes—or when his Canadianisms kicked in, *runners*. I rarely ever touched his shoes if I didn't have to. It wasn't as if his feet smelled—strangely, they didn't—but they did get sweaty, and I mean really sweaty. He'd been training so hard the last two months, the sweat had reached an all-time high. My fingers tried not to go anywhere near them if it could be avoided.

I was in the middle of looking through a cookbook, trying to decide what to make for dinner, when the thunder that followed a 280-pound man jogging down the stairs started. Seriously, every time he came down the stairs any faster than a slowpoke, the walls trembled. I wasn't sure how the stairs survived. Whatever kind of materials the builder used on them, it had to be good stuff.

I didn't need to turn around to know he'd made his way into the kitchen. The refrigerator door opened and closed, followed by the sound of him munching on something.

"Pick up some more sunblock for me. I'm almost out," he said in a distracted tone.

I'd already ordered him some days ago, but I didn't see the point in telling him it was cheaper to order it than to buy it at the store. "You got it, big guy. I'm taking two of your shorts to the seamstress later. I noticed when I was washing them that the hems were loose." Considering he got half of his clothes specially made because "size behemoth" wasn't widely carried, I was a little unimpressed those same shorts already needed to get patched.

Juggling the pear he was eating and two apples in his other hand, he tipped his chin up. "I'm running some drills tonight. Anything I need to know before I leave?"

Fiddling with the leg of my glasses, I tried to think about what I had planned on telling him. "There's a few envelopes I left on your desk this morning. I'm not sure if you saw them already or not, but they look important."

That big, handsome face went thoughtful for a second before he nodded. "Did Rob cancel the signing?"

I almost winced from thinking of the conversation with his agent, another asshole I wasn't fond of. Honestly, I wouldn't be surprised if his own mom wasn't fond of him either. Rob was that much of a dick. "I told him to, but he never called back to tell me if he did or not. I'll find out."

He nodded again, crouching that massive six-foot-four frame to pick up his duffel bag. "Make sure you do that." He paused. "Leslie's birthday is this month. Send a card and a gift card over, would you?"

"Your wish is my command." In the entire time I'd worked for Aiden, Leslie was the only person who got a gift from him. I couldn't even be remotely jealous that I didn't get at least a verbal "happy birthday" on mine. Not even Zac received anything, and I'd know, because if he did, I'd be the one buying the present. "Oh, I made those granola bars that you like in case you want to take some with you," I added, pointing at the plastic container I'd left by the fridge.

He headed to where I'd indicated, opening the container and pulling out two wax-paper-wrapped bars before shoving all his snacks into his duffel bag. "Come by the gym tomorrow with the camera and my breakfast. I'm going in early and staying until lunch."

"Sure." I had to make a mental note to set my alarm for half an hour earlier than usual. Most days when he was in Dallas during the off-season, Aiden did cardio at his house, had breakfast, and then left to do his weightlifting and other kinds of workouts with whichever trainer he'd deemed to honor with his presence. Some days, he woke up earlier and went straight to the gym.

The facility was located on the opposite side of town, so I'd either have to make him breakfast at my house and go straight there or wake up even earlier to drop by his house, which was out of the way, and then head over. No thanks. I barely survived on my usual four to five hours of sleep most nights. I wasn't about to lose what little I had left.

I stepped back from the counter and grabbed the gallon of water I'd refilled earlier, holding it out for him, locking my gaze on his thick neck before forcing myself to look him in the eye. "By the way, I talked to Trevor about me leaving, and he said he'd start looking for someone else."

Those dark orbs met mine for a second, only just a split second, cool and distant like always, before he looked away. "Okay." He took the jug from me as he threw his bag over his shoulder.

Just as he reached the door that connected the garage with the kitchen, I called out, "Bye."

He didn't say anything as he closed the door behind him, but I thought he might have wiggled a finger or two. I was probably imagining it.

Who was I kidding? Of course I was imagining it. I was just being an idiot for even thinking there was a possibility he'd done otherwise. While I wasn't the bubbliest person in the world, Aiden had me beat by a landslide.

With a resigned sigh, I shook my head at myself and started making my way around the kitchen when my personal cell phone started ringing. Taking a quick peek at the screen, I hit the answer button.

"Herro," I said, slipping the phone between my ear and my shoulder.

"Vanny, I don't have time to talk. I have an appointment in a minute," the bright voice on the other line explained quickly. "I just wanted to tell you Rodrigo saw Susie."

Silence hung between Diana and me on the phone. Two moments . . . three moments . . . four moments. Heavy and unnatural. Then again, that was what Susie did best—messed things up.

I wanted to ask if she was sure it was Susie that her brother, Rodrigo, had seen, but I didn't. If Rodrigo thought he saw her, then he had. She didn't have the kind of face that was easy to mistake, even after so many years.

I cleared my throat, telling myself I didn't need to count to ten, or even five. "Where?" My voice came out in a slight croak.

"In El Paso yesterday. He was visiting his in-laws this weekend with Louie and Josh, and said he saw her at the grocery store by the old neighborhood."

One, two, three, four, five, six, seven.

Nope. That wasn't enough.

I had to start counting all over again, all the way to ten the second time. A thousand different thoughts went through my head at the mention of Susie's name, and they were all pretty terrible. Each and every single one of them. It didn't take a genius to know what she was doing in the old neighborhood. Only one person who we both knew still lived there. I could still remember our old stomping ground so clearly.

It was where Diana and I had met. Back when I lived with my mom, Diana's family had lived next door to us. They'd had the pretty house—the freshly painted blue one with white trim and a nice lawn—with the dad who played with his kids outside, and the mom who kissed boo-boos. The Casillases were the family I had always wanted when I'd been a kid, when things had been at their worst, and the only thing I found consolation in was my notebook, not the mess within the walls of my house.

Diana had been my best friend for as long as I could remember. I couldn't count the number of times I'd eaten over at their house with my little brother until Mom had lost custody of us. Diana had always done what my own family hadn't, and that was watch out for me. She was the one who had found me—

Stop it. Stop it. It wasn't worth the energy it took to think about things in the past I was over. It really wasn't.

"Huh. I had no idea she was back." My voice sounded just as robotic out loud as it sounded in my head. "I just talked to my mom a week ago and she didn't say anything." Diana knew I was referring to my real mom, the person who had actually given birth to me and my four siblings, not my foster mom of four years who I still kept in touch with.

At the mention of my birth mom, Diana made a small noise I almost missed. I knew she didn't understand why I bothered trying to have a relationship with her. Honestly, half the time I regretted it, but that was one of those rare things I never told the person I was closest to in the world, because I knew what she would say and I didn't want to hear it.

"I figured you would want to know in case you were planning on visiting," she finally said in kind of a mutter.

I didn't visit El Paso often, but she was right. I definitely wouldn't want to go now that I knew who was there.

"I really have to go in a sec, Vanny," my best friend quickly added before I could say anything. "But *did you tell Miranda you're leaving?*"

The "Miranda" went in one ear and out the other. I'd been calling him that for so long, it sounded so natural it didn't even register. "I just told him yesterday."

"*And?*"

She couldn't just let me sulk in my reality. "Nothing." There was no point in lying or making something up that would make me seem more important to Aiden than I was. While I didn't tell anyone a whole lot about him because of the nondisclosure agreement I signed when I first started working for him, Diana knew enough to get why his name was saved on my personal phone under "Miranda Priestly" from *The Devil Wears Prada*.

"Oh," was her disappointed response.

Yeah. I thought so too.

"He'll miss you once you're gone. Don't worry about it."

I highly doubted that.

"Okay, I gotta go, my client is here. Call me later, Van-Van. I get off work at nine."

"I will. Love you."

"Love you too. Oh! And think about letting me dye your hair once you're out of there," she added before hanging up on me.

Diana's comment made me smile and kept me smiling as I headed into Aiden's office to tackle his inbox. Talking to Di always put me in a good mood. She never gave me shit for how much I worked because she worked a lot too.

But I told her the same thing my foster dad had told me when I was seventeen and I told him I wanted to pursue my artwork: "Do what you need to do to be happy, Vané. Nobody else is going to watch out for you but you."

It was the same belief I held on to when I first told my foster parents I wanted to go to school a thousand miles away, and what I told myself when I didn't get a scholarship and my financial aid was merely a drop in the bucket to go to said school. I was going to do what I needed to do, even if I had to leave my brother—with his blessing—in the process. I'd told him the same thing when he was offered a scholarship for a college right after I moved back to Texas to be closer to him.

Sometimes it was easier to tell other people what they should do than to actually practice what you preached.

That had been the real root of my problem. I was scared. Scared that my clients were going to disappear and my work would dry up. Scared that one day I'd wake up and have absolutely no inspiration anymore when I had my photo-editing program open. I was worried that what I'd worked so hard for would crash and burn and everything would go to hell. Because I knew firsthand that life could be taking you in one direction, and the next moment you'd be going in a completely different one.

Because that was the way surprises worked—they didn't tend to pencil themselves into your schedule and let you know they were visiting ahead of time.

THREE

T his place smells like armpits, I thought as I made my way past the cardio equipment at the facility where Aiden had been training since we'd gotten back from Colorado.

Located in the business warehouse district on the outskirts of Dallas, the facility had the equipment necessary for all levels of weightlifting, plyometric exercises, calisthenics, strongman, and powerlifting. The building itself was new, nondescript, and easy to miss unless you knew what you were looking for. It had only been open about three years, and the owner had spared no expense on any square inch of the gym. The facility boasted that it trained some of the most elite athletes in the world in a wide range of sports, but I only paid attention to one of them.

Aiden's schedule had been as consistent as it could be in the two years I'd been with him, considering everything that had happened in the last ten months. After football season ended, and after he'd been cleared to train this year, Aiden headed to a small town in Colorado where he rented a house from some ex-football star for two months. There, he trained with his high school football coach. I'd never outright asked him why he chose there of all places to spend his time, but from everything I knew about him, I figured he enjoyed the time away from the spotlight. As one of the best players in the NFO, there was always someone around him asking for something, telling him something, and Aiden wasn't exactly the outgoing, friendly type.

He was a loner who happened to be so good at his sport, there wasn't a way around the spotlight he'd been thrust into from the moment he'd been drafted. At least, that was what I'd learned from the countless articles I'd read before sharing on his social pages and the hundreds of interviews I'd sat through with him. It was just something he put up with on his road to being the best—because that's what fans, and even people who weren't fans, referred to him as.

With a work ethic like his, it wasn't a surprise.

After his seclusion in the middle of nowhere—I'd gone with him twice, because apparently he couldn't live without a chef and housekeeper—he, we, flew back to Dallas, and his high school coach went back to Winnipeg. Aiden then worked on other aspects of his role with another trainer until the Three Hundreds called him in for team camp in July.

In a couple of weeks, official practices would begin and the insanity that surrounded an NFO season with one of the highest-caliber players in the organization would start all over again. But this time, I wouldn't be part of it. I wouldn't have to wake up at four o'clock in the morning, or have to drive around like a crazy person doing the hundreds of things that seemed to pop up when he was busy.

This August, instead of dealing with planning meals around two-a-day practices and preseason games, I'd be in my apartment, waking up whenever the hell I wanted, and not having to cater to anyone else's needs but mine.

But that was a party I could throw in the near future, when I wasn't busy looking for Aiden while my hands were full.

Past the cardio machines and through two swinging double doors was the main part of the training ground. At a cavernous 10,000 square feet, red-and-black decor swam in front of my eyes. Half the floor looked like turf and the other half had lightly cushioned black flooring for a weight-training section. Scattered around the building at six o'clock in the morning were only about ten other people. Half looked like football players and the other half looked like some other sort of athlete.

I just had to look for the largest one of them all, and it only took a second to spot the big head on the turf section by one of the 1,100-pound tires. Yeah, *1,100-pound tires.*

And I thought I was badass when I managed to carry all of my grocery bags to my apartment in one trip.

A few feet away, a familiar-looking man stood by watching the Wall of Winnipeg. Finding a spot out of the way but still close enough to take a decent picture, I sat cross-legged at the edge of the mats perpendicular to Aiden and his current trainer, and pulled out the DSLR camera I'd suggested he should buy specifically for this purpose a year ago. One of my duties was to update his social media pages and engage his fans; his sponsors and fans enjoyed seeing live shots of him working out.

No one paid me any attention as I settled in; they were all too busy to look around. With the equipment out of the bag, I waited for the perfect shot.

Through the lens, Aiden's features were smaller; his muscles seemed not as detailed as they were when you saw them in person. He'd been cutting his calories for the last two weeks, aiming to drop ten pounds before the start of the season. The striations on his shoulders popped as he maneuvered around the massive tractor tire, squatting in front of it, making the full muscles of his hamstrings look even more impressive than they usually did. I could even see the cleft that formed along the back of his thigh from how developed his hammies were.

Then there were those biceps and triceps that some people seemed to think had gotten the size they were due to steroids, when I knew firsthand that Aiden's body was fueled by massive amounts of a plant-based diet. He didn't even like taking over-the-counter medications. The last time he'd gotten sick, the stubborn ass had even refused to take the antibiotics the doctor had prescribed. I hadn't even bothered to fill the painkiller prescription he'd been given after his surgery, which might have been why he'd been so grumpy for so long. I wouldn't even get started on his aversion to sodium laurel sulfates, preservatives, and parabens.

Steroids? Give me a break.

I snapped a few pictures, trying to get a really good one. His female fans always went nuts over the shots that showcased the power contained within that great body. And when he had tight compression shorts on while he was bent over? "BAM. I'M PREGNANT," one of his fans had written last week when I posted a picture of Aiden doing squats. I'd almost spat water out of my mouth.

His email inbox got flooded after those kinds of posts went up. What the fans wanted, they got, and Aiden was all for it. Luckily for him, between semesters, I'd taken a photography class at the local community college in hopes of snagging a few gigs during the summer doing wedding photography.

The tire started its path to getting flipped. Aiden's face contorted as sweat poured down his temples and over the thick two-inch scar that slashed white vertically along his hairline before melting into the beard that had grown in overnight. I'd overheard people talk about his scar when they didn't know I was listening. They thought he'd gotten it during a drunken night in college.

I knew better.

Through the lens, Aiden grimaced and his trainer urged him on from his spot right beside him. I snapped more pictures, suppressing a sleepy yawn.

"Hey, you," a voice whispered a little too closely into my ear from behind.

I froze. I didn't need to turn around to know who it was. There was only one person in the group of people that circled Aiden's life who made my creeper-radar go off.

And this will hopefully be one of the last few times you see him, I told myself when I had the urge to flinch.

There was also the fact my gut said that making my dislike of him known would just make this situation worse, and it wasn't as if I would tell Aiden his teammate gave me the heebie-jeebies. If I hadn't told Zac, who *was* my friend, that Christian made me feel uncomfortable, I sure as hell wouldn't tell the person who wasn't. But it was the truth. I minded my own business when I showed up to anything Three Hundreds-related and tried to be nice, or at least polite, to the people who were kind to me. Trevor had drilled it into my head when he'd interviewed me that I wasn't to be seen or heard. The attention always had to be on the big guy and not some crazy-ass assistant, and I was totally fine with that.

Plastering a tight, forced smile on my face, even though I wasn't facing him, I kept the camera where it was, ready for action. "Hi, Christian. How are you?" I asked in a friendly voice that I really had to dig in there for, easily ignoring the good-looking features that disguised a man who had gotten suspended a few games last season for getting into a fight at a club. I thought that said a lot about him to begin with, because who did something that stupid anyway? He made millions a year. Only a total idiot would jeopardize a good thing.

"Great now that you're here," Creeper Christian said.

I almost groaned. It wasn't like I'd known he was training at the same place Aiden was. I doubted Aiden even knew or cared.

"Taking pictures of Graves?" he asked, taking a seat on the floor next to me.

I brought the viewfinder eyepiece to my eye, hoping he'd realize I was too busy to talk. "Yep." Who else would I be taking pictures of? I snapped a couple other shots as Aiden managed to flip the tire again, resuming that wide-legged, squatted position after each time.

"How you been? How long has it been since I've seen you?"

"Good." Was it bitchy to be so vague? Yes, but I couldn't find it in me to be more than cordial to him after what he'd done. Plus, he knew damn well how long Aiden had been out for the season. He was the team's star player. Someone from the team had been constantly in contact with him since his injury. There was no way Christian wouldn't have kept up with Aiden's progress. It seemed like every time I flipped through the Sports Network, some anchor or another was making a prediction about Aiden's future.

The heat of his side seared into my shoulder. "Graves sure got back on his feet real quick."

Through the lens though, I found Aiden glowering over in my direction, his trainer a few feet away jotting down something on the clipboard he was holding.

I was torn between waving and getting up, but Aiden beat me to decision making by saying loudly, "You can leave now."

You can—?

Lowering the camera to my lap, I stared over at him, pressing my glasses a little closer to my face with my index finger. I'd heard wrong, hadn't I? "What did you say?" I called out the question slowly so he could hear me.

He didn't even blink as he repeated himself. "You can leave now." *You can leave now.*

I gawked. My heart gave a vicious thump. My inhale was sharp. *One, two, three, four, five, six, seven, eight, nine, ten.*

"Kill them with kindness," Diana's mom would say when I'd tell her about my sisters picking on me. I hadn't necessarily taken her words into account when dealing with my family, but they had made sense to me once I was old enough to have to put up with other people's bullshit.

Being the kind of person who smiled at someone who was being a jackass usually pissed off the assholes a lot more than being rude in return did.

In some cases though, people might also think you had brain damage when you did it, but it was a risk I was willing to take.

But in this case, in that moment, forcing myself not to obviously flip Aiden off was a lot harder than normal.

It was one thing for him to ignore me when I tried to be playful with him, or when I said goodbye or good morning, but for him to act that way with me in front of other people? I mean, he wasn't exactly a teddy bear on the best of days, but he usually wasn't a model for Asswipe & Fitch. At least, not when we were around other people, which was rare.

One, two, three, four, five. I had this.

I raised my eyebrows and beamed over at him like nothing was wrong, even though I was pretty much seething on the inside and wondering how to give him diarrhea.

"What the fuck is his deal?" Christian muttered under his breath as I settled the camera back into its case, and then into my bag. I couldn't decide whether to leave as quickly as possible or stay where I was, because he was out of his damn mind if he thought I was going to do his bidding when he talked like that to me.

The reminder that I didn't need to take his crap anymore hit me right between the eyebrows, and my shoulder blades. I could take him being aloof and cold. I could handle him not giving a single crap about me personally, but embarrassing me in front of other people? There was only so much you could forgive and ignore.

One, two, three, four, five, six.

"Is he always like that?" Christian's voice jump-started me out of my thoughts.

I shrugged a shoulder, conscious not to put my foot in my mouth in front of someone who was practically a stranger, even though said man wasn't exactly on my list of people I would pull out of a burning building at the minute. "He's a good boss." I let the bland, forced compliment out, getting to my feet. "I don't take it personally."

Usually.

"I need to get going anyway. See you," I said as I slipped the strap of my bag over my shoulder and picked up the insulated bag with the big guy's food inside.

"I'm sure I'll see you soon," he noted, his tone just a little too bright, too fake.

I nodded before noticing Aiden taking a knee on the turf, staring over with a perfectly impassive expression on his face. Fighting the uneasy feeling I got from him practically telling me to scram, I went to stand on the other side of the tire. He was sweaty; his T-shirt was clinging to the muscles of his pectorals like a second, paler skin. His face was tight, almost bored—so basically the norm.

I tried to steady my words and heart. Confusion, anger, and, honestly, a little hurt soured my stomach as I watched him. "Is there something wrong?" I asked slowly, steadily as I tapped my fingers along the stitching of the bag with his camera and my things inside.

"No," he answered sharply, like he would have if I'd asked him if he wanted something with fennel for dinner.

I cleared my throat and rubbed the side of my hand against the seam of my pants, warily, counting to three that time. "Are you sure?"

"Why would anything be wrong?"

Because you're being a massive douche bag, I thought.

But before I could make up something else, he kept going. "I don't pay you to sit around and talk."

Oh *no*.

He leaned his entire upper body forward to rest against the length of his leg in a deep stretch. "Did you bring my breakfast?"

I tried to be patient. I really did. For the most part, I had patience on lockdown. There was no sense of "this is mine" when you had three older sisters who didn't respect anyone's boundaries, and one little brother. Needless to say, I didn't get my feelings hurt particularly easily, and I didn't hold 99 percent of things against my brother or sisters when they said something they wouldn't mean later on.

But that was the problem, Aiden wasn't my brother. He wasn't even my friend.

I could take a lot, but I wasn't obligated to take anything from him.

In that moment, I realized how over this shit I was. I was done. *Done*.

Maybe I was scared as hell of quitting, but I would rather take a gamble on myself than stay there and get insulted by someone who wasn't any better than me.

Calmly, calmly, calmly, despite the angry ringing in my ears, I made myself focus on his question and answered, my voice stony, "Yes." I held up the bag he clearly would have seen when I walked up to him.

He grunted.

As much as I could respect Aiden for being so determined, focused, and logical, sometimes . . .

It grated on me just how blind he was to everything else in his life. In all the time I'd worked for him, he still couldn't grace me with more than an occasional "thank you" or "good lunch." Sure, I knew that you shouldn't expect someone's gratitude for doing things just because it was good manners, but still. I could count the number of times he'd smiled at me or asked me how I was doing on one hand. *One freaking hand.* I was a person who filled a role, but I could have been any person filling this role and it wouldn't have mattered.

I did a good job, hardly ever complained, and always did what needed to be accomplished even if I didn't want to do it. I tried to be nice to him, to mess with him, even though he definitely didn't care for it, because what was life if you took it too seriously?

But he'd pretty much just told me to shoo in front of other people.

"Is that all?" Aiden's rough voice snapped me out of my thoughts. "I have a workout I need to finish."

It was an oddly relieving sensation that pierced through my chest right then. I felt . . . like I could breathe. Standing there, I felt *right*. "Yeah, that's all, boss." I swallowed, forced a smile on my face, and walked out of there with my head held high, thinking, *I'm done. I'm so done.*

What was wrong with him?

I'd been around Aiden dozens of times when he was having a bad day. Bad days with Aiden Graves were nothing new or anything to particularly hold on to. Even practices with the Three Hundreds were serious business for him. Every mistake he made was like a strike against his soul that he dwelled on. He'd said so in interviews plenty of times in the past, how he'd lie in bed going over plays until he'd fall asleep.

He was cranky on days that the sun was out and he was cranky on cloudy days too. I could handle grouchy men who preferred their own company. Usually he just glared and maybe snarled a bit.

No big deal. He didn't throw things or yell.

But acting like an asshole with me in public? Saying that kind of stuff? That was new even for him, and that was probably why I was handling it so badly. Sometimes the worst things you could ever hear were wrapped in sweet tones and calm voices.

I walked out of the facility distracted. I even drove my car muttering to myself under my breath. Twenty minutes later, I pulled into Aiden's subdivision and parked on the street like usual. When I opened the front door, I realized something was wrong when the alarm system wasn't beeping.

The alarm wasn't beeping.

"Zac?" I yelled, reaching into my purse for my pepper spray at the same time I made my way through the kitchen, toward the door that led into the garage, to see if there was a car in there.

I didn't make it that far.

Sitting on the onyx countertop right next to the refrigerator were dangling long legs stuffed into brown leather cowboy boots. I didn't need to look at the upper body above them. I knew what I would see: a threadbare T-shirt, a narrow, handsome face, and light brown hair hidden beneath that black Stetson he'd owned for years.

Zachary James Travis was draped across the counter with a bag of chips in his lap. At six-foot-three, Zac was the second-string quarterback of the Dallas Three Hundreds. Plagued by one injury after another, Austin, Texas's once-upon-a-time star had stumbled through the last six years of his career. Or so the sports analysts said.

But that wasn't how I knew Zac. With a twang in his accent, clothes that told everyone the only thing he worried about was them being clean and comfortable, and a smile that made most women swoon, he was my buddy. My confidant where his roommate was not.

And I hadn't seen him in almost three months since he'd left to go back home for part of the off-season.

In that instant though, I didn't miss him that much. "You almost got sprayed in the face! I thought you were coming next week." I panted with my hand on my chest, the other hand clutching my pepper spray.

Dropping his boot-clad feet to the floor, I finally let my eyes go up to find that he was standing there with his arms open, smiling wide. He was fresh-faced, tanner than usual, and, eyeing his middle section, maybe a little thicker. "I missed ya too, darlin'."

Temporarily pushing aside the veil Aiden's crappy mood had put over my head, I couldn't help but smile. "What are you doing here?"

"I figured it wasn't gonna kill me to come back a little early," he explained as he rounded the kitchen island and came to stand in front of me, pretty much towering over my five-foot-seven frame. Before either of us could say another word, his arms were around me.

I hugged him back. "The only person that might be getting killed soon is you-know-who. I've almost poisoned him a few times these last couple of months." I took a sniff of him and almost laughed at the scent of Old Spice he insisted on wearing.

"Is he still alive?" he drawled the question lazily but seriously.

Thinking about his comment at the facility had me scowling into his shirt. "Barely."

Pulling back, the smile Zac had on his face withered, his eyes narrowing as he studied my features. "You look like hell, sugar. You're not sleepin'?" he asked as he kept eyeballing what I was sure were the circles under my eyes.

I shrugged beneath his palms. What was the point in lying? "Not enough."

He knew better than to give me shit; instead, he simply shook his head. For a second, I thought about how Aiden would react to the four to five hours I usually squeezed in. He was even more religious about getting anywhere from eight to ten hours of snooze time daily. That was also part of the reason why he didn't have any friends. Thinking about Aiden reminded me of the conversations I'd had recently and how I hadn't talked to Zac in two weeks.

"I finally told Aiden," I blurted out.

His thin mouth fell open, those milky blue eyes going wide. "You did?"

Zac had known what my plans were. Soon after we started getting to know each other, he'd seen me working on my tablet while I was having lunch one afternoon and asked me what I was doing. So I'd told him.

He'd simply grinned at me and replied, "No shit, Van. You got a website or somethin'?"

Since then, I'd redone the logo for his personal website—after I'd insisted how much of a good idea it was for branding himself—and done various banners for his media pages. As a result, he'd gotten me more work through a couple of the other players on the team.

I threw my hands up and put a smile on my face at the same time I wiggled my fingers. "I did it. I told him," I practically sang.

"What he say?" the most unapologetically nosey man I'd ever known asked.

I fought and lost the urge to grimace at the memory of how much Aiden hadn't said. "Nothing. He just told me to let Trevor know."

One of Zac's light brown eyebrows twitched. "Huh."

I ignored it. It didn't matter if Zac thought the same thing I did: *What a dick thing to do.* "Yay," I muttered, still giving him spirit fingers, because even memories of Aiden weren't going to rain on my parade of quitting soon.

He eyed me speculatively for a moment before the emotion was wiped off, and he slapped me on the shoulder hard enough to make me go *Oof.* "It's about damn time."

I rubbed my arm. "I know. I'm relieved I finally sucked it up. But between you and me, I still want to hurl when I think about it."

He watched my hand for a second before making his way back around the island. With his back to me, he said, "Aww, you'll be fine. I'm gonna miss the hell out of your meatloaf when you're gone, but not all of us get to do what we love for a livin'. I'm glad you finally get to join the club, darlin'."

Some days, I didn't completely understand why I wasn't madly in love with Zac. He was a little full of himself, but he was a pro football player, so it wasn't exactly a surprising trait. Plus, he was tall, and I loved tall guys. In the end though, all I felt and had ever felt toward Zac was friendship. The fact that I'd gone out to buy him hemorrhoid cream a couple of times probably helped solidify the lines in our friend zone.

"I'll make you meatloaf anytime you want," I told him.

"You said it." Zac grabbed a banana from the metal tree next to the fridge. "I'm so damn happy to hear you did it."

I shrugged, happy but still a tiny bit nervous about the situation despite knowing it was mostly unreasonable. "Me too."

For a second, I thought about telling him how Aiden had been acting an hour ago, but what was the point? They had polar-opposite personalities as it was, and I knew they got fed up with each other at times. Really, when I thought about it, I wondered how or why they still lived together. They didn't spend much time together or go out and do stuff that friends did.

But with one guy who felt so uncertain with his position on the team that he didn't want to buy a house, and another who wasn't even an American resident, I guess they both found themselves in weird situations.

"How much longer are you—" Zac started to ask just as his phone rang. With a wink, he pulled it out of his pocket and said, "Gimme a sec it's—damn, it's Trevor."

Ugh. He and Aiden had the same manager; it was how they ended up living together.

"He knows?" he asked, pointing down at the illuminated screen of his phone.

I scrunched up my nose. "He hung up on me."

That earned me a laugh. "Lemme see what he wants. Then you can tell me what he said."

I nodded again and watched as he answered the call and headed toward the living room. Setting my bag on the counter, I started cleaning up the kitchen, remembering at the last minute that it was trash day. Pulling the bag out, I put another one in there and then headed into the garage to grab the city-issued can.

I slapped the button to open the garage door. I held my breath before opening the bin lid, throwing the bag in, and then dragging the can down the driveway toward the curb. Just as I was setting it in place, a woman ran by across the street at a steady pace, heading in the direction of where one of the subdivision's walking trails started.

Something, which was as close to jealousy as I thought I could get, panged through my stomach. I eyed my knee and flexed it a little, knowing I could jog if I wanted to, but most of the time I was too tired. Years of physical therapy had done a lot and I knew my knee would ache less if I actually exercised regularly, but I just didn't have the time . . . and when I did have the time, I spent it doing other things.

What a bunch of excuses.

I wanted all these things out of my life . . .

I had finally put in my notice to quit and everything seemed to be going okay. Or at least, things could have been a lot worse than they were. Maybe it was time to start working on other things I wanted to do. I'd been so focused on building up my business the last few years that I'd put off doing a hundred other things I could remember wanting to do when I was a kid.

Screw it.

I only had this one life to live, and I didn't really want to sit back and not accomplish the things I wanted.

It was time, damn it.

FOUR

The thing with having a terrible day is that a lot of times, you don't know it's going to be a bad one until it's too late; it isn't until your clothes are on, you've eaten breakfast, and you're out of the house, so it's too late to go back to request a sick day and bam! The signs stare you right in the eye, and you know your day has instantly gone into the shitter.

I woke up that morning at five o'clock, slightly earlier than usual because it was going to be a busy day of running around, to the smell of my coffee machine going and my alarm clock blaring the most obnoxious tone in its programming. I showered, slipped a thick headband on to keep the hair out of my face, and threw on a pair of slim, red, cropped pants, a short-sleeved blouse, flats, and my glasses. My two cell phones, tablet, and laptop were all sitting together on the counter in the kitchen. I grabbed my things, poured a travel mug with coffee, and hauled ass out of my apartment when the sky was still sleepier than it was awake.

I managed to make it all the way to the parking lot when things started to go wrong. I had a freaking flat. My apartment complex was too cheap for working outside lights, so it took me three times as long to change the tire than it would have usually taken me, and I stained my pants in the process. I was running late, so I didn't go back to change.

Luckily, the rest of the drive went by fine. There wasn't a single light on at any of the other houses surrounding my boss's, so my usual spot in front of the 4,000-square-foot home was empty. I went inside through the front door, disarmed the security panel, and headed straight to the kitchen just as the pipes began humming with use up-stairs.

I put on the apron hanging from a hook in the corner of the kitchen because one stain was enough for only having been up two hours. I pulled fruit out of the freezer, the kale and carrots I'd washed and prepped the day before out of the fridge, measured a cup of pumpkin seeds out of a glass container on the counter, and dumped it all into the five-hundred-dollar blender on the countertop. On the mornings when he didn't leave the house to go to training first thing, he had a big smoothie, worked out a little at home, and afterward had a "normal" breakfast. As if a sixty-four-ounce beverage could be considered a snack.

When I was done blending the ingredients, I poured the mixture into four big glasses and placed Aiden's portion in front of his favorite spot on the kitchen island. Two apples out of the fridge later, I set it all right next to the glasses of smoothie. Like clockwork, the sound of thunder on the steps warned me the Wall of Winnipeg was on his way down.

We had this routine set up that didn't require words to get through it.

The second sign I'd been given that today wasn't going to be my day was the scowl Aiden had on his face, but my attention had been too focused on washing the blender to notice it. "Good morning," I said without glancing up.

Nothing. I still hadn't been able to give up greeting him even though I knew he wouldn't respond; my manners wouldn't let me.

So I went on like always, washing dirty dishes as the man sitting on the stool in front of me drank his breakfast. Then, once he was ready, he finally cracked the silence with a low, sleep-stained and hoarse-voiced, "What's the plan for today?"

"You have a radio interview at nine."

He grunted his acknowledgment.

"Today is the day the Channel 2 news people are coming by."

Another grunt, but that one was especially unenthusiastic.

I didn't blame him; at the same time, I didn't understand why his manager had even gotten him that kind of publicity with the local news. It was one thing for him to get through an interview in a hotel room in the pressroom after a game, or in the locker room, but one at his house? I'd spent the day before dusting the hell out of the living room and kitchen in preparation for it.

"Then you have that luncheon you were invited to at the seniors center you donated money to. Last month, you had me confirm with them." I kind of eyed him after I said it, half expecting him to say he'd changed his mind and wasn't going.

He didn't. He nodded that tiny baby nod that could have been easy to miss.

"Did you want me to go with you?" I asked just to be sure. Most of the time, I accompanied him anywhere he went in Dallas, but if I could get out of it, I would.

"Yes," he grumbled his sleepy reply.

Damn. "All right. We should get going by eight just to be on the safe side."

He lifted a couple of fingers in acknowledgment or agreement, whatever. Five chugs of smoothie later, he got up and handed over the empty glasses. "I'll be in the gym. Get me fifteen minutes before we need to leave so I can shower."

"You got it, boss."

"VANESSA!"

I peeked my head into the green room Aiden was waiting in until his radio interview, and hit send on the message to my little brother before slipping my personal phone into the back pocket of my jeans.

"Yes, sir?" I called out.

"I want more water," he replied. He sat on the edge of the couch, busy doing whatever it was he did on his phone. It wasn't like he responded to any fan mail unless I insisted, and he didn't pay his own bills, or do his own posts on his social media websites. That was my job. What exactly he did was beyond me.

I didn't care enough to snoop.

"Okay, I'll be back," I replied, trying to remember where I'd seen the break room.

It took me a lot longer than I expected to find the vending machines because, of course, no radio station employee happened to be roaming the hallways in my time of need. But I bought two bottles with the cash I had on hand and found my way back to the green room.

"Did you go all the way to Fiji to get the water?" Aiden asked abruptly when I entered.

Umm.

What?

I frowned and then blinked. I focused in on my boss and the fact there were two women sitting on the couch perpendicular to him now, catching a glimpse of boobs in a low-cut blouse, and too much makeup. I wasn't worried about them. The only thing I was paying attention to was my boss. My temporary boss. *My temporary boss*, I reminded myself.

"Is something wrong?" I made myself ask carefully as I stood there, staring him right in the eye, even as the two women seemed to squirm in their seats, like when you're a kid and your friend's parents scold them right in front of you; it was that awkward.

He watched me right back, his answer more of a pop than a statement. "No."

No.

Why did I bother asking stupid questions? Really. For a moment, I thought about keeping my mouth closed, but this moody crap was getting old real quick. His usual grumpiness was one thing, but this was a total other. The fact he was being an asshole *again* in public hummed a quiet song that was too easy to ignore and push away before mulling over, because I didn't know the women in the room and I would never see them again. What he'd said in front of Christian had been a different story.

Picking at the material covering my headband, I glared at that whiskered face and that whiskered face alone. "I know it's not my position to say anything, but if there's something you want to talk about . . ." My voice was rough, anger tinting each syllable.

His sole focus was on me. The big guy straightened his spine and set his phone on top of one of his thighs. He wore his usual baggy shorts and T-shirt. "You're right. I don't pay you for your opinion."

One, two, three, four, five, six, seven, eight, nine, ten.

I balled up the sensation burning my esophagus and willed myself to keep it together. I knew what it was like to be picked on. I knew what it was like to be treated like crap by the people you were supposed to care about.

I wasn't going to cry over Aiden. I didn't cry over people who didn't deserve my tears, and Aiden—especially not fucking Aiden—wouldn't be the person to break me. Not now, not ever.

One, two, three, four, five, six, seven, eight, nine, ten.

He was right. I was his PA, and that was what he paid me for no matter how hard I gritted my teeth. I was leaving soon. He wouldn't be my business any longer. Biting the inside of my cheek, I made myself let the moment go, even though I would later look back on it and realize it was the hardest thing I'd ever done.

In a calm, even voice, I set the bottles of water on the table, maybe slightly breathing like a dragon. "Do you need anything else right now?"

"No," the rude bastard muttered.

I smiled at him, even though I was positive my nostrils were flaring, and kept right on ignoring the women who had gotten to their feet. I didn't need to ask to know that they had invited themselves in and were now regretting that decision. Good. "I'll be out here then."

I got out of there and leaned my back against the wall right next to the door, my fists clenching at my sides. A second later, the two strangers who had magically appeared were out of the room, two dark heads pressed together as they walked down the hall and out of sight. It wasn't the first time women had tried to approach Aiden and gotten shut down immediately; either way, it wasn't like I even cared. I was too pissed off to give a crap about anything other than the asswipe in the green room.

What the hell was his deal?

I hadn't told him about the multiple emails he'd gotten from angry fans in San Antonio over the canceled signing—he wouldn't have given a crap about them either way. Trevor and Rob hadn't been blowing up my phone or his about anything lately. He didn't seem to be having any issues with his tendon either. What was it then? He had everything and anything he wanted.

What the hell could possibly be wrong in his nearly perfect little world?

This was the last year of his contract and he'd been putting off talking about what he wanted to do after it was over, but he had options. Probably too many options, if that was possible. Getting bent out of shape over that didn't make sense, at least this early. Aiden focused on the now. I could see him worrying about the future once the season was at least halfway over.

So what else could it be?

"Hi, miss," a voice called out from down the hallway with a wave. "We're ready for Mr. Graves," the radio station employee said.

I forced a smile on my face and nodded. "Okay." I dropped the smile before peeking into the room and giving Miranda a flat, expressionless look, as everything in me raged at the sight of his face. "They're ready for you."

AFTER THE INTERVIEW, the ride back to Aiden's place had been quiet and tense. As soon as we arrived, he disappeared into his gym without a single word. I raged to myself as I swept and mopped the living room and kitchen floor again, angrily, in anticipation of the camera crew coming. I knew what Aiden had done hadn't been the floor's fault, but it was the only thing I had around that I could take my frustrations out on.

I had just started working on the hallway that led from the front of the house to the half bathroom and the gym when I overheard Aiden.

"I'm about sick and tired of hearing what you think is best for me. I know what's best for me," Aiden's familiar voice spat.

Uh . . . what?

"No, you listen to me. Maybe I'll re-sign with them, maybe I won't, but don't make promises I have no intention of keeping," Aiden kept going with venom in every vowel.

Was he contemplating leaving Dallas?

"Don't glorify what you've done. I have what I have because of my hard work, no one else's," Aiden added after a brief pause.

Who was he talking to? Trevor? Rob?

"I don't care," Aiden growled a moment later.

The silence after that was heavy, almost ominous, and extremely alarming.

"All I'm asking is for you to do what's best for me. That's what you're supposed to do. You work for me, not the team."

Well, someone wasn't just being bitchy to me today. That should have made me feel better, but it didn't.

"I don't need to remember anything," Aiden said carefully, his tone controlled and cool. "Don't open your mouth; it's that easy. Don't promise them anything. Don't even talk to them. I'm telling you to listen to what I want. That's what I pay you to do, isn't it?"

Then, just like that, it was over.

I must have stood completely still for at least five minutes, listening, but there was nothing else said. I stayed rooted in place, breathing as quietly as possible until I figured enough time had passed to not make a suspicious sound.

"Slackin' on the job?" Zac asked, his head hanging over from the top stair rail.

I froze. What if Aiden thought I might have overheard his conversation? Damn it. I coughed and smiled innocently up. "You're barely waking up?" I tried to play it cool.

"It's my day off," he explained as he jogged down the steps.

"Hasn't every day been your day off?" I teased, not waiting for him to answer. "Ask me what time I woke up this morning," I said, putting my chin on the top of the Swiffer handle.

"I don't wanna know, darlin'." He patted my shoulder as he walked by me into the kitchen. "I don't wanna know."

I snorted and pushed the dusting device around the hardwood floor as the sounds of Zac messing around in the kitchen kept me company while I thought about Aiden's conversation. He had never said anything about leaving the team, and I guess I hadn't assumed he would. Judging from the digits in his bank account—at least the account I had access to—his contract extension a few years ago had been more than lucrative. Plus, he'd only improved. He was the face of the Three Hundreds. They would give him anything he asked for, but who the hell actually knew what that was? I sure didn't.

Aiden should be singing praises for the Three Hundreds all day every day for what they'd given him in exchange for his skills.

"The house is lookin' good, *Cinderella*," Zac snorted as he held a bowl to his chest and snuck by me before I could whack him with the handle. He dashed through the doorway that led into the living room. The television was turned on a moment later.

Before I knew it, Aiden was in his bedroom getting dressed in something other than workout clothes for the first time in months, and a Channel 2 news truck was parking on the curb across the street. With a quick glance around, I made sure the house looked even more spot-free than usual. By the time the doorbell started ringing, Zac was zooming up the stairs with a panicked expression on his face.

"I don't live here," he muttered on his journey just as I reached the door and opened it.

A man in a suit and two cameramen stood on the other side. "Hi, come in," I said, waving them forward. "Aiden will be down in a second. Would you like something to drink?"

All three of them glanced around carefully as I showed them into the living room, where a producer and Trevor had already agreed would be the best place to film. I caught the camera guy looking at the walls when Aiden jogged down the steps. I'd never lived through an earthquake, but I was sure him on the steps might register on the Richter scale.

He filled the entrance to the living room—his shoulders and arms looking spectacular in the white polo shirt he'd somehow squeezed into, and the khaki pants he had to get specially made for his oversize thighs. I edged my way out of the corner of the living room, not nec-essarily wanting to but knowing I needed to. Just because I was pissed off at him didn't mean I stopped doing my job.

"Need anything before you start?"

His eyes were everywhere, except on me. "Get them some water."

Oh, ye of little expectations.

I blew out a breath, ground down on my molars, and nodded. "I was already going to do that. I was just waiting for you to come down-stairs."

When the doorbell rang, I frowned and walked around Aiden, wondering if one of the crew had been outside taking a smoke break. Peeking through the hole, I saw a face I'd seen enough of recently through video chat.

Trevor.

Of all the people in the world . . .

Undoing the lock, I slowly let it swing open, but put my body between him and the crack in the door.

"Vanessa," the fortyish man greeted me.

My eyelids lowered. "Trevor."

Dressed in a steel-gray suit with his hair combed back, he looked every bit the high-powered sports manager he was . . . and a douche. "Can I come in?" He didn't make it sound like a question.

Could he? Yes. Did I want him to? No. But considering his two clients lived here, I didn't really have a say. "I didn't know you were in town," I commented as he stepped past me inside.

"Only for the day," he said, casually strolling in and heading into the living room.

Had he been in town talking to the team about Aiden? Was that who Aiden had been on the phone with?

To give Aiden and Trevor credit, they both acted like they hadn't just been arguing recently. What a bunch of fake asses. I held back my eye roll and headed into the kitchen to grab enough bottles of water for the entire crew, Aiden, and the White Devil. I set the bottles on the coffee table and headed toward the half bath to take a quick pee.

"Van!" Zac whisper-hissed when I was in the hallway.

I tipped my head back to find him peeking over the railing and couldn't help but grin. "What are you doing?" I whispered, eyeing the living room to make sure no one was paying attention.

"I'm beggin' you. I'll love you forever, darlin' . . ." he started.

That had me groaning. I knew I was going to say yes to whatever he was about to ask of me, just because he was being so cute.

"I don't wanna go down there, but I'm starvin'. I have two sandwiches in the fridge; can you toss 'em up to me?"

I blinked. Did he not know who he was talking to? Me tossing stuff? "Give me a second."

He pumped his hands in front of his chest before retreating behind the bannister. What a goofball.

As I passed by the doorway of the living room to go into the kitchen, I could see the crew arranging white umbrellas and bright lights by the couches as the man in the suit talked to Aiden and Trevor. I snagged the two foot-long sandwiches, still in their wax-paper wrapper from the fridge, and hustled up the stairs with them and a bag of sweet potato chips. I knew him. He'd get hungry in half an hour on just a sandwich.

Sure enough, Zac was waiting at the top of the stairs, his back against the guest bedroom's closed door, just far enough away from the staircase so that anyone standing at the bottom couldn't see him.

He beamed when he spotted my offering. It didn't escape me that he still hadn't gotten dressed for the day. I couldn't wait until I didn't have to either. "I love you, Vanny. Do you know I love you?"

I handed him his things. "So you've said."

"I do. Anything you ever need, I'm your loyal servant," he said, busy peering down the stairs as he whispered.

"How about a million bucks?"

Zac glanced at me over his shoulder. "Well, anything but that. I don't even have a million bucks for me. I'm the poor guy in the house."

Considering he probably made eight times what I did—at least—I wouldn't call him poor. But comparing him to Money Bags of Winnipeg in the living room, I could see his point.

"Have you seen Vanessa?" Aiden's voice carried up the stairs from below.

Just as I opened my mouth to let him know where I was, Trevor answered. "Since when do I keep track of your dinner roll?" he replied in a voice that definitely wasn't a whisper.

Did that asshole just call me fat?

Zac's eyes met mine as if he was thinking the same thing. I frowned and put my index finger up to my mouth so I could focus on listening. Apparently, I was a masochist who liked to do things that caused myself pain and anger.

"She was here a second ago."

"I know this isn't the time, but I will find you somebody else." That was the asshole talking. "She did tell you she was quitting, didn't she?"

Aiden's "Uh-huh" made it up the stairs.

"Good. I'll find you a replacement soon. Don't worry."

"I'm not," the traitor replied, which only slightly insulted me.

"I was worried you weren't going to handle it well," Trevor admitted, but I was so focused on what was being said, I didn't pick up on the hints he was leaving with his word choice.

"She can do whatever she wants," the Wall of Winnipeg replied in that cool voice that held zero emotion, a confirmation of its own that he meant what he said.

What a damn dick. Did anyone appreciate me?

"I never liked her much anyway," the devil's advocate continued.

I hadn't liked Trevor much either, but sheesh. Weren't there more important things in the world to talk about than me behind my back?

Aiden, on the other hand, grunted, and the insults just kept on coming . . .

"Maybe I can find you someone a little easier on the eyes. What do you think?" Trevor's tone lightened at his joke.

I waited. Then I waited a little longer for Aiden to tell him to shut up and do his job.

But I waited in vain. He didn't say a word.

After everything I had done for Aiden . . .

Everything . . .

He was going to let Trevor talk shit about me? I mean, I just figured a decent person wouldn't do that. I would never let anyone talk
badly about Aiden, unless it was Zac and me doing the shit-talking,
but I figured we both had get-out-of-jail passes with it, since he was his
roommate and I was his lackey.

But the entire conversation—this moment—felt like a betrayal at
the highest level.

It was one thing to be his employee, but for him not to care even
a little bit that I was leaving? On top of that, for him to let this asshole
talk about me? About my freaking looks of all things? I'd never shown
up to work a sloppy mess. My straight, auburn hair was usually fine
because I didn't do much with it other than let it loose around my
shoulders. I put makeup on and put some effort into my clothes. I
wasn't gorgeous, but I wasn't ugly—at least I didn't think so. And sure,
I wasn't a size zero or a three or a five, but *was Trevor fucking kidding
me? Me? A goddamn dinner roll?*

I was hit on every once in a while. If I wanted a boyfriend, I could
have a boyfriend, and he wouldn't look like Shrek either, damn it.

Fucking asshole. Who did he think he was? He wasn't exactly
Keanu Reeves to begin with.

I managed to count to two before thinking "fuck it" and letting
myself get mad.

What was I doing here? It had been weeks since I told them I was
quitting. Aiden had been bossier and moodier than usual. Colder. I
couldn't completely blame it on his injury at this point either.

And here I'd been stressing out about keeping his house clean,
putting chocolates on his pillow, and delaying my dreams because
I felt bad leaving him, and he couldn't even tell Trevor not to talk
about me.

I swallowed and blinked once. Only once. I met Zac's eyes and
found his jaw clenched. Biting the inside of my cheek, I thought
about what I told myself out on the curb with the trashcan. I'd begun
going for walks that day. I'd even done a little jogging. I'd gotten paid
last week.

This was my life, and I was the one to choose how to spend it, wasn't I? Hadn't I done enough? Put up with enough? Sucked it up enough?

If I didn't put up with people who should have mattered, why the hell was I putting up with people who didn't? Life was what you made out of it, at least that was what those *Chicken Soup* books my foster father thrust on me when I was a teenager imprinted on me. When life gives you lemons, you get to choose what you make out of them; it doesn't always have to be lemonade.

With a mental slap to my own butt, I nodded at the only loyal person in this house. "I'm out of here."

"Van—" he started to say, shaking his head. His long face was tight.

"Don't worry about it. They're not worth it."

Zac scrubbed at the side of his jaw before tilting his head in the direction of the stairs. "Get outta here before I try to go kick both their asses."

That had me sucking in a watery snort. *Try to kick both of their asses.* "Give me a call or a text every once in a while. All right?"

"Nothin' would stop me from doin' it," he assured me, putting his fist out.

Thinking of my psychopath older sisters, I filled my veins with every inch of hard-earned resolve I had within me and fist-bumped him. We looked at each other for a moment before hugging, just a second, not a goodbye but an "I'll see you later."

Down the stairs, I ignored the bare walls I'd be looking at for the last time. The sound of voices in the living room almost had me glancing over, but I didn't care enough to waste the energy.

I was over this.

In the kitchen, I pulled my work phone out of my bag, fished my keys out of my purse, and pulled Aiden's house, mailbox, and PO box key off the ring. Setting those four items on the kitchen island, I rubbed at my eyebrow with the back of my hand, adjusted my purple-framed glasses, and tried to make sure I hadn't left anything lying around. Then again, if I left something, Zac could grab it for me.

I rubbed my pants with the palms of my hands and slung my purse over my shoulder, nervous anticipation flooding my stomach. I was doing this. *I was fucking doing it.*

"Could you go out and grab me something to eat?" Trevor asked, suddenly standing in the kitchen when I turned around to leave.

While I knew I was supposed to kill even this dipshit with kindness, I couldn't dig deep enough inside of me to be an adult. This was the last time I'd have to put up with his crap; I'd never have to see him again, deal with him again. Amen and thank you, Jesus.

"No," I replied with a little smirk on my face. "Dinner Roll is leaving now. Please make sure to tell Aiden later on when no one else is around that I said he can eat shit."

Trevor's mouth gaped. "What?"

Going out in a mini blaze of glory, I wiggled my fingers at him over my shoulder as I walked out of the kitchen. Just as I reached for the door, I turned to peek in the living room to find Aiden on one couch talking to the reporter. For a brief split second, those brown eyes met mine across the room, and I'd swear on my life a crease formed between his eyebrows.

Just as I opened the door, and before I could talk myself out of it, I mouthed, "I deserve better, asshole," making sure he read my lips as I did it. Then I raised my middle finger up at him and waved goodbye with it.

I hoped they both got syphilis.

FIVE

One week turned into two, then three, and finally four.

In the days that followed me walking out of Aiden's house, and subsequently quitting my job, I thought about Aiden a lot more than I would have ever expected when I wasn't busy working. Most of those times didn't even revolve around me wanting to kill him, either.

After I walked out of his house, my foot couldn't hit the gas pedal fast enough to get me home. The first thing I did was start on a new project, more determined than ever to succeed at what I loved doing. I was ready and willing to bust my ass to make things work, no matter the cost.

The ties had been cut as far as I was concerned.

Aiden had been a fucking jackass, when I had never accused him of being anything other than practical and determined. I could relate to that, but I couldn't connect with him being such a traitor. I was no Trevor or Rob. I didn't make extra money off the choices he made, and if anything, things were better for me when he was happier. Hadn't I tried to do what was best for him? Hadn't I tried to do things that made him happy?

Yet he'd let that asswipe talk about me when I'd spent last Christmas in Dallas, instead of going to see my little brother, because he still hadn't been able to move around much at that point.

Unfortunately, I thought about Aiden first thing in the morning for days after I walked out. My body wasn't used to sleeping in until eight; even on my days off, I was usually up and about by six. I thought about him as I made my breakfast and chomped on breakfast sausage.

Then I thought about him again at lunchtime and dinner, so used to making his meals and eating part of them.

Each day for those first two weeks of freedom, I thought about him often. You couldn't work with someone five, six, or even sometimes seven days a week for two years without getting into a routine. I knew I couldn't just erase him from my life like he'd been drawn in with a pencil.

Much less erase that moment when I realized I'd been holding on to a job with a man who wouldn't come to my funeral, even if it fell on a day he was supposed to rest. The fact I had family members who wouldn't go to my funeral didn't really help ease the sting of it enough.

After a few days, my anger abated, but that feeling of betrayal that had seared my lungs didn't exactly go away completely. Something had been going on with him; that much had been obvious. Maybe under normal circumstances, he wouldn't have acted like such a massive prick.

But he had crossed the thin little line I'd drawn in the imaginary sand. And I did what felt right.

So it was done.

I kept living my life as my own boss, which was exactly what I'd planned on doing anyway.

And I didn't look back at what I'd done.

I WAS SPEED-WALKING toward my apartment one night after a visit to the gym, finalizing the last brainstorming touches I wanted to add to a paperback design I was aiming to finish before I went to bed, when I spotted a figure sitting at the bottom of the stairs. Patting the pepper spray I always kept within reach, especially when I was in my complex, I narrowed my eyes and wondered who the hell would be sitting there right then.

It was nine o'clock at night. Only drug dealers hung around outside our complex after dark. Everyone else knew better. Plus, who liked sitting outside with the summer heat and mosquitos?

With that in mind, I walked a little faster, conscious that my knee ached only a little after my two-mile run. Two miles! It had only taken me half a month of jogging four times a week to work up to a steady one-mile distance, and then I'd added another mile, going just a bit faster. It was something, and I was proud of myself. The plan was to up another mile this week.

My hand was still on my pepper spray as I kept a wary eye on the . . . man; it was definitely a man sitting at the foot of the steps. I squinted. My keys were in my free hand, ready to get put to good use, either to open my door or to stab somebody in the eye if it came down to it.

I had just started pulling my spray out when a male voice spoke up. "Vanessa?"

For one split second, I froze at the sound of the rumbling, raspy tone, more than slightly caught off guard at the fact that this stranger sitting on the stairs knew my name.

Then it hit me. Recognition.

I stopped in place just as the not-a-stranger stood up, and I blinked.

"Hey." My ex-boss straightened to his impressive full height, confirming it was him. Aiden. It was Aiden. Here.

Crouched down, he could have been any guy who worked out, especially when he had his arms tucked into his sides, hiding the girth of muscles that made him famous. The possibility that this was the first time he'd ever used the H-word with me was the first thought that ran through my head before I blurted out, "What are you doing here?"

I was definitely frowning. My forehead was creasing and scrunching up as I took him in, in his T-shirt and shorts, for the first time in a month.

His face was that same immovable mask as always. Those brown eyes I'd seen hundreds of times in the past bore down on me, his eyes going over the bright ruby red I'd let Diana color my hair two weeks ago. He didn't comment on it. "You live here?" His question cut the air between us abruptly. His gaze dropped to the hand I had on my pepper spray and the set of keys clutched between my fingers.

I thought about my neighbors, the crappy building, the number of cars parked in the lot that were always in some sort of disrepair, and the cracked sidewalk with a dying lawn straddling it. I rarely had people over, so it wasn't like I had any reason to care about where I lived. All

I'd needed was a roof over my head. Plus, it could be worse. Things could always be worse. I tried to never forget that.

Then I thought of the beautiful gated community Aiden lived in, and the awesome kitchen I'd cooked in so many times before . . . and finally, I envisioned the stained carpet in my apartment and the peeling vinyl countertops with only a slight cringe.

I wasn't going to be ashamed that I didn't live in an upscale condo. It was the first place I'd ever had all to myself, and it had done what I needed it to do: give me a place to sleep and work in peace.

So I nodded slowly, surprised—okay, I was shocked as hell—to see him. I'd talked to Zac a few times since I quit and had gone to eat with him twice, but except for once, he hadn't brought up Aiden in any of the conversations we'd had. The extent of what he'd told me about my ex-boss was that they'd been working out together. That had been more than enough.

Aiden's gaze didn't waver for a moment. His remote, clean facial expression didn't change at all either. "I want to talk to you," he demanded more than said.

I wanted to know how he found out where I lived, but the question was trapped in my throat. The one syllable word I knew I needed to tell him had taken a stroll down the block . . . and then I remembered: dinner roll.

That fucker Trevor had called me a dinner roll of all things, and this man had said nothing.

I couldn't help but squeeze the loose side of my shorts. I'd lost almost ten pounds over the last five weeks, and it had taken its toll on most of my clothes. But thinking about Trevor's comment only made me angry and more resolved.

"No." There, I said it. Easy. It was so easy to say it. "I don't have time. I have a lot of work to do."

Guilt nipped at my head for being so rude, but I squashed it. I didn't owe him a single thing, not a moment of time or a single extra thought.

That stubborn, strong chin tipped up, that full, masculine mouth flattening, and he blinked. "You don't have a few minutes for me?"

I swallowed hard and fought the urge to fidget under his gaze. "No. I have a lot of work to do," I repeated, looking at that familiar face evenly.

The lines that came over his forehead settled the emotion he'd been fighting with a second ago. Shock. He was shocked for what was more than likely the first time in his life, and that gave me a boost of strength and confidence not to waver under his glare.

"We need to talk," he said, brushing off my comment in typical Aiden fashion.

What the hell did we need to talk about? Everything that needed to be said between us had been said. He'd been an asshole, and I was done. What more was there?

"Look, I really am busy."

I was just about to make up some other excuse when one of the doors in the building in front of mine closed with a loud snap. I didn't want to find out what could possibly happen if anyone in my complex found out who was standing in the stairwell to my building. I'd been home enough Sunday evenings to know there were football fans everywhere.

With a sigh and a promise to myself that he wasn't going to get whatever he came here for, I waved him toward the door. "I don't think there's anything for us to talk about," was the only thing I managed to respond with. Did I want to stand outside my apartment? No. Did I want to go inside? No. But I definitely didn't want my neighbors finding out a semi-famous millionaire was standing right outside my door. "But you can come inside for a little bit before anyone sees you," I said in more of a mumble than anything, turning back to unlock the door. "I guess," I added just because the sight of him made me pretty bitchy.

You should have told him to beat it, Van, my brain said. And it was the truth.

I held the door open for him, watching out of my peripheral vision as he squeezed inside. Once the door was locked, I flipped on the lights as the big defensive end took a few hesitant steps inside. I could see his head turning one way and then the other, looking at the pieces of stretched canvas art I had on the wall—not that he knew they were my work unless he looked closely at the initials in the corners. He didn't make a comment and neither did I. He'd never asked what I did when I wasn't at his house or with him, and I'd never mentioned it either.

Which was funny when I thought about it, because there were players on his team who knew exactly what I did. Players who had sought me out to redo their website banners; two of the guys I'd actually done tattoo designs for—and here was this guy. This guy who I had twice said to, "I was thinking your promo shots could be a little simpler. The font they used for your name doesn't look very clear, and the placement looks weird. Do you want me to change it for you?" And what had he done in return each time?

He'd said, "Don't bother."

He'd brushed me off. It had taken me weeks to get the nerve to make that suggestion to him, and I would have done it for free. But it was fine. It was his career and his branding, not mine.

He planted himself on the love seat in my living room, and I spun my desk chair around to face him, looking at him as evenly and unattached as I possibly could. The room was pretty small. The entire apartment was sized for one person. The only furniture that fit, cramped, was the two-seater couch, my desk, a chair, and a bookshelf that doubled as a TV stand.

Nerves didn't pound through me as I watched him practically consume the space. I was over this thing with him, and I just didn't have the faintest urge to try and be friendly. I didn't feel like joking with him or making it seem like there weren't any hard feelings. If anything, I was annoyed he was at my apartment.

I had nothing left to lose, and he wasn't in charge of my paychecks anymore. I hadn't even stressed when I realized I wouldn't get paid for the last few days I was with him, because there was no way I was contacting Aiden or Trevor. Walking out the way I had and flipping him off in the process had been worth every penny lost.

"Why are you here, Aiden?" I finally broke the silence when a minute or two had passed after we'd sat down.

Aiden had his hands on his lap, his face was as remote as it was before a game; even his shoulders were as tight as ever, his spine eternally straight. I didn't think, even when he was at home, that I'd ever really seen him at ease. His hair was freshly buzzed, and he looked fine and healthy. Like he always had. As if a month hadn't passed since the last time we'd been in each other's presence.

He leveled his dark gaze on me and said, "I want you to come back."

I was dreaming. That probably wasn't the best word to use. Nightmaring? Delusional, maybe?

"Excuse me?" I breathed as I took in the whites around his eyes to make sure they weren't bloodshot. Then I took a brief sniff to make sure he didn't smell like a skunk. He didn't, but apparently anything was possible. "Are you . . . are you on drugs right now?"

Aiden gave me one hard, slow blink. His short but incredibly thick lashes went to rest for a brief second. "Excuse me?" His tone was subdued, guarded.

"Are you on drugs?" I repeated myself, because there was no way he'd be here asking me this sober.

Right?

He stared at me with his unflinching eyes and hard, no-nonsense mouth. "I'm not on drugs," he said, clearly insulted.

I eyed him like I didn't believe him, because I didn't. What the hell would give him the idea that I'd go back to work for him?

Drugs.

Drugs would make him think that wasting his time by coming here was a good idea. Hadn't the parting comment I'd asked Trevor to deliver for me been enough?

What I was thinking must have been apparent on my face, because he shook his head and repeated himself. "I'm not on drugs, Vanessa."

I'd grown up with an addict, and I was well aware they denied they had a problem, even if the signs they were out of control were right smack in front of their face. I narrowed my eyes and searched his features again, trying to find a sign he was on something.

"Stop looking at me like that. I'm not on anything," he insisted; faint lines crossed his tan forehead—the children of the time he spent in the sun and a marker that he was thirty years old and not twenty-two.

I glanced at his arms to make sure there weren't any weird bruises on them and came up with nothing. Then I glanced at his hands, trying to peer at the delicate flesh between his fingers to see if there were any track marks there. Still, nothing.

"I'm not on anything." He paused. "Since when have you ever known me to want to take a painkiller?"

It was my turn to pause, to meet his eyes in the safety of my apartment, and slowly say, "Never." I swallowed. "But then I also didn't know you to be an asshole either," I replied before I could stop myself.

For one second, he reared back. The motion was minute, tinier than tiny, but I'd seen it. It had been there. His nostrils flared wide, the gesture so exaggerated I couldn't help but take it in. "Vanessa—"

"I don't need you to apologize." My hands fiddled at my lap as that small hint of betrayal scourged its way right between my breasts, reminding me that maybe I hadn't completely gotten over what had happened. *Maybe.* But I made myself tell him, "I don't need anything from you."

He opened his mouth, and I would swear on my life the muscles high up on his cheeks twitched. He made a small sound, the beginning of a stutter, like he wanted to say something substantial to me for the first time since we'd known each other, but didn't know how to go about it.

The thing was, I wasn't in the mood for it.

Whatever he might have contemplated saying was a month too late. A year too late. Two years too late.

I had lied to my loved ones about why I'd suddenly quit. Adding up another lie to add to the list of things I'd refrained from telling them over the years because I didn't want them to worry or be angry over something so dumb and insignificant.

It didn't matter though. I didn't work for him anymore, and I'd honestly expected never to see him again. What was the point in getting all bent out of shape? I tried to tell myself that leaving the way I had had been the best way to go about it. Otherwise, who knew how much longer I would have hung around waiting for my replacement? Maybe they would have tried to get rid of me quickly, but I would never know.

We were as even as we possibly could be. I didn't feel anything except the barest hum of recognition for someone I'd seen hundreds of times. This guy who I had admired, who I had once respected, who had slightly broken my heart and disillusioned me.

I have moved on with my life though, I thought, forcing my hands still. "I just want to know why you're here. I really do have things to do," I said in a calm voice.

The man who had earned his nickname in high school, because even back then he'd been a big son of a gun, cocked his head to the side, his tongue sweeping over his upper teeth. The big knot of his Adam's apple bobbed before he finally aimed his gaze back at me, accusingly. "I kept expecting you to come back after a few days, but you never did."

Had I been that much of a pushover? "You honestly thought I would do that?" I gave him my best "are you serious?" look.

His eyes slid to the side briefly, but he didn't admit or deny anything. "I want you to come back."

No matter what, he wasn't going to guilt-trip me. I didn't even have to think about my response. "No."

He decided to ignore me. Shocking. "I tried to get Trevor to find you, but no one even knew you had another cell phone or had your right address."

Of course no one did, because neither one of them had ever made an effort to know anything about me, but I kept that to myself. The address they had was from the place where I'd lived with Diana and her brother in Fort Worth, a sister city to Dallas. Rodrigo had moved out a year and a half afterward when his girlfriend had gotten pregnant, and when I got my job with Aiden, I got my own place, needing to be in Dallas instead of traveling back and forth almost an hour every day. Since then, Diana had moved into her own place.

It also didn't escape me that Aiden didn't drop Zac's name. He was the only one in our small circle who knew my personal number, and I was sure he wouldn't share it.

"Come back."

I pushed the bridge of my glasses up and used one of the strongest, most resilient words in the English language: "No."

"I'll pay you more."

Tempting, but . . . "No."

"Why not?"

Why not? Men. It was only freaking men who would be so . . . so *dumb*. He hadn't apologized to me for what he'd said. He wasn't even trying to be nice and win me over to come back—not that I would. It was the same old shit it always was.

Come back.

Why not?

Blah, blah, blah.

Why not?

Why the hell would I?

I almost said I was sorry for not doing what he wanted, but I wasn't. Not even a little bit. As I took in Aiden, his overwhelming size swallowing my couch, demanding that I come back and not understanding why I wouldn't want to, I realized that being nice wasn't going to accomplish anything. I had to tell him the truth, or at least the closest thing to the truth as possible. A small, immature part of me wanted to be mean.

I wanted to hurt him the way he'd hurt me, but as I took him in, I took in the man who had provided me with a job that had allowed me to fund and fulfill my dreams. This was the same person who I'd seen at his worst, when he'd faced the possibility he would never play the only thing in the world he loved again.

This was Aiden. I knew some of his secrets. I didn't want to care about him, but I guess I couldn't help it, even if it was a subconscious, mutilated version of what it had once been. And I didn't want to be like Trevor, or Susie, or any other person I'd ever met who was mean for the sake of being mean.

So I kept it as simple as I could. I stuck my fingers under my thighs and said, "I told you. I deserve better."

SIX

"Oh shit."

I spotted the black Range Rover in the parking lot the instant the taxi pulled up in front of the complex by the guest entrance. There was no way I could miss it; I'd taken it to get an oil change and a wash a few times in the past. It wasn't necessarily the nicest car in the lot—a few of my neighbors had Escalades and Mercedes that I wasn't sure how they afforded—but I recognized Aiden's license plate number.

Yet it still caught me off guard to see it there.

He hadn't exactly left my apartment with a smile on his face a few days ago. After I clearly told him I didn't want to go back to work for him, he'd looked at me like I was speaking a different language, and asked, "Is this a joke?"

There went arrogance for you.

I'd answered the only way I would. "No."

He had gotten to his feet, turned his attention toward the ceiling for a moment, and left. And that was that.

The last thing I expected was for him to come back. Then again, maybe I shouldn't have been surprised. I'd learned that this was a person who, once he put his mind to something, nothing deterred him from his goal. This was the person who only heard what he wanted to hear. That didn't exactly leave me with a warm, fuzzy feeling. I guess a big part of me just wanted and expected to make a clean cut with him, especially after he'd made his lack of loyalty so apparent.

The fact that he'd somehow gotten my address and gone out of his way to come to my apartment when he hadn't even been able to put in a single effort to ask me how I was doing frustrated me more than it probably should have. It was too little too late. All I would have wanted from him in the past was at least a little bit of loyalty, if not friendship, and he hadn't even been able to give me that.

"Everything all right, ma'am?"

"Everything is fine, thanks," I lied, gripping the handle. "I thought I lost my keys, but I found them. How much do I owe you?"

Paying my fare, I slipped out of the car and hurried through the gate.

I made my way toward my apartment with one hand wrapped around my pepper spray and the other with my keys and wristlet, all too aware that I'd had too much wine to drink to deal with this crap right now.

My visitor was in the same spot on the stairs I'd found him days ago.

Aiden's gaze almost immediately landed on me, hovering on the hem of the dress I'd worn to dinner as he climbed to his size 13 feet. Dressed in workout shorts that reached his knees and a T-shirt, I was pretty sure he'd left practice and come straight over. If my dates were right, the team was halfway through preseason training camp, focused more on the rookies than on veterans like Aiden.

"We need to talk," he stated immediately, his eyes scraping their way to my chest and catching on the low dip of the cotton sundress right between my breasts.

Huh.

I gave him a side look as I approached my door, ignoring the curious expression he was giving me. It wasn't like I hadn't worn dresses around him before, but none of them had been above my knees, and they had all covered the Girls. The one I had on now? Not so much. But it had been my "I'm meeting up with a man for the first time in almost two years on a blind date, someone who I'd met on the matchmaking website I'd signed up for a few weeks back" dress. While we'd gotten along pretty well in the messages we'd exchanged, we hadn't hit it off in person. Paranoid about meeting a stranger that could write down my license plate, I'd taken a cab to the Italian restaurant we were having dinner at.

"Give me a few minutes," he said in a slightly less confident and aggressive tone, his eyes still dipping to my dress.

The temptation to say "Oh, you finally want to talk after two years?" was on the tip of my tongue, but I held it back and raised my eyebrows at him before sliding the key into the lock.

A muscle in his cheek twitched and he ground out, "Please."

Hell was about to freeze over. He said please?

Before I could think about it much more, voices suddenly came from one of the apartments above mine. Damn it. Aiden's big frame was a little too eye-catching, especially when he happened to be a celebrity in Dallas. Just a few days ago, I'd seen a handful of Three Hundreds jerseys around the complex with GRAVES stitched on the back. The last thing I needed was for someone to see him when I had made sure for years not to let anyone find out he was my boss.

"Come in," I muttered, waving him in quickly before someone spotted him.

He didn't need to be told twice. Aiden squeezed his way inside with just enough time for me to close and lock the door just as three men came down the stairs. I walked around him and headed into the kitchen overseeing my living room, frustrated with myself for inviting him in.

"You look different." His comment had my steps faltering for a moment.

"I've worn dresses in front of you before," I snapped a little more bitterly than I would have liked.

"Not one like that," came the quick, nearly brash retort that came out aggressively enough for me to frown. "I wasn't talking about your shirt."

My shirt?

"*You* look different."

I sniffed and circled around the kitchen counter. "My hair is a different color, and I lost weight. That's all."

Aiden took a seat at my small table, then his gaze brushed over the part of my body he could see: my face, neck, chest, and bare arms. Good lord, he made me self-conscious. As those dark orbs took another sweep over me, his thick eyebrows climbed up his forehead and he made an indiscriminate noise, like a "hmm." Like most things with Aiden, another thought immediately forgotten. The next comment out of his mouth confirmed it. "I want you to come work for me again."

I couldn't hold back my groan as I turned to the refrigerator.

"I mean it," he kept going, as if I doubted him.

I took my time opening the fridge and ducked inside to pull out the water jug in there. I was stubborn. I accepted my flaw honestly. But Aiden? Good grief. He had me beat by a landslide; he took stubborn and hardheaded to a whole new level. He was supposed to have just forgotten my existence after a couple of days.

Keeping my attention down as I closed the fridge door, I took a calming breath in and let it out. I knew him, and the way he was acting really shouldn't be a surprise. It was like spoiling a kid his entire life and then trying to put your foot down once it was too late. I'd let him get away with too much over the course of the time we'd known each other, and I had to deal with it now. "I meant what I said too. I don't want to, and I'm not going to."

Silence ticked by, second on top of second, buoyant and endless with the things I thought we both could have said to each other but didn't.

The chair Aiden was sitting on creaked with his weight. I didn't want to look at him. "You don't get on my nerves," he noted, almost as if I'd cured cancer.

I couldn't look at him. I couldn't even look at him. *You don't get on my nerves.* I had to set the jug on the counter and grip the sharp edge of the countertop with my free hand. How did he expect me to respond? Did he want me to thank him for such a heartfelt compliment?

I counted . . . *one, two, three, four,* so that I wouldn't just blurt something out in frustration. Picking and choosing my words carefully, I lifted my head and pulled a glass out of the cabinet. "Tell your next employee that talking isn't required," I said as I poured water into my cup.

"I never told you that," his rough, low voice responded.

"You didn't have to." Actions spoke louder than words after all.

He let out an exasperated noise and followed it up by saying something that stopped me in the middle of putting the water jug back in the fridge. "You're a good employee."

One, two, three, four, five.

Of all the things he could have said . . .

I could have smacked him in the face right then. I really could have. "There are plenty of good employees in the world. You pay well enough for someone to not half-ass their duties." I set the water into the fridge and closed the door. "I don't know why you're here. Why you're insisting that you want me to come back *when I don't want to be your assistant anymore, Aiden.* I can't make myself any clearer."

There. I'd said it, and it was painful and relieving at the same time. "Do you remember when I first started working for you? Do you remember how I'd tell you good morning every day and ask how you were doing?"

He didn't reply.

Perfect. "And do you remember how many times I've asked you if there was something wrong, or tried to joke around with you only for you to ignore me?" I licked my lips and paused where I was, one shoulder against the refrigerator, able to see him at the kitchen table. "I don't think anyone could get on your nerves unless you let them. And anyway, I told you that none of this matters anymore anyway. I don't want to work for you."

The big guy sat forward in his seat, his nostrils flaring. "It matters because I want you to come back."

"You didn't even care that I was there to begin with." Sudden irritation at what he was trying to do set the nerves of my spine on fire. *You will not bang your head against the fridge. You will not bang your head against the fridge.* "You don't even know me—"

"I know you."

Exasperation like I didn't know gripped my chest. "You don't know me. You've never tried to know me, so don't give me that," I snapped, and immediately felt guilty for some stupid reason. "I told you I was quitting, and you didn't give a shit. I don't know why you care now, but it doesn't matter. This work relationship between you and me is done, and that was all we had to begin with. Find someone else, because I'm not going back to work for you. That's the end of the story."

Aiden didn't blink, didn't inhale or exhale; he didn't even twitch. His gaze was locked on me like his pupils were all-knowing lasers capable of emotional manipulation. For the longest moment in time, there wasn't a single sound in my tiny apartment. Then abruptly, in a tone that was completely Aiden, as if he hadn't just heard a single word that came out of my mouth, he said, "I don't want someone new. I want you."

I suddenly wished I could have recorded his comeback so I could sell it on the internet to the hundreds of girls who filled his inbox every week with offers of dates, blowjobs, companionship, and sex.

But I was too busy getting more and more aggravated by the second to do so.

Where the hell was he getting the nerve to say that to me?

"Maybe—and I just want you to think about it for the future—you should consider what other factors are important in employee retention. You know, like making people feel appreciated, giving them a reason to stay loyal to you. It isn't just about a paycheck," I replied as gently as I could, even though I knew damn well he didn't exactly deserve to get handled with kid gloves. "You'll find someone. It's just not going to be me."

His brown eyes sharpened and left an uneasy feeling in the pit of my stomach. "I'll pay you more."

"Listen to me. This isn't about money, for freaking sake."

About a thousand different thoughts seemed to go through his head in that instant as one of his cheeks pulled back into what seemed like half a grimace.

I had no idea what he was thinking, and I sighed. How did we get to this point? Six weeks ago, I couldn't get him to tell me "Hello." Now, he was at my apartment, sitting at my hand-me-down dining room table, asking me to work for him again after I'd walked out.

It was like an episode of *The Twilight Zone*.

His chin tipped back in a determined gesture I was too familiar with. "My visa expires next year," he ground out.

And . . . I shut my mouth.

A few months ago, I remembered opening his mail and seeing something about his visa in an official-looking letter. A letter that I thought he might have gotten again right before I quit, when I'd told him he needed to check the things I'd left on his desk.

I didn't get how a visa could be used as an excuse for being a jerk.

"Okay. Did you already send the paperwork to renew it?" The words had no sooner come out of my mouth than I was asking myself what the hell I was doing. This wasn't my business. He'd made it not my business.

But I still wasn't expecting it when he said, "No."

I didn't understand. "Why not?" Damn it! *What the hell was I doing asking questions?* I scolded myself.

"It's a work visa." His words were slow, like I was mentally impaired or something.

I still didn't get what the problem was.

"It's subject to me playing for the Three Hundreds."

I blinked at him, thinking maybe he'd taken one too many hits to the skull in his career. "I don't get what the problem is."

Before I could ask him why he was worried about his visa when any team he signed with would help him get a new one, he cleared his throat. "I don't want to go back to Canada. I like it here."

This was the same Winnipeg native who had only once gone back to his motherland in all the time we'd worked together. I'd grown up in El Paso, but I didn't go "home" much either, because nothing really felt like home anymore. I hadn't had a place that made me feel safe or loved or warm, or any of the feelings I figured could be associated with what home should feel like.

I glanced at the wall to the side of his head, waiting for the next revelation to help make sense of what he was saying. "I'm still not understanding what the issue here is."

With a deep sigh, he propped his chin on his hand, and he finally explained. "If I'm not on a team, I can't stay here."

Why wouldn't he be playing? Was his foot bothering him? I wanted to ask him but didn't. "Okay . . . isn't there some other kind of visa you can apply for?"

"I don't want to get another visa."

I blew out a breath and shut the refrigerator door, my fingers instantly going up to my glasses. "Okay. Go talk to an immigration lawyer. I'm sure one of them can help you get your permanent residency." I chewed on my cheek for a second before adding, "You have money to get it worked on, and that's a lot better than most people have it." Then an idea entered my head, and before I thought twice about suggesting it, or talked myself out of not saying anything because I wasn't feeling particularly friendly, I blurted it out. "Or just find an American citizen to marry you."

His gaze had drifted to the ceiling at some point, but in that moment, he shifted it to scrutinize me. Those broad features were even and smooth, and not even remotely close to a scowl.

"Find someone you like, date them for a little bit or something, and then ask them to marry you. You can always get divorced afterward." I paused and thought about a distant cousin of Diana's. "There's also people out there who would do it if you paid them enough, but that's kind of tricky, because I'm pretty sure it's a felony to try to get your papers fixed by marrying someone for that reason. It's something to think about."

I blinked, noticing his expression had gone from scrutinizing to contemplating. Thoughtful. Too thoughtful. This weird sensation crept over my neck. Weird, weird, weird, telling me something was off, telling me I should probably get out of his line of view. I took a step back and eyed him. "What is it?"

Nothing in this world could have prepared me for what came out of his mouth next.

"Marry me."

"*What?*" It came out of my mouth as surprised and rude as I imagined it did, I was positive of it.

He was on drugs. He was seriously on fucking drugs.

"Marry me," he repeated himself, like I hadn't heard him the first time.

I leaned back against the kitchen counter, torn between being weak from shock and dumbfounded from how ridiculous his statement was, and settled for just staring blankly in the general direction of his granite-like face. "You're on dope, aren't you?"

"No." The usually taut corners of Aiden's mouth relaxed a fraction of an inch; the tension in his body diminishing just a tiny amount, but it was enough for me to notice. "You can help me get my residency."

What in the hell was going on with him? Maybe it was brain damage after all. I'd seen some of the guys he went up against; how could he have gotten off scot-free after so many years? "Why would I do that?" I gaped. "Why would I even *want* to do that?"

That strong jaw seemed to clench.

"I don't want to work for you, much less marry you to help you get your papers fixed." An idea rang through my brain, and I almost threw my hands up in joy at the brilliance behind it. "Marry someone who can do all your assistant stuff too. It makes perfect sense."

He'd started nodding when I brought up the assistant idea, but the emotion in his eyes was a little disturbing. He looked way too determined, too at peace with whatever crazy crap was going on in his big head. "It's perfect," he agreed. "You can do it."

I choked. As badly as I wanted to say something—to argue with him or just tell him he'd lost his mind—nothing managed to come out of my mouth. I was flabbergasted. *Fucking flabbergasted.*

Aiden was on crack.

"Are you insane? Did you drop a barbell on your neck bench pressing?"

"You said it; it's a perfect plan."

What had I done? "It's not perfect. It's nowhere near perfect," I blabbered. "I don't work for you anymore, and even if I did, I wouldn't do it." Seriously? He was thinking I would? I didn't know him to be anything but practical, and this was just outrageous.

But he wasn't listening. I could tell. He had his thinking face on. "Vanessa, you have to do it."

Did he not understand that we weren't friends? That he'd treated me in the opposite way you would treat someone you cared about?

"No. I don't and I'm not." If I met the right person, I wasn't opposed to getting married someday in the future. I didn't think about marriage often, but when I did, I kind of liked the idea of it. Diana's parents had been a perfect example of a great relationship; of course, I'd want something like that in the future, if it was possible. Realistically, I knew I would be fine on my own too.

And I wasn't going to scratch kids off my list of things I'd like if I also had the right person in my life. I faintly knew what I wanted in a partner, but more than anything, I knew what I didn't want.

And Aiden, even on his best days, wasn't that person. Or anywhere near it. Sure he was good-looking; anyone with eyes could see that. His body alone had women of all ages turning in their seats to get a good look, because Aiden breathed virility, and what woman didn't like a man who looked like he drank testosterone in gallons? He was a big drink of cool water, or so I'd been told. Okay, and he had money, but that wasn't a hard requisite for a future boyfriend or husband. I could make my own money.

That was it though.

Except for the first three months of my employment, I had never once thought to myself that I had feelings for the Wall of Winnipeg. I was physically attracted to him, sure. But for me, and because of everything I'd seen my mom go through, jumping from one relationship to another my entire life, that wasn't enough. My last boyfriend hadn't been the best-looking guy on the planet, but he'd been funny and nice, and we liked the same things. We got along. The only reason we'd split up was because he'd been offered a job in Seattle, and I hadn't been convinced I was head over heels in love with him enough to move across the country, even further away from the few people in my life who mattered to me. I'd done it once already going to school in Tennessee.

Aiden didn't fit any of the same qualifications my ex had. He wasn't funny or nice, we didn't like the same things, and based on the last two weeks of our work relationship, we didn't get along.

And why the hell was I even thinking about reasons why this was a bad idea? It was a terrible one point-blank. One I wasn't going to go through with. No way, no how.

Aiden, on the other hand, wasn't paying attention. He didn't have to say a word for me to know he was ignoring everything coming out of my mouth.

"Aiden, listen to me"—*for the second time in your life,* I added in my head—"I'm sure Trevor can find you someone. Just ask."

That comment had him snapping to attention. His thick, dark eyebrows straightened. "I'm not telling Trevor."

I pushed at my glasses, even though they were in place.

"Would you?" he questioned.

Yeah, that had me wincing. I wouldn't trust Trevor to put something in the mail for me. "What about Rob?"

No response.

Huh. Touché. "Zac?"

Aiden simply shook his head in denial.

"Your friends?"

"I would have told them already if I wanted them to know," he explained in a careful tone that made too much sense.

Of course he'd been serious about coming back from his injury. But on top of that, his extra-terrible mood at the fear of being deported if he was let go by the organization added to that. Even more so, dealing with his manager and agent, who didn't seem to be totally on board with whatever it was Aiden wanted once his contract came to the end, only made matters worse. But there was one thing that didn't really add up once I thought about it, and it wasn't the reason why he didn't want to go back to Canada or why he didn't want to stay in Dallas.

"Why are you telling me this?" I asked hesitantly.

Those brown irises settled on me, lines scorching his broad forehead.

Before I could talk myself out of it, I frowned in return. "You've never really told me anything before." I blinked. "Ever. But now I quit, and you're suddenly over at my apartment, asking me to come back to work for you when you hadn't given a single crap that I was quitting, and you want me to marry you to get your papers fixed. You're telling me things you don't want to tell anyone else about and . . . it's weird, man. I don't know what the hell you expect me to tell you."

"I'm telling you because . . ." He opened his mouth and closed it just as quickly. Opened it once more before closing it again, the muscles in his cheeks moving, as if he didn't really know why he was doing so. Hell, I didn't get it. Finally, Aiden shrugged those massive, rounded shoulders and made sure our gazes met. "I like you as much as I like anyone."

Damn it.

God damn it.

Diana had told me once that I had no backbone. Actually, I'm pretty sure her exact words had been, "You're a sucker, Van."

I like you as much as I like anyone shouldn't have been a compliment. It really shouldn't have. I wasn't that dumb. But . . .

A rough laugh tore its way out of me unexpectedly, and then I was snickering, raising my eyes to the popcorn ceiling.

Coming from someone like Aiden, I guess it was the biggest compliment I could ever get.

I like you as much as I like anyone. My word.

"Why is that funny?" Aiden asked, a frown curving his mouth.

I slapped a hand over my eyes and leaned forward over the kitchen countertop, giggling a little as I rubbed at my brow bone in resignation. "There's a huge difference between me not irritating the hell out of you and us being friends, Aiden. You've made that perfectly clear, don't you think?"

His blink was innocent, so earnest, I had no idea what to do with it. "I don't mind you."

I don't mind you.

I started cracking up—really cracking up—and I was pretty sure it sounded like I was crying when I was really laughing.

"You're the most even-tempered woman I've ever met."

Even-tempered. He was killing me.

This was what my life had come to. Taking half-assed compliments from a man who only cared about one thing: himself. A man who I'd tried to make my friend over and over again to no avail.

To give him credit, he waited a bit before saying carefully, way too calmly, and almost gently, "This isn't funny."

I had to squat down behind the kitchen cabinets because my stomach was clenching so badly.

"You're asking me—oh hell, my stomach hurts—to perform a felony, and your reasoning for having me do so is because you 'like me as much as you like anyone,' because you 'don't mind me,' and because I'm 'even-tempered.'" I held my hands up to do air quotes over the top of the cabinets. "Holy crap. I didn't think you had a sense of humor, but you do."

The best defensive player in the NFO didn't hesitate with the opening I gave him. "You'll do it then?"

I couldn't even find it in me to be annoyed by his persistence after that. I was still laughing too much over my greatest attributes as a possible fake wife. "No, but this has been the highlight in my time knowing you. Really. I wish you'd been like this with me from the beginning. Working for you would have been a lot more fun, and I might have even thought about coming back for a little bit longer."

It still wasn't enough though. Working for him permanently wasn't part of the plan, especially not after everything that happened, and everything he was asking of me now. *Marry him.*

He was out of his damn mind.

The plan after becoming entirely self-employed on my graphic design work was to pay off the terrifying amount of student loans I still had, buy my own house, buy a new car, and the rest . . . it could all fall into place in its own time. Travel, find someone I liked enough to be in a relationship with, maybe have a kid if I wanted one, and continue my financial independence.

And to make money, I needed to work, so I forced myself to my feet and shrugged at my old boss. "Look, you'll find someone if you just try a little. You're attractive, you have money, and you're a decent guy most of the time." I made sure to pin him with a look that emphasized the *most of the time*. "If you found someone who you liked, even a little bit, I'm sure you could make it work. I'd give you one of my friends' phone numbers, but they'd drive you nuts after ten minutes, and I'm not mad enough at you to give you any of my sisters'."

I bit the inside of my cheek, not knowing what else to say, fully aware that I would more than likely never understand what had led him to this time and moment with me.

And what did he do?

His eyes roamed my face as his forehead wrinkled and he shook his head. "I need your help."

"No you don't." Shrugging again, I offered him a reluctant smile, a gentle one, because I was well aware he wasn't used to having someone tell him no. "You'll figure everything out on your own. You don't need me."

SEVEN

Flipping my grilled cheese sandwich over, I snickered into the phone. "I'm not going. I don't think he liked me much anyway either."

"I didn't like Jeremy until our third date and look at us now." Diana's argument was probably the worst one she could have chosen.

The five times I'd met him over the last six months was five times too many. I knew for a fact her brother felt the same way about him. We'd hung out with him for Diana's birthday and within minutes we'd shared a "he's a jackass" glare. Neither of us tried to hide our dislike, and in this instant, nothing actually came out of my mouth, which said more than enough, I figured.

Not surprisingly, she knew what the silence was for and sighed. "He's really nice to me."

I highly doubted that. The times we'd gone out, he'd tried to pick a fight with someone . . . for no reason. He seemed high-strung, moody, and way too cocky. Plus, I didn't like the vibe he gave off, and I'd learned to listen to my gut when it came to people.

I'd told her enough times how I felt, but she'd continuously brushed it off. "Hey, I don't have anything nice to say, so I'm not going to say anything," I told her.

The big sigh that came out of her let me know she didn't want to talk about Jeremy anymore—well aware it was a lost cause. Nothing would get me to change my mind about him unless he saved my life or something. "I still think you should go on another date. At least you can get a few drinks out of it."

Why had I even told her my date last night had invited me out again? I knew better. I really did. "I drank about as much wine as my liver could handle last night just to get through two hours. I'm good."

She made a "meh" noise. "There's no such thing as too much wine."

We both burst out laughing at the same time.

"When are you free?" I asked. I hadn't seen her since she'd dyed my hair.

"Oh, ah, let me get back to you. I have plans with Jeremy."

Yeah, I might have rolled my eyes a little. "Well, let me know when you don't." I let the Jeremy thing in one ear and out the other.

"I will. I wanted to try a different color on you. Are your roots showing yet?"

I was in the middle of mulling over how she hadn't asked if she could dye my hair again when three sharp knocks rattled my door. "Hold on one second." Turning off the stovetop range, I made my way toward the door. It wasn't either of my neighbors; neither of them knocked hard enough so that the door rattled on the rare occasion they dropped by.

With that thought, I knew exactly who it was before I even made it to the peephole.

"Fart breath, let me call you back later. I, uh, someone's knocking on my door," I explained abruptly. I still hadn't told her, or anyone, about Aiden coming by to ask me to come work for him again, much less tell them that a week ago he'd asked me to marry him so he could become a permanent resident. I had thought about calling Zac, but decided against it.

"Okay. Bye." I didn't get a chance to say bye before the dial tone filled the receiver.

"Who is it?" I asked, even though I would have bet twenty bucks I already knew.

"Aiden," the voice on the other side of the door answered just as I went up on my tippy-toes to peer into the peephole. Sure enough, a tan complexion with chocolate-colored eyes and a familiar, tightly pressed mouth greeted me through the glass.

It wasn't until I opened the door that I realized he had a hoodie on over his dark hair. I raised my eyebrows at him as he stood there, resembling his nickname as his shoulders took up the door-frame. He really did look like a damn human wall. "You're back." I blinked. "Again."

While I grudgingly accepted that sometimes I didn't have a back-bone, I was also well aware that once you gave me a reason to stop liking you, it was nearly impossible to win yourself back into my good graces. You could ask Susie. While I could get over Aiden being a grumpy little B, the Trevor thing had gotten him into irreconcilable territory. Basically, he'd made it to the Land of the Forgotten. When it came down to it, he'd hurt me.

He gave me a look I wasn't sure how to interpret before slipping inside my apartment—without an invitation—his chest brushing against my arm in the process. He was radiating a massive amount of heat, and I didn't need to look at the clock to know he'd just gotten out of a training session. He also smelled like he'd skipped a shower in the locker room.

I had just closed the door when Aiden stopped in the hallway, hands on his hips, giving me a hard glare that I didn't understand. "You live with drug dealers."

Oh.

I shrugged a shoulder at him. "They leave me alone." Sure, I'd had to tell them "No thanks" about a dozen times, but I didn't clarify that point.

"You *know* that they're drug dealers?"

I shrugged again, deciding right then that this judgmental ass wasn't going to find out some of the people in the buildings on either side of mine were in a notorious gang that hung blue bandanas out their pockets. So I went with changing the subject, thinking about my sandwich sitting in the pan waiting for me. "Do you need something?" The words were out of my mouth before I could stop myself, damn it.

Sure enough, Aiden nodded, still standing there in the hallway between the door and the rest of my place. "You."

Me.

In another world, with another person, I'd like to think that I would love to hear someone say they needed me. But . . . this was Aiden. Aiden who thought he "needed" me to marry him; Aiden who had only shown up to my apartment because he needed something from me. "No."

"Yes."

Good grief. "No."

"*Yes*," he insisted.

My stomach growled, reminding me I hadn't eaten anything since having breakfast hours ago. Grumpiness started climbing up my shoulders, edging me on to getting an attitude with this delusional human being. Shoving my glasses up so that they rested on the top of my head, I rubbed at my eyes with a sigh, peeking at him with a blurry eye. "I'm honored, really," if I was being honest with myself, *not really*, "but I'm the last person you should be asking."

His nostrils flared, and he tipped his chin up high, his jawline accentuating. This massive man who faced other big men for a living was glowering at me. *At me.* "Do you have a boyfriend?"

"No—"

"Then there isn't a problem."

I rubbed at my eyes with the meaty part of my palms some more and tried to rein in my frustration. Blowing out a breath, I set my glasses back on my nose and stared at the behemoth in my hallway. Obviously, we were going to have to go there. "Where would you like me to start?"

When all he did was give me that look that made me want to stick my finger in his nose, I figured that expression was going to be the best answer I would get out of him. If he wanted to be a pain in the ass, I could be a pain in the ass too. What did I have to lose? We weren't friends, and he hadn't cared about my feelings before, so I shouldn't feel guilty for being honest with him.

So I started. "Okay." I rolled my shoulders for battle, eyeing the canvas piece with one of my favorite hardback covers for moral support. It was a heart made out of multicolored stilettos for a book called

Heeling Love. I'd been pretty proud of myself for that one. "One, we don't know each other."

"We know each other," Delusional argued.

I wanted to move on to my next claim, but apparently we weren't going to be able to until he understood each of the more-than-apparent reasons why me helping him fix his immigration status was a terrible idea. "I know you pretty well, but you don't know a single thing about me besides my first name. Do you even know my last name?"

"Mazur."

I *knew* him. I freaking knew him, so I folded my arms over my chest and narrowed my eyes. "You looked up my name, didn't you?"

He was giving me the same face that drove me nuts. It was so damn smug. There was this one popular shot of him during a press conference after a game with a similar glare aimed at a reporter who had asked him a stupid question. Panties all over the U.S. were dropped that day. Yet the only thing that pointed chin, flat mouth, and cool eyes did to me was frustrate the shit out of me. "I don't see what the problem is."

One, two, three, four, five, six, seven, eight.

"I don't know whether you're just pretending to be ignorant or if you really are just that hardheaded," I gritted. "I worked for you for two years, and you didn't know my last name. You couldn't even tell me 'Hi.' Aiden, this isn't you asking me to let you borrow twenty bucks or give you a ride to the airport. You don't know me, and you don't even like me. And that's okay, I'm not worried about it, but we can't 'get married,'" I busted out the air quotes, "to fix your papers when you don't like *me*. You can't ignore me for years, not give a shit that I'm leaving, treat me like crap, and then expect me to jump to help you when you ask."

"I told you. I like you as much—"

Oh my word. I was dealing with a brick wall. My eye almost twitched as I fought the urge to not make a pun about his nickname. "As you like anyone. Is that why you let Trevor talk about me? Because you like me?"

His hand went up to rub at the side of his neck, a color that was nearly pink staining his cheeks. "I do—" he started to argue. The pink managed to make its way down to his throat.

Damn it.

I had to count to six, my spine going rigid as I did it. My vocal cords went tight. This was so pointless. "Fine. *Fine*, Aiden. I don't even know what the hell that means, but okay; you've sure shown me in the last two years. Now you don't have an assistant and you want to become a resident and you're here. That seems real genuine, don't you think? But okay, I'll give you the benefit of the doubt. Maybe you can tolerate me for some strange reason, and you didn't want me to get all conceited so you didn't make it noticeable." That sounded like total bullshit to my ears. "How about, what you're asking me to do is a felony? I could go to jail and you could get deported. What about that?"

"It's only illegal if you get caught."

My mouth dropped open. I was at a total loss for words. Was this a dream? Was this even real life?

"I have a plan," he concluded in that low, low voice that reminded me of an eighteen-wheeler revving its engine.

Too late, I had a feeling this was a lost cause. "The government takes this stuff seriously, you know. I would be the one going to jail, not you." Okay, I didn't know if I would really get jail time or not, but maybe.

"I've done my research. I have a plan."

Here he went with his freaking plan again. "I have a plan too, and part of my plan isn't to marry someone to help them get their immigration paperwork together. I'm sorry, Aiden. I'm really sorry, but you're in about the best place you can be to find someone to marry you if that's what you want. You shouldn't have to though. Maybe you can pay somebody a lot of money to fast-track your paperwork."

"Getting married is the best way to go about it." He paused. His big hands visibly clenched at his sides, and I swore he looked even bigger in that moment. "I don't want another visa."

My heart reacted a little because it was weak and pathetic, and because I felt like a jerk for telling him no. I hated not helping people who needed it. But this was ridiculous. Here was a man who had never been particularly kind to me or tried to be my friend until I'd quit on him. Now it seemed like he was asking the world of me, and I didn't feel entitled to give it to him. "I don't know what to tell you." I shook my head. "You're out of your mind. I'm not doing it, and I don't know where you're getting the balls to ask me to."

His gaze locked on mine, irrepressible and unflinching, like I hadn't just told him no again. His chin tipped up as his lips disappeared for a moment, curling behind his teeth. Teeth that I knew were white and perfect. "You're that mad at me?"

"Even if I would have left on good terms, I still wouldn't go back to work for you, much less help you get your visa or your residency, or whatever it is you want to do."

His eyes roamed my face slowly, making me extremely aware of the fact that I wasn't wearing makeup . . . or a stinking bra. Luckily, I'd only seen Aiden look at something other than my face once, and that had been that night when he'd showed up and I had been in a short dress. Then again, I'd also never seen him glance at a woman's chest or ass either. He'd told the media a dozen times in the past how he didn't have time for relationships, and he was right. He didn't. "I can see it in your face, Vanessa," he stated, making me temporarily ignore the situation I was in.

The word *stupid* ricocheted around in my head. "I haven't been mad at you since I walked out of your house."

"You're lying. You're making that face you do when you're trying not to show you're angry," he explained, even as his gaze stretched over me, making me feel pretty self-conscious.

"I'm not," I practically grunted out.

His impassive face said what words didn't. *Liar.*

I lost it. I was hungry, grumpy, and irritated. That was the absolute truth. From the way a vein in my forehead pulsed, I was still holding a not-so-insignificant amount of residual anger toward him too. "Okay. Fine. Yes, I'm still a little pissed at you. You let Trevor of all people talk about me behind my back." I blinked. "*Trevor.*" By that point, my blood didn't know whether to rush to my face or away from it. "Trevor would sell his own kid for a price. Maybe we're not friends, but you have to have known I cared about you a lot more than fucking *Trevor* does."

Just saying his name out loud made me angry, and I had to tell myself to reel it in.

One, two, three, four, five.

I bit the inside of my cheek and blinked at him. "You've never said a single freaking 'sorry' to me ever. Do you understand how rude that is? You never apologize for anything, *anything*. After everything I did for you, everything I've ever done for you, things that went above being just your employee, and you just . . . I would never ever let anyone talk shit about you," I said, making sure his gaze met mine when I said it so he could understand, or at least see, that I wasn't just being an asshole to be an asshole.

"On top of that, you were acting like a major prick before I quit," I accused him, feeling that familiar burn of disappointment scorch my chest. "Why would I want to do anything for you? There's no loyalty between us. We aren't friends." I shrugged. "You might not know anything about me, but I know almost everything there is to know about you, and that means nothing now. I'm done. I respected you. I admired you, and you just . . . didn't care. I don't know how you can expect me to brush all that off as nothing."

Honestly, I was surprised I'd lost it, and I might have been even more shocked that I wasn't panting at the end of my spiel.

The vein in my head was pulsing. My hands fisted, and I felt angrier than ever in the past. Yet, when I really focused in on the hoodie-wearing man standing five feet away in the hallway of my apartment, I couldn't help but pause.

The cords in his neck pulled taut. The hard slashes of his cheekbones seemed more prominent than ever. But it was the emotion in the shape of his mouth that I had never seen before. "You're right."

It wasn't that I didn't expect him to sort of apologize—a small part of me did. But . . .

What?

"I shouldn't have let him say that."

"No shit."

He ignored my comment. "I should have treated you better."

Was I supposed to disagree?

As if sensing how much his words were failing, Aiden's shoulders pulled back in resolution. "I'm sorry."

My hands opened and closed at my sides. I wasn't sure what to say, even as I tried to steady the angry beat of my heart.

"You were a great assistant," Aiden added.

I still kept on eyeing him. Of course I had been a good one, but I was also the only assistant he'd ever had so . . .

With a hand to his neck, his Adam's apple bobbed. I'd swear those impressive shoulders slumped forward. "You've always been loyal to me, and I didn't appreciate it until you were gone."

Neither one of us said a word for a few extended moments. Maybe he was waiting for me to rail at him again, and maybe I was waiting for him to ask me to do something that I didn't want to do. Who knew? But it must have been long enough for Aiden to finally clear his throat.

"Vanessa, I'm sorry for everything."

I could believe he was slightly sorry, but a bigger part of my conscience believed he wouldn't be apologizing if he didn't want something from me. I couldn't help but feel skeptical, and I was positive that emotion was written all over my face.

But Aiden wasn't an idiot or anywhere close to it, and he kept going. "I've been angry over other things that have nothing to do with you. I haven't tried to be nice, that's true, but I've never gone out of my way or wanted to be mean to you either."

I snorted, the scenes at the gym and at the radio station at the front of my brain.

He must have known exactly what I was thinking about because he shook his head, frustrated or resigned, I didn't know or care. "I'm sorry I took that out on you. Apologizing doesn't change anything, but I mean it. I'm sorry."

Did I want to ask what other things he was angry with? Of course. Of course I did. But I knew if I asked him to elaborate it would seem like a sign he was on the road to maybe, possibly winning me over.

He wasn't.

So I kept my mouth shut. There were a lot of things I would be willing to forgive, but the more I thought about it, the more I realized he'd let me down when I didn't have high hopes for him to begin with. Aiden became just another person who didn't live up to the expectations I had. What kind of crap was that? Plus, the stresses surrounding him being an asshole for a short period of time didn't explain the rest of the months and years he'd never given me the time of day.

Aiden kept watching me with those coffee-colored eyes, watching, watching, watching. "I've been incredibly stressed lately," he said, his words like bait.

All this stuff I already knew.

He licked his top lip and tilted his head down before letting out a long, low exhale. "Can I use your bathroom?"

I pointed in the direction of my bedroom and nodded. "It's in there."

He disappeared through the door between my living room and kitchen a second later, and I took that moment to let out my own shaky breath. My head had started hurting just a little bit at some point, and I knew it was the result of hunger and tension. In the kitchen, I grabbed my now cold sandwich, and leaned over the sink while I took a few bites out of the grilled cheese.

I wasn't even halfway done eating when Aiden appeared, leaning against the doorway that led from the kitchen into my bedroom, crossing his arms over his chest. If I wasn't in such a shitty mood, I would have appreciated the breadth of his shoulders, or how his arms were perfectly proportionate to the rest of his massive size. I didn't need to look at his thighs to know those things had the width of a redwood tree.

"I'll pay you," he said while I was not checking him out.

Ready to tell him one more time that I was fine money-wise, Aiden kept going before I could.

He laid the bomb. "I'll pay off your student loans and buy you a house."

I dropped my sandwich in the sink.

EIGHT

To say that I had an Achilles' heel would be an understatement.

Growing up in a family with five kids and a single mom, money had always been tight. So, so tight. Scarce, really. My crayons in elementary school were those off-brand ones that didn't color so well. I'd worn mostly hand-me-downs exclusively until I was old enough to pay for new things myself, and that hadn't been until I was with my foster parents.

But if there was one thing that having so little for so long had taught me, it was the value of money and appreciation of belongings. No one respected money more than I did.

So, it had been to my utmost horror when I applied to college and received zero scholarships. None. Nada. Not even $500.

I was smart, but I wasn't an extraordinary student. I was shy in school. I didn't raise my hand much in class, or join every extracurricular activity available. I didn't play sports because there wasn't disposable income lying around to buy uniforms, and there hadn't been any for us kids to join league teams either. My favorite thing had always been hanging out by myself, drawing and painting, if I had paints. I didn't excel at anything that could have gotten me a scholarship. My high school hadn't had a fine arts program worth anything; the closest class I'd been able to take was woodshop, and I'd excelled at it. But where did that lead me?

There was a very clear memory of my high school guidance counselor telling me how average I was. Really. She'd said that to me. "Maybe you should have tried harder."

I'd been too shocked to have to count to ten after that.

All As and a couple of Bs hadn't been good enough. Yet I'd still been horrified and disappointed when I got accepted to every decent school I applied to, but received no financial help other than a federal grant I qualified for because of my financial need, but that only covered 10 percent of my total yearly tuition.

And, of course, the school I wanted to go to was out of state and incredibly expensive. I'd loved it more than I loved any other one I'd gone to check out with my friends the fall of my senior year.

So, I did the unthinkable. I took out loans. Massive student loans.

Then I did the next most unthinkable thing in the world: I didn't tell anyone.

Not my foster parents, not my little brother, or even Diana. No one knew except me. There was no other person in the world who carried the burden of nearly $200,000 on their conscience but me.

In the four years since graduating with my bachelor's, I'd been paying off as much as I could from my loans while also attempting to put money aside in savings to eventually be able to dedicate myself full-time to my dream. A debt as large as the one I had was a bottomless pit that you had to accept like it was hepatitis—it wasn't going anywhere. But it only served to make me work harder, which was why I didn't mind going to work for Aiden, and then doing my design work well into the middle of the night afterward. But there was only so much you could take, and I'd saved and paid off a significant enough of a chunk to get to the point where I felt like I could breathe for the first time in years . . . as long as I didn't let myself look too closely at the loan statements I got in the mail every month.

But . . .

"What do you think?" the big man asked, leveling his stare right at me as if he hadn't just busted out the greatest secret in my life.

What I thought was he was out of his damn mind. What I thought was my heart shouldn't have been beating so quickly. What I also thought was no one else should have known about how much money I owed.

Mostly though, a small part of me was thinking there was a price for everything.

"Vanessa?"

I blinked at him before looking down at my poor contaminated sandwich sitting in the sink. Then I took a deep breath, closed my eyes, and opened them once more. "How do you know about my loans?"

"I've always known."

What? "How?" I felt . . . I felt a little violated, honestly.

"Trevor did a background check on you." That sounded vaguely familiar now that he mentioned it, even though it was disturbing to hear they knew something I'd tried so hard to keep to myself. "There's no way you've managed to pay them off," Aiden stated.

He was right.

Vomit. Vomit. Vomit.

"Whatever you owe, I'll pay it."

Just like that. *I'll pay it.* Like $150,000 was no big deal.

I liked to watch that show on television where bosses went undercover at their businesses, and then at the end, they surprised their employees with some crazy amount of money to go on vacation, or to pay off whatever it was they owed money on. More often than not, I got teary-eyed watching it. The employees would usually always cry and say how they never expected something like that to happen to them, or they would talk about how much of a blessing the money was going to be for their families. Or how much the gift they were being bestowed was going to change their lives.

Yet here I was.

My hands shook. The ability to breathe was stolen from my lungs. My loans were my Achilles' heel.

I was only slightly ashamed of myself for not immediately thinking his offer was preposterous. Why wasn't I kicking him out or telling him to go eat shit? Why wasn't I laughing at his idea? Or telling him to get the hell out because he couldn't buy me? He hadn't treated me well. He didn't deserve for me to do him a "favor" and put my life on the line for him.

Clenching my hands at my sides, I let the sensation of being overwhelmed wash over me. He was offering to pay off this thing that weighed on my soul like a cement block in a pool. Who did that?

Better yet, who said no to an offer like that? I liked to think I made wise decisions, that I did what was the best for me, or would be the best for me in the long run. But $150,000? Holy *shit*.

"I'm willing to compromise," Aiden offered, his eyes even, his voice steady, which didn't help any.

I sputtered.

Shut up, Van, I told myself. *Shut up, shut up, shut up and just say yes, you idiot. Don't talk him out of this. Don't be that dumb. You can get over anything for that much money. This is the opportunity of a lifetime, even if he hurt your feelings, even though it's stupid and illegal, and doesn't make any sense, because there are a million other women in the world who would do it for less.*

But I couldn't shut up. I just couldn't. It was that nagging little part of my personality that I'd had to hone over the years—the one that didn't know how to keep quiet sometimes.

I lifted my eyes and looked at the bearded man standing in my apartment offering me a lifeline, an opportunity. A *felony*, I made myself remember. He was asking me to do something that was essentially illegal. This man who had never given two single shits about me until now that he needed something, and he had no one else to ask. "Aiden . . ."

The most muscular man I'd ever known took a step forward and dropped his hands to his sides, pinning me in place with his gaze alone. "It has to be you. I've thought about it. No one understands my schedule the way you do. You don't get on my nerves, and you're . . ." He shook his head and crucified me on the spot. "I'll do whatever it takes. Tell me what you want and you'll have it. Anything."

The headache that had been hanging around my temples from hunger suddenly intensified.

Tell him no, the smart part of my brain said. I could pay off my loans eventually. I still had time.

But the other part of my brain, the logical one, told me it would be dumb to waste this opportunity. All I had to do was marry the guy, right? Sign a piece of paper? Save a fortune worth of interest?

Oh, hell. I couldn't seriously be changing my tune from one minute to the next. I'd just been telling him how we weren't friends and how much he'd hurt my feelings, and how dumb he was being for even bringing it up . . . and now I was thinking about his offer all in a matter of a few minutes. Then again, over a hundred thousand dollars was riding on this offer. This wasn't nothing.

His gaze was totally fixed on me standing there, in my tiny kitchen in baggy Dr. Pepper pajama pants and a spaghetti strap tank with no bra. This incredibly handsome and intimidating man wanted . . .

There was something wrong with me. There was something seriously wrong with me.

Tell him to screw off. Tell him to screw off.

I didn't.

"Let me think about it," I said, my voice breaking, unsure.

He didn't cry victory at me not immediately telling him to go to hell, which was surprising. Instead, Aiden said very calmly, "That's fine." He hesitated for a second, rocking from one foot to the other. "I am sorry I messed up."

A knot formed in my throat at the expression on his features.

"I'm used to being on my own, Vanessa. Nothing that I did or said had anything to do with you. I want you to understand that."

Without another word, the man known as the Wall of Winnipeg let himself out. The only sound signaling his departure was the door slamming shut behind him.

I was going to think about it. Going to think about marrying a guy for money when I'd walked out on him a month ago for not defending me to his manager, for not upholding the tiny bit of a bond I thought we shared. What the hell was I doing?

Being smart, that logical part of my brain whispered.

I DIDN'T GET any sleep the next two nights, and that wasn't exactly surprising. How the hell was I supposed to sleep when all I thought about was if I was really considering committing fraud—marriage fraud it was called—to make a lot of money? Was this what thieves went through?

I felt guilty, and I hadn't even done anything.

I felt slightly cheap too, for not saying "hell no" right off the bat, but I didn't feel *that* cheap.

Getting my loans paid off—and the possibility of having a house bought for me—enticed me a lot more than my morals would have ever expected. Then again, morals didn't exactly mean much when you were shelling out what was a mortgage worth on loans each month. I lived in an apartment that would horrify my foster parents if they knew what it was like. My car was twelve years old. I kept my expenses to the absolute minimum, just to spend my money the way I needed to.

And then I started thinking to myself . . . if I did this, I would have to get divorced one day. I would have to tell my future husband—if there was one—that I'd been married once, and I would never ever be able to tell him the truth as to why I'd done it. It wasn't like I could lie and pretend it had never happened, even if it would be fake and in word only.

Was that cool? Was that fair? Maybe it was, because my mom never married while I was young, but I'd always envisioned it as being this ultraserious, special thing that not everyone got to do. A union of two people who decided they were going to tackle the world together—so you should be picky with whom you chose as your partner. 'Til death do you part and all that stuff; otherwise, you would just be wasting your life. Right?

When I wasn't contemplating all that stuff, I asked myself what in the world I would tell the people in my life. They would know I was up to my neck in shit if I suddenly said I was marrying Aiden. I would have to bring up the loans if I told them the complete truth, and I would rather stick my hand in a boiling pot of water than do that.

It was all too much. Way too much.

And so, I finally picked up the phone and called the only person who I wouldn't be able to fool with my lies. I couldn't live with it any longer. I was tired, grumpier than ever, and I wasn't focusing because I was too distracted. I needed to make a decision.

"Diana, would you marry someone for money?" I asked her out of the blue one afternoon when I called her during her lunch break.

Without missing a beat, she made a contemplative noise. "It depends. How much money?"

It was right then that I knew I'd called the wrong person. I should have dialed Oscar, my slightly younger brother, instead. He was the levelheaded one in my life, the basketball player studying mechanical engineering. He'd always been wise beyond his years. Diana . . . not so much.

I only told her the partial truth. "What if someone bought you a house?"

She hmmed and then hmmed a little more. "A nice house?"

"It wouldn't be a mansion, you greedy bitch, but I'm not talking about a dump or anything either." I figured at least.

"All I had to do was marry someone, and they would buy me a nice house?" Later on, I could laugh over the entire situation leading up to this conversation, and how easily Di was considering it.

"Yes."

"Would I have to do anything else?"

What else would there be? The marriage would just be to get his residency; it wouldn't be a forever thing. "I don't think so."

"Oh." Her tone perked up. "Sure. Why not?"

Sure. Why not? Good grief. I snorted.

"Wait a second. Why are you asking? *Who's doing it?*" she finally chimed in, extremely interested.

When I was done explaining to her just about everything minus what had been my tipping point to quit, I waited for her sage—usually not so sage—advice.

What I got was: "Do it."

"That's it?" I scoffed. I was asking her for her opinion on a life-changing decision, and that was how she was going to respond?

"Sure. Why not? He has money, you know the worst things about him, and he's willing to pay you. What do you have to think about?" she said in a matter-of-fact tone.

She was definitely the wrong person to call for advice. "It's illegal."

"In that case, make sure you don't get caught."

Okay, Aiden Junior, I thought before she continued on.

"People do it all the time. Remember Felipa?" That was her cousin; how could I forget? "That Salvadoran guy she married paid her five thousand dollars. You might get a house, Vanny. You could be a little more grateful."

Definitely the wrong person. "We're not each other's biggest fans."

That had her exasperated. "You like almost everyone. He can't exactly hate you if he's asking you and not someone else. I'm sure he'd have bitches lining the block if he even remotely put in some effort."

Her comment had me groaning. "You really think I should do it then?"

"There's no reason why you shouldn't. You don't have a boyfriend. You have nothing to lose."

She was making this too easy, making me feel dumb for not immediately jumping at the chance, but something had been lingering in my gut, and it wasn't until she said the thing about bitches lining the block that I realized what it was. My pride. I cracked my knuckles. "I don't know how I'd feel about being married and having my *husband*"—I almost choked on the word—"being with other people during. Even if it was fake. Someone would find out that we'd gotten married, and I don't want to look like the poor idiot wife whose husband cheats on her and everyone knows."

Diana hummed again. "Did he date around while you worked for him?"

He didn't. Ever. He didn't even have any females saved in his contacts on his phone. I would know. I was the one who had gone to the store to get him a new phone and have his contacts transferred, and I might have looked through them. There had definitely never ever been any sleepovers at his house, or any women hanging around. There couldn't be any after away games because, according to Zac, Aiden always went straight back to his hotel room afterward.

So, yeah, I felt a little dumb. "No."

"So then there's nothing to worry about, is there?"

I swallowed my saliva. "I can't date anyone either."

That had her cracking up and I suddenly found myself insulted at how hard she was laughing. "You're funny."

"It's not funny." So I hadn't had a boyfriend in a couple of years. What the hell was the big deal?

Her hysterical laughing reached a peak. "*I can't date anyone either,*" she mocked me in a voice that I knew was supposed to be mine. "Now you're just making shit up."

It was a well-known fact that I didn't date much.

Diana sounded like she was covering her mouth with her hands to smother her laughs. "Oh, V. Do it and stop thinking about it so much."

She wasn't being any help, and I found myself still torn in half. "I'm going to keep thinking about it."

"What's there to think about?"

Everything.

BUT I THOUGHT about it. Then I kept thinking about it some more.

I looked online at how much I still owed on my loan, and I almost threw up. Looking at the balance was like looking at an eclipse; I wasn't supposed to do it. The six digits before the period that glared back at me from the screen made me feel like I was going blind.

This thing with Aiden was a lottery, and I happened to be the only one with a ticket to it. It also happened to be the winning ticket. This small nugget of uneasiness jiggled around in my chest, but I ignored it as much as I could until I couldn't handle it anymore.

I would be helping someone whose sincerity I couldn't judge completely.

I would be signing away years of my life.

I'd be doing something illegal.

And I would be doing this all as technically a business transaction. It wasn't that complicated, because I understood what Aiden was doing and why he was doing it, for the most part.

I just didn't completely understand why he insisted on trying to reel me back into his life.

Regardless of everything else though, a part of me was resentful that Aiden I-get-everything-I-want Graves had his mind set on me to be the one to help him out. I guess I didn't feel like he deserved my help or my loyalty when he'd never exactly done anything to deserve it.

But . . .

My student loan debt wasn't just a paycheck; it wasn't payable in five years like a car loan. Plus, if a house would also be a form of payment . . . We were talking a lot of money, a lot of heartache, and a lot of interest. Thirty years on a mortgage. It would be a massive relief.

Wouldn't it?

Could I just forgive Aiden and do this?

I knew people made mistakes, and I understood that you didn't always know what you had until you didn't have it. I had learned that myself the hard way about small things I'd taken for granted. But I also knew how resentful I could be, how I held on to grudges sometimes.

I found myself driving to Aiden's house, heart in my throat, risking my life and freedom for a freaking student loan that I couldn't just forget about or disregard.

The security guard at the gate grinned at me when I pulled into the community Aiden lived in. "I haven't seen you in forever, Miss Vanessa," he greeted me.

"I quit," I explained after greeting him. "He shouldn't be surprised I'm here."

He gave me a look that said he was a little more than impressed. "He's not. He's been reminding me every week to let you in if you came by."

He was either a little too confident or . . .

Well, there was no "or." He was a little too confident. I suddenly had the urge to turn my car around to teach him a lesson, but I wasn't egotistical or dumb enough to do it. With a goodbye wave at the guard, I drove past the gate and toward the home I'd been to too many times to count.

I knew he'd be home, so I didn't worry about the absence of cars in the driveway as I parked on the street, like I had every time in the past, and marched up to the front door, feeling incredibly awkward as I rang the doorbell.

I wanted to turn around, walk away, and tell myself I didn't need his money. I really wanted to.

But I didn't go anywhere.

It took a couple of minutes for the sound of the lock getting tumbled to let me know he was there, but in no time, the door was swung open and Aiden stood there in his usual attire, his towering body blocking the light from inside the house. His expression was open and serious as he let me in and led me over to where everything had begun—the big kitchen. It didn't matter that his couch was incredibly comfortable; he always seemed to prefer to sit in the kitchen at the island or in one of the chairs of the nook to eat, read, or do a puzzle.

He took a seat on his favorite stool, and I took the one farthest away from him. It was weirder than it should have been considering what was at stake.

I was a person, and he wasn't any more or any less special than I was, and regardless of what happened, I had to remember that point.

So I sucked in a breath through my nose and just went for it. Honesty was the best policy and all that, wasn't it? "Look, I'm scared," I admitted in one breath, taking in his familiar features, the slants of his cheekbones, the thick, short beard that covered the lower half of his face, and that ragged white scar along his hairline.

For two years, I'd seen his face at least five times a week, and not once had we ever had a moment remotely close to this. I couldn't forget that, because it mattered to me. It would be one thing to have a stranger ask me to marry him because he wanted to become a U.S. resident, but it was a totally different thing to have someone who I *knew*, who had never cared for me, ask.

Honestly, it was worse.

Aiden's long lashes lowered for a moment, and the man who was as greedy with his attention and affections as I was with the red and pink Starbursts lifted a rounded, hunk of a shoulder. "What are you worried about?" He commanded the words.

"I don't want to go to jail." I *really* didn't want to go to jail; I'd looked up marriage fraud on the internet and it *was* a felony. A felony with up to a five-year prison sentence and a fine that made my student loans seem like chump change.

Apparently the male version of my best friend said, "You have to get caught to go to jail."

"I'm a terrible liar," I admitted, because he had no idea how bad of one I was.

"You knew you were planning on quitting for months before you did. I think you might be okay with it," he threw out suddenly in a slightly accusing tone.

That might have made me wince if I felt guilty about what I'd done, but I didn't. It also didn't occur to me right then that he somehow knew I'd been planning on quitting for a long time. It just sort of went in one ear and right out the other. "I didn't lie to you. I only stayed because you had just gotten better, and I felt bad leaving you so soon afterward. I couldn't talk myself into doing it, and I was only trying to be a nice person. There's a difference."

His thick eyebrows went up a millimeter but no other muscle in his face reacted to my comment. "You told Zac," he pointed out like an accusation.

An accusation I wasn't going to grab on to. "Yeah, I told Zac because he's my friend." I damn sure wasn't going to apologize for it. "Please tell me when I was supposed to casually tell you, and expect a high five. Or were you going to give me a hug and congratulate me?" I might have nailed him with a look that said *Are you fucking with me?*

"When I did finally tell you, you didn't care, Aiden. That's what half of this comes down to. I'm still . . . *I'm so mad at you,* and I accept that I shouldn't be. I just can't help it. You're not my friend; you've never tried to be my friend. You haven't once given a shit about me until you needed something, and now for some strange reason, you're making it seem like you can't live without me. And we both know that's bullshit."

He stayed quiet for a moment, taking a sharp sniff, his eyes seemingly trying to pierce a hole straight through my head. "I've apologized to you. I meant it. You know I meant it," he insisted, and I could grudgingly admit to myself that the logical part of my brain recognized that statement as a truth. Aiden didn't apologize, and for all the things he was, he wasn't a liar. That just wasn't in his genes. For him to actually say the A-word? It wasn't insignificant. "I don't have time for friends, and if I did, I wouldn't go out of my way to make them anyway. I've always been this way. And I really don't have time for a relationship. You understand that. I'm not worried about getting caught—"

So he was changing the subject. "Because you won't be the one going to jail," I reminded him under my breath, frustrated at his tactics.

He raised one of his eyebrows another millimeter, but it was his flaring nostrils that gave away his irritation. "I've done a lot of research, and I consulted an immigration lawyer. We can pull it off. All you would have to do at first is file a petition for me."

Aiden didn't say *I think we can pull it off*; he said we could do it, and I didn't miss that nuance.

"You know, Aiden, you make saying yes so damn difficult. I would have done just about anything for you if you'd asked me when I worked for you, but now, especially when you act—you still act— like one single 'sorry' makes up for disrespecting me in front of other people, and letting someone talk about me, it pisses me off. How can you ask me to do this huge favor for you when I feel zero obligation to? We wouldn't even be having this conversation if I didn't want my loans paid off."

I bit the inside of my cheek. "I want to tell you to leave me alone, that I'll pay off my debt on my own like I had always planned on doing. I don't need your money." Meeting his eyes, I had to fight the urge to tear up. "I wished you had respected me enough to appreciate me back when it would have meant something. I liked you. I admired you, and in the course of a few days, you killed all that."

The words came out of my mouth before I could stop them.

We stared at each other. And stared at each other. Then stared at each other a little more.

When I was a kid, I learned the hard way how expensive the truth was. Sometimes it cost you people in your life. Sometimes it cost you things in your life. And in this life, most people were too cheap to pay the price for something as valuable as honesty. In this case, I could tell the price tag had hit Aiden unexpectedly.

Slowly, after a few breaths, he ducked his head and rubbed at the back of his neck with that great big hand. His breathing got harder, raspier, and he sighed an Alaska-sized breath. "Forgive me." His tone was rougher than ever, seemingly dragged through sand, and then covered in shards of glass. Yet somehow it sounded like the most real, heartfelt thing to ever come out of his mouth, at least in front of me.

But it still didn't feel like enough.

"I can forgive you. I'm sure you regretted it later on when I wasn't around but—" I shoved my glasses to the top of my head and rubbed my forehead with the back of my hand before lowering them again. "Look, this isn't a good start to a fake relationship, don't you think?"

"No." He moved his head slightly, just enough so that I could see those dark coffee irises with that bright amber ring surrounding the pupil peering up at me beneath the fanned cover of his long eyelashes. "I always learn from my mistakes. We made a good team once. We'll make a good team again."

Lifting his head completely, a dimple in his cheek popped out of nowhere, and he raised his hands to cup the sides of his head. "I'm no good at this kind of stuff. I would rather give you money than have to beg, but I will if that's what you want," he admitted, sounding about as vulnerable as ever. "You're the only person I would want to do this with me."

Why wasn't this so black-and-white?

"I'm not asking you to beg me. Come on. All I've ever wanted from you was . . . I don't even know. Maybe I want to think that you care about me at least a little bit after so long, and that's pointless. You want this to be a business deal, and I understand. It just makes me feel cheap, because I know if Zac was asking me, I would have probably said yes from the beginning because he's my friend. You couldn't even find it in your heart to tell me 'good morning.'"

He sighed, his index finger and thumb pulling at his ear. Dropping his gaze to the kitchen countertop, he offered, "I can be your friend."

Two years too late. "Only because you want something."

To give him credit, he didn't try to argue with me otherwise. "I can be your friend. I can try," he said in a low, earnest voice. "Friends take a lot of time and effort, but . . ." Aiden looked up at me again with a sigh, "I can do it. If that's what you want."

"I get so angry thinking about everything; I don't know if that's even what I really want anymore. It's probably not what I ever wanted. I don't know. I just wanted you to see me as a person instead of just that person you don't ever have to say 'thank you' to. So for you to tell me you can *try* to be my friend, it's so forced."

"I'm sorry. I know. I'm a loner. I've always been a loner. I can't remember the last time I had a friend who didn't play football, and even then, it usually never lasted. You know how much it means to me. You know how seriously I take it, maybe better than most of my teammates do," he explained like it was taking everything in him to make that admission.

I just kind of side-eyed him.

He continued. "I know you know. I can also accept responsibility for not being very nice to you either, all right? I said I'm not good at this friendship thing; I never have been, and it's easier not to bother trying."

If that wasn't the most slacker comment to ever come out of his mouth, I didn't know what was. But I didn't say it out loud.

"If you got on my nerves, I would have fired you the first time you flipped me off."

I found myself not exactly feeling honored.

"You're a good employee. I told you that. I needed an assistant, Vanessa; I didn't want a friend. But you're a good person. You work hard. You're committed. That's more than I can say about anyone else I've met in a long time." That big Adam's apple bobbed as he stared right at me. "I need a friend—I need you."

Was he trying to bribe me with his amazing, once-in-a-lifetime friendship? Or was I just being a cynical asshole?

As I stared at his facial features trying to decide, I realized I was being dumb. This was Aiden. Maybe he'd done something shitty by not defending me, but if I really thought about it, he probably wouldn't have defended Zac either. He'd said time and time again in interviews that he solely wanted to focus on his career while he had it. From every interview that had ever been made with one of his coaches, they all said the same thing: he was the most single-minded, hardworking player they had ever come across.

He started playing football his junior year of high school. *Junior year.* Most NFO-caliber players had been on the field since they were old enough to walk. Yet Aiden had a calling, Leslie, his high school coach, had said. He became a phenomenon in no time at all, and attended a university on a football scholarship. Not just any run-of-the-mill school either, but a top one. One that he'd won a few championships with, and even graduated with a degree from.

Damn it.

God damn it.

He wouldn't be asking me to do this if he didn't think he had to.

And I was well aware that people didn't change unless they wanted to, and this was a man who did whatever he put his mind to.

This pitiful, resigned sigh pulled its way out of my lungs. An answer to what he was asking of me sat at the front of my brain, at the tip of my tongue, curled in the pit of my belly. Was there any other possible response that wouldn't lead me to being the biggest idiot on the planet?

"Let's say we can. How long . . . how long would we have to stay marr—" I couldn't say it on the first try. "Stay married for?" I rushed out in a small voice.

He made sure to look me right in the eye when he answered. "Five years would make it seem less suspicious. I would only be given a conditional green card at first. After two years, I could get a permanent one."

Five years? Aiden was thirty now; he'd be thirty-five. I was twenty-six for the remainder of the year. I'd be thirty-one when we'd technically get divorced. Thirty-one wasn't old, not even close to it. The number didn't seem as atrocious as it should have . . . if I was really considering agreeing.

But still. Five years. A lot could happen in that period of time. What I knew most though was that there was no way in hell I could manage to pay off my loans in ten years, much less five, even if I sold my car, rode the bus everywhere, disconnected my cell phone, and ate ramen noodles for breakfast, lunch, and dinner.

"Five years," I repeated, blowing out a breath. "Okay."

"Makes sense?"

I eyed him, reminding myself that I wasn't saying yes to him yet. We were just talking. "Yes, it makes sense . . . if I were saying yes, which I'm not doing right now, so calm your horses." I'd give myself a pat on the back later for being so ballsy and firm.

He stared at me evenly, unfazed. "What else are you worried about?"

I huffed. "Everything?"

Aiden blinked at me. "About what? I'll pay off what you owe and buy you a house."

Think, Van. Think. It couldn't go this easily. I had some honor, and I hadn't completely forgiven him for being a jackass, despite his possibly manipulative and forced apologies earlier. My pride had a price too, and it was that idea that had me swallowing hard and meeting the gaze that for so long had forced me to look elsewhere.

"What if your career ends tomorrow?" I asked, despite how much of a gold digger it made me sound. This was a business deal, and I was going to treat it like one.

One of his eyebrows went a little funny. "You know how much money is in my bank account."

He had a point.

"If I didn't work the rest of my life, I would be fine. You know I don't handle my money irresponsibly either," he stated in an almost insulted tone. By that, he meant he could still go through with what he was offering me and be okay in the end.

"I'm not going to be your assistant again either." I made sure to keep my eyes on him, even though I really, really didn't want to. "I've worked really hard to do my design work full-time, and I'm not going to give it up."

That wide, square jaw hardened, and I could tell his teeth were grinding, which gave me an oddly victorious sensation in my chest. "Vanessa—"

"I'm being serious. I'm not doing it. We tried it and it didn't end well, and I won't put myself through that again. You know I don't even really want to do this, but you're offering me something that's hard to say no to," I explained. "I'm not trying to take advantage of you, but I didn't ask for this. You asked me. You've gone out of your way to get me to agree. I told you there are a million women in the world who would do this for you and not want anything in return"—except to maybe sleep with him, but I kept that to myself. "You don't need me. You have the world at your fingertips, big guy. I don't know if you know that or not."

After saying that, I realized I might be the dumbest person in the entire universe. The *dumbest*.

I half expected him to tell me to screw off then, but this was a deal breaker, and I needed him to understand that. If he told me I was out of my damn mind, then twenty years from now, I could more than likely live with myself for turning down his offer. I'd planned to quit working for him to further my dream; I wasn't going to tie myself down for another five years with the same amount of work I'd been juggling. I just wasn't. There was a lot I'd be willing to sacrifice, but not that.

Folding my hands on my lap, I squeezed one set of fingers tight, focusing, and keeping my breathing even.

He was frustrated. Aggravated. But he wasn't saying yes or no. I had nothing left to lose, and I needed him to understand that yes, maybe I was being a little bit of a bitch, but it wasn't for no reason. He did what he did for his dream, and I was going to do what I needed to do for mine. If anyone could understand that, it should have been him.

I reached up and played with one of the legs of my glasses, forcing myself not to look away. I licked my lips nervously and raised my eyebrows. I'd done it, said what I needed to say, and I could live the rest of my life with the consequences, damn it.

What seemed like a month later, the Wall of Winnipeg sighed.

I set my elbow on the counter and mirrored his position in resignation. "Are you fine with me not being your assistant or not?"

Aiden nodded gravely.

I wasn't sure whether to be disappointed or relieved, so I went with neither. Business mode, I needed to get into business mode. "I'm not going to go to jail for you, so we need to figure everything out. What are we going to tell Zac?" Speaking of Zac, where was he? I wondered.

"Even if I told him to find his own place, he would know something was going on. We have to tell him. We would need people to confirm we're in a real relationship together."

Was that the truth? I nodded, thinking of Diana, and how I had told her everything already. "Yeah. I have to tell my friend. She would know something was going on. I can get away with not telling anyone else." I'd thought about it, and I was fairly certain I could embellish Aiden trying to win me over to come back as some sort of love story. At least, that's what I hoped. Not being super close to anyone, including my little brother, who had his own busy life, obviously helped in this situation.

Aiden nodded, practical and understanding.

But . . . I raised both of my shoulders. "What about everyone else?" *Everyone else*. Literally. Everyone in the world. Just thinking about it made me want to puke. Any idea or hope of possibly being able to hide a possible marriage had gotten flushed down the toilet when I remembered an article on Aiden years ago, when he'd been spotted eating dinner with a woman—a woman who turned out to be a rep for a company that was trying to endorse him. Who cared? I'd originally thought.

Then it had hit me. Some people did. And too many people cared about all things involving Aiden Graves. He couldn't cut his hair without someone posting about it. Someone in the world would find out we'd gotten married at some point. There would be no hiding it.

And that made me feel uneasy. I hadn't even liked the attention I'd gotten from people when they found out I worked for him. Getting hitched to him would be an entirely different ballpark.

I had to swallow the saliva in my mouth to keep from gagging.

"We could keep it quiet for a while. . . ." the big guy started to say. I gave him a look that he just returned with a blink. "But someone will find out eventually. We can get married without making a big deal over it, and divorce the same way. What happens on the field is for my fans, everything else isn't their business." The way he stated that didn't give me room to doubt him.

I would be living the rest of my life as Aiden Graves's ex-wife.

The thought almost made me cross my eyes at how absurd it was. Then immediately afterward, I wanted to put my head between my knees and pant.

Instead of doing any of those things, I made myself process his words, and then nod. His idea made sense. Obviously, someone in the world would eventually find out, but Aiden was intensely private with the people he knew, and so much more with folks he didn't. It wouldn't look strange if we kept it a secret as long as possible.

The thought had just entered my head when I asked myself, *What the hell had I gotten myself into?*

"We wouldn't be able to sign an agreement that says you get a house and your loan paid off, but I hope you trust me enough to know I wouldn't back out on you." Those dark eyes seemed to laser a message on my forehead. "I would trust you enough not to sign a prenup."

No prenup? Uh . . .

"I won't begin a relationship while the marriage is intact," he continued out of the blue. "You can't either."

That had me raising my gaze. My relationship status wasn't going to be changing anytime soon. It hadn't in years, and I didn't foresee it doing so anytime soon, but my conversation with Diana seemed to haunt me. Even as a fake wife with a paper marriage, I wouldn't want to look like an idiot. "Are you sure you can promise that? Because you might meet—"

"No. I won't. I've only loved three people in my entire life. I don't plan on loving anyone else in the next five," he cut me off. "I have other things to worry about. That's why I'm asking *you* to do this and not finding somebody else." What he wasn't saying in that moment was that he was in the prime of his career, but I'd heard him say those exact words countless times in the past.

I wanted to cry horseshit, but I kept it to myself. I also wanted to ask who the only three people he'd ever loved were, but I figured this wasn't the time. Leslie had to be one of them, I imagined. "If you say so."

From the way his throat bobbed, he wanted to make a comment, but instead he kept going. "I'll help you pay off your loan over the next three years."

And negotiations suddenly came to a screeching halt. For a moment.

Then I made myself think about it. Taking a few years to pay off the loan would look an awful lot less sneaky than if it was done in one or two big payments. If I made a few payments here and there, that would look a lot better too, wouldn't it? Like if we waited a few months until after we signed the papers and everything? I had to think so.

"Okay." I nodded. "That works for me."

"My lease on this house is ending in March. We can rent another house afterward or sign another lease here. When my residency comes through, I'll buy one that you can keep afterward."

Afterward was the second thing I paid attention to.

The main thing I didn't miss was the beginning of his statement and the "we" in the following sentence.

"I'd have to move in with you?" I asked slow, slow, slowly.

That big, handsome face went a bit squinty. "I'm not moving in with you." I couldn't even find it in me to be offended; I was too busy processing whether he'd made a joke or not. "You're the one worried about making it believable. Someone is going to check our licenses."

He had a point. Of course he had a point. But . . . but . . .

Breathe. Loans and a house. Loans and house.

"Okay. All right. That makes sense." My stuff. What was I going to do with it? My apartment with all my things that I'd collected over the years . . .

I was going to have a panic attack at some point.

I'd known I wasn't always going to live there—at least I'd better not. But that didn't change anything. This house wasn't mine and it didn't feel like mine. It felt like Aiden's place. Like the house I'd worked in for years. But I could move in if I needed to, especially if it was the difference between making this hoax of a marriage seem legitimate and not.

I had to. Had to.

"When do you want to do this?" I pretty much croaked.

He didn't ask me. He just said, "Soon."

I was going to have a panic attack. "Okay." All right. Soon could be a month from now. Two months from now.

"Fine?" Aiden raised his eyebrows in what seemed like a challenge.

I nodded dumbly, finding myself becoming more and more in tune with the idea that we were really doing this. I was going to marry him to get his papers fixed. For money. For a lot of money. For financial security.

Aiden stared at me for a while, the bobbing of his throat the only sign that he was thinking. "You'll do this, then?"

I would be an idiot if I didn't, wouldn't I?

That was a dumb question in itself. Of course I would be an idiot, a massive, gigantic idiot who owed a lot of money.

"Yes." I gulped. "I will."

For the first time in two years, the Wall of Winnipeg's face took on an expression that was as close to joyous as I had ever seen. He looked . . . relieved. More than relieved. I'd swear on my life his eyes lit up. For that one split second, he resembled a completely different person. Then the man who wore a jockstrap on a regular basis did the unthinkable.

He reached forward and put a hand on top of mine, touching me for the first time. His fingers were long and warm, strong, his palm broad and the skin rough, thick. He squeezed. "You won't regret this."

NINE

didn't call Aiden and he didn't call me.

I couldn't blame the lack of communication on him not having my cell phone number; I'd given it to him before I left his house the day I'd agreed to do what we were doing.

A week passed, and when he hadn't bothered getting into contact with me, I didn't think much of it. The Three Hundreds were in the middle of preseason games according to the news. I knew how busy this time of the year was for him.

Plus, there was the small chance that maybe he had changed his mind. Maybe.

Well, I didn't know why else he wouldn't call, but I made myself not think about it more than I needed to, which I figured wasn't much, and I sure as hell wasn't going to stress about it.

The reality that there was a chance he had found some other way of getting his residency petition filed wasn't as crippling as I would have imagined considering there was over a hundred thousand dollars riding on our deal. I wouldn't even say I was disappointed but . . .

Okay, maybe by the fifth day into the week I might have accepted that I was a little, tiny bit disappointed. Having my loans paid off would have been . . . well, the more I thought about having that amount of money resting on my shoulders, the more I realized just how repressing it was. It would be one thing if I owed that much money on a house, but in freaking school loans?

If twenty-six-year-old Vanessa could talk to eighteen-year-old Vanessa, I wasn't sure I would have still gone to such an expensive school. I probably would have gone to community college for my basics then transferred to a state college. My little brother had never made me feel guilty for leaving; he'd been the one to tell me to go. Every once in a while though, I regretted the decision I'd made. But I was a stubborn jackass idiot who wanted what she wanted come hell or high water, and I'd done what I wanted to do at an incredibly high expense.

By the seventh day into our no-communication spree, I was more than halfway through coming to terms with the fact that I would be in debt the next twenty years of my life, and that I'd already assumed that would be the case the instant I'd gotten that first statement in the mail after graduation.

So why cry over it?

I had told him the truth. I didn't need him or his money.

But I would have taken it because I was an idiot, but I wasn't that much of an idiot.

I WAS IN the middle of uploading a Facebook cover file to DropBox for a client when my phone rang. Peeking over at it sitting on the coffee table behind my work desk, I couldn't help but be a little surprised at the name appearing on the screen.

Miranda P.

I should probably change the contact information since he technically wasn't my version of Miranda anymore.

"Hello?"

"Are you home?" the deep voice asked.

"Yes." I'd barely finished pronouncing the *s* when a now familiar, heavy-handed knock banged on my door. I didn't have to check my phone to know he'd hung up. A moment later, the peephole confirmed who I thought it would be.

And, yep, it was Aiden.

He barreled inside the instant the deadbolt was turned and slammed the door shut behind him, locking it without a second glance. Those dark eyes pierced me with a look that made me frown and freeze at the same time.

"What is it?"

"*What the hell were you thinking moving here?*" he pretty much growled in a disgusted tone that immediately put me on the defensive.

Sure, I knew my complex was slightly scary, but he didn't need to make it seem like I lived in a slum. "It's cheap."

"You're kidding," he muttered.

Where the hell did this smart mouth come from? "Some of my neighbors are nice," I claimed.

The expression on his face was dubious as he said, "Someone was getting jumped right next to the gate when I pulled in."

Oh. I waved him inside to change the subject. He didn't need to know that happened on a weekly basis. I'd called the cops a couple of times, but once I realized they never actually showed up, I stopped bothering. "Do you need something?"

Walking ahead of me toward the living room, he answered over his shoulder, "I've been waiting for you to let me know when you're moving in."

That had been one of the first things I'd stopped wondering back when I began considering that he might have changed his mind. So hearing it again was like having ice thrown on me. Almost. I didn't bother telling him I'd thought we weren't going through with it anymore. "Were you . . . did you . . ." I coughed. "Was I supposed to do it soon?"

Turning around to face me, he tipped his chin down before crossing his giant biceps over his chest. "The season is about to start; we need to do it before then."

I didn't remember hearing about that being part of the plan. I mean, I figured sooner than later, but . . .

He was paying off my student loans if I did this. I should have moved in the day after we came to a decision, if that was what he wanted.

"When do you think I should?" I asked.

Of course he had a date in mind. "Friday or Saturday."

I almost hacked out a lung. "*This* Friday or Saturday?" That was only five days away.

That big head tipped to the side. "We're on a time crunch."

"Oh." I swallowed. "My lease is up in two months."

Sometimes I forgot Aiden didn't believe in obstacles. "Pay it off. I'll give you the cash."

This was happening. This was really happening. I was moving in. With him.

I eyed him—the wide muscles of his shoulders, the dark hair dusting his jaw, those freaking eyes that seemed to glare at everything and everyone. I was going to be living with this guy.

My loans. My loans, my loans, my loans.

"Which day is better for you? Friday or Saturday?" I made myself ask.

"Friday."

Friday it was. I peered at my belongings for the first time and felt a pang of sadness.

Just as I was thinking about my things, Aiden seemed to be doing the same thing, glancing around the small living room. I thought he might have lifted a foot to toe my couch. "Do you need help packing . . . or something?" he asked in an unsure voice, like this was his first time asking someone if they needed help.

I wouldn't be surprised if it was.

"Umm . . ." Right after I'd gotten home from his house, I'd decided what I would keep and what I would donate or give away. In conclusion, I assumed it would have to be most of my stuff.

I figured I'd be taking the guest room, since it was the only room not being used on a full-time basis. The other three rooms besides the master were Zac's, the home office, and the huge in-home gym.

"The only things I want to keep are my bookcase, my television, and my desk." I didn't miss the judgmental eye he slid toward the small, sixty-dollar black desk behind me. "The rest I'm going to give to my neighbors. There's no point in keeping any of it in storage for"—I almost gagged on the words—"five years."

He nodded even as he took in my television. "Everything can fit in a couple of trips."

I nodded, sadness nipping my throat at the idea of leaving my apartment behind. Sure, it wasn't luxurious or anything, but I'd made it my own. On the other hand, an apartment I hadn't been planning on staying at forever anyway wasn't going to be the difference between living in debt and not.

I could cry at Aiden's later if I needed to . . . and that thought almost made me crack up out loud. What had my life come to? And why the hell was I complaining so much? I'd be moving into a nicer place, getting my loans off my back, and getting a house, all in return for "marrying" a man. So I couldn't date anyone if I wanted to. Whoop-de-do. The last date I'd gone on two weeks ago hadn't exactly left me excited for a repeat. It was a fair exchange, more than a fair exchange if I didn't calculate the risk of what would happen if someone found out that our marriage was a fraud. Then again, you didn't get anywhere in life unless you took a risk.

"Okay," I muttered out of the blue, more to myself than Aiden.

Then we just stared at each other, letting that same awkward silence that had been between us as boss and employee come out.

I cleared my throat.

Then he cleared his throat. "I talked to Zac."

"You did?"

"Yes."

"And?"

Aiden shrugged his shoulders carelessly. "He said he understood."

In that case, I needed to call him; I didn't want to be a total coward and just move in without talking to him about it.

Aiden dipped his chin once before turning his body to face the door. "I need to go. I'll see you Friday," he said as he moved toward it.

And then he was gone.

He didn't tell me to call him if I needed help with anything, and he didn't say bye. He simply left.

This was what I'd signed up for.

This was the next five years of my life. It could be worse, couldn't it?

IT WAS SEVEN-THIRTY in the morning, and I was at my dining room table for the last time ever when that now familiar, three-rap knock made my door rattle. I'd just gotten out of bed twenty minutes ago, and I was sitting around waiting for the waffle iron to heat up. Hell,

I still had my pajamas on, hadn't washed my face, or even brushed my teeth yet. My hair was up in something that looked like a baby pineapple.

"Aiden?" I called out as I dragged my feet toward the door.

Sure enough, his dark facial hair greeted me through the peephole before I let him in with a yawn and a small frown.

The man who was apparently going to be my new roommate, amongst other things, strolled in, not muttering a "good morning" or anything. Instead, he waited until I locked the door before giving me a lazy look. "You aren't dressed yet?"

I had to stifle another yawn, covering my mouth with my hand. "It's seven-thirty. What are you doing here?"

"Helping you move," he said, like I was asking a dumb question.

"Oh." He was? He'd said something about it only taking a few trips to move my things, but I'd assumed it would take *me* a few trips. Huh. "Okay. I was just about to make waffles . . . do you want some?"

Aiden eyed me for a moment before turning around and continuing on to the kitchen. His head turned from left to right in what I assumed was him either making sure that I had actually gotten some packing done or taking inventory of what I had left to go. I'd bubble-wrapped all my artwork two days ago. My clothes were all in boxes the people at the grocery store were nice enough to let me have. My books and knickknacks were packed. My television and desktop computer were the only items that hadn't been prepped, but I had almost every blanket and comforter I owned in the living room waiting to get put to good use.

"Which recipe?" he had the nerve to inquire.

"The cinnamon one." Before he could ask, I added, "I'm not using eggs."

He nodded and took a seat at the table, still not exactly subtle in his perusal. All my dishes, utensils, and pots were already out and stacked on the countertops, waiting for their new owners to come and take them. I'd been lugging them around since college, and I figured they'd gone above and beyond the call of duty.

I made more batter and then poured it into the hot waffle iron, keeping an eye on Aiden as he kept taking in my belongings. "What are you doing with the rest of your furniture?"

"My neighbor upstairs is taking the mattress, dining room table, and the dishes." She was a single mom with five kids. I'd seen her mattress during the few occasions I'd babysat, and my things were definitely an improvement. The dining room table was also a nice addition to the empty space she had where one would have normally sat, even though there weren't enough chairs for her and all the kids. "My next-door neighbor is taking the couch, the bed frame, dresser, and coffee table for his daughter."

"They're coming to get it today?"

"Yep, but my neighbor upstairs is a single mom, and I want to help her."

"Did you pay the rest of your lease off already?"

I glanced at him from the other side of the kitchen. "Not yet. I was going to go to the business office before I leave."

"How much do you owe?"

I might have muttered the amount.

There was a pregnant pause before Aiden asked, "For a month?"

I coughed. "No, that's two months."

Was he breathing louder than normal? "Did I really pay you that little?"

Again with a comment about my place. "No." I fought the urge to scowl. I had other things to spend my money on. I didn't need to explain myself to him.

Did he roll his eyes? "I brought enough cash."

Was I supposed to say "No, don't worry about it. I have it?" or was it okay for me to accept it? Ideally, he was already doing more than enough for me for the next five years when I really didn't have to do much more than sign some paperwork, and make sure I didn't fall in love with someone . . .

Okay, that was guilt sweeping along the lining of my stomach, and I knew what it meant. "Don't worry about it. I can pay for it." I didn't want to take advantage of his kindness, or whatever it could be called.

Aiden just shrugged.

A few minutes later, the waffles were ready and we ate in silence at the table, both of us eating efficiently and quickly. I washed off our dishes and dried them, leaving them on the stack with the others.

"Let's get the things your neighbors are taking out of here first, then pack up the cars," Aiden suggested, his fingers dipping into the front of his shirt to pluck at the medallion hanging around his neck. He moved it so that it lay against the back of his neck, the chain it was on tight around the front of his throat. I'd always wondered where he'd got it from—especially since as far as I knew, he wasn't a religious person—but it was another one of those things he'd never bothered sharing.

"Sounds like a plan," I said, eyeing the hint of gold one more time. Oh well.

Once on the floor above mine, the single mother opened the door on the second knock, accepting the box of glasses I'd carried up the stairs. "You're leaving now?" she asked me in Spanish.

"Yes. Do you want to send some of the kids down with me to help carry some things?"

Mrs. Huerta nodded and called her three oldest children to help. The eleven-, nine-, and eight-year-old hugged my hips and then ran down the stairs ahead of me, already fully aware of what they were keeping. The three of them barged in and headed straight toward the kitchen, slowing down when they spotted the big man transferring boxes from my bedroom into the hallway.

One by one, they each grabbed cups, pots, pans, or utensils and headed back out. I grabbed two chairs from the dining room table and made my way toward the stairs, shooting Aiden a tight smile when our eyes met on the way out. I had just deposited them in my neighbor's living room when a shadow appeared at the doorway, carrying the other two chairs under his arms effortlessly.

"*Dios santo. ¿Es tu novio?*" the slightly older woman asked from her spot on the couch.

Boyfriend? I felt my eyes bulge, but nodded, maybe a bit robotically. "*Sí.*" What else was I going to call him? I was probably lucky enough that she didn't have time to watch football and had no idea who he was.

She glanced in Aiden's direction once more, balancing her three-year-old on her lap, and gradually nodded, impressed. "He's handsome," she said in Spanish. "And those muscles." Mrs. Huerta added a grin to the end of her comment that had me giving her a timid smile.

"*Ya se,*" I said in a mutter before darting back out of the apartment and heading downstairs. *I knew?* Well, it was the truth. I did know he had some guns. And a chest. And that ass. I could have done worse. Maybe he had little desire for social skills and maybe he didn't really care about anyone but himself, but he could be worse. He could be a psychopath who did bad things to animals, I guess.

I found Aiden in my apartment with the table flipped on its back, unscrewing the top of it from the legs with a pocket multi-tool I wasn't sure where he'd gotten. He glanced up when he sensed me standing there. "What else are they taking?"

"The mattress."

He hummed and nodded.

Forty minutes later, I had sweat pouring down my face, but Aiden and I had managed to carry the mattress up the stairs. Weight-wise, he could have carried it up by himself without a huff or a puff, but apparently, it was too big to carry alone, and my puny muscles had struggled. We set the older mattress where my neighbor's blow-up bed had been the last time I'd come over. I'd offered the bed frame to her but understood why she hadn't wanted it—two mattresses would barely fit in the tiny one bedroom that was built for *maybe* two occupants but not six.

Luckily, by the time we were done, my next-door neighbor's sons were waiting outside my door to help move the rest of the furniture into his place. Aiden and I sat across from each other in the bedroom, taking the bed apart so it could be easier to move. I caught him looking at the multiple night lights I hadn't gotten a chance to pack away. He didn't ask about them, and I was pretty grateful.

I noticed both of the neighbor's sons eyeing Aiden more than a little bit when they peeked into my bedroom, and then I heard one whispering to the other, but none of them said a word to us before carrying out the first of the things in the living room.

I had just taken a pee break when I opened the door and overheard talking coming from the hallway.

"Sure." That was Aiden.

I grabbed two of the boxes left in my bedroom and made my way out to leave them in the living room. Standing in the hallway was Aiden, one forearm against the wall while his left hand was up, scribbling away on something with one of the Sharpies I'd left around the apartment so I could write on boxes. Next to him were my neighbor's sons, their eyes glued on Aiden.

Yeah, it didn't take my not-so-genius brain to figure out they knew who he was, and what Aiden was busy doing.

"I appreciate it," one of them thanked him when he handed over the piece of paper he'd signed.

The big guy nodded, his attention turning toward me. "No problem. We should really finish packing up. We need to get going."

The guys kind of hesitated. "We could help."

Aiden shook his head dismissively. "We got it."

"Thanks though," I threw out when the rude-ass didn't.

They nodded and one of them said, "Man, Vanessa, I had no idea you were together. Dad's gonna lose it. He's a huge fan."

I already knew that, and it only made me feel guilty. My neighbor had a Three Hundreds mat outside his door. During the holidays, he hung up a wreath with team ornaments on it. "Yeah . . ." I just kind of trailed off. I mean, what else was I supposed to say?

Luckily, they quickly thanked Aiden again and took off, closing the door behind him.

"All right." I took a breath. "Let's get the rest of this done."

Between the two of us, we carried my television over to Aiden's Range Rover as my arms trembled with exhaustion. My desktop computer followed. The fact that he could have carried it on his own didn't escape me at all, but I wasn't going to complain, so I kept my mouth shut. In the back of my Explorer, we put my bookcase, desk, and chair. The rest of the boxes were split up into both of our vehicles.

Aiden was in his SUV when I closed my apartment door one last time, nostalgia hitting me dead center in the chest. I always thought about moving on with my life and taking the next step toward whatever upcoming goal I had. Like when I left Aiden, a part of me missed him—or some weird variation when you're so used to doing things a certain way for a long time and suddenly you don't—but I'd known I was going to move on. I was doing something better for myself, and doing this for him, no matter what my conscience said, was a smart step. A weird one, but a smart one.

It was a giant leap for my future, and I was going to hold on to that reminder with both hands.

I dropped off a check for the last two months of my lease, signed a few papers with the office manager, and I was out of there.

IT TOOK AN hour just to get to Aiden's house from my apartment thanks to a ten-car pileup on the highway. Between being a little overwhelmed with moving, especially since I wasn't feeling exactly stoked to have to move in with another person—that person being my ex-boss of all people—and trying my best to convince myself that I wasn't going to go to jail if or when officials found out the truth, I was trying not to become paranoid.

I smiled at the security guard when we got to the gated community and ignored the curious expression on his face when he saw my car loaded up. Aiden backed into the garage, and I parked in the driveway for the first time ever.

When I got out and spotted him toting boxes inside, I grabbed the most I could carry on my own from my Explorer. I followed after him, nervous, anxious, and a little bit scared.

Everything looked familiar, but it felt foreign at the same time. I made myself march on up those stairs I'd climbed a thousand other times and kept on going when all I wanted to do was turn around and head back to my apartment.

I was moving in with Aiden and Zac, signing some papers that would unite us in paper matrimony, and this would be my reality for the next five years. When I thought about it in bits and pieces . . . yeah, it didn't help. It still seemed like a huge white elephant I couldn't ignore.

The door to the empty guest room was open as I approached it, and I could hear Aiden inside setting things down. I'd been in there many, many other times in the past to dust or wash the sheets. I was pretty familiar with the layout.

But it wasn't the same as it had been the last time I'd seen it.

Aiden didn't have a bunch of crap all over the house. Every room except the gym was pretty sparse and utilitarian. He didn't have artwork or knickknacks. He hadn't even bothered painting any of the rooms. There wasn't a single trophy or jersey hanging around anywhere. The boxes of that kind of stuff were hidden in his closet, something I couldn't completely understand. If I had the kind of trophies he did, they would be up so everyone could see them.

In his bedroom, he had a bed and two dressers. He didn't even have a mirror in there, much less a single picture of anything or anyone. The guest bedroom had been even more barren, with only a bed and a nightstand in a relatively large-sized room—it was twice the size of the room at my apartment.

But when I walked into the room that would now be mine, I didn't just find a bed. There was a large matching dresser with a big vanity mirror mounted to it, and a new smallish bookshelf that also seemed to match the rest of the dark brown, contemporary furniture. It didn't hit me until much later that it was all the exact same furniture I'd had in my bedroom at my apartment . . . just nicer and matching.

"Your bookshelf from home would look better in the office," Aiden casually suggested when I just stopped and stood at the doorway, too busy taking in the new furniture.

I tried to keep my surprise to a minimum, but I wasn't sure if I succeeded or not, so all I managed to scrape together as a response was a nod. He was right though; my bookshelf would match better in there.

"Your desk can go there." He vaguely pointed at the empty section of the wall right between the two bedroom windows. "I bought the mattress right before you started working for me. It's only been slept in . . . What do you think? Three times? But if you want a new one, order one. You know which card to use."

I snapped my mouth closed and batted away the surprise that had stolen my words, blinking over at Aiden at the same time I hesitated. He'd done all this? For me? When I'd left working for him, he hadn't even known where to order his soap. He didn't even run his own dishwasher. Now there was new furniture?

Who was this man? I shook my head, my forehead scrunching. "No, this is all great. Thank you."

I didn't even have to put any effort into remembering how comfortable it had been when I'd had to climb on top of it to strip the sheets or dust the headboard. Not too soft, not too firm. "It's perfect." I almost said *Don't worry about it,* but then again, I was sure he wasn't worried; he was just trying to be accommodating, and considering I didn't expect much, it was more than I would have planned on. "This is better than what I'm used to."

I took another breath and slowly lowered the things I was holding to the floor. "Thanks for helping me move, by the way."

I'm really doing this. I'm moving in. Holy shit.

"I appreciate it," I wobbled out. I was really doing this. *I'm really doing this.*

He tipped his head down just slightly, then brushed past me on the way out, back downstairs, from the sound of the creaking staircase. There was no way I was going to slack off and make him do the majority of the hauling, even if he was in way better shape than me, and had four times the muscles.

Okay, I wasn't going to be a lazy shit.

Downstairs, I kept up with the rest of the moving. It took a little more than half an hour for both of us to get the boxes from the vehicles into the bedroom. Then we carried my television up while my arms convulsed from how tired they were, and my fingers turned slippery with sweat. The freaking thing seemed to have gained twenty pounds on the trip from my complex to his house.

It was really heavy, and I had a feeling I was going to pull my lower back. I did manage to smash my fingers into the doorjamb, hissing "Motherfucker" under my breath.

We were heading to grab the next piece of furniture when Aiden said over his shoulder, "You should think about doing some upper-body training."

I made a face behind him. I might have even stuck my tongue out as I held my poor, mangled fingers with my good hand.

Luckily, moving the bookcase into Aiden's office was a lot easier, and we didn't have any problems. My new roommate carried the desk upstairs all on his own, and I hauled the chair. Apparently, either we both needed a break or Aiden recognized the signs of exhaustion that I was sure were all over my face, so we took a break to have lunch.

Then the awkwardness began all over again.

Was I supposed to make lunch or was he? Or were we each going to make ourselves food? I hadn't gone grocery shopping yet, obviously, but Aiden had never been stingy with his groceries or complained when I had some, but . . .

"I have two pizzas in the freezer."

"Pizzas?" Were we in the right house? This was Mr. Whole-Food-Plant-Based-Diet. The most processed he got was quinoa pasta, tofu, and tempeh every so often.

He muttered something under his breath that sounded like "with soy cheese and spinach."

I bit my cheek and nodded, watching and wondering what the hell had happened to him over the last month and a half. "Okay."

With that, I turned on the oven like I had a thousand other times in the past. Unlike every other time, the Wall of Winnipeg went to the freezer and pulled out food on his own, getting the pizza stones out from a cabinet in a way that surprised me a little. At least when I was around, he never messed around with any of the kitchen items besides plates and utensils.

I went into the garage to throw the cardboard in with the rest of the recyclables and paused. Container after container of frozen micro-wavable vegan meals filled the bin.

The tiniest bit of guilt nipped at my stomach as I went back into the kitchen just as Aiden set the pizzas into the oven. I took the same seat I'd taken almost two weeks ago when I'd come by to talk to him about his offer. That strange silence seemed to grow as he took his favorite seat.

"Where's Zac?" I asked, watching the huge muscles in his fore-arms ripple as he rotated his wrist in a stretch.

A tendon in his thick neck seemed to pop, and I knew it was in annoyance. "He didn't come home last night." Before I could say any-thing, he added in a voice I recognized as a disapproving one, "He said he'd be here."

But he wasn't. Zac going out wasn't unheard of; he actually went out pretty often. Not coming back home wasn't exactly a rare occur-rence either. I'd talked to him a couple days ago briefly just to make sure he was going to be fine lying to authorities if he was questioned, and that he was okay with me moving in. He'd seemed to be more than okay with both.

"It's fine," I said, knowing full well from the way that tendon was straining it genuinely bothered Aiden. "So . . . what's the next step with your green card thing?"

Aiden had his attention on his arm. "We should go ahead and get the paperwork over with first." *Paperwork.* He was going with *paper-work* to describe what we were doing. Was I nauseous or did I suddenly get heartburn? "Soon."

"How soon?" My voice sounded more cryptic than what was really necessary, considering I knew exactly what I was getting myself into.

Those thick eyebrows kind of quirked, his jaw slightly twitched. "Before the season. I don't want to wait until bye week," he said, refer-ring to the week off the team got during the season.

He still wasn't answering my question. "Okay . . ."

"I have an early preseason game next week. Let's do it then." I choked and he ignored me, barreling straight through into his explanation. "We can't file the petition until the paperwork is done. You should change the address on your license as soon as you can, but you need to have mail coming here."

What could I say? *Let's wait?* What he was saying made sense. He really didn't have more than a day off after each preseason game, and from what I remembered, most of them were always in the evening. That probably would be the best chance we had of getting it done.

But it still made the part of my personality that liked to plan things in advance and mentally prepare cringe.

Next week. We were "doing it" in a week.

It was that easy. We needed to live in a house together, sign some papers, maybe take some pictures—was that even necessary?—and then . . . live the next five years of our lives.

I almost expected him to give me spirit fingers and say "Ta-da."

That simple. It was that simple apparently.

I took in the man who was sitting across from me—the biggest man I had ever seen, the most restrained, who was for all intents and purposes, technically my fiancé—and let nausea and nerves roll around in my belly like puppies.

"My lawyer said it'll be several months between you filing a petition for me and having my status adjusted until I get a conditional green card. We're going to need a lot of paperwork; they're going to ask for your bank statements. You'll have to go with me once everything is approved to have someone at the immigration office interview us. Will that work?" he asked, eyeing me warily, like he wasn't positive how I was going to take his plan.

I swallowed my heart. I'd already read all of that stuff online in the days between when he'd showed up at my place and when I came to his and agreed, so I was mentally prepared. Mostly. "Yeah." But the smile on my face was pretty damn faint.

What in the hell had I just agreed to?

TEN

The weekend came way too quickly and way too slowly at the same time. I'd woken up each night sweating profusely. I was going to commit a felony. I was getting married. And of all the people in the world, it was Aiden I was doing this with and for.

It didn't matter how many times I reminded myself that what we were doing wasn't real, my body couldn't be fooled. All these changes—the moving, the living in a different room, the sleeping in a different bed—they were all battling my brain for attention at all hours of the day, giving me a case of insomnia.

The only thing that eventually managed to lull me to sleep was the knowledge that I knew exactly what I was doing, what I was getting out of the hoax of a lifetime. *Debt freedom and a house.* I reminded myself of that repeatedly.

And we were going to Vegas to get it over with.

"It will make more sense if we do it there. We've gone twice together already," he'd explained to me after I'd agreed with him that speeding into it was fine. "If we did it here, we'd have to go to the courthouse to apply for a marriage license and get a Justice of the Peace to perform a ceremony."

He was right. We'd gone to Vegas twice. Once for a signing and the other time for a commercial he shot. Plus, I completely understood where he was going with doing it in Dallas. Someone would recognize him the instant he got out of the car at the courthouse. I could already picture a crowd if we tried to get our marr—the word gave me indigestion. License. There'd be a crowd if we went to get our license.

Actually, I think it was the word *our* that gave my insides gas.

"Everyone goes to Las Vegas to elope," the big guy had added, as if I didn't know.

Obviously, I did.

"There's no waiting to apply for a marriage license," he had ended with as he'd polished off a sandwich.

Another truth.

How can you argue practicality? There wasn't a point in having any of my few loved ones there, and honestly, I really wouldn't have wanted them to be in attendance. This wasn't some everlasting marriage built on love. I'm pretty sure I had told Diana more than once that I was going to have a beach destination wedding if the time ever came.

If the time came, that had been my plan. Maybe someday in the distant future, it'd be a possibility.

For now, *for this*, Las Vegas would work.

With his credit card in hand, the morning after I moved in, I reserved two first-class plane tickets, because explaining to Aiden that flying economy was cheaper was a pointless argument I'd tried once and failed at miserably. I also scored a two-bedroom suite at the hotel we'd stayed at in the past. We'd fly in Sunday evening and leave Monday afternoon. In and out, we would sign some papers, maybe take a picture, and then head back.

On the day before we were supposed to leave, I was at the grocery store when I spotted the customer in front of me wearing a wedding band, and it hit me.

Was Aiden going to need a ring? Was I going to need one?

He'd never said anything about engagement rings or wedding rings, and I wasn't sure if that was something we'd need to pull off the believability factor. Would they check that out at the interview? Would they care? I remembered Diana's cousin Felipa had worn a wedding ring way before things got serious between her and her husband. But I'd also met couples before who didn't bother with rings.

So . . .

I looked online to see if there was anything about whether agents checked that kind of thing or not, and I knew *The Proposal* wasn't a good example of how immigration issues actually worked. What was I supposed to do?

Chances were, he wouldn't wear it. But . . .

Get one anyway, my brain said. I could worry about one for myself when the time came, but it would be months until then.

I'd learned to trust my instincts, so that evening when he was running drills after hours by himself at the Three Hundreds' training facility, I fought the nagging feeling in my belly and snagged his College National Football Championship ring from the drawer where he kept it. Holding on to it for dear life, I headed to a small jeweler I'd visited in the past to get my favorite pair of earrings fixed when I'd messed them up.

The jeweler had a lot of rings to choose from, but not much in sizes large enough to fit Aiden's fingers. Luckily, he said he could get something resized for me in record time, and I chose a basic fourteen-karat white gold band. It was nothing remotely fancy or even eighteen karat, but . . . no one likes a picky bitch, and I was paying for it out of my own pocket, so he'd better not complain.

I was buying my soon-to-be fake husband a wedding ring that he may or may not wear.

After all, we had to make it believable. So even if he didn't wear it, at least he'd have it, I figured.

It only made me not want to get it more.

"ARE YOU READY?" Aiden called up the stairs.

I was never going to be ready. Ever.

I'd been up since four in the morning, waking up to find my heart pounding and a hundred million thoughts going through my head one after the other. We were leaving. We were going to Vegas to *sign paperwork* that would legally make me able to change my name to Graves if I wanted to.

That was another thing we hadn't talked about, but I didn't see a point in bringing it up. Plenty of women didn't change their names when they got married nowadays, right? If he didn't ask me to, I sure as hell wasn't going to bring it up. That just seemed like a nightmare waiting to happen at the social security office.

"Vanessa," he hollered. "We need to go."

With a nervous sigh that bordered on a growl, I got off the edge of the bed, where I'd been sitting for the last fifteen minutes while I waited for the nausea and the nerves to go somewhere else, and grabbed my duffel bag. We were only staying one night, but I didn't know what to pack or what to wear to . . . *do it* . . . so I brought a casual dress I'd worn ten times before, dressy jeans and a blouse, and two T-shirts to be on the safe side, along with one of my favorite pairs of heels. Underwear, socks, a toothbrush, travel toothpaste, a hairbrush, and deodorant rounded out my bag. I was wearing my tennis shoes on the way. For one day, it was definitely more than I really needed, but I hated not being prepared, so I'd live with what I'd packed.

Packed to go get married.

It was just as big a deal as I was trying not to make it out to be.

"Vanessa," Aiden bellowed, not impatiently, more just so I could hear him. "Come on."

"I'm coming. Hold your horses!" I yelled back from the top of the stairs, before hightailing it over to Zac's room real quick. Knocking on the door, I pressed my ear against it. "Zac Attack, we're leaving!"

The door opened a few seconds later. His dark blond head peeked out, a big smile already plastered on his face. He had been teasing me nearly nonstop since he'd gotten home right after I moved in, apologizing for not making it home in time and not needing to hint that he'd stayed over at a woman's house. The first chance I had with him alone, I'd asked him again if he was really fine with what was going on. His response: "Why wouldn't I be, darlin'? You're the one marryin' him, not me, and I like havin' you around."

And that was that.

With them being away from the house so much, it wasn't like we'd been inconveniencing each other or anything.

"Gimme a hug then, bride-to-be," Zac said, already holding his arms wide.

"Ugh." I scowled even as I leaned into his embrace.

"*Vanessa!*"

"Your future hubby is waitin'," Zac said before I reached up and pinched his lips together.

"We'll be back tomorrow."

"*Vanessa!*"

I sighed and took a step back. "Wish me luck."

Zac waved his hand in a dismissive gesture, an ornery smile taking over his tan face. "I sure will, Mrs. Graves."

He was so full of shit, but I knew if I didn't get downstairs, Aiden would probably come up here and drag me down—he hated being late—so I let Zac's comment go and ran down the stairs. At the bottom, Aiden's expression was his typical exasperated one. He was dressed in jeans and a black V-neck that stretched across the wide width of his muscular chest. His favorite hoodie dangled from his fingertips.

He gave me a look as I jogged down the steps, nerves making my knees weak. Aiden didn't wait for me to make it down before he was on his way to the garage. I hauled ass through the kitchen, closed the garage door behind me, and carried my bag to his SUV.

"You got everything?" he asked with a curt look once we were both buckled in as he turned his head to back out of the driveway.

I ran my fingers over the small lump in the front pocket of my jeans and felt the flutter of nerves remind me they hadn't gone anywhere. I took in his face quickly; the stern line of his mouth, the hard jut of his chin, and the constant tension creasing his eyebrows. Reality flowed over me. I was marrying this guy.

Oh, brother.

"Yep," I squeaked.

The trip to the airport went well, with the sports talk show on the radio keeping us company. Luckily, they were only discussing professional baseball. Aiden parked his car in one of the covered lots. From there, we took a shuttle to the terminal. I eyed him a few times on the way over, my hands getting sweatier by the second. Just as the minibus rolled up to the drop-off, Aiden slipped his hoodie on despite the ninety-something degree weather in Dallas, and pulled the zipper all the way up to his throat.

When the bus stopped, he was the first to get up, reaching for his backpack with one hand and my duffel in the other. If he wanted to carry my bag, I wasn't about to insist.

I let him lead us toward the check-in. In no time, we had our boarding passes, and Aiden signed autographs for the four airline employees working behind the counter before the trek toward security. It was impossible not to notice the people around us stealing glances and gawking at him. It wasn't like he didn't stand out in a hoodie, even if it was only to women checking him out. While he wasn't the tallest man in the world, the sheer size of him was eye-catching. Even in a double-extra-large hoodie, the size of his shoulders and the outlines of his biceps were unmistakable.

Together, we walked up to the first TSA agent, who looked at both our licenses, went a bit pink-faced for a moment, and then waved us forward. Gentleman that he was, Aiden let me get in line first. Making sure his attention was elsewhere when we got to the part of security where our carry-on luggage was checked, I put the white gold band on one of the trays with my cell phone and snuck it back into my pocket the instant I finished passing through the detector.

"I want a cup of coffee," I said when Aiden caught up to me. "Do you want something?"

He shook his head but walked along with me to the closest Dunkin' Donuts, his frame a big, imposing shadow that I couldn't help but constantly be aware of. In all the times we'd traveled together, I didn't think we'd ever been so close to one another. Usually I was trailing behind him, or he'd go off to sit somewhere by himself. This time though, he wasn't standing fifty feet away, much less ten, with his headphones in, oblivious to everyone and everything around him.

And that might have made me feel a little bit better. He wasn't exactly ignoring me or acting the way he usually did, AKA pretending I didn't exist. I had to give him some credit for that, didn't I?

Once we were in line, I glanced over to find his attention straight ahead, focused on the menu; a crease formed between his eyebrows. The customer in front of us moved aside, and I took a step forward as the employee peeked up from the cash register, briefly glancing at Aiden before looking back down. "How can I help you?"

"Can I—?"

Double taking, the employee's gaze went up to Aiden again. His nostrils flared.

I knew he was going to gasp before he did it. The employee's eyes went wide first. His mouth slammed shut second. Then he sucked in a breath. "Fuck," the cashier whispered, his gaze locked on the behemoth next to me.

The behemoth who was, at that point, looking around and not paying any attention to the individual freaking out in front of him. So I elbowed him. Aiden's attention snapped down to me so quickly it was a little alarming. He was frowning. I tipped my head to the side discreetly in the direction of the donut shop employee. Not anywhere near being an idiot, those brown eyes went where I indicated.

The employee was still gazing at him with huge eyes.

"Are you . . . you're . . . you're Aiden . . . Aiden Graves," the guy who had to be a couple years younger than me blubbered.

Aiden nodded tightly.

Oh, brother. Mr. Social Skills was at it again.

"You're . . . I'm . . ." The guy was panting. "I'm such a fan. Holy shit." He sucked in another breath, and I swear his face paled. "You're even bigger in person."

He really, really was.

Aiden shrugged, carelessly, like he usually did when someone mentioned his size. I thought people made him uncomfortable when they brought it up, but mostly because I'd heard him tell Leslie before that it wasn't like he'd done something for it. His genes had given him his stature and the framework of his build; all he'd done was work out and eat well to develop what he'd been given. His lack of a reply wasn't arrogance; I was pretty positive he just didn't know what to say.

The poor guy continued gaping at him, completely unaware I existed, much less that behind us were at least four other people wondering what the hell was taking so long for us to order.

Aiden didn't help the situation either by standing there, looking back at his fan with that unreadable, borderline bored expression on his face. "Could you get my girl a coffee?"

His girl?

It took every ounce of my self-control not to look up at him with an expression that said exactly what I was thinking: *What the hell did you just call me?*

Thankfully, I didn't physically react. When the cashier finally snapped out of his trance, he glanced at me and blinked. I smiled at him even as I pulled my phone out of my pocket, ignoring the strange feeling coursing through my spine at the fake term of endearment that had just come out of Aiden's mouth.

"Oh, sure. Sure. My bad. What can I get you?" the guy asked, blushing.

I placed my order, quickly looking down to make sure I was texting the right person, and typed out a quick message.

Your girl? I sent the man next to me before handing over my card.

The guy cast another glance at Aiden while he swiped it hastily, nervously. I thanked him when he gave it back, but he was back to not paying any attention to me; he was still staring at Aiden, and on closer inspection, I realized the poor guy's hands were shaking.

"Thanks," I mumbled one more time as I took my cup and moved aside. Aiden shifted over along with me, seeming to be in his own little world, oblivious to the text message I'd sent him, or maybe just deciding to ignore the phone I knew he usually kept on vibrate in his pocket. It was right then that I noticed the people in line behind us were all staring at him.

I couldn't blame them. He didn't exactly give off a welcoming vibe, standing there with his backpack on both shoulders, his arms crossed over his chest with my bag resting at his feet while he waited for me. Then I realized they were glancing at me too. Measuring me. Seeing who was with the guy the employee was freaking out about.

Just me.

—

THE NERVES AND the urge to throw up didn't go anywhere. I was nauseous the entire flight to Vegas. Aiden said maybe five words to me before he put his head against the window and fell asleep, which wasn't a bad thing, considering I was stuck in my own world of denial and terror. I kept telling myself everything was fine, but it didn't feel like it. If Aiden was battling any nerves or insecurity, he didn't let it show as we walked out of the airport and caught a cab to our hotel off the Strip. We checked in and made our way up the elevator to the suite.

He swiped the card through the door and let me in first.

I had to let out a whistle as I took in the clean, contemporary furnishings. I'd forgotten how nice this hotel was and it made me feel a little guilty. When I was a kid, we hadn't traveled much, mostly because my mom never had the money, much less the time or inclination, to take us anywhere. But on the rare occasion that Diana's parents invited me to go along with them on a trip, we would stay at the really cheap motels on the side of the road that looked like something out of a horror movie, and we'd all crammed in to a room—or two, if her parents could swing it.

And I always had a good time, even more so if the motel had a pool.

Yet here I was at this five-star hotel, staying with a man who was a millionaire. I'd paid the rate for the room with his card. I was well aware of how much everything cost. I knew that no one in my family, with the exception of my little brother, would ever stay in a place like this. And it made me feel slightly uncomfortable. Guilty. A little sad.

"You all right?" that gruff, low voice asked from behind me when I'd stopped just through the door.

I had to clear my throat and force myself to give him a nod and a smile, which was about as insincere as you could get. "Sure."

Yeah, he read it on my face easily, his eyes swinging around the room in confusion. "You chose the hotel." His tone was slightly accusing. "You don't like it?"

"No." I shook my head, now feeling like a dick on top of everything else. "I mean, of course I like it. This is the nicest place I've ever stayed." That was saying a lot, because when I traveled with Aiden, we always stayed somewhere nice. "I was just thinking about how fancy it is, and how I never would have imagined when I was a kid that I could stay somewhere like this. That's all."

The fact I was staying here with Aiden, to marry him, just sent that nail straight home into my heart. Younger Vanessa, pre-twenty-six-year-old Vanessa, had no idea what she had in store for her.

There was a pause, and I swore we both looked over our shoulders to glance at each other. The tension between us was awkward and uncertain. The Wall of Winnipeg blinked those big brown eyes. "You could have invited your family if you really wanted to."

"Oh, uh, no. It's all right." In hindsight, I realized I'd shot down his offer too fast. "I only keep in contact with my little brother, and he's already back in school."

Why was he looking at me so strange?

"I don't . . ." Good grief, why was this flustering me so much? And why couldn't I just shut up? "I only talk to my mom every once in a while and never my sisters. And my best friend works a lot." I wrung my hands and finished up the spiel of stupidity. "I don't have anyone else."

Aiden stared at me for so long, I frowned. "You're acting weird," he stated so casually I almost ignored the actual words that had come out of his mouth.

"Excuse me?"

"You're being weird with me," Aiden repeated himself.

That had me slamming my mouth closed and my frown growing.

The man who didn't keep things to himself kept on barreling through what he apparently felt he needed to say. "I told you I was sorry."

Uh.

"Look, everything is fine—" I started to say before he cut me off with a shake of his head.

"It isn't. You don't smile anymore. You haven't called me big guy or given me hell," he stated.

Wait a second. I hadn't, had I? And he'd noticed? The possibility that he'd noticed made me feel strange, almost uncomfortable. "I thought

I annoyed you," I mumbled, trying to figure out what was the right response and whether he was saying these things because he genuinely missed them or not.

"You do." And there we went. "But I'm used to it now."

Wait another second. . . .

"You've never made me feel awkward before, but you look at me differently now. Like you don't know me, or you don't like me." The fact he leveled an even gaze at me, without shame, without embarrassment, without playing games, hit me right in the solar plexus. "I get it if you're still pissed, if you don't think of me the way you used to, but I liked the way we were before," he went on. With his face open and completely earnest, he only slightly made me feel bad for how obvious I'd been with my frustrations with him, especially since he seemed to have not just noticed, but also missed the way things had been despite going out of his way to ignore me for so long.

"I know." I swallowed and bit the inside of my cheeks. "*I know*. Look, I'm just . . ." I shrugged. "We'll be back to normal in no time, I'm sure. This has all just been a lot for me to handle, and I'm trying to get used to it. It's hard for me to forgive people sometimes. I don't know how to act around you anymore, I guess."

"The same way you used to," he suggested evenly, as if it was the easiest answer in the world.

I swallowed, stuck between being stubborn and holding on to the fear and resentment I'd felt and unsure of how to move forward with this version of Aiden I was trying to get to know.

As if sensing I had no idea how to answer, he rolled his shoulders back and asked, "Other than that, you're sure you're fine?"

"Yes."

"Positive?"

I nodded, letting out a breath that had somehow gotten stuck deep in the pit of my belly, bloating it with insecurity and anxiety and probably a dozen other things I wasn't aware of. "Yeah. I, ah, changed my address on my bank statement a couple days ago. I'll change my license as soon as I can," I explained, and suddenly felt a little awkward. "Are *you* sure you're okay with all this? You're sure you still want to be stuck with me for the next five years?"

That dark, almost caramel-colored gaze landed on me, even, intense, determined. "Yes," that smoke-wrapped voice replied effortlessly. "We need to go pick up the paperwork for the petition right after we sign the papers."

Sign the papers. We were back at it. I gulped. "Yeah. Okay."

Something in my tone must have been apparent, because he shook off that pinning focus, leveling a frown in my direction. "You're not backing out on me."

It occurred to me he wasn't asking. He was telling. I was a little offended he'd even assume I would do that. "I'm not backing out on you. We're here already. I wouldn't do that."

"I didn't think you would, but I wanted to—"

What? Remind me? Make sure? "I'm here. I'm not going anywhere. We're doing this," I assured him.

It took him a moment to nod. "I know we're rushing into it, but this is the only chance we'll have. Next month is going to get busier for me."

"*Aiden*, I know. I understand. That's why I'm here, isn't it? It's fine. I have things to do too." Without thinking about it, I reached over and touched his bare forearm lightly. "I'm not going to disappear on you in the middle of the night. I always go through with my promises, all right? The only place I'm going soon is to El Paso next month for a weekend, but I'll be back after a few days. I'll be around in two years, and I'll still be here three years after that. I don't take my word lightly."

Something flashed across his eyes so briefly it was there in one blink and gone the next.

Feeling a little shy, I pulled my hand back and smiled up at him, feeling something loosen up inside of me. "Look, I guess I haven't completely gotten over what happened, even though I know you're sorry. I know what it's like for someone to do something unforgivable, and it's unfair for me to take it out on you, okay? I'm sure I'll be back to flipping you off in no time. Don't worry."

He nodded slowly, his features never loosening up enough to be considered relaxed.

"Everything will work itself out. I know you're sorry." I made myself shrug and let out a long exhale that made me feel like I lost a few pounds. "I'm grateful for everything, but I need to go pee right now. Come get me when you're ready to leave."

I smiled at him before I hightailed it to the bathroom in the bedroom on the right, needing a minute to myself. Inside, I leaned against the door and let out a choppy exhale. What was I doing?

Everything would be fine, I figured, as I used the bathroom and then headed into the bedroom.

It was only five-ish in the afternoon thanks to the time change, but knowing Aiden, he'd want to get *the paperwork* signed and over with as quickly as possible. So I wasn't surprised when he knocked on the open door connecting my room to the living area and raised his eyebrows when he found me sitting in the middle of the bed, trying to rein in the eighty different emotions battling their way through my nerves.

I was doing this. I was really fucking doing this. I was getting married.

And if that wasn't enough, apparently Aiden missed me giving him shit. Who would have thought?

But most importantly, I was about to marry Aiden Graves.

I wasn't sure whether to laugh or cry. Or both.

"You want to go get this over with?" he asked from his spot at the doorway.

Get this over with.

That decided it. It broke me.

I couldn't help it. I face-planted on the bed. It was either crying or laughing, and I was going to go with the latter so I wouldn't lose it over Mr. Romance. "Sure. I don't have anything else to do," I snorted, muffled by the comforter. *I was about to go commit a felony.* Little Vanessa had no idea what she would be capable of as an adult.

"Why are you laughing?" His question reached me as I lost it even more.

It took a second for me to get it together, but eventually, I managed to sit up and rub my hand over the side of my face as I let out a shaky, nervous smile. He, on the other hand, was standing there looking at me like I'd lost my mind. "You make it sound like we're having to go to the DPS to get your license renewed, and you don't want to go." I scooted off the edge of the bed and stood up, stretching my jaw from how hard I'd cracked up. "Do you know where you want to do this?"

He tipped that bearded chin down. "There's a chapel two blocks away from here."

I nodded, that familiar sense of anxiety fluttering through my chest once more. "Okay." I took in the clothes he was still wearing from the flight. "Let me change my shirt at least." He wasn't dressed up. Why should I be?

He cast a glance at the T-shirt I had on and backed out.

I changed into the slightly dressier work blouse I'd worn in front of him plenty of times in the past and met him in the living room. He was still in his hoodie and V-neck, looking handsome and casual at the same time. Show-off. That small medallion peeking at the apex of the cut of his shirt was what caught my eye the most though.

I followed after the big guy. We walked through the lobby and out into the hot Vegas sun. He'd said the chapel was only two blocks away, but they felt like the longest blocks of my life. I'd been to Vegas two other times in the past, but it had always been with him for work, so I hadn't gotten a chance to walk around and check it out. Most of my sightseeing had been done through the window of whatever car we were traveling in.

During the day, it didn't look anything like it did at night. I could see Aiden just a foot or two ahead, but I was too busy looking around at the different shops and restaurants to put in much effort to keep an eye on him. Sure enough, exactly two blocks away from our hotel, he stopped in front of a little white chapel that I was pretty sure I'd seen in movies before.

"Are you ready?" the Wall of Winnipeg asked like we were heading for battle.

No.

I wasn't, but as I looked at Aiden's hard face and thought about how badly he wanted to live in the U.S. without worrying about his visa, how could I have told him no? Okay, I could have, but that huge part of me that was 100 percent pushover understood. I knew what it was like to not want to live somewhere.

Goodbye to the next five years of my life.

"Yes," I finally answered. "We need pictures. The immigration official is going to ask for them at your interview."

The corners of his mouth moved in a way that was as much of a smile as I'd ever witnessed on him, and might ever see. My nerves were like live wires and my stomach hurt, but it seemed like I was doing the right thing.

"What? I looked it up. I want to be prepared." To not go to jail and get what had been promised to me. And wasn't that what Aiden should have realized? I was going off his word, relying on him to go through with what he'd promised me at the end of this upcoming journey. Hell, when we divorced, I could ask him for half of everything he owned. Obviously, he had to trust me enough to know I would never do something like that.

"Everything will be all right," he seemed to promise me after a moment, that partial smile still tipping the fullest part of his cheeks.

"Okay." My hands were sweaty. "Let's do it."

He nodded and in we went.

The two people working at the main desk had obviously done this a thousand times in the past. They didn't blink a single eyelash at us in our street clothes; they didn't gush or ask any questions that would have made me feel strange. I thought about the ring I was carrying around in my pocket and . . . I chickened out. I left it there, promising myself I'd take it out later.

We filled out the paperwork they gave us, chose a wedding package for $190 that included a ceremony in the chapel, a silk rose bouquet, a boutonniere that had Aiden eyeing it with disdain, a photographer, and a CD with five high-resolution pictures to document our "big day."

The minister was another $60.

So, for $250, Aiden and I stood at the front of the aging wedding chapel with a man who might have been inebriated, and we listened to him say words that seemed to go in one ear and out the other. At least for me.

Was I freaking out? A little bit. But I kept my eye on the boutonniere that Aiden had shoved into the front pocket of his jeans, and I squeezed the ribbon-wrapped stems of my bouquet with damp fingers until the words "Are you exchanging rings?" came out of his mouth.

Aiden shook his head at the same time my trembling fingers pulled the white gold band out of my pocket and handed it over. I didn't want to put it on for him; it just seemed too intimate of a gesture.

Those dark irises shot to mine as he tried to slide it over his knuckles. It didn't fit. Why was that so surprising? Of course he would have gotten bigger in the eight years since he'd won the national championship in college. He moved the ring over to his pinky finger and it slid on easily. That penetrating gaze went back to mine and stayed there, heavy and insurmountable, making me feel so vulnerable that I had to look down at the bouquet that wasn't going to make it much longer under how much I was wringing my hands. I kept my expression down until the words "You may now kiss the bride" came out of the minister's mouth.

When I peered up, I found Aiden's eyes on me and I widened mine, slanting a look to the side, not knowing what the hell we were supposed to do. I'd been too busy stressing about the ceremony to worry about this part.

Then I thought about the photographer and knew what needed to be done, even though I didn't want to do it.

But more than that, I really didn't want to go to jail or pay out of my butt for fines. Screw it. I didn't have to make out with him . . . even if it wouldn't have really been a hardship if I had to.

I took a step forward. Aiden's gaze shifted to the side in uncertainty, something I didn't want to focus on too much right then because I had my own nerves to worry about. Then I took another step forward, put my hands on those muscle-packed upper arms, and went up to my tippy-toes, still coming up short.

He was frowning even as he lowered his head, our gazes locked on each other, and I pressed my mouth against his. It was nothing grand, just a peck, the center of my lips against the fullest part of his. They were softer, more pliable than I ever would have imagined. The whole contact lasted maybe two seconds before I fell back to my heels and stepped away. My chest and neck were hot.

And this handsome, stern man I was *signing paperwork* with, was frowning even more after I put three feet between us.

"Congratulations!" the minister cheered as the other chapel employee literally threw glitter at us. I was glad I was wearing glasses when Aiden rubbed at his eyes with the back of his hand.

"One picture of you two together," the photographer said, already gesturing me back to Aiden's side.

I swallowed and nodded. *Believable.* A quick shuffle later, I was at his side. When he didn't put his arm around me or do anything remotely couple-like, I slipped my arm through his, pressed my hip against him, and held on just as the flash blinded us.

The photographer smiled as she took a step back and lowered her camera. "Give me ten minutes, Mr. and Mrs. Graves, and I'll have the CD ready."

Mr. and Mrs. Graves.

Diana's favorite saying described the situation perfectly: shit just got real.

IT WAS STRANGE to think that by eight o'clock on a Sunday in mid-August, I was legally a married woman.

After the chapel gave us our CD with our five photographs and *paperwork*, we headed back to the hotel in a dreamlike state. At least for me it seemed like a dream. A weird, weird, weird dream that resembled more of an acid trip than reality. Neither one of us said much, but I was busy thinking about what we'd done, and knowing Aiden, he was thinking about his next preseason game.

We headed into our respective rooms, only exchanging a forced smile from me and a slightly pinched mouth from him. I must have sat on the edge of the bed for at least thirty minutes, simply getting my thoughts together. The walls seemed to close in on me, and I started to feel itchy and restless.

Married. I was freaking married. The woman at the chapel had called me Mrs. Graves.

I married Aiden.

There was no way I could have stayed in that room all night. I was too amped up to work or draw. Crawling out of my skin, I needed something else to keep my mind on. So I thought about all the things I used to imagine doing when Vegas came to mind, and there was really only one thing on the list: I wanted to see a show.

After making sure I had my ID and debit card, I got up and walked into the living area of the suite to find it empty. Peeking into Aiden's room, I found him asleep on the bed, fully clothed and completely passed out. One big palm was being used as a pillow and the other was tucked between his thighs, a super-soft, barely audible whistling sound coming out of his mouth.

I glanced at my watch and hesitated for a second. He probably wouldn't want to go, would he?

Nah.

He didn't seem like the type to get excited over acrobats and clowns in extravagant costumes, much less crowds. Grabbing the notepad on the nightstand next to the king-sized bed he was on, I jotted down a message.

> Aiden—
>   Going for a walk around the Strip. I might try to
> catch a show if there are still tickets available. Be back
> later. I have my phone on me.
> —V

I tippy-toed out of the room, slowly closed the hotel door behind me, and I was out of there.

Las Vegas wasn't exactly the best place in the world for a single female traveler, but with all the people on the street walking around,

I figured it could have been a lot worse. It was easy to blend in. I walked down the street and took my time going in and out of some of the shops. Tourists of all ages and nationalities filled the stores, and I didn't feel as lonely as I thought I would have walking around this unknown city all by myself on the same day I'd married my ex-boss.

I was looking around the M&M's store when my phone started vibrating in my pocket. When I pulled it out, **Miranda P.** flashed across the screen.

"Hello?"

"Where are you?" the raspy, sleepy voice asked.

I named the store with a frown as some asshole shoved me from behind to get to the display in front of me.

Aiden cursed, and I had to pull the phone away from my face to make sure it really was him calling and not his evil twin. "Wait there," he demanded.

"For what?" I asked just as the line went dead.

Was he coming? And had he just cussed or was I imagining it?

I wasn't sure. I browsed the store for a while and was barely walking out when I happened to glance in the direction I'd come from. Towering over everyone down the block was what had to be Aiden's big head. I couldn't see his face, because his hood was up, but I knew it was him just from the way he held his shoulders. I was too far away to see his eyes, but I could tell he was looking around.

It was a fact that even with his hood on, I could tell he was irritated. I stood off to the side by the doors and watched him make his way around the tourists oblivious to his presence. The second his gaze landed on me, I sensed it and waved.

His mouth went a little funny in a way that I recognized all too well.

What the hell was he mad about anyway?

"What are you doing?" he snapped the instant he was close enough to be heard.

I lifted my shoulders, shoving my glasses up the bridge of my nose in the process. "Walking around."

"You could have woken me up to come with you," he practically hissed, stopping a foot away from me.

First off, his attitude was getting on my nerves. Secondly, I wasn't a fan of the tone of voice he was using. "Why would I wake you up?"

The few inches of his jaw that were visible were tight. "So I could come with you. Why else?"

He was giving me that look.

One, two, three, four, five.

I narrowed my eyes. "I didn't know you'd want to come. I figured you would rather stay in the hotel room and rest." After all, he'd been taking a nap when I looked for him.

The long line of his throat rippled. "I would've rather stayed in, but I also don't need you getting kidnapped and being used as a drug mule."

God help me. I looked around at the thousands of people making their way up and down along the Strip to make sure I wasn't imagining them. "You really think someone's going to kidnap me here? *Really?*"

Aiden's nostrils flared. He stared down at me.

I stared back.

"You're already giving me a headache and it's been four hours."

"I was trying to be nice and leave you alone, not give you a headache. Come on." I huffed. "I'm just walking around. I have gone places without you." A few. But not by myself. I wasn't going to admit that out loud though, especially now when he was getting all bent out of shape for no reason.

He kept glaring at me, that look that got on my nerves taking over his features inch by inch. "That's stupid. You're—what? Five-seven? Five-eight? A hundred and forty pounds? *You can't walk around Las Vegas by yourself,*" he stressed, his tone so tight I reeled back.

I blinked in confusion and surprise. "Aiden, it isn't a big deal. I'm used to doing things by myself."

The lids over those big, brown eyes lowered slowly, a deep breath blowing from pursed lips, as if we were the only people on the Strip when that absolutely wasn't anywhere close to the truth. "Maybe you're used to doing things by yourself, but don't be an idiot." He started off calmly, totally in control. "I didn't know where you were. There's crime here—don't give me that face. I know there's crime everywhere. We might not be *doing this* for the reasons most people do, but I made a vow, Van. And I promised you we would try to be friends. Friends don't let friends wander around alone." He pinned me with a glare. "You aren't the only one who takes their promises seriously."

Uh. What was happening?

Those dark eyes were the steadiest thing I'd ever seen as he said, "I can't do this without you."

Well, shit. I wasn't sure I even knew how to talk after that.

Our marriage—vomit, hurl, and diarrhea—wasn't real, but he had a point. *We had made vows I couldn't seem to remember because I hadn't been listening.* But the point was, we had made promises to each other even before that, and I didn't ever want to be the type of person who backed out on their word.

"I won't go anywhere until you're a resident, big guy. I promise."

His gaze swept over my face for the longest second of my life, and eventually, *eventually*, he cleared his throat. "What is it you want to do?" he grumbled suddenly, as if he hadn't just said the most meaningful words I'd ever heard come out of his mouth.

To give him credit, he didn't complain once after I told him the name of the production I wanted to go watch. But I was also clasping my hands together in front of my chest like I was a little kid begging for something. "It's all I want to go see."

And I was going to do it regardless of whether he tagged along or not, but he didn't need to know that yet.

He simply looked back up at the nonexistent Nevada stars and sighed. "Fine, but I need to get something to eat afterward."

I might have bounced up to my toes. "Really?"

"Yes."

"Really-really?" I swear I might have been beaming.

Aiden gave me the most pained nod in the history of the world. "*Yes.* Sure. Let's go buy the tickets."

I'd never in my life wanted to pull a Dorothy and click my heels together, but the idea of not walking around Vegas by myself, and with this gigantaur who could have passed for a bodyguard, I found myself grinning at him and clapping. "Okay, let's go."

For the sake of his life, I decided to ignore the grimace on his face.

Off we went. The hotel was on the opposite side of the Strip, but we made it with time to spare, snagging the two best tickets possible, which I paid for since I felt guilty he'd been paying for everything, and they were third-row seats, so I figured it would be worth every penny spent dipping into my savings.

As we got in line at the concession stand, I could feel myself shaking for the second time in the same day, but this time it was with excitement. *Cirque du Lune* had come to Dallas in the past, but I'd always talked myself out of shelling out the cash to go. Now that I wasn't paying rent and business was steady, spending the money didn't send me into heart palpitations, or have me falling over with guilt over the extravagance. Plus, I was so pumped, I even signed the receipt with a smile on my face.

"Do you want to share a popcorn?" I asked after we got into the super-long line at the concession stand, so overjoyed I didn't care that the popcorn was going to cost an arm and a leg.

He started to dip his chin just as I spotted a finger reaching up to tap his arm from behind. Aiden hesitantly turned to come face-to-face with a woman in her forties and a man in the same age range. They were both smiling.

"Could we take a picture with you?" the woman blurted out, her cheeks coloring.

"We're huge fans," the man added, his face more red than pink.

"We've been following your career since Wisconsin," the woman continued on in a rush.

Aiden did that tiny little half-assed smile he conjured up for fans as he nodded. "Thank you. I appreciate it." That big head turned to face me. "Take the picture?"

The woman smiled sheepishly at me before handing over her phone. I got the camera in focus as the older couple sandwiched Aiden between them—*they looked so small in comparison!*—and was taking a step back when I caught movement in the sliver of space between Aiden and the female fan. He never put his arm around people in pictures, I'd noticed from the beginning, but always kept his hands at his sides. It was because of that, that I almost missed the small hand motion, but I didn't, and when Aiden scowled almost immediately, it took everything inside of me not to burst out laughing as I took the shot.

By the time I handed the phone over, we were next in line, and I left Aiden to finish listening to his handsy fans as I ordered popcorn with no butter, a medium soda, and a bottle of water.

"It was so nice meeting you!" the woman called out as Aiden headed toward me once I was out of line.

I barely managed to raise the bag of popcorn to face level when I lost it, peeking at him when I wasn't blinking away tears.

The fact that Aiden's ears turned red as he watched me crack up said he knew what I was dying over. "Don't say a word," he gritted.

"Did she grab a handful?" I choked out.

The look he gave me was a mix of "you're an idiot" and "fuck off," which only made me laugh harder.

He'd gotten molested. By a fan. Right in front of me.

That split second look of surprise on his face when he got fondled would probably stay with me for the rest of my life.

"Shut up, Vanessa."

I was dying. He usually just ignored me, but this was so much better. "I'm not saying anything!" I wheezed from behind the bag of popcorn.

Aiden narrowed his eyes, waiting patiently. "Are you done?" he asked after a few more seconds of me cracking up.

I had to wipe at the tears in my eyes with the back of my hand, shaking my head. "I—I—"

He gestured me toward the doors to the theater. "Get inside before they close the doors." His tone was exasperated and maybe even a little embarrassed. Maybe. Why would getting his butt cheek squeezed rile him up?

I had to swallow raggedly as I wiped at my face one more time, picturing that epic look of shock once more. I lost it again. "Does that kind of thing happen often?"

"No. *Would you stop laughing?*"

—

IT WAS ALMOST two in the morning by the time we made it back to the hotel. I felt happier than I had in forever. The show had been amazing, and dinner at the restaurant in the same hotel as *Cirque du Lune* after the show had been great. The host had recognized Aiden and gave us the best and most secluded table so Aiden could be left in peace. It had seriously been nice, even if Aiden hadn't talked much while we ate. I didn't go out often, but deciding to explore instead of staying in to work that night seemed like one of the best ideas I'd had in forever.

So when we got inside the living area to the suite and started going in opposite directions toward our rooms, I stopped at the doorway to mine and turned to look at the man I'd signed papers with hours ago. He was visibly tired; after all, he usually went to bed by nine at the latest, and he looked beyond exhausted.

Why wouldn't he though? He'd played a preseason game twelve hours ago and only managed to nap twice since then. Damn it. This sense of unwanted affection seeped its way into the place between my breasts.

"Thank you so much for staying up and coming with me," I said, squeezing my hands at my sides as I smiled at him. "I had a really good time."

Aiden nodded, one corner of his mouth moved a millimeter, but it was a millimeter that could have moved a mountain. "Me too."

I was too soft to be excited by that sliver of a smile. "Good night."

"Night."

It wasn't until after I showered and had snuggled under the covers that I finally let myself sink into reality. I was a married woman.

ELEVEN

"Where are you going?"

With one hand on the staircase handrail, I finished thrusting my heel into my tennis shoe and glanced up at the man standing in front of me with a wary look on his lightly bearded face. "I'm going for a run. Why?"

The big guy glanced down at the overpriced accessory on his wrist, an expensive workout watch I know he'd gotten for free, because I'd been the one to open the box when he got it. "It's five o'clock," he said, as if I didn't know how to read time.

I did, and I'd learned how to a long, long time ago.

He'd gotten home about an hour ago while I was upstairs going over the fifth draft of a paperback cover for an author I'd decided never to work with again. The guy was driving me nuts, changing his mind from one revision to the next, and if it wasn't for my motto—never leave a client unhappy because they'll tell everyone you suck—I would have told him to shove his money down his throat and find someone else.

Yeah, I was feeling on edge, and I knew I needed to get out of the house for a little while, even if it was already later than I normally would have liked to go for a run. So I'd been surprised when I first heard Aiden make his way from the kitchen into the foyer, where I was trying to finish getting ready to leave.

We hadn't seen each other much since we'd gotten back from Las Vegas a little over a week ago, but things had been fine. It was kind of weird how the trip had sort of relaxed me around him, and it seemed like the sentiment was mutual. Aiden had even started knocking on my doorframe when he walked by my room when he got home. He didn't say much more than "Hey," loud enough to be heard over the music I liked to play while I worked, but it was something, I thought.

"I'm only doing five miles," I let him know right then, grabbing my other shoe off the floor and balancing on one foot to slip it on, like I had the other one. It was a lot harder than it should have been, mainly because I was too aware he was watching me, probably expecting me to fall.

"It's going to get dark soon," he said, as I struggled to get my heel into my tennis shoe.

"I'll—damn it—I'll be fine." I started to fall over, flailing an arm out for balance, and instead, getting a big hand catching my elbow to keep me steady. I flashed him a sheepish look and let some of my weight lean on him as I finally got my heel in. "Thanks." I took a step away. "Anyway, it shouldn't take me more than a little over an hour. I'm still running a little slow, but I won't be gone long."

Aiden blinked those great, dark eyelashes at me before reaching up to scratch at his chin, those lean cheeks puffing just slightly. Resignation, that clear, clear emotion that seemed to melt its way down from his hairline and over that perpetual wrinkle between his eyebrows and the sides of his mouth had me blinking.

"Give me a minute," he sighed as he moved around me and jogged up the stairs, two at a time, the house shaking in response. Briefly, I feared for the life of the stairs. Then I realized what he was doing.

Was he . . .

"You don't have to come with me," I shouted, taking a moment to absorb those perfect glutes and rock-solid calves defying gravity as they made their way up the stairs. Why would he even want to come along anyway? The memory of what he'd said in Las Vegas when I took off on my own suddenly came back to me. *You aren't the only one who takes their promises seriously.*

"I'm not asking," he yelled back just as he reached the clearing.

Torn between thinking it was nice and cute that he didn't want me going out for a jog alone at dusk, I remembered how important it was for him—for big guys in his position in general—to keep their cardio to a minimum. They couldn't afford to lose weight when they needed to keep their size, especially someone with a diet like Aiden's, where he had to consume more physical food than someone who ate meat to get an appropriate amount of calories and not go hungry. It was why Aiden worked out so hard during the day and made a severe effort to rest as much as he could during his off time.

Then I wondered, could he even run five miles?

I took a step closer to the staircase. "You really don't. I won't be gone long. I'll take my phone."

There was a pause, and if I really focused, I could hear his dresser drawer slamming shut. "One minute."

This stubborn ass. "No, Aiden, stay here!"

"Thirty seconds," the hardheaded mule replied.

Why was I even waiting around arguing with him? He really should stay home. He didn't have any business putting strain on his tendon if he didn't have to.

"I'll be back soon!" I took my glasses off and set them on the table right by the door, waiting for my eyes to adjust. I wanted to buy a strap to keep them from falling off when I ran, but I hadn't gotten around to it yet. I'd almost always been farsighted, but I swear my vision was getting worse and worse every year. It was probably time to get a new prescription. Just as I reached the door, I heard that giant, 280-pound body stomping around before the stairs took another beating.

"I told you to wait," he grumbled on the way down.

I glanced at him over my shoulder and scrunched my nose. "I told you to stay. You're not supposed to be doing a whole bunch of cardio."

He was apparently going to pretend I hadn't said anything. "Let's go."

I patted the fanny pack clipped around my waist in case he hadn't seen it. "I have a flashlight and pepper spray. I'll be fine."

The expression on his face wasn't an impressed one. "That's nice. Let's go."

"Aiden, I'm being serious."

"Vanessa, let's go."

He had busted out that damn tone of voice again, which only meant one thing: This was one of those times that it was pointless to argue with him. I realized that now.

Waving me to go through the doorway first, he set the alarm to stay, since Zac was napping in his room, and followed me onto the paved stone walkway leading up to the house. Facing each other, I took a long step back with my right leg and got into runner's pose. "Aiden, I'm not joking. Stay home."

"Why?" He mirrored my stretch, making the material of his shorts squeeze those massive thighs like a second skin. I didn't even know a leg had as many perfect, delineated muscles until I'd seen Aiden in compression shorts.

I had to force myself to quit fondling those big hams with my eye-balls. I didn't know what it was about muscular thighs that drove me nuts. I could live without a six-pack, but developed quads and calves were my Kryptonite. "Because you shouldn't be running." Before I could think twice about what was in my mouth, I said the worst thing you could possibly tell a highly competitive person. "And I don't know if you can run five miles, big guy. Plus, your Achilles—"

What had I done?

The Wall of Winnipeg, the man who had dragged himself into becoming the greatest defensive player in the NFO, leveled a gaze at me that for the first time in the years we'd known each other made me uncomfortable. It was unsettling. Beyond unsettling. And I wished I had something to hide behind.

"You worry about running your own five miles, all right?" he quipped in a quiet, rough voice.

God help us. I lifted my hands up, palms toward him, and shrugged, backing away in surrender. "Whatever you say."

My middle finger twitched, but I kept it under wraps and with its brothers and sisters. We stretched in silence for the next few minutes, our quads, hamstrings, and calves getting needed attention. I did it because of my knee injury, and Aiden because his body was worth millions. Millions and millions.

The fact he was breaking the strict rules he put on himself just so I wouldn't go out for a run alone definitely made an appearance in my heart and head, chipping away a little more at that aggravation I'd built up with him since I had quit. I just hoped he didn't regret it tomorrow.

"I'm ready," the stubborn mule reported.

I nodded and kept my eye roll to myself. "The trail around here is only two miles. I've been circling it."

He simply jerked his chin down and followed me toward the gated entrance. I waved at the security guard as we slipped through the side door, and soon enough, we started jogging.

As big as Aiden was, it was amazing how he didn't lumber. He definitely wasn't a sprinter by any measure, but he was constant, consistent. His stride was even, his breathing good, and those long legs, which had to weigh at least eighty pounds apiece, somehow made it so he wasn't a half mile ahead or behind me. I had no idea how much distance he usually covered when he did cardio, usually on the bike or doing sprints, but I knew he kept track of that sort of thing religiously.

But he kept up, mile after mile, even as his breathing got heavier and each step became more of a fight for him. And when we rounded the last corner, about a quarter of a mile away from the house, I slowed down. Neither one of us said much as we walked side by side. I had my hands on my hips as I caught my breath, and when I happened to look over, his hands were in the same position as mine.

As if sensing me checking him out, Aiden raised those thick, nearly black slashes called his eyebrows.

I raised my eyebrows back at him. "Are you all right?"

"I'm fine." He gave me a smug and slightly sour look. We walked for a little while in silence before he asked, "When did you start running?"

Wiping at my brow, I made a face at myself. "Right before I quit."

Aiden did a double take I couldn't miss.

I remembered the day I'd been outside of his house and I'd seen that woman running. "I didn't have time for it before." And I hadn't exactly been motivated to, but I kept that part to myself. "I want to run a marathon in a few months. I just need to get up to six miles without going into cardiac arrest afterward."

We walked a little longer before he added, "One of our condition-ing coaches runs marathons. I'll ask him if he has any tips. You should really be following a training guide so you don't get injured."

"Oh." Huh. "Thanks. It'll still be at least a month before I can even start at the rate I'm going, but we all have to start somewhere, I figure."

He made a thoughtful noise but didn't say anything else as we walked the rest of the way home. I could tell he was busy thinking about something from the way the creases at his eyes intensified, but he didn't voice whatever it was going through that big noggin.

We made it back to the house just as the streetlights switched on. Taking positions on the lawn, we each dropped into stretches. I smiled at him and he kind of quirked up his mouth a bit in a delayed response.

"Has your preseason been going okay?" I asked.

"Yes."

I switched legs and shot him a look at his evasiveness, but he was busy inspecting the ground. "How about your tendon?"

"Fine."

"Really?"

That had those brown eyes up. His peaceful, serious face turned mildly irritated. "*Really.*"

"Okay, smart-ass. I'm just making sure." I snorted, shaking my head as I dropped my gaze to the ground.

There was a pause before he spoke up again. "I'm all right. I'm being careful. I know what'll happen if I'm not."

We both knew. He could lose everything.

I suddenly felt just a little bit like an asshole. "I just wanted to be sure you were doing okay. That's all."

Even though his face, by that point, was tipped down, I noticed the ripple in his trapezius muscles telling me what I wanted to know. He was all right, but he was stressed. "Everything is going better than anyone expected. The trainers are happy with my progress. I'm doing everything they're telling me to."

I couldn't help but smile a little at that. "You know that's one of the things I used to like the most about you. You know what you want and you'll do whatever you have to do to get it. It's really . . ." Attractive wasn't the right word, and it definitely wasn't the one I would choose to willingly say out loud in front of him. "Admirable."

Honestly, looking back on my word choice fifteen seconds later, I knew that I'd meant what I said with the best intentions, but when I took in the lines bracketing the mouth I'd kissed a week ago, maybe it hadn't come out that way.

"You don't anymore?" His question was low.

Shit. "No, I do," I backtracked and reached up to mess with my glasses, remembering right then that I'd taken them off, and dropped my hand. "I don't know why I said I used to. I still do. You inspired me to quit, you know. I figured you of all people would understand why I did it."

He turned his head so slowly it was honestly a little creepy. But the way he looked at me? . . . I wouldn't know how to describe it. The only thing I knew for sure was it made the space between my shoulder blades tickle.

His Adam's apple bobbed as he swallowed, that hard mouth twitching as he nodded almost reluctantly. "I understand." He cleared his throat and turned his attention back to the ground, getting to his feet and pulling his heel back toward his butt. "How's your work going?"

Oh, lord. This might be the longest and most personal conversation we'd ever had. It was kind of exciting. "It's been steady. I've been able to take on more projects, so I can't complain." I glanced at him to see if he was listening, and he was. "I actually just got invited to go to one of the biggest romance novel conventions in North America, so that's pretty exciting. I should be able to get more work if I go."

"I thought you do book covers?" he asked.

"I do, but they let other people have tables as long as they pay, and if I go, I might be able to get more work out of it. Half my clients are authors, the rest is a mix of whatever anyone asks me to do."

He switched legs as he asked in a genuine voice, "Like what?"

And it was moments like these that made the distance between us in the past so apparent. "Anything really. I've had some commissions for business cards, business logos, posters, and flyers. I've made a few designs for band T-shirts. A few tattoo designs." I pointed at the shirt I was currently wearing. It was off-white with a neon-colored sugar skull and ruby red roses surrounding the crown of the head. THE CLOUD COLLISION was spelled out just below the jaw. "I made this for my friend's boyfriend's band. I've also done some work for Zac and a couple of guys on your team." I didn't miss the way his head jerked up when I mentioned that. "Mostly redoing their logos and doing banners for them and things like that," I told him, almost a little shyly, self-conscious about my work.

"Who?" he asked, perplexed and more than slightly surprised.

"Oh. Um, Richard Caine, Danny West, Cash Bajek, and that linebacker who got traded to Chicago during the off-season."

"I never heard anything about it."

I shrugged, trying to smile to play it off like it wasn't a big deal.

He made this soft, little, thoughtful sound of his, but didn't add anything. The silence that wrapped around us wasn't awkward at all. It just was what it was. After a few more stretches, Aiden touched me on the shoulder before disappearing into the house, apparently done.

By the time I made it inside and slipped my glasses back on, I found Zac standing at the stove in the kitchen. Aiden had taken a seat at the kitchen island with a glass of water. Grabbing a glass from the cabinet, I filled it up with the same.

"What are you making for dinner?" I asked Zac as I peeked over his shoulder.

He gave what smelled like onions and garlic a stir. "Spaghetti, darlin'."

"I love spaghetti." I batted my eyelashes when he glanced at me, earning me a grin. I took a seat on the stool one down from Aiden's.

The tall Texan let out a soft laugh. "There's more than enough. Aiden, you're on your own. I put meat in the sauce."

He just lifted one of those rounded shoulders dismissively.

I got up to get another glass of water when Zac asked from his spot still at the stove, breaking up the two pounds of ground beef he'd added to the vegetables: "Vanny, were you gonna want me to help you with your draft list again this year?"

I groaned. "I forgot. My brother just messaged me about it. I can't let him win again this year, Zac. I can't put up with his crap."

He raised his hand in a dismissive gesture. "I got you. Don't worry about it."

"Thank—what?"

Aiden had his glass halfway to his mouth and was frowning. "You play fantasy football?" he asked, referring to the online role-playing game that millions of people participated in. Participants got to build imaginary teams during a mock draft, made up of players throughout the league. I'd been wrangled into playing against my brother and some of our mutual friends about three years ago and had joined in ever since. Back then, I had no idea what the hell a cornerback was, much less a bye week, but I'd learned a lot since then.

I nodded slowly at him, feeling like I'd done something wrong.

The big guy's brow furrowed. "Who was on your team last year?"

I named the players I could remember, wondering where this was going and not having a good feeling about it.

"What was your defensive team?"

There it went. I slipped my hands under the counter and averted my eyes to the man at the stove, cursing him silently. "So you see . . ."

The noise Zac tried to muffle was the most obvious snicker in the world. Asshole.

"Was I not on your team?"

I gulped. "So you see—"

"Dallas wasn't your team?" he accused me, sounding . . . well, I didn't know if it was hurt or outraged, but it was definitely something.

"Aah . . ." I slid a look at the traitor who was by that point trying to muffle his laugh. "Zac helped me with it."

It was the *thump* that said Zac's knees hit the floor.

"Look, it isn't that I didn't choose *you* specifically. I would choose you if I could, but Zac said Minnesota—"

"Minne-sota."

Jesus, he'd broken the state in two.

The big guy, honest to God, shook his head. His eyes went from me to Zac in . . . yep, that was outrage. Aiden held out his hand, wiggling those incredibly long fingers. "Let me see it."

"See what?"

"Your roster from last year."

I sighed and pulled my phone out of the fanny pack I still had around my waist, unlocking the screen and opening the app. Handing it over, I watched his face as he looked through my roster and felt guilty as hell. I'd been planning on choosing Dallas just because Aiden was on the team, but I really had let Zac steer me elsewhere. Apparently, just because you had the best defensive end in the country on your team didn't mean everyone else held up their end of the bargain. Plus, he'd missed almost the entire season. He didn't have to take it so personally.

It only took a second for him to see who I had on there and he flicked his dark irises back up at me. "Zac helped you?"

"Yes," I muttered, feeling so, so bad.

"Why didn't you put Christian Delgado on your team?"

Just the sound of his name made my upper lip begin to snarl.

But before I could say anything, Zac chipped in, "I know I told you to add Christian."

He had. I just hadn't because he was a scumbag. Getting up, I went back to the fridge, refilled my glass, and muttered, "I didn't want to."

The master of "Why?" didn't let me down.

The fact was, I was a terrible liar, and I wouldn't be surprised if both Aiden and Zac realized I was making things up if I did. "I don't like him," I answered bluntly, hoping but knowing that wasn't going to be a good enough answer for either one of their nosey asses.

"Why?"

"I just don't. He's a slimeball."

"I don't like him much either, darlin'," Zac claimed.

Keeping my gaze on my glass for longer than necessary, I gradually lifted my head and immediately noticed Aiden's dark irises on me. He was thinking, and I was pretty sure disbelieving at the same time, that intelligent face making me antsy. Did he know I was hedging around the answer?

If he did, he let it go for the time being when he dropped his attention back to my phone. That little line between his brows left me on guard. The line deepened as he asked Zac, "Why did you tell her to choose Michaels?" Zac responded something that left Aiden shaking his big head. "Don't listen to him. I'd help you if you asked."

We were having another moment like the one earlier when he'd asked about my work. I thought about not bringing it up, then decided against it. "I did once. Two years ago. I asked you a question about wide receivers and you told me to look it up on the internet."

He winced. Aiden literally winced. And I felt just the teensiest bit guilty for reminding him of something that hadn't been important enough for him to remember.

In the spirit of being nice, since he'd gone for a run with me, I reached across the counter and patted his hand. "Hey, we have the next five years for you to help me out."

TWELVE

I t was amazing how easily you could settle into a major change in your life.

Or maybe it just amazed me how easy it was for me to live with Aiden and Zac, and keep living my life in the same way I'd been doing in that month after I quit. Really, it wasn't that life itself had changed much; I was just in a new environment, but still doing the same thing I'd done back at my apartment.

A few weeks passed in the blink of an eye, and before I knew it, I'd been at my new house for a month. I'd *signed paperwork* two weeks ago. The season had started for the guys last week. Basically, life was going and heading in its same old trajectory.

Except the house didn't completely feel like my own. It reminded me of back when I was a kid, sleeping over at Diana's, when I couldn't walk around in my underwear or go braless, because it wasn't my house. Then again, I spent the majority of my time in my room working and no one was ever home, so I could pull off whatever outfit—or lack of an outfit and underwear—I felt like wearing, only running up the stairs like a crazy person when the garage door opened. Then there was the small issue of having to turn down the volume on my computer's speakers when one of the guys was home and I was working.

I still hadn't talked myself into spending time in the living room watching television even when the guys weren't around. Fortunately, claustrophobia hadn't gotten to me yet, considering most of my time was spent in the same place, and that was because I made sure to go to the gym a couple of times a week, to see Diana once a week or every other week, and took my time going to the grocery store. I watched Netflix on my TV when I was bored. I drew in my sketchpad when I felt like it. Sometimes I hung out with Zac, but that didn't happen often, because he'd been spending a lot of time away from the house after practices and meetings, seeing his girl of the season.

By the time I woke up each morning, both guys were already gone. They were basically the best roommates ever. Best of all, Aiden was the type of roommate who you didn't have to pay rent to.

I'd brought it up, of course. That day that I'd moved in, I'd asked him what bills I could help him pay, and all he'd done was give me that bored face that my temper hadn't become immune to. Then I'd asked again, and he'd just ignored me.

He'd said he would work on being my friend, but I couldn't expect a miracle overnight, could I?

If it was strange for either one of them having me in this house, they didn't say anything about it or make me feel like an intruder, mostly because they both had enough on their plates. Zac had passingly mentioned to me how stressed he was about another quarterback the team had picked up, and Aiden lived and breathed for his sport, never allowing himself to slack off. Not that that was anything new. He nodded at me every time we happened to be in the same room together and offered me his leftovers if there were any, which there usually weren't, because the poor guy seemed to be surviving off smoothies, fresh fruit, sweet potatoes, canned beans, nuts, brown rice, and at least one frozen meal daily.

That wasn't my business though, was it?

But every day, I would find the recycling bin filled with more card-board containers than the day before. It made me feel bad, guilty.

It also made me wonder again why Trevor hadn't hired him some-one who did all the same duties I'd been responsible for. I knew he'd hired Aiden someone to answer his emails, because I'd logged on to his account just to see what the damage was and found that every few days there were replies, but no one ever appeared at the house, and sometimes I'd find mail from his PO box sitting in the kitchen after he got home. Where was his Vanessa 2.0?

THE PROBLEM WITH being friends with someone is that unless you want to be a shitty friend—or at least a fake friend because real ones shouldn't be shitty—you couldn't pretend you don't notice if something is wrong with your buddy.

The biggest problem with my newfound friendship with Aiden was how complicated it was. What we'd done was technically a business transaction. But we sort of knew each other, and I knew that even if he wasn't perfect and wasn't truly my friend-friend who would donate a kidney if I needed one, I still cared about him anyway. I was a sucker like that. I figured, best-case scenario, he liked me enough to chip in for someone to donate whatever I needed. I mean, he'd gone running with me so that I wouldn't go by myself when it was late out.

On top of that, we lived together. We were technically married.

Complicated was the best word to describe the situation.

So when I found Aiden in the breakfast nook with his leg propped on one of the other chairs and an icepack over his foot, mere weeks after the regular NFO season had started, I couldn't pretend not to see it. Friends didn't do that. Not people who had known each other for two years. Not when I knew Aiden well enough that I was aware he treated his body like a temple. So for him to have an icepack on his ankle?

Guilt flooded my chest. The Three Hundreds had some of the best trainers and physical therapists in the country. They had all kinds of advanced technology to get their players back in shape. The staff wouldn't have let Aiden leave the facility until they'd done as much as they could for whatever was troubling him.

His facial expression only confirmed something was wrong. His jaw was jutting out and the cords lining his thick neck were more pronounced than usual. He was in pain, or at least incredibly uncomfortable.

This man whom I'd seen walk off the field like his ribs hadn't just been fractured two years ago, much less without crying out "Owwie," was in clear and visible pain.

And I couldn't ignore it. Because friends didn't do that, did they?

I took my time circling the kitchen island, watching him, not minding that all he'd done was lift an index finger to greet me. He was eating a sandwich and reading a book on . . . it had the word "dumb" on the front. I opened the refrigerator door to grab ingredients to make a soup, and turned my attention back as discreetly as possible to watch the big man at the small table.

"I'm going to make some soup, do you want some?" I offered.

"What kind?" he had the nerve to ask without looking away from his hardback.

I held back my smirk. "A kind you like."

"Okay." There was a pause. "Thanks."

I chopped a few vegetables while occasionally glancing up. Running through a few different scenarios in my head on how to go about approaching him to find out if he was in pain or not, I realized I was being dumb.

"Aiden?"

"Hmm?"

"What's wrong with your foot?" I just blurted out.

"I sprained it." That was easy, effortless, no bullshit Aiden for me.

Unfortunately, his comment didn't help or reassure me. I wouldn't be surprised if someone had hit him with a car and the tendon wasn't even attached to his leg anymore, and he was insisting it was just a sprain.

But was I going to say that? Nope.

"High sprain or low sprain?" I asked carefully, as casually as I could. Between his injuries and Zac's, I'd become familiar with the different kinds possible.

"High," he replied just as nonchalantly.

"What did the trainers say?"

That had his jaw tightening. "I'm questionable for the next game."

Not probable, *questionable*. Oh, brother. Questionable statuses made Aiden Graves a grumpy goose.

I lowered my gaze back down to the cutting board and the celery I had on there. "It might be a good idea for you to go see that acupuncturist you went to last year when your shoulder was bothering you." The more I listed his past injuries, the more it made me wince. Zac had told me once that every football player he knew constantly lived with pain; it was inevitable.

"That might be a good idea," he murmured, turning a page in his book.

"Do you want some Advil?" I suggested, glancing up, knowing damn well he never took painkillers. Then again, he rarely ever busted out the icepack.

When he said, "Two would be nice," I had to hold back my gasp.

EARLY THE NEXT afternoon, the sound of the garage door opening and closing told me enough about what was going on. When the television came on a few minutes afterward, I stayed upstairs with my colored pencils and a tattoo commission I was working on for a client.

Three or four hours later, once I finished my project, started on another one, and had showered to get ready for bed, I crept down the stairs, hearing the drone of the TV on in the background. The living room was directly to the left at the bottom of the staircase, the kitchen to the right.

I peeked in and found Aiden stretched out on the couch, the foot of his injured leg propped on the armrest. He had one arm twisted behind his head as a pillow; the other one was along his side, his palm resting on his stomach. His eyes were closed. I knew he hadn't accidentally fallen asleep on the couch. I knew it with every fiber of my being. He'd done it on purpose.

The worry that swam around my stomach didn't surprise me. Here was this seemingly indestructible man who I believed with every cell in my body had stayed on the couch to avoid climbing up the stairs to get to his room.

Damn it.

I went back up to the second floor and pulled the pristine white comforter from the top of his bed and grabbed his favorite pillow. Once back downstairs, I crept back into the living room and laid the comforter across his lower body, tucking it in so that it didn't drag on the floor. I took a step back, chewing on my lip, and that was when I saw . . .

His eyes were open and he was watching me.

I smiled at him and held out the pillow.

A small smile cracked across his full mouth as he took it from me and stuck it under his head. "Thank you."

Taking a step back, I nodded, feeling caught. "You're welcome. Good night."

"Good night."

HE'D BEEN SITTING in the garage for a while.

The fact that he hadn't left the house to go to practice was the next thing that sent alarm bells ringing in my head. He wasn't the suicidal type, but . . .

Leaving my bowl in the sink, I opened the door and stuck my head out to see what was going on. Sure enough, he was in the driver's seat of his Range Rover with his head in one of his large hands, looking down. I walked over and knocked on the window. His head lifting, he frowned before rolling it down.

"Do you want me to drive you?" I offered, thinking about the project I'd wanted to finish working on that morning and shoving it to the back of my head.

Aiden's nostrils flared, but he nodded. To give him credit, he only slightly limped around the car, but it was more than enough to worry me. I'd been thinking about him since the night before when I'd found him on the couch, but I knew better than to baby him. Instead, I ran back in the house, grabbed my purse, and set the alarm before going back to the garage and getting behind the wheel.

It wasn't the first time I'd driven his car, except the last time I'd been behind the wheel it was to take it to get an oil change and a wash. "Where are we going?"

"To the acupuncturist."

"Did you put the address into the navigation?" I asked as I backed out of the garage, extra careful, incredibly self-conscious about my driving skills.

"Yes."

I nodded and followed the gentle female voice all the way to the acupuncturist's office, though after a while of driving, I remembered exactly where we were going. Just like every other time I'd ever taken Aiden, what seemed like all of the female employees at the homeopathic clinic seemed to find their way to the front desk while he was signing in. I took a seat and, with a smirk on my face, watched as one woman after another approached the counter, asking the big guy for an autograph or a picture. Aiden spoke with a low, calm voice, his movements measured, and his entire body tense the way it always was around people he didn't know.

He didn't even get a chance to sit down before the door leading to the main part of the clinic opened and another employee called his name. Aiden glanced back at me and tipped his head toward the door before disappearing. The crowd of women disbanded too. I hadn't really been thinking straight before we rushed to leave, so I'd forgotten to bring something along to keep me entertained. I grabbed one of the magazines on the table and started flipping through it, trying to tell myself that Aiden was fine.

An hour later, the door Aiden had gone through opened again and his bulky frame slowly crept out, one obviously pained step at a time. A man in a short white coat behind him at the doorway shook his head. "Get crutches or a cane."

Aiden simply lifted a hand before approaching the window where only two employees were waiting at that point. I dropped the magazine on the table and got up. The Wall of Winnipeg hunched over the counter, signing something.

"It's such a pleasure to see you again," the receptionist crooned just as I stopped right behind Aiden. Was she batting her eyelashes?

If she was, he didn't notice. His attention was on what looked like the invoice in front of him.

"I'm such a huge fan of yours," she added.

A fan of that ass, more than likely, I figured.

She kept going. "We all hope you get better soon."

Yeah, she was definitely batting her eyelashes. Huh.

That had Aiden responding with one of those indecipherable noises of his as he straightened and slid the paperwork over to her.

"Mr. Graves, I can settle your visit with your assistant if you'd like to take a seat," the receptionist said in a sugary sweet voice, her green eyes flicking to my direction briefly.

Aiden settled for shrugging a shoulder as he turned his body to face me. Nothing about his expression or body language gave me a warning. "She's my wife."

Time stopped.

What the hell did he just say?

"Handle it for me, would you, Muffin?" Aiden asked casually, digging into his back pocket and handing over his wallet like he hadn't just said the freaking W-word in front of strangers.

And wait a second, *did he just call me Muffin? Muffin?*

My mouth went dry and my face went hot, but somehow I managed to smile when the woman's curious and slightly shocked attention slid over to me, more than extremely aware of the weight of Aiden's gaze on me.

His wife.

I was his freaking wife and he'd just said so out loud.

What the fuck?

There were words for everything, and I understood that a lot of times, they meant nothing. In this case, I recognized that yeah, "wife" didn't mean crap, but still, it was weird. It was really, *really* weird to acknowledge the title for a hundred different reasons.

It was even weirder to hear the word out of Aiden's mouth, especially when it was me he was talking about.

The Muffin thing was its own beast, something I definitely wasn't prepared to deal with in that moment.

Picking Aiden's wallet from his hand, I turned my hopefully not-so-shocked face to the receptionist and handed over Aiden's debit card. With a fake, strained smile that was more of a grimace, she took it from me and swiped it. After she handed a receipt over, I found Aiden waiting for me at the door and walked out alongside him. I resisted the urge to ask if he wanted to use me as a crutch for support. Once we were in the car and before I did anything else, I turned to him in the seat, acting as if nothing out of the ordinary had happened.

"Aiden . . . uh . . ." I scratched at my forehead, trying to keep my features even. First things first. "Did you just call me Muffin?"

He looked at me. His blink was so delayed, I started thinking maybe I'd imagined it. "I figured it was too soon to call you Dinner Roll."

I stared at him, and as I did, my mouth might have been open at the same time. Slowly, eventually, I nodded at him dumbly, attempting to absorb what I realized was a joke he'd just made. A joke he'd made aimed at me.

"You were right. It would have been too soon," I muttered.

He made this face that irritatingly said, "I told you so."

Who the hell was this human being? He looked like Aiden. He smelled like Aiden. He sounded like Aiden, but he wasn't the same Aiden I knew. This was the Aiden who had sought me out in Vegas and told me to shut up when I was teasing him. Okay. I swallowed and nodded, accepting that this was what I'd wanted from him. And I'd finally gotten it.

I liked this version more, even though he seemed like a completely different person. Messing with the leg of my glasses, I sniffed and floundered around for the other thing bouncing around in my head. "Why did you call me your wife in there?" My voice sounded all weird.

That heavy-lidded, smart-ass gaze was as cool as a damn cucumber. "Why wouldn't I?"

"I thought we were going to keep this under wraps for as long as possible." And he could have at least warned me he was going to do it so I could have mentally prepared.

The Wall of Winnipeg didn't look remotely apologetic. "You are my wife, and I don't have patience for flirts," he said in that calm, detached voice that made me want to club him. "You're not my assistant. Did you want me to deny it?"

"I just . . ." My nostrils flared on their own. Did I want him to? I wasn't sure. But it wasn't like he'd called me his bitch or anything. "It's fine that you did it. You caught me off guard, that's all."

Stretching that long body out in his seat, Aiden didn't add anything else. I sat there for a moment thinking about what he'd done, and thinking about this unconventional fake marriage we had and this new, oddly shaped, blossoming friendship. And it was when I was thinking about those things that I remembered what Aiden had said to me in Vegas. How we'd made promises to each other and how he was going—in his own strange way—to keep up with them.

With my hands wrapped around the steering wheel, I looked at him over my shoulder and asked outright, with a choppy exhale, "What's it going to be? Crutches or a cane?"

He went with nothing.

"Crutches or a cane, big guy," I repeated.

Aiden shifted in his seat. "Give me a break."

Give me a break. I had to count to five. Turning the ignition, I reminded myself that he'd called me what I was: his friend and, weirdly, his wife. He knew me. He'd missed the Vanessa I'd been back when things had been okay between us.

"I'll find you a walker if you don't make a choice by the time I get on the freeway," I threatened, keeping my attention forward. "The faster you heal, the better. Don't be a pain in the butt more than you need to be."

He sighed. "Crutches."

That was way too easy, and I wasn't dumb enough to bring it up more than necessary so that he wouldn't change his mind. I didn't say anything else as I drove to the pharmacy and parked. Aiden stayed silent too when I hopped out of his SUV. In no time, I found crutches and bought a new bottle of over-the-counter anti-inflammatory pills.

The ride home was pretty quiet. I made sure not to watch as he slowly hobbled inside and made his way to the couch, where the comforter I'd brought downstairs the night before was neatly folded, stacked under his pillow. Leaving the crutches I'd bought propped against the couch, I hesitated for a second by the stairs as I watched him settle in.

"I'll be upstairs," I said.

He nodded stiffly, palming the remote in one of his hands, his head turned toward me. "Thanks for taking me."

"Yeah." I shuffled my feet. "What are friends for?" I teased him in a small voice, unsure of how he'd react.

"For that, Van."

The man I'd seen kind of, sort of, maybe smile a couple of times, had a tentative grin crack across his mouth. The expression on his face completely caught me off guard. For a man who never ever physically reacted, even when he won a game, his smile . . .

Heaven help me.

It was beautiful. There was no other word to describe it. It was like a double rainbow. Better than a double rainbow.

I felt stunned. Rooted in place forever.

His features didn't necessarily soften, but the way his entire face seemed to lighten . . .

I touched my mouth to make sure it was closed and not wide open.

I couldn't respond. I could only stand there nodding in place, with something that was pretty close to a deranged smile making an appearance on my face.

"Holler if you need me. I, uh, have work to do." Yeah, I tucked my imaginary tail in and ran upstairs.

Good lord. My heart pounded as I sat at the chair behind my desk, and I set my palm over it. What the hell was that? That smile was like a nuclear bomb he had within his reach. I mean, I knew Aiden was attractive, obviously, but when he smiled, there was nothing to prepare you for that weapon of mass destruction.

Hello, I had eyes. Even if I had become mostly desensitized to those muscles on top of carefully sculpted muscles, I knew they were there. I knew his face was handsome despite how unyielding it usually was.

I sucked in a breath and let it out, trying to clear my head. But it wasn't as easy as it should have been. When I was looking for photographs of male models for an e-book cover, I thought about Aiden one or two times more than necessary.

Good grief, he needed to keep that thing in check.

THIRTEEN

A couple of weeks later, after Aiden had completely recovered from his sprain, I was in my room working on a paperback cover for one of my favorite clients when I heard the garage open and close, followed by the beeping of the alarm, and finalized by the loud slap of the door being slammed shut. Lowering the volume on my computer speakers, I sat there a minute.

I didn't need to look at the culprit to confirm who it was. Aiden wasn't the slamming-the-door-shut-out-of-anger type of person. He tended to stick to venting his grievances with words or on the field or gym, or more often than not, he went into his room and stayed there doing who knows what. I'd never figured out what he did in there for hours.

That was what alarmed me. It had to be Zac, and Zac was usually too laid back to react to anything like that . . . unless he had a reason to be really pissed.

I stayed in my room and faintly listened to the angry noises coming from the first floor: the cupboards being forcefully closed, the loud clatter of plates on the counter, and the "*Goddammit!*" that was shouted twice. It all wafted up the stairs and wrapped around me in my room. But I stayed where I was.

If Zac was angry, he needed space to cool off. At least that was the best way to deal with my sisters when they were pissed.

So I left him alone, despite wanting to know what happened.

Sometime later, stomps echoed their way up the stairs and down the hall.

And that was how I knew something was really wrong. Zac *always* told me hi. Then his bedroom door closed with a bang just down the hall from my room.

For one brief second, I thought about texting Aiden to ask if he knew what was going on, but if he didn't text me back, it would just make me mad. So I waited instead.

ZAC DIDN'T COME out of his room the rest of the day.

I didn't hear him in his room either, and that was when I started to worry.

The following afternoon, I made my way downstairs after he still hadn't come out. I found Aiden in the kitchen, fiddling with the knobs for the stove while he held a pan in one hand. He briefly peeked at me over his shoulder before muttering a "Hello" that seemed almost natural.

"Hi," I greeted him back, not getting hung up on the H-word as I tried to decide how to best go about asking him about my main concern: Big Texas.

It must have been apparent I wanted something, because not a few seconds later Aiden spoke up. "What's wrong?"

"I think there's something wrong with Zac."

He said, "Oh," so casually I wasn't anticipating what came out of his mouth next. "The team released him yesterday," he explained like the news wasn't the most devastating thing to happen to Zac ever. Hell, it would be the worst thing just about any professional athlete on any team could ever hear. Even I found myself sucking in a breath.

"Why?"

He'd turned to face the stove again, those mountainous shoulders and wide lateral muscles greeting me through the thick, white T-shirt he had on. "He's been too inconsistent. He hasn't been listening." Aiden lifted his shoulders. "I told him it was going to happen."

I blinked. "You *knew*?"

"He hasn't been taking his training seriously enough and it's noticeable. The other QBs have been playing better." He made a humming noise as he moved toward the refrigerator. "He's pissed off, but it's his fault and he knows it."

I winced, feeling bad for Zac's situation but understanding the point Aiden was trying to make, despite how brutal the truth was. Even I had brought up how much time he took off when he should have been working out during the off-season. Hurt for him clung to edges of my soul though. Just a couple months ago, he'd been the one telling me how happy he was that I would be joining the "do what you love" team. Now?

"Have you talked to him?" I asked.

"No."

Of course not. When a normal person would try to commiserate with a friend after something crappy happened to them, Aiden wouldn't. I sighed and scratched at my temple. Damn it, I couldn't believe it.

I wondered what Zac was going to do now, but it was still too soon to ask. Figuring he probably needed a little more time to stew on what happened, I made myself let it go. Maybe he'd gotten a little complacent, but that didn't mean he had to get his dreams ripped away from him.

I wanted to talk to him, but I couldn't help but think about how terribly some people handled disappointment in their lives. I'd grown up with three of them. It wouldn't hurt to wait.

Toeing the floor with my sock-covered foot, I glanced at Aiden to find him spreading hummus all over two tortillas on the counter. "You doing okay?"

"Yes," he answered quickly.

"That's good." I stared at his broad back and bit the inside of my cheek, that same uncertainty with talking to him filling my guts. Did he want me to leave him alone? Should I try to make more of a conversation with him?

"How's the running going?" he asked suddenly.

Small talk. Heaven help us, he was trying to make small talk. "Good. I'm getting faster." I puffed my cheeks up with air and gave the fridge a side look. "Why? Do you want to go with me again?"

His snicker was soft and it made me laugh.

Rome hadn't been built in a day.

"No? Okay. I'm going back to my room. Let me know if you talk to Zac though, would you?"

TWO DAYS PASSED and I didn't see Zac once. I wasn't sure when he ate, because I never saw him, and if it wouldn't have been for his car in the driveway and the occasional flush of the toilet from the bathroom adjacent to his room, I wouldn't have known he was home.

I knocked on his door once but he didn't respond.

But by the third full day of not seeing him, I figured he'd had enough time to stew in his pot of pity. Finishing the two projects I'd assigned myself for the day, I headed across the hall to his bedroom and gave the door two raps.

Nothing.

So I knocked again a little harder.

Still nothing.

"Zac Attack?"

And nothing.

"I know you're in there. Open up." I pressed my ear to the door and listened. "Zac, come on. Open the door or I'll pick the lock."

No response.

"I know how. Don't tempt me." I waited a beat and then kept going. "I used to break into my boyfriend's locker in high school." Not necessarily my most mature moment, but it had come in handy a couple of times.

He wasn't biting.

"Zac, buddy. Come on. We don't have to talk about it if you don't want, but let's go get some Mexican food."

The mattress creaked loudly enough for me to hear and I smiled.

"If you're a nice boy, I'll take you to do some two-step at that honky-tonk place you like. What do you think?" I tried to bribe him.

He definitely made some stirring noises. It took what felt like a couple minutes before he finally spoke up like I had hoped he would. He'd never say no to going to a country-western club. Which I guess worked out in his favor, because if he had the kind of status that Aiden had, he wouldn't be able to do that sort of thing without getting hounded, and now wasn't the time for that. In that kind of club, he wouldn't stand out.

Then finally, he answered, "You'll drive?"

"I'll drive."

"Give me an hour to get ready."

I couldn't help but snort. "It doesn't even take me that long to put on my makeup."

There was a pause, and what sounded like his bedsprings squeaking confirmed he really was moving around. "I gotta straighten my hair too, sugar. Gimme a break."

I smiled at the door. "That's my girl."

"I HATE TO be the one to say this to you, but you need to go on a diet."

Zac managed to take a step forward before he swayed so much most of his weight ended up on me. Again.

He was no Aiden, but he definitely wasn't anywhere near underweight either. Good grief. I started panting as we took another two steps closer to the house, seriously reconsidering the big guy's suggestion that I start doing some weight training. I'd been walking, jogging, and running nearly five days a week for the last two months so I could begin training for a marathon, but that didn't prepare me for carting around Big Texas. I was planning on starting to do some cross-training soon but hadn't gotten around to it yet.

To make matters worse, like an idiot, I'd parked on the street like I usually did, but the difference was that I didn't usually have a 200-pound drunk man hanging off my arm for dear life.

Instead of drinking away his sorrows with margaritas like I'd originally suggested, Zac had gone straight for the Coronas. Many, many Coronas. So many I'd lost count, even though my wallet hadn't.

But I wasn't going to say anything, because the moment he'd arrived at the doorway to my room, dressed, I saw "devastation" in the flesh.

Zac, who was normally a vision of health, vitality, and friendliness, looked like shit.

I didn't comment, and I had to settle for smiling in his direction and giving him a slap on the butt as we headed down the stairs and toward my car for our evening. Sure enough, he hadn't wanted to talk about getting let go from the team, and instead he'd slapped on a somewhat bright smile after a few minutes and made every effort to have fun.

Up until he'd gotten wasted.

"Hey, hold on to the wall a second so I can get the door unlocked," I ordered, poking him in the side at the same time; I tried to angle him so he could grab hold.

"Sure, Vanny," Zac muttered, smiling at me dreamily, lips pressed tight, his eyes closed.

I snickered, made sure he had one hand firmly planted on the wall, and then slipped under his arm. It didn't take me long to unlock the door and turn off the alarm. With Zac's arm over my shoulder again, I shuffled him three feet inside before he started tilting side-ways, one clumsy foot in front of the other until he crashed into the side table next to the couch. The lamp on top teetered as Zac tried to right himself, but it lost the battle with gravity and clattered to the floor, the shade flying off, the bulb cracking into a thousand pieces.

Damn it.

I sighed. *One, two, three.* "All right. You're done for the night, buddy." Grabbing Zac's arm, I led him onto the couch like he was a little kid. Opening them just as his butt hit the cushion, his eyes were glassy, wide, and so completely guileless I couldn't even be irritated with him longer than a second. "Sit here." He did. "Let me go get you some water, but don't move, okay?"

He forced himself to blink up at me, totally dazed, and I was pretty sure he couldn't see me, even though he was obviously trying. He smacked his lips. "Yes, ma'am."

Ma'am? It took everything inside of me not to crack up. "I'll be right back," I croaked, pinching my nose and taking a couple steps back to avoid the broken pieces of light bulb before heading toward the kitchen. I flicked on the lights, filled up a plastic cup with water—because I wasn't about to trust him with glass—and grabbed the broom and dustpan from the pantry closet.

Zac sat on the couch where I'd left him, his boots kicked off in the middle of the room, and his butt scooted up to the edge. His eyes were closed.

But it was the big smile on his face that killed me.

This surge of affection filled my heart as I squatted down to poke him in the shoulder. The second he lazily cracked those blue eyes open, I held the cup of water toward him. "Drink up, buddy."

He took the cup without argument, and I went over to the mess on the floor. I swept up what I could, poured the shards in a small cardboard box I'd found in the recycling bin, and tossed it all into the trash. Taking the vacuum from the pantry, I pulled it after me and into the living room, where I moved the suction all over the floor just to be on the safe side.

I'd barely unplugged the vacuum and turned around to put everything back when I sucked in a breath and let out the girliest, most pathetic squeak in the universe. It wasn't "aah" or "eep." It just sounded, well, I'm not sure what it sounded like, but I would never take credit for it.

Aiden stood there, not even two feet away, literally cloaked in the darkness of the hallway like a damn serial killer.

"You scared the hell out of me!" My heart . . . I was going to have a heart attack. I had to slap my hand over my chest, like that would help it stay in place. "Oh my God."

"What are you doing?" His voice was raspy and low.

Hand still over my chest, I panted. "Somebody broke a light bulb." I gestured toward the drunk Texan on the couch, oblivious to everything and everyone around him at that point.

I eyed Aiden, his sleepy face, the wrinkled white T-shirt he had on, the thin lounge pants I know he'd thrown on to come down the stairs, because in the two years I'd been responsible for doing his laundry, I'd only washed them a handful of times, and I immediately felt guilty. The big guy usually went to bed at the earliest possible time he could to ensure he got a minimum of eight hours of sleep, and here I'd been vacuuming, waking him up.

"I'm so sorry. I didn't mean to wake you," I whispered, even though I was sure I could have walked around the living room banging pots and pans and Zac wouldn't have woken up.

He shrugged one of those big shoulders, his eyes going from me to his now ex-teammate. I didn't need to look at Zac to know he was more than likely passed out on the couch by that point, especially not when Aiden's stray gaze stayed on the spot behind me. "How much did he have to drink?" he asked, yawning.

A pang of guilt hit my belly. "Too much." As if to explain, I added, "I just wanted to get him out of his room for a little while. I thought it would be good for him." Maybe too good for him, but it was too late to take the evening back by the time I figured getting shit-faced wasn't the best thing for him to do.

To be fair, it had been a lot of fun.

A loud, rough snore ripped through the air and the sharp, sudden rumble of Zac snoring had me glancing over my shoulder. "I need to go grab something. I'm sorry if I woke you."

Before he could say anything else—or not say anything else—I hauled ass upstairs and into Zac's room, internally cringing at the mess he'd made since he began locking himself in; and the smell, it was bad. Real bad.

Grabbing the corner of the wrinkled comforter on the bed and his pillow, I ran down the stairs and found Aiden standing next to the couch talking to Zac in a low voice and . . .

Was he patting the armrest?

"Here." I handed over the pillow.

Aiden took it, his attention still on Zac, and set it alongside the armrest I'm pretty sure he'd been petting a second ago. "Lie down," he ordered the drunk one in a quiet, no-nonsense voice that obviously left no room for argument to even someone who was mostly out of it.

Sure enough, Zac lay down without opening his eyes. His arms crossed over his chest, one shoulder cocooned into the couch cushions. I tossed the comforter over his long body and smiled at Aiden, who was still standing over the couch, looking extremely, ridiculously serious at what was essentially us tucking a grown man in.

Zac made some funny kind of puttering sound that made his lips flutter, and I snorted. "He looks like a little kid, doesn't he?" I whispered.

"He acts like a little kid," Aiden grunted, shaking his head in total disapproval.

"What is he going to do now?" I found myself blurting the question out.

The big guy hummed. "What he should do is quit acting like the world has ended and get back to training so another team will pick him up later on in the season," he stated. "What he's going to do—I don't know. If he waits too long, it'll hurt his chances of getting another opportunity in the future. Every day we get older and our bodies can't . . ." Aiden tipped his chin to the side and cast me a long look. "I'll talk to him tomorrow."

"That's a good idea. I think he'll listen to you."

"He'd probably listen to you more."

That had me frowning at him at the same time I shoved my glasses farther up my nose. "You think?"

His attention didn't stray from the couch as he answered, "I know."

I didn't necessarily believe that was true, but okay. "I'll try, I guess. The worse he'll do is not listen to me, and it wouldn't be the first time it's happened."

That had his head turning. "Are you talking about me?"

I pressed my lips together. "I wasn't talking about you, but . . ."

"But?"

I kept my gaze on the wall away from Aiden. "You haven't listened to me before, if you want to get technical."

Aiden didn't respond.

"A lot of times," I added in a mutter.

Nothing. Okay.

I tipped my head toward the kitchen. "I was going to make a sandwich before I went to bed. Do you want one?"

"What kind?" he asked, like I'd offer him a turkey club.

FOURTEEN

"So how's it going, living in sin?"

I gave an awkward laugh, shaking the wok in my hand at the same time. Uncomfortable laughs were what you got when you felt guilty. I still hadn't told Diana that Aiden and I had gone to Las Vegas.

It was a damn miracle. She usually knew I started my period ten minutes after I did. We liked to celebrate another month of not being pregnant.

I could only think about two other things I'd ever lied to her about. Apparently, I liked to live life on the edge, because I knew I was in for a reckoning the likes of which I'd never seen when she found out the truth. Because, at this point, I was in too deep and there was no way in hell I was going to admit what I'd done.

The biggest problem with lying to your closest friend was finding the right line to straddle. Enough truth to be believable but not enough of a lie so they could notice you were full of shit, which was exactly what I needed to find, so I went with diverting her attention by going for middle ground. "It's going fine."

"Fine? That's it?"

"Yeah. Fine." What the hell else could I say? While things between Aiden and me were better than they ever were, nothing amazing had happened. He lived his life and I lived mine. He was a busy guy; I'd always known that and nothing had changed. "The most exciting thing I've found out was that Aiden gets his groceries delivered *once a week*, and that he hired some lady who lives in Washington to answer his emails. Crazy stuff, huh?"

She hummed, paused, and then asked, "Why does it feel like you're lying to me?"

She could already tell. What the hell? And why was I surprised? "Because you're crazy?" I offered, making a face into the phone in panic.

"Doubtful."

"It's more like a fact, but anyway, there's nothing *to* tell you. We don't see each other that much. The most he does is wave at me." Sometimes he talked to me, but we didn't have to be technical, did we?

"B-o-r-i-n-g."

I groaned. "S-o-r-r-y."

"Really? You don't have anything juicy to tell me?"

"Nope." I'd already worked for him for two years, if there was something bad to tell her, I couldn't have told her anyway. I'd signed a nondisclosure agreement.

The disgruntled sound out of her mouth made me grin. "Fine. Are you going to El Paso this weekend after all?" she asked, already moving on, knowing if I hadn't already told her something, I probably wouldn't.

"Yes," I confirmed with only the smallest bit of anxiety going through my stomach.

I was going to El Paso for my mom's birthday.

Did I know I was more than likely going to regret taking the trip hours after I got there? Yes. Nine times out of ten, that had been the case.

But it was her fiftieth birthday, and her husband was planning a party for her. She'd love to see me there, he'd said to me. Lay on the guilt-trip, why didn't he? I talked to her once a month. I figured that wasn't too shabby to begin with considering everything.

From the way he'd made me feel, one call every four weeks wasn't good enough. At least enough for me to feel obligated to go, even though my gut said it was a stupid idea.

"Where are you staying?"

"At a hotel," I responded. I could stay with my mom if I wanted to, but I didn't. The last time I'd stayed with her had ended terribly. There were also my two oldest sisters, but I'd rather camp out under a bridge than do that. Finally, there were my foster parents, who I was planning on dropping by and visiting while I was in town, but I didn't want to impose on them.

"Is Oscar going?" she asked about my little brother.

"No. He already started school."

"Are you going by yourself?"

"Of course I'm going by myself," I answered before thinking about just what I was saying.

Wasn't the Three Hundreds' bye week coming up? That was the week they got off a season to let the players rest. Should I go by myself? Would it be a good idea to take Aiden around my mom? My sisters? That idea had me cringing.

But I could have him around to break the news. Now that idea seemed like the only one that could have convinced me. There was no chance of my family members telling Diana or her family, so I wasn't worried about it getting around that way. "Actually, maybe I won't."

The nosey broad took a swift intake of breath. "Really?"

"I might ask Aiden, so keep your mouth shut."

"I will." She was such a damn liar. I didn't believe her at all. I didn't believe she hadn't told at least her brother that I was living with Aiden.

The opening and closing of the garage door let me know someone was home. "I'll tell everyone about your porn bookmarks if you don't," I threatened her, with a snicker.

"I'm never going to live that down, am I?"

You never forget accidentally coming across your friend's— predominantly man on man—porn bookmark folder, no matter how hard you try. "No."

"Like you've never seen gay porn," she sniped bitterly. "You think Susie might be at your mom's?"

And just like that, my nice, fine day was kicked in the shin. I bit the inside of my cheek and reached up to push my glasses farther up my nose. "I don't know. I talked to my mom a few days ago, but she didn't mention anything."

Not that my mom would.

If I did see Susie, chances were high it wasn't going to end well. It never had. Even people I didn't know who knew about our situation were well aware that was a fact. We were like two magnets constantly repelling each other.

Damn it. I knew Diana was just trying to be helpful, but simply thinking about Susie made my head start hurting.

"I don't think you should go by yourself or with Aiden, for the record."

That wasn't surprising. I just wished she wouldn't have brought up Susie. "I know."

"But you're still going?"

I'd already given my word I would. How could I take it back? "Yes."

She didn't approve, and it was evident over the phone.

"I want to finish eating so I can get back to work. I'll text you later. Give the demons a hug from me next time you see them, and tell Drigo I haven't forgotten he still has the DVDs I let him borrow a month ago," I said to her, rubbing at one of my throbbing temples.

"I will. I'm babysitting them tomorrow. I'll let you know when I'm off next week so I can do your hair again, 'kay?"

We hung up just as the door that connected the garage to the kitchen opened and Aiden came in, his duffel in hand.

"Hi," I said, turning off the stove.

"Hi, Vanessa." Aiden dropped his bag on the floor by the door and then made his way toward where I was standing, his nostrils flaring at the smell of lentils, chopped vegetables, and sundried tomatoes mixing together. "Smells good."

I gave him a side-look, only letting what seemed to be an extra-large shirt on his double-extra-large frame distract me for a second. "There's enough for both of us, if you have a normal, human-sized meal instead of a Hulk-sized one."

He sniffed, and I think it was more at my comment than to actually smell the food again. "Thank you," he said, making his way toward the sink to wash his hands. He seemed to hesitate at the island for a minute before taking two plates down from the cupboard and setting them on the counter by the side of my hip.

When the timer for the noodles went off, I drained them, splitting up half the pot on two plates and leaving the other half in the pot. I scooped up the stir-fry and placed it on top of the noodles as Aiden put two red apples side by side in the spot he usually ate at.

We sat down to eat. Each of us just sitting there, not on our phones or computer or anything. Just . . . sitting there.

"Has Zac come down?" he suddenly asked.

"Once. He came out of his room around noon, but that's it." It had been almost a week since he'd been let go from the team, and apart from the day we'd gone out, he hadn't left his room more than he needed to, which was solely for meals. He didn't want to talk to anyone or do anything, and I wasn't sure what to do, if I should even do something.

Aiden made a hmm noise.

"I don't know what to say to him, or if I should do something," I admitted. I wasn't good at consoling people. I really wasn't. Some people knew what to say in all types of situations, knew what words were needed, and they used them perfectly. Me? I usually just settled for an "I'm sorry." I wasn't good with words even though I did want to do something for Zac. I just didn't know what.

The big guy raised his shoulder. "Give him some time," he suggested.

Mr. Congeniality right here was trying to give me advice on what I should do? Did that mean I should do the opposite?

"Yeah, I guess I will," I said, before my conversation with Diana came back to me. "Umm, I'm going to El Paso for a few days this weekend. Remember I told you?" I stabbed at a few pieces of pasta scattered around the plate. "It's my mom's birthday."

He shifted in his stool, the side of his knee touching mine. "Okay."

There was no reason for me to feel awkward. None. If he said he'd go, great. If he didn't want to go, it wasn't a big deal. "I was thinking . . . maybe you could come with me. I haven't told her we got married, and I would rather tell her in person than let her find out some other way." I fidgeted in my seat and slanted him a look out of the corner of my eye.

Aiden simply forked some food into his mouth, chewing slowly.

I scratched at my ear. "If you want." Then I added, "It's just for the weekend."

Dumb. Dumb. Dumb, dumb, dumb.

Why had I even bothered saying anything?

Aiden scratched at his jaw with the end of the fork in his hand. He twisted his lower body in his seat, his knee hitting the side of my leg again before he said, "I'd need to be back Sunday night."

I almost had to do a double take. "Really?"

He shrugged down at his food, super casual, or at least as casual as someone his size could be. Honestly, I was surprised he could fit that butt onto one stool. I was even more surprised the stool's legs hadn't given out yet under his weight. "Yeah," was his reply.

"Oh . . . okay. I was planning on leaving Friday. It's an eight-hour drive."

That had his face swinging to me, his expression going from blank to disturbed in a second flat. "You want to drive there?"

I nodded.

He stared at me for a second longer before reaching into his pocket, pulling out his black leather wallet, and then holding a silver credit card out in my direction. "Buy two tickets and rent a car. I don't do long road trips."

Did I know he didn't like riding in a car for longer than absolutely necessary? Yes, but I wanted to cross my eyes anyway. If I didn't have to do an eight-hour road trip, I wasn't going to, especially not if I wasn't paying for it.

He couldn't be considered my sugar daddy if we were legally married, right?

Shoving the thought aside, I hesitantly took the card from him. "Are you sure?"

He didn't hold back his eye roll. "Get an afternoon flight, they usually let us out around three." He eyeballed me from the side. "Don't rent one of those tiny economy cars either just to save money."

Yeah, his bossiness was bringing back not the best of memories. I nodded anyway and held his card between my fingers. "Is this supposed to be a test?" I asked hesitantly.

Back to being busy eating, it took him a second to answer before he turned to me with a furrow between those thick eyebrows. "What are you talking about?"

"Is this a test?" I wiggled his credit card. "To see if I'll spend your money or offer to pay for my own ticket."

That full bottom lip of his dropped just a little, his eyelids hanging low. Then he shook his head slowly, so slowly I knew he was exasperated . . . or he thought I was a complete idiot. One or the other. Maybe both. "Don't be dumb. I wouldn't offer to pay for the tickets if I didn't want to. You know me better than that."

He had me there. I shrugged. "Okay. All right." Sheesh. "I just wanted to be sure, because if you want to pay for them, I'm not going to tell you no."

"Just buy the tickets and rent the car." He got up with his plate in hand and walked around to the sink before adding, "Where are we staying?"

"I was planning on staying at a hotel."

"Good. What are you going to tell your family?"

I scratched at the back of my neck before picking at my food. "Just my mom. I don't—my sisters don't need to know. Either way, no one's finding out the truth. They don't know I'm living with you. I figured—" Shit. What? Was I expecting my mom to not remember who I worked for? Of course she remembered. *Now.* Ten years ago, she didn't remember half the time that she'd given birth to me and I relied on her. That was an easier truth to consider than the idea that she loved drinking more than she loved her kids.

I needed to stop. I needed to stop five seconds ago. Everything in my life had worked out for the better. I had no reason to complain. My life was better than fine. Way better.

With that reminder, I cleared my throat and pasted a playful tone to my words. "If she asks, I'll just tell her I quit and you came after me. You realized how madly in love with me you were—"

Honest to God, he snorted.

I put my hand on top of the table and extended my middle finger at him even though I smiled. "—and you can't live without me, so we eloped. I figured I should stick with at least a partial truth so it doesn't get too complicated. You got a problem with that?"

Aiden shook his head, the corners of his mouth pulled tight in a smirk that eased my soul a little more. *Everything in my life had worked out.* "No."

Jackass. I couldn't help but snicker. "You'll take one for the team then, so that can be the story we tell everyone who finds out?"

"What team?" he asked.

"You and me. Team Graves-Mazur. We signed a contract together. Sort of." I smiled.

That bearded chin dipped to his neck, and I could see his mouth twitching. "All right. I'll take one for the team."

IT WAS FIVE minutes before we were supposed to be leaving for the airport, and Aiden wasn't home yet.

He hadn't answered the three times I'd called, and there was no way for him to know about the ten other times I'd picked up the phone but talked myself out of dialing. Where the hell was he?

I'd been ready all morning. I'd even made him lunch so he could eat it on the way to the airport since I'd known he'd be hungry after watching game footage for a few hours before the players were dismissed for the week.

But he wasn't home. *He wasn't home.* And we needed to leave.

I was pacing. My bag was already by the front door, and if I didn't leave in five minutes, I would more than likely not make the flight.

The abrupt ringing of my phone from its spot in my back pocket immediately snapped me out of my freak-out. Sure enough, Miranda P. appeared on the screen and a bad premonition pinched my gut.

"Hello?"

"Vanessa." There was a noise in the background that sounded like someone laughing. "I'm not going to make it."

Disappointment like I hadn't known in forever—if I let myself think about it, I would realize the last time had been back when he'd let Trevor talk about me—squeezed the base of my skull. I wanted to ask him why. I wanted to ask him why he'd waited so long to call or why he hadn't at least texted me if he'd known he wasn't going to make it, but I couldn't make myself do it. Chest tight, head suddenly hurting, I asked, "Are you okay?" even as anger fisted my fingers.

"Yes" was his curt, distracted response.

"Okay." I swallowed hard and clenched my eyes closed. *One, two, three, four, five, six, seven, eight, nine, ten.* Yeah, that didn't help as much as it should have. "I'm leaving the house then. I'll be back on Sunday."

"Leslie is coming into town."

That's fine swam along my tongue, but I bit it back. It wasn't fine. I was pissed off at him for wasting my time and making plans for him to go along with me. I was mad at myself for expecting—for getting a little, tiny bit excited—about him coming with me. I'd never taken anyone with me to El Paso before.

That only made me angrier. "I understand. I need to get my stuff in the car. I'll see you in a few days."

He might have said bye, but he might have not. I didn't know because I hung up on his ass.

One, two, three, four, five, six, seven, eight, nine, ten, eleven, twelve.

What the hell had I been thinking? I knew the only person I should blame was myself. Why had I even bothered inviting him? I should have kept my mouth shut and not said anything. I'd made him food and wasted hours of my life stressing about having to explain to him my family situation.

God, I was so, so stupid.

What had made me think he would actually cut into his bye week to go somewhere with me when the last two bye weeks he'd stayed at home to train?

I was an idiot.

I ran up the stairs to my bedroom and yanked my checkbook out of my desk drawer. I wrote out a check for the cost of my plane ticket and the entire amount for the SUV rental I'd booked with him in mind. My soul wept a little—it was ten jobs' worth of money—but I signed the damn check and eyed the Hello Kitty image printed on the background with a little grumble of my own. In less than a minute, I was down in the kitchen, slapping the stupid check on the counter and flipping it off while imagining it was Aiden's face before walking away.

I threw my bag into the backseat of my Explorer a little more forcefully than I needed to and took off, hoping to catch my flight.

"I THOUGHT YOU were bringing a friend," my mom noted almost immediately after ushering me through the door.

I blew out a breath and rolled my shoulders, pasting a tight smile on my face. I took in the tall, slim, and nearly blond woman who I used to think was so beautiful when I was a little kid and in her few and far between moments of being wonderful. Especially then. I'd loved the hell out of her before I knew better, and that thought made my heart ache for kid-Vanessa, who hadn't known any better for a while.

It was easy to forget someone so perfect-looking had once been a functioning alcoholic. Then again, that's why she'd gone so long without anyone noticing she had a problem. Luckily, she was fine now, which was why I'd come so far for her birthday.

On the flight over, I'd mentally prepared myself for this situation and what was the best way to handle it. We already had one idiot in the family thanks to Susie. We didn't need another one. So I was going to play dumb and downplay it.

"He had something come up at the last minute," I explained vaguely, looking around the house I'd only been in a handful of times before. It was nice. Really nice. Her husband of the last five years was a divorce attorney she'd met at AA. He seemed like a nice enough guy, and my little brother had spoken very highly of him.

"That's too bad," my mom said. I could sense her looking me over. "You don't want to bring your bag inside?"

I made sure to meet her eyes before I answered. I didn't want to feel ashamed for not wanting to stay with her, and I wouldn't let myself be. If she really put her mind to it, she'd remember how shitty things went when I stayed with her. "I checked in to my hotel already."

The truth was, I'd checked into my hotel the day before. Afterward, I'd gone to see my foster parents and had dinner there. I talked to my foster dad pretty often—in my case once every few weeks was often—and told them I'd married Aiden. My foster dad had looked at me from across the table where I'd eaten dinner seven days a week for four years of my life and asked in a serious voice, "You couldn't have married someone who plays for Houston?"

I'd forgotten how much he hated the Three Hundreds.

This morning I'd had breakfast with my foster mom. But I didn't tell my mom about any of those things. Anytime I brought up my foster parents, this glazed look came over her eyes that I wasn't fond of.

"Oh." It was the sharp inhale before her smile that told me she understood enough. "In that case, I'm glad you're here early."

I smiled back at her, a small one, a half-assed one. "Do you need help with anything for the party?"

"We almost have everything together already . . ." she trailed off, her features turning unnecessarily bright. Forced.

This sudden feeling of dread put me on alert. "Who helped?"

She named her husband. Slipping her arm over my shoulder, she pulled me into her side, kissing my forehead—I fought that tiny urge to pull away from her—and I knew. *I fucking knew what she was going to say.* "And Susie and Ricky."

My entire body went rigid. I swear, even my knee started aching in recognition. My heart went double-time.

"Vanessa," my mom said my name like it was made of eggshells, "they've been staying with us. I didn't want to tell you because I was worried you wouldn't come."

I wouldn't have. She had that right.

"She's your sister," Mom said, giving me a shake that wasn't distracting me from the fact I was going to have to count to a thousand so I wouldn't lose it. "She's your sister," she repeated.

Susie was a lot of things, and a fucking bitch was at the top of the list. Anxiety and a not insignificant amount of anger flooded my veins. How could she do this?

"Vanessa, *please*."

Why would she try to ambush me like this? First it was Aiden. Now it was my own mom ambushing me with Susie and her asshole.

"Be nice. For me," she insisted.

I was going to end up at the liquor store before the day was over. I could already feel it.

The urge to be mean gripped my tongue. I wanted to ask her about the hundreds of times she hadn't done something for me. I really did. On my best days, I was convinced I'd forgiven her for the days at a time she never came home. For making me resort to having to steal money from her purse to buy groceries, because she'd forgotten *again* how there wasn't anything to eat at home. For leaving me alone and forcing me to deal with three angry, mean older sisters who couldn't have cared any less about my little brother and me.

But I couldn't get myself to go there. Regardless of how many years she'd been sober, I knew now that my mom hung by a thread. She had a problem and she was dealing with it, even if it was twenty years too late to take back her mistakes.

All I could do was grunt; I couldn't promise her anything. I really couldn't, no matter how badly I wanted to tell her this could be the first time since we were kids that Susie and I wouldn't end up wanting to kill each other within minutes of being face-to-face. Good grief, that was sad. It seemed like we hadn't ever gotten along, and by that I meant my slightly older sister—only by a year and a half—had singled me out and hated my guts for as long as I could remember.

I'd taken a lot of shit from her for those first few years. She'd bullied the hell out of me. It had started off with her pinching me whenever our mom wasn't around, which was always, then progressed to name calling, evolved to stealing the few things I had and then ended with physical confrontations. She'd been an asshole *forever*.

Then one day, when I was probably fourteen, I decided I was done taking her shit. Unfortunately, she kicked my ass and I'd ended up in the emergency room with a broken arm after she'd pushed me down the stairs. It was that broken arm that had led Child Protective Services to our house, because our mom hadn't shown up to the hospital after she'd had people try to contact her. The five of us got split up after that night, and it was only at one other point, four years later, that I lived with my mom or sisters again. That hadn't ended well at all.

It was a painful, miserable history I'd given up on a long time ago.

I had accepted that there was something wrong with all of my sisters, but mainly Susie. As I got older, I realized that chances were high my mom had drank while she'd been pregnant with them. They were all small, unlike my little brother and me, and had learning and behavioral problems. While I accepted now that they couldn't help most of the things that were wrong with them, it didn't help ease my resentment much.

For the sake of my relationship with my mom, we avoided bringing Susie up, and she only briefly mentioned my other two sisters once a year.

Until shit like this.

I seriously couldn't believe Susie and Ricky were staying there, and that no one had warned me. Diana was going to lose it when I told her.

"Vanessa, please. I'm so happy you're here. I've missed you. You never come visit enough," my mom laid the guilt-trip road down for me thick.

One, two, three, four, five, six, seven, eight, nine, ten.

There was nothing in this world I couldn't do, I reminded myself. Everything in my life had worked out. I had more than I'd ever imagined. The past didn't matter anymore.

With a deep breath, I forced out an "Okay," gritting my teeth the entire time.

"Yes?" she asked, beaming with hope.

I nodded, urging my muscles to stop locking up. I knew what I was going to say was an asshole comment. I realized I was being immature, but I really couldn't find it in my soul to care. "Yeah. I'll play nice as long as she does."

The sigh she let out?

Yeah, she knew. She knew Susie didn't know how to be nice.

FIFTEEN

"I can't believe it."

"Believe it," I snarled as I tried to shake off my anger for about the millionth time in the last day.

Diana scoffed as she moved around me, a stained plastic bowl in one hand, a brush in the other. Her brown eyes temporarily shifted from the section of my head she'd already put color on to meet my gaze before she blew a raspberry. "You know I don't want to talk about your family, but when I think they can't get any shittier, they do." Liar. She didn't mind going over the finer defects of four-sixths of my family. How many times had we sat in her room and acted out the hundreds of things we'd do and say to my sisters in retaliation for whatever they'd put me through? A hundred? Not that we'd ever gone through with any of it. They were older than us, and you didn't mess with crazy.

"The worst part was after Ricky grabbed my arm, no one said anything. They all wanted to act like nothing had happened."

"Jesus, V," my best friend muttered. "I told you not to go."

She had, and I'd been stubborn and didn't listen. "I know."

Her hand touched my shoulder. "I'm sorry."

Not as sorry as I was.

I made it three hours at my mom's before everything went to hell. Three hours before I stormed out of her house, pissed out of my mind. I was honestly surprised that I had managed to spend the night at my hotel before heading to the airport first thing in the morning to catch a flight back to Dallas on standby. The anger hadn't abated as much as I'd hoped on a good night's sleep, and the flight back hadn't helped much either.

As soon as I landed, I'd texted one of the only people in the world who was loyal to me, and then headed over to Diana's so I could tell her everything and get it off my chest. Did it help? Not much, but it was something. So I told her everything that had happened as she dyed my hair some surprise color I told her she could choose. It was one of the benefits of being your own boss.

"Wait, so you didn't tell me what happened with Aiden," she finally noted.

Good grief. There I went getting pissed off all over again. At least that was one issue I'd managed to set aside for a while since the day before, but all of a sudden it was another fresh wound to add to my already existing one. "He called and canceled on me at the last minute."

She winced. Her "ooh" just barely audible.

"Yeah," I mumbled as her boob passed about an inch from my face. "His old coach was coming into town or something, and he was busy watching game film or something with the team when he called, but it doesn't matter. It was a stupid idea to invite him anyway."

"I'm sure he had a good reason to cancel," Di tried to assure me.

There was only one reason, and it was the most important one to him. I didn't need the details to know what the exact wording would be. "Yeah. I'm sure he did." I let out a shaky breath. "I'm just in a shitty mood. Sorry."

"No, I can't believe it," the smart-ass gasped.

I reached forward and tried to pinch her through the apron she'd put on, but she danced out of the way with a big grin on her face. "Leave me alone."

She stuck her tongue out. "Put your potato head down for a second, would you?"

I mocked her as I did what she asked. Diana took a step toward me, her belly inches away. She must have reached forward because her shirt went up an inch, exposing a sliver of skin.

I frowned.

Reaching from under the hem of the cape she'd put on me, I pulled her shirt up even higher, exposing a row of small bruises shaped like a smaller version of the ones on my forearm.

"What are you doing?" She took a step away.

I looked up at her, at her face, her neck, her arms, and saw nothing that shouldn't have been there.

"What?" Her tone was a lot less harsh the second time, but I knew, I knew from the way she rubbed her pant leg that something was going on. That was her nervous tic.

One, two, three, four, five, six, seven, eight, nine, ten.

I had to count to ten again before I could manage to not lose it. "What happened?" I asked her as coolly and calmly as possible, even though I was already on my way to becoming even angrier than I'd been when I first showed up.

Diana tried to brush it off a little too quickly. "Nothing. Why?" She had the nerve to look down and pull up her shirt in the same way I had. She even frowned as she touched the bruises I'd bet my firstborn she knew damn well about.

"Where did those come from?"

She didn't look up as she answered. "I remember hitting my hip."

"You hit your hip?" She was lying. She was damn well lying out of her ass.

"On the counter."

"On the counter?" I asked slowly. This felt like a terrible dream.

My best friend—my best friend of my entire life—lied again. "Yeah," she insisted.

"Di—" I wasn't going to lose it. I wasn't going to lose it in front of her.

"Let me finish putting this on your hair," she cut me off.

"Diana—"

"Tip your head down one more time, Vanny."

"*Di.*" I grabbed the hand she had extended toward me. Her brown eyes shot to mine, her expression startled. "Did Jeremy do that?"

"No!"

A knot formed in my throat, growing bigger and bigger by the second. "Diana Fernanda Casillas." Yeah, I went with her whole name. My hand shook. "Did Jeremy do that?"

This fucking liar supreme met my gaze evenly, and if it weren't for her palm hitting her pant leg again, I would have believed she was telling me the truth, that this person I loved, who I would do anything for, and who I felt would do anything for me, wouldn't lie to me.

I wasn't even about to focus on the fact that I'd kept things to myself in the past. That I hadn't told her I'd married Aiden. That she didn't know about my student debts. None of that figured into my thoughts in that instant.

"No, Van. He loves me. I hit my hip."

That knot in my throat swelled and I could feel my eyes well up as her gaze met mine unflinchingly. That was the problem. Diana was just like me. Once she was in too deep, she wasn't about to dig herself out of the hole she was in. She wasn't about to back down and tell me the truth.

"I'm fine, Van. I swear."

She swore. The tingling in my nose got worse. "Di," I kind of croaked out.

The smile that took over her mouth hurt me. "I hit my hip, stupid. I promise."

I didn't think Diana would ever know how badly she was hurting me. I'd like to think the lies I'd told her had been to protect her, so she wouldn't worry about me being in disastrous debt, and I hadn't told her Aiden and I eloped because she had a big mouth and she'd tell everyone. I knew she'd grudgingly understand that after she was done being mad for not being the first person I told. She didn't know how to keep a secret; we all knew it.

But this . . .

I didn't have it in me to keep my mouth shut, even though I knew there was no way in hell she was going to backtrack and admit the truth. Tightening my hold on her, I tried to ignore the severe beating of my heart and made sure her eyes met mine. "Di—"

She was lying. She was being a massive liar as she said, "It's just a bruise, Van."

But it wasn't.

It wasn't.

IT WAS THE conservative sedan parked in the driveway when I got home that told me we had a visitor. Leslie.

Oh Leslie.

The one person in the world who I actually liked, but every once in a while, specifically this weekend and every June 15th, made me just a teensy bit jealous. Leslie was the only person in the world who I could honestly say Aiden cared about, and I guess I was just a greedy, selfish asshole. I couldn't even get a "happy birthday" on my special day, while Aiden didn't just remember Leslie's birthday, but he cared enough to get me to send him a present.

Was I seriously complaining about Aiden caring about someone who wasn't me?

I was in a bad mood—a worse mood than I'd been in when I'd first gotten back to Dallas five hours ago. Hell, I'd been in a bad mood since I left for El Paso. All I wanted to do was get home, stew in my anger, and maybe watch a movie to get my mind off all the things that were bothering me. My mom; Susie; her husband, Ricky; Diana; her boyfriend; and Aiden. I wanted to be alone.

Parking on the street, I grabbed my suitcase from the backseat, ignoring the pain radiating from my wrist, and trudged up the driveway, then the path.

I counted to ten over and over again as I unlocked the door and slipped inside as quietly as possible.

"Vanessa?"

I was halfway up the stairs with my suitcase gripped in hand when Aiden's voice reached me from the foot of them. Slowly lowering my bag to the step I was on, I ground down on my molars and glanced over my shoulder at the man who had stood me up, standing there in between the living room and the foyer in his sweatpants and a tank so loose I could see the ripped sides of some of the sexiest muscles in the universe.

Did I love sexy lateral muscles? Of course. I had ovaries.

But I also had a brain, a heart, and some pride, and huge, brawny arms on someone who left me hanging weren't going to make me forget a single thing.

Things might have gone worse if he'd been there, I tried to remind myself as I tugged at the sleeve of the hoodie I'd put on before leaving Diana's, drawing it farther down my arm. But the other half of my brain wanted to believe that maybe the weekend would have gone differently if Aiden had been there.

Then again, maybe I just wanted to blame someone other than myself for not listening to my instincts when they told me to do something, and then I did otherwise.

"Yes?" I asked, sensing my cheeks go tight.

The big guy was examining me, something about the way he was pursing his lips said he was hesitating. "Leslie's here."

The words were barely out of his mouth when a white head of hair peeked out from the living room. Nearly as tall as Aiden and way more fit than any man who should have been considered elderly could be, Leslie Prescott flashed those perfect white veneers at me. "Hello, Vanessa."

A sharp pain thudded right between my eyebrows unexpectedly. I set my suitcase down in place and smiled at the man I'd met in the past. We'd spent months together in Colorado on two separate occasions, and he'd visited Aiden the rest of the times. I liked him; I really did like him, but I was in a shitty mood, and it wasn't fair to take it out on him.

"Hi, Leslie," I pretty much muttered as I jogged down the steps and held out my hand.

He shook it, flashing me an open, easy smile. "Congratulations," he said, shaking my hand. "I heard the big news." Leslie's other hand came forth to clasp mine between both of his, his smile growing bigger by the second. If he thought it was strange that I didn't give Aiden a hug or a kiss when I got home, it wasn't evident on his features. "I'm a bit hurt I wasn't invited, but I understand."

"Oh, thanks." I gave him a tired smile, pointedly ignoring the big body standing in my peripheral vision, watching on.

"I couldn't be happier for you two. I was disappointed you were out of town this weekend, but I'm sure we'll have more time to see each other in the future."

I forced myself to keep the smile on my face. Aiden and I had nearly five years left together; I was positive I'd see Leslie again at some point. "I'm sure we will."

Leslie beamed. "We finished watching some footage, so I'll get out of your hair to give you both some alone time tonight, eh?"

The tender, amused look that came over Aiden's face more than slightly irritated me. "Eh." *Aye.*

Then the fact that his Canadian had snuck up on him—when it only came up in the times he was really comfortable—made my little-girl immaturity that much worse.

"I'll leave you two to it. I have some work I need to catch up on." I focused on Leslie as I talked.

The older man nodded. "Sure, sure. I understand. If you'll excuse me, I need to make a pit stop before I go." He smiled again, easing the tension in me just slightly.

He hadn't done anything wrong, and I was being an asshole. "You'll be by tomorrow?"

"Eh. My flight leaves the day after. I have to get back home."

"I'll see you tomorrow then. Drive safe."

Leslie agreed and then made his way toward the half bath around the corner. That was my cue to get the heck out of there. Grabbing my bag with my good hand, I managed to make it halfway up the staircase before I heard, "You all right?"

I didn't bother stopping. I kept going up. "I'm fine."

"Vanessa." His voice was low, careful. "Look at me."

One hundred and eighty percent ready to be in my room, I stopped and turned around, raising my eyebrows at the figure standing at the bottom of the staircase with one palm on the handrail.

He had that dark gaze narrowed on me. "When you say you're fine, I know you're not."

"Hmm," was the only thing I could manage to get out without saying something really bitchy. I tried to tell myself it wasn't a big deal he hadn't gone with me; I'd told myself that at least a dozen times over the weekend. I also told myself I understood that he'd stayed to see someone he cared about, but it didn't help, and it didn't work.

My damn pride couldn't handle being stood up and let down by not just him but by everyone this weekend.

"That's what I thought," Aiden stated as he tipped his chin up at me almost defiantly.

I squeezed my fingers around the handrail, envisioning it was his neck I was wringing. "Yeah, I guess so," I admitted with a sniff. "I don't want to talk about it. I'm going to bed."

I barely managed to turn around when Aiden's raspy, low voice spoke up. "I don't care if you don't want to talk about it. I want to talk about it," he said in that authoritative, demanding voice that scratched at my nerves. It wasn't a loud voice by any measure, but it didn't need to be.

Rolling my eyes, I shook my head as he continued his bullshit explanation. "Leslie called, said he was in San Antonio, and asked if he could drop by for a few days. Coach wanted to go through some more footage before I left, and I lost track of time." And he kept going. "I figured you of all people would understand. I don't get what the big deal is."

For one moment, I thought about picking up my suitcase and throwing it at him. Immature, sure. Unnecessary, yes. But it would have made me feel better. Instead, I counted to seven, and while looking at the stairs, I said to him, "I do understand, Aiden. I get it. Your job is the most important thing in your life, and I'm fully aware of how much Leslie means to you. I know that, and I've always known that."

"Yet you're still mad."

There wasn't a point in even lying, was there? Setting my luggage on the stair ahead of me, I turned back around to face that dark head of hair and tanned face I'd seen more of when I worked for him than I did now that I lived with him. "I'm not mad, Aiden. I'm just . . . look, I'm in a terrible mood. Maybe now isn't the time to talk, all right?"

"No." His back straightened and he took his hand off the handrail. "I stayed to watch footage with the staff and see Les," he stated, a furrow between his eyebrows.

"I understand why you stayed. I'm not telling you I don't. I'm frustrated over this entire fucking useless weekend, and I don't want to take it out on you." That was a lie. I sort of did. "Can we please stop talking about this?"

I knew what his reply was going to be before it came out of his mouth: *nope*. He didn't fail me. "I didn't do anything for you to be mad over."

Heaven help me. *Heaven fucking help me.* My fingers went up to press over the top of my eyebrows, as if that would keep my headache at bay. I hissed, "Aiden, just let it go."

The man never let anything go. Why would this moment be any different? "No. I want to talk about it. I didn't go with you to your mom's house. I'll go next time."

The problem with some people was that they didn't understand the principle of things. The other thing with people was that some guys didn't understand when to let shit go, so they kept pushing and pushing and pushing until you just said "fuck it." That was exactly what Aiden did to me then. The pain in my head got even worse. "I invited you so you could meet my mom and my foster parents. And stupid me, I got disappointed when you bailed on me at the last freaking moment."

In hindsight, that sounded a lot more melodramatic than it needed to.

The fact that my mom had knowingly lied to me had been bad enough. Susie going into psycho mode had definitely made things worse. Diana's lies only magnified every ruthless, hurt emotion in me, but I didn't tell him any of that. Every piece of anger in me had been sprouted from the seeds Aiden's absence had left.

"I had to," he stated in that cool, crisp tone that said he definitely didn't understand why I was so upset about it.

Sighing, I pulled my hand away from my face and shook it off. "Forget it, Aiden."

"I don't understand why you're so pissed off," he snapped.

"Because! I thought we were getting to be friends, and you couldn't even bother to remember to tell me until the last minute you weren't going with me. Do you have any idea how unimportant that makes me feel?" I snapped back.

Some strange emotion flickered in his dark eyes, the long length of his face loosening for a second before the normal, bland expression took over his face. "I stayed for a good reason."

"I get it. I know your priorities. I know where we stand. I know what this is and what it isn't. I'll try to adjust my expectations from now on," I cut him off, completely over this stupid conversation.

Aiden's dark pink mouth had been open, but at my comment, he slammed it closed. His forehead creased, and that pouty mouth that belonged on a woman with some kind of cosmetic enhancement went tight at the corners. He blinked those long brown eyelashes as his forehead scrunched.

He was at a loss for words.

Words that could have gone along the lines of "We are friends" or "I'm sorry." Instead, I got nothing. No excuse, no promise, *nada*.

So frustrated—so *freaking* frustrated—I held back the eye roll tempting me by the second and plastered a tight, completely fake smile on my face. "I'm really tired." And my arm hurt. "Good night."

Two steps up the staircase later, I heard, "It isn't that big of a deal."

Why? Why me? Why couldn't he just drop this before I decided to slit his throat in his sleep? "Forget I even said anything," I tossed over my shoulder for his sake and mine. God, I was being bitchy, but I couldn't find it in me to care too much.

Aiden snickered loudly. "I don't understand why you think it's such a big deal. I'm not asking you to pay me back for the airline ticket or the rental car. I'm sure I can meet your family another day. It isn't like we don't have time. We've got five years, Vanessa. I don't want to spend them with you being pissed at me the entire time. You knew what you were getting yourself into."

"Trust me, I haven't forgotten for a second how long we're in this for." I pulled my suitcase up another step angrily.

When I didn't say anything else, he took it upon himself to continue. "What the hell is your problem?"

I turned completely around to face him, my hands going instinctively to my hips. "I already told you what my problem is. I'm in a shit mood and you left me hanging, and that bothers me way more than it should, I know that. But I know I should have known better."

He scoffed. He scoffed so hard his nostrils flared and he shook his head, his eyes going everywhere except at me. "What the hell is that supposed to mean?"

I felt my blood rush away from my face, but I'd be damned if I walked back up to my room now. Sometimes facial features said so much more than words could, and I hoped the smart-ass smile I was giving him said exactly what I wanted it to say. *Fuck you.*

A sharp noise that could have been mistaken for a bitter laugh exploded out of Aiden's mouth. "I'm not paying off your loans and buying you a house to have to put up with this, Van. If I wanted someone to nag at me, I would have gotten a real wife."

Oh . . . hell . . . no.

Every drop of blood in my upper body went south. Ugly, hurtful words pinched my throat and I couldn't talk. I couldn't think. I couldn't even breathe.

I didn't have to take this shit.

Standing there on the step, I nodded, my hands shaking. "You know what? You're right. You're completely right. I'm sorry I opened my fucking mouth. I'm sorry I gave a shit and started looking forward to you coming along with me." And I was sorry I was blaming him for starting off a chain of events that spiraled downhill.

I really was being a wee bit of an asshole, but I couldn't muster up enough fucks to give in that moment to let the situation go.

Clenching my hands together, I jogged up the steps with my suitcase in my bad hand and slammed the door shut behind me once I was in the room. I wasn't sure how long I stood there, staring around me at what suddenly felt like a five-year prison sentence. If we weren't already "married," I'd pack my stuff up and leave.

But I'd signed the papers and made a promise to him. *Five years. I won't go anywhere until you're a resident, I promise.*

That was the difference between Aiden and me though.

I actually kept my word.

Dropping my bag on the floor, I scrubbed at my cheeks with my hands, trying to calm down. My eyes felt oddly dry. This hole the size of Crater Lake took residence where the important parts of my soul used to be. I wasn't going to cry. I wasn't going to fucking cry.

I bent down to unzip my suitcase and took all the clothing out to wash later when the Wall of Asswipe wasn't hanging around. That knot in my throat I'd gotten back at Diana's seemed to swell back to its original size. I wasn't going to cry. I wasn't going to cry even if the urge to was more overwhelming than it had ever been.

I was in the middle of sliding my suitcase beneath the bed a little more forcefully than was necessary when a knock rapped at my door, two taps too low to be Aiden.

Controlling the anger and the not-tears creeping around in my eyeballs, I called out, "Yes?"

"Van." It was Zac.

"Yes?"

"Can I come in?"

Taking off my glasses, I rubbed at my eyebrow bone for a moment with the meaty part of my palm and let out a shuddering breath. "Of course. Come in."

Sure enough, Zac opened the door and slid inside my room, a funny, wary smile on his face as he closed it behind him. "Hi, darlin'," he said in an almost delicate voice.

I gave him an equally wary smile, trying to suppress my aggravation with the guy downstairs, with my family back in El Paso, and with the idiot known as my best friend in Fort Worth. I played with the sleeve of my hoodie again to make sure it was down to my wrist. "Hey."

"I like your hair."

"Thanks." I probably would have liked the teal color a lot more than I did, in any other circumstance, but I was so pissed and disheartened, I couldn't find it in me to care my hair was now like something straight out of Candy Land.

"You all right?" he asked, moving to take a seat on the edge of my bed just a couple feet away from where I was kneeling.

Reluctantly, I kicked my luggage the rest of the way under the bed frame and got to my feet. "Yeah."

"You sure?"

Shit. "You heard all that, huh?"

"I heard," he confirmed, with a blink of those wonderful blue eyes.

Of course he had. I'd been pretty much yelling toward the end. "He gets on my nerves so easily sometimes, I don't understand." I took a seat right next to him with a sigh.

"I know."

"He doesn't care about anyone but himself."

"I know."

"Then he gets mad when someone is disappointed in him," I grumbled at the floor.

"I know," Zac agreed again.

"I didn't beg him to go with me. I just mentioned it. I would have been fine if he'd said he was too busy."

"I know."

"Why is he such a pain in the ass?"

In my peripheral vision, Zac held out his hands. "The world will never know, darlin'."

I snorted and shifted my gaze over to him finally. "No, probably not." I nudged his elbow. "You wouldn't have backed out on me, would you?"

"No way." He nudged me back with his thigh, drawing my attention down to the reindeer-print pajamas he had on. "Bad trip home?"

I hadn't told him much about my family situation in the time we'd known each other. Besides a few casual mentions of how I wasn't close to my mom, how much of a pain in the ass my sisters were, and possibly bringing up my foster parents in passing once or twice, I'd never gone into too much detail with Zac. But he knew enough.

Drawing my gaze up, it settled on the stubble he'd let himself grow out over the course of some time; he usually shaved that baby face every day. Light blue circles were nestled under his eyes and his cheeks looked hollower than they had two weeks ago, making me feel like a self-centered asshole. Some people had real things to worry about, and here I was losing it over people who didn't care about me.

"Yes." That was an understatement. I shook my head, bottling up the argument with Susie and her husband for the time being. "It sucked. A lot."

Zac fed me a pity smile that I ate up. "Why do you think I haven't gone back home?"

Aah, hell. "I hear ya." Tilting my head to look at him, I took him in. "I've been worried about you, you know."

He made a dismissive noise in his throat. "I'll be fine."

How many times had I said those exact same words to myself when it felt like the world was falling apart on me? Reaching over, I put my hand on his thigh. "Of course you're going to be, but that doesn't mean I'm not going to worry or wonder what you're going to do."

That sandy head dropped back and his sigh seemed to fill my room. "I don't fucking know, Vanny," he admitted to me in a tired voice. "I have no idea what I'm going to do."

Maybe I couldn't fix the situations with Aiden, my sister, and Diana, but I could try to help Zac as much as possible now that he finally wanted to talk about it. "Do you still want to play?"

He chuffed. "Of course."

That was easy enough. "Then you know what you're going to do. You're going to start training again, and you're going to get your agent to find you another team to join. Maybe not this season, but at least next. No if, ands, or buts about it. Don't give yourself another option," I told him. "What about that?"

Zac's sock-covered toes tapped against the floor and the sound of his steady puffing told me he was there. His hand came to rest over mine and I elongated my fingers upward to link through his.

"Maybe things won't work out, but maybe they will. You'll never know unless you try, and if you don't try, you'll probably end up an old geezer wondering what would have happened if you hadn't given up," I warned him before letting go of his hand and reaching around to give him a one-armed hug.

That had him snickering.

"You're okay on money?" I wasn't rich by some standards, but I had my savings still, and I was proud of how much I'd set aside all on my own.

"I'm okay," he assured me.

I figured he was. He wasn't extravagant. "If you decide to stay, I'll even let you run this marathon in February with me if you're a good boy," I added, pulling him into my side for another side hug.

His back stiffened. "You're going to run a marathon?"

"Why do you think I've been running?"

"Because you're bored?"

I'd done more research on the training process that was suggested for people running their first marathon, and I couldn't see anyone doing it because they were bored. "No. I just want to do it. I haven't had time to train for one before, and I like the idea of it being a challenge." Plus, I wanted to prove something to myself. Do something for my poor knee. I wanted to remind it that it could do whatever it wanted to. That it wasn't anyone's bitch.

I wanted to know that nothing was impossible and to give my sister a big fuck you for what she had done to me.

I leaned into his side and let out a shaky breath, suddenly feeling overwhelmed over the entire weekend. "Are you in or what?"

The long Texan let out a deep sigh.

"What? You're going to be a loser and back out?"

His face angled slightly toward me. The corner of his mouth hooking up. "What do I get out of it?"

"The same thing I do—personal satisfaction that you did something you couldn't do before."

The smile that came across Zac's face wiped out any lingering resentment I had right then over Aiden's behavior, at least. Those blue eyes twinkled and he radiated something awesome. "You are just a ray of sunshine, aren't you, darlin'? *Do something you couldn't do before.* Well, fuck it. Count me in to this trial of terror."

Yeah, I might have squealed, surprised he'd actually taken up my offer. *"Really?"*

"Yes, really." Just like that, his smile drooped a little. "How many miles is a marathon again?"

I winced, not wanting to kill our agreement before it even got started. "You don't want to know, Zac." Sliding my arm off, I gave the middle of his back a solid pat. "You don't want to know."

"Fuck me, huh?"

"Basically."

He grinned and I grinned right back at him.

"Are you going to be okay?"

I nodded. "I'm always going to be okay."

AN HOUR OR two later, I was lying in bed with one of my favorite movies on, the volume on ultra-low—I had the captions on—when three soft knocks tapped on my door.

Three. It was Aiden.

After a moment, three more low, low, low knocks hit the door.

I kept my mouth shut and went right on watching *Independence Day*.

He could take his real wife and shove her up his ass.

SIXTEEN

"You're up early," I noted dryly as Zac dragged his feet behind him into the kitchen.

The big Texan raised two sleepy eyebrows in my direction. If I didn't know any better, the expression on his face would lead me to think he was drunk, but he was just really tired. "Mm-hmm."

Okay. Someone wasn't in the mood to talk, and that was fine by me. It wasn't like I'd woken up in a fantastic state of mind. It didn't help that the first thing I did after I was awake was call Diana's brother so I could tell him about what I'd seen the day before, only for him to let me know that one of his sons had already told him about the bruises a couple days ago.

"I tried talking to her, but she said she hit her hip," he'd explained.

So she was keeping her story straight; I still didn't believe it. "I don't believe her."

Her brother had made a hesitant sound that left a bad taste in my mouth. "I don't know, Van. I don't like that douche as much as you don't, but I don't think D would lie about it."

That was the problem with growing up in a family that was usually honest and open with each other—you didn't know the lengths someone would go to hide something shameful. And I knew right then that unless Diana blatantly told her brother that Jeremy was getting physical, or unless she ended up with a black eye, he wouldn't assume the worst.

The conversation had been pointless, only adding to the aggravation simmering under my veins for days. I was perfectly fine admitting to myself that when I hadn't been tossing and turning last night, I'd been

wide awake, thinking about all the things I shouldn't. All the things
I knew better than to let bother me, but it was impossible to ignore
them when they'd all hit me so hard. One after another, nip, nip, nipping away at my resolve.

Aiden. My mom. Susie. Diana.

My technically husband. My mom. My sister—though I still
wanted DNA reports to confirm that connection. My best friend of
my entire life.

Was there anyone in this world I could trust? I could rely on? Only
myself it felt like sometimes. You would figure I'd know better by now.

The sound of weights clinking together in the gym down the hall
had me scowling. *Someone* had already been busy working out by
the time I'd come down the stairs. While most athletes took their bye
week off to vacation or spend time with their families, the big guy
didn't. Hadn't.

I should have known better.

By the time I was done talking myself into pushing thoughts of them
away, Zac had nuked some oatmeal in the microwave and dumped a
cup full of toppings on it, taking the seat opposite mine at the breakfast
nook. A part of a puzzle Aiden was working on decorated the middle of
the table. Zac and I happened to glance at each other at the same time,
and we smiled at one another, his a tired one and mine an aggravated-
but-I'm-trying-not-to-be one.

My tablet sat next to my bowl of cereal; I had been absently flipping
through page after page of a website that sold T-shirt designs from free-
lance artists. I'd sold some of my work on there in the past, and I was
looking to see if any designs gave me ideas to work on today, unless I got
an unexpected last-minute request.

The doorbell ringing once—not long enough to be annoying but
not too short to be ignored—had me getting to my feet. "I got it."

The face on the other side of the peephole had me smiling a little.
Leslie didn't deserve my bitch face when I only saw him a couple
times a year. "Good morning," I greeted as I opened the door.

"Wonderful morning to you, Vanessa." Leslie smiled back. "After
you."

A gentleman. That had me genuinely smiling as I stepped back and let him in, watching as he closed the door.

"How are you?"

My chest gave a dull throb in response. "I'm okay," I answered about as honestly as I could. "And you?"

The expression on his face caught me off guard completely. It was like he was surprised I told him the truth, or maybe he wasn't at all surprised I wasn't fine, and was just acknowledging that I'd been honest with him. "I'm alive. I can't ask for more."

That had me sniffing in near indignation. I could be mopey every once in a while if I wanted. That sounded pathetic even in my own head. Letting out a slow, controlled breath, I nodded at the older man. "Good point." I gestured with my head toward the gym. "Aiden's working out. Would you like something to drink?"

"Do you have any coffee?"

I was the only coffee drinker in the house. "I'll make some right now."

With his hands behind his back, he dipped his chin in thanks. "I appreciate it. I'm going to check up on Aiden."

Leslie peeked into the kitchen and raised his hand, giving Zac a no-tooth smile. "Morning, Zac."

I headed into the kitchen as Leslie went to the gym and scooped out the pre-ground coffee beans into the coffeemaker, hitting the button to start the brew. By the time I made it back to my seat, Zac was scraping the sides of his bowl, looking way more awake than he had half an hour ago. "You feelin' better?" he asked.

"Not really." Was I that obvious? I lifted a shoulder. "What are you doing today?"

"Gonna work out."

I held out my fist for him to bump, and he only slightly shook his head as his fist connected with mine.

"You want to go for a run today?"

To give him credit, he tried to control his facial features so that they didn't resemble a grimace. "*Sure.*"

"Don't sound so excited." I laughed.

Zac grinned immediately. "I'm foolin' ya, Vanny. What time do you wanna go?"

"Is four okay?"

He nodded. "I'll be back by then."

I held up my hand again and he fist-bumped it.

"I'm gonna get dressed so I can get outta here," Zac said, already pushing his chair back.

We agreed to see each other later, and after rinsing off his plate and sticking it in the dishwasher, he disappeared up the stairs. With the intention of finishing looking through the rest of the current posts on the website I still had up on my tablet, I made it through one more page before Leslie appeared.

"Thank you for making this," he said once he was at the coffee-maker, pulling out a cup from the correct cabinet without needing direction.

"Oh, you're welcome." I put my tablet to sleep, figuring I didn't have much time before Aiden appeared. I wasn't in the mood to deal with his crap right then. Just thinking his name had my blood boiling.

A *real wife*.

Fucking asshole.

"I'm sorry for dropping by so early," Leslie chimed in from his spot at the counter, pouring coffee.

That had me snapping out of cursing Aiden in my head. "Don't worry about it. It's okay."

"It isn't okay. I felt terrible after Aiden told me you were going home."

Home. What a word to use for El Paso.

"I didn't mean to take up your time alone. I remember what it was like to be a newlywed," the man who had put into motion Aiden's future said.

Newlyweds. I wanted to puke. "It really is okay. I know how much you mean to him." Or at least, I had a good idea of how much the older man meant to him.

Aiden had two friends he kept in touch with semi-regularly. He saw them in person maybe once a year. Other than them, there was only Leslie. Leslie who had been his coach in high school. Leslie who Aiden had said repeatedly had groomed him and pushed him to succeed. In the twelve years since he'd graduated high school, they still saw each other often enough. Leslie continued to train Aiden in Colorado when the season was over. Then there were the other times that the former coach came by to visit.

If that wasn't its own form of love and respect—at least in Aiden's case— I had no idea what was.

My comment though had him chuckling. "Only because he knows how much he means to me."

As bitter as I felt, I couldn't help but soften a little as Leslie walked around the island with his cup in hand. His eyes strayed to the table, a smile coming over his face. "He's still doing those?" He gestured toward the puzzle.

"All the time. Especially when he's stressed."

Leslie's smile grew even wider, turning wistful. "He used to do them with his grandparents. I can't remember there ever not being a puzzle at their home." He snickered softly. "You know, after his grandmother died, he didn't speak to me for almost a year."

Uh. What? His grandmother?

"I can't tell you how many times I tried calling him, left him voicemails. I even went to several of his games at Wisconsin to see him, but he went out of his way to avoid me. It damn near broke my heart." He took the seat that Zac had just left. His white eyebrows rose as he looked at me from over the top of his cup. "That's between you and me, eh? He's still sensitive about that time period."

Aiden? Sensitive?

"When his grandfather died, he was devastated, but when Constance, his grandmother, passed away . . . I've never seen anyone so distraught. He loved that woman like you couldn't imagine. He doted on her. She'd told me he called her every day after he went away to school," he continued on like this wasn't the greatest secret I'd ever heard.

There was no way I could pull off being casual about what he was saying. Plus, I had a feeling that the second he really looked at my facial expressions, he'd know damn well I had no clue about anything relating to his grandmother and grandfather.

And because I was tired of being lied to so much over the course of the last few days, I went with being honest with this man who had never been anything but kind to me. "I didn't—he's never even mentioned his grandparents to me before. He doesn't like to talk about things," I admitted, messing with the leg of my glasses.

Leslie set his cup on the table and gave me a little shake of his head. "That shouldn't surprise me." Of course it shouldn't. "Between us"—he tipped his forehead forward—"he's the most remarkable man I've ever met, Vanessa. I've told him that before a hundred times, but he doesn't listen. He doesn't believe, and I'm not sure he cares. When I first met him, I couldn't get a single sentence out of him. One sentence, can you imagine that?"

I nodded, because yes, yes I could imagine that.

"If I would have asked him to try out for the football team on any other day than the one I did, he never would have agreed. His grandfather was alive back then, you know; Aiden was already living with them. He had gotten in trouble with the lacrosse coach again the day before for fighting with his teammates, and his grandfather had told him *something*—he's never told me what—that got him to agree to try out. It took me four months to get him to really talk to me, and I was persistent. Even then, the only reason why he did was because his grandfather had a heart attack and I had this feeling he needed someone to talk to." Leslie let out a sigh at whatever memory was bouncing around in his head. "You can't live your life bottling everything up. You need people, even if it's only one or two, to believe in you, and as smart as that boy is, he doesn't understand that."

At some point, I'd planted my elbows on the table and set my chin in my hands, caught up in every detail he was telling me. "Did you know his grandparents well?"

"His grandfather was my best friend. I've known Aiden since he was in diapers." Leslie's mouth twitched. "He was the fattest baby I have ever seen. I remember looking at his eyes and knowing he was sharp. Always so serious, so quiet. But who could blame him, with his parents?"

I had about a million more questions I wanted to ask but didn't know how to.

"He's a good man, Vanessa. A great one. He'll open up to you in time. I'm sure of it," Leslie added. "He used to say he would never marry, but I knew all it was going to take was him finding the right girl to convince him otherwise. Even mountains change over time."

And that had me feeling like a schmuck. Like a giant, fake schmuck. It messed with my head.

I wasn't his real wife. He didn't love me. This was all a charade.

The knot from the night before swelled in my throat again, leaving me unable to speak for a moment while I tried to collect my thoughts. "I know he's a good man," I finally managed to get out with a tremulous smile that felt way too transparent. "And, hopefully, we have a long time ahead of us," I added even more weakly.

The way Leslie's features lit up made my stomach roll.

I was a fluke. A con woman. Imaginary.

I was what I made myself to be.

"Is he almost done?" I forced myself to ask as I snuck my hands under the table and clenched them.

"Almost. He should be—oh, here he is. Were you eavesdropping on us?" Leslie joked.

I pushed my chair back, trying to school my emotions, my face, and my body all to behave and get through these next couple of minutes until I could disappear to my room. Before I could even make it to the island, the big guy was in the kitchen, heading to the sink.

"No." Those brown and caramel irises were on me.

Rinsing off my bowl, I set it in the sink as I faintly listened to Leslie and Aiden discuss his workout. I ignored the way his shirt clung to his sweaty chest, ignored the way he kept glancing at me. Regardless of what Leslie had said, I wasn't in the mood to deal with him, even if he'd loved the hell out of his grandparents.

Somehow, I managed to paste something similar to a grin on my face as I walked right by Aiden, purposely letting my shoulder brush his arm, because I was positive Leslie was watching. "I have a lot of work to do. I'll be upstairs if you need me," I said more to the older man than to the one I was married to.

Only Leslie responded.

Which was fine. It was totally fine, I assured myself as I climbed the stairs. Aiden could be pissed at me all he wanted. I was mad at him.

I had just gotten to the top when my phone started ringing. Closing the door behind me—because anyone who would be calling me right then was not going to be on my list of people I'd want to talk to—I picked up my cell from where I'd left it on the nightstand. MOM flashed across the smooth screen.

To give myself credit, I didn't flip the phone off, curse, or even think about not taking the call. I was going to take the damn call, because I wasn't petty. Because I had nothing to feel bad about.

I just didn't want to talk to her. Now or anytime soon. That was all.

"Hello."

"Hi, baby."

Okay. That had me rolling my eyes. "Hi."

"I've been so worried about you," she started off.

Was that why she'd waited almost two days to call? Because she was so worried? Damn it, I was being a bitch. "I'm fine," I let her know in a dull tone.

"You didn't have to leave like that."

There was only so much a person could handle, and I was at my tipping point. I'd been at my tipping point, and it was all my fault. If I hadn't ignored my instincts and gone to El Paso, this could have been prevented. I'd been the idiot. Then I'd given everyone else the ability to piss me off. "You—"

"I love you both."

"I know you do." Once upon a time, when I was a lot younger and a lot more immature, it had killed me that she loved us equally. I wasn't a borderline psychopath like Susie. I hadn't been able to understand how she didn't take my side each time there was an issue. But now that I was older, I realized there was no way I could ever ask that of her. It was just one of those things. On a bitchy day, I thought broken things couldn't help but love other broken things.

I might not be flawless, and I might have hairline fractures all over the place, but I'd sworn to myself a long, long time ago that I wouldn't be like either of them.

It was a terrible, shitty thought. Mostly because I held my mom and Susie as the prime examples of who and what I didn't want to ever be.

But there was only so much I could take. "I'm not asking you to not have a relationship with her, but *I* don't want one with her. Nothing is ever going to change between us. I might get along okay with Erika and Rose *sometimes*, but that's it."

"Vanessa—"

"*Mom.* Did you hear what she said? She said she wished she'd hit me harder with her car. She tried to spit on me. Then Ricky grabbed my arm. I have bruises. *My knee still hurts every single day from what she did.*" Damn it, my voice cracked at the same time my heart seemed to do the same. Why couldn't she understand? Why? "I'm not trying to argue with you, but there's no way I could have stayed after that."

"You could have walked away," said the woman who had walked away a hundred times in the past. This was the person who couldn't deal with her problems if there wasn't some sort of bottle around.

Damn it. I was so angry with her in that moment, I couldn't find a single word that wouldn't be brutal, that wouldn't hurt her feelings. She said some things that I didn't listen to because I was too focused on myself. I shoved my sleeves up my forearms in frustration. Squeezing my free fists closed, I didn't even bother trying to count to ten. I wanted to break something, but I wouldn't. I fucking wouldn't. I was better than this. "You know what? You're right. I really have to go. I have a lot of work to catch up on. I'll call you later."

And that was the thing with my mom. She didn't know how to fight. Maybe it was a trait I'd picked up from my dad, whoever the guy was. "Okay. I love you."

I'd learned what love was from my little brother, from Diana and her family, and even from my foster parents. It wasn't this distorted, terrible thing that did what was best for itself. It was sentient, it cared, and it did what was best for the greater good. I wasn't going to bother analyzing what my mom viewed as love again; I'd done it enough in the past. In this case, it was just a word I was going to use on someone who needed to hear it. "Uh-huh. Love you too."

I didn't realize I was crying until the tears hit my chin and plummeted to my shirt. Fire burned my nose. Five-six-seven-eight-nine-ten-eleven-twelve-thirteen-and-fourteen-year-old Vanessa all came back to me with the same feeling that had been so strong in those years: hurt. The Vanessa who was fifteen and older had felt a different emotion for so long: anger. Anger at my mom's selfishness. Anger at her for not being able to clean her act up until years after we'd been taken away from her. Anger for being let down for so long, time and time again.

I had needed her a hundred times, and ninety-nine of those times she hadn't been around, or if she had been, she'd been too drunk to be of any use to me. Diana's mom had been more of a mother figure to me than she had been. My foster mother had been more maternal than the woman who had given birth to me. I had practically raised Oscar and myself.

But if it weren't for everything I'd been through, I wouldn't be where I was. I wouldn't be the person I was. I'd become me not because of my mom and sisters, but in spite of them. And most days, I really liked myself. I could be proud of me. That had to be worth something.

I'd barely managed to wipe off my teary face and set down my phone when a familiar bang-bang-bang called a knock rattled my door. If I was capable of snarling, I'm sure the facial expression I made would have been called exactly that.

"Yes?" I called out in a sarcastic tone, resisting the urge to throw myself back onto my bed like a little kid. Not that I'd ever done that, even back then.

Considering "Yes?" wasn't exactly an invitation to come in, I was only slightly surprised when the door opened and the man I didn't exactly want to see in the near future popped his head inside.

"Yes?" I repeated, biting the inside of my cheek to keep from calling him something mean. I was sure my emotions were written all over my face, my eyes had to have some trace of the tears that had just been in them, but I wasn't going to hide it.

Aiden opened the door completely and slipped inside, his eyes sweeping across the room briefly before landing back on me sitting on the edge of my bed. His eyebrows scrunched together as he witnessed what I wasn't trying to hide. His mouth depressed into a frown. One of his hands went up to reach behind his head, and I tried to ignore the bunched biceps that seemed to triple in size at the action. His Adam's apple bobbed as his gaze swept over my face once more. "We need to talk."

Once upon a time, all I'd wanted was for him to talk to me. Now, that wasn't the case. "You should really be spending time with Leslie while he's here."

Those big biceps flexed. "He agreed I should come up here and talk to you."

I narrowed my eyes, ignoring the tightness in them. "You told him we got into a fight?"

"No. He could tell something was off without me saying anything." Those massive hands dropped to his sides. "I wanted to talk to you last night."

But I'd ignored his knock. I made a vague noise. What was the point in lying when I'm pretty sure he was well aware of the fact I'd been awake then?

Aiden fisted his hands for a moment before bringing them back to cross his arms over his chest. "I'm sorry for what I said yesterday."

I wasn't remotely impressed by his directness and I was sure my face said that.

In true Aiden fashion, he didn't let my expression deter him from what he'd come to say. "I don't like things hanging over my head, and if you and I are going to have a problem, we're going to talk about it. I meant what I told you in your apartment. I do like you as much as I like anyone. I wouldn't have come to you for all of this if I didn't. You always treated me as more than just the person who paid your check and I see that now. I've seen it for a while, Van. I'm not very good at this crap." Did he look uncomfortable or was I imagining it? I wondered. "I'm selfish and self-centered. I know that. You know that. I bail on people all the time." He had a point there. He did. I'd witnessed it firsthand. "I get it, you're not that kind of person. You don't go back on your word. I . . . I didn't think you'd care if I didn't go," he said carefully.

I opened my mouth to tell him that no one liked being bailed on, but he trudged on before I could.

"But I understand, Van. Just because people don't complain to my face when I do it, doesn't mean it doesn't piss them off, all right? I didn't mean to be an asshole downstairs. I only wanted to make sure you made it back fine and you weren't going to kill me in my sleep for flaking out on you. Then I got mad."

I *had* thought about killing him, but it surprised me just a little bit that he assumed I would think that.

Before I could linger on that thought too long, Aiden leveled that dark gaze on me. "If you had done that to me . . ." He looked a little uncomfortable at whatever he was thinking and let out a shaky exhale. "I wouldn't have handled it as well as you did."

That was a freaking fact.

"I wasn't nagging," I stated, then thought about it and, in my head, amended the statement to add "mostly" to it.

He tilted his head to the side like he wanted to argue otherwise. "You were nagging, but you had a right to. I have a lot going on right now."

My first thought was: The end has come. He's opening up to me.

My second thought was: it's so obvious he's stressed as hell.

I hadn't caught on to his body language, or the tightness he carried both in his shoulders and his voice as he spoke, but now up close, it was obvious. He'd been through a lot in just the first month of the regular season. He'd already sprained his ankle. Zac had gotten kicked off the team. On top of that, he was worried about his visa and his future with not just the Three Hundreds but in the NFO, period. His injury would be a factor in his career for the rest of his life. Anytime he made a mistake, people would wonder if he hadn't come back as strongly as he'd been before, even if it had nothing to do with his Achilles tendon.

The guy looked ready to snap, and it was barely the end of September. I wanted to ask him if he'd heard anything back from the immigration lawyer, or if our marriage license had shown up, or if Trevor had quit being a pain in the ass and started to look for another team or a better deal or whatever it was that he wanted out of the next stage of his career but . . .

I didn't. Today would be a bad day for me to ask and for him not to answer. I was too raw and tired and disillusioned.

And it was in that moment, with that thought, the slightest bit of remorse flickered through my brain, because I realized that maybe I had been itching for a fight. Maybe. And maybe this really had been the worst time—for him—to give him so much shit when he already had so much on his shoulders.

Plus, I wasn't in the best state of mind either.

But apologizing wasn't my forte and doing so wasn't easy, but a good person recognized when they were wrong and accepted their faults. "I'm sorry for exploding on you. I was angry that you didn't go, but I know why you bailed. I just don't like it when people say they'll do something and then don't, but I've been like that for a long time. It has nothing to do with you." I took those words straight from the Bank of Aiden. On top of that, there was everything else that had built up over the course of the weekend that wasn't his fault. Not that I would bring it up.

His response was a nod of acceptance, of acknowledgment that we'd both handled the situation badly.

"So, I'm sorry too. I know how important your career is to you." With a sigh, I held out my hand to him. "Friends?"

Aiden glanced from my outstretched palm to my face before taking my hand in his. "Friends." It was midshake that he looked down at his giant hand swallowing mine, and the most disgusted expression came over that perfectly stoic face. *"What the hell happened to your wrist?"*

Yeah, I didn't even bother trying to pull my sleeve down and play stupid. Like an idiot, I'd forgotten that I'd tugged them up. I slipped out of his hold and let the familiar flow of anger creep down the back of my neck once more at the memory of my sister's idiot husband.

Specifically, him grabbing my arm and yanking me away after I'd yelled at Susie, because she'd practically said she wished she'd have killed me. I'd told her she was out of her goddamn mind. But I hadn't asked her for the millionth time why she hated me so much. What could I have possibly done before I was even four years old to make me her archnemesis? I was mad at myself for not preventing the entire situation, mostly. Then again, her husband had dropped his grip of steel the minute I'd charged my leg upward to try and knee him in the balls, ramming him straight in the inner thigh instead.

"It's nothing."

Those dark brown eyes blazed up to meet mine, and I swore on my life, the fury in those irises was enough for me to stop breathing. "Vanessa," Aiden growled, literally growled, as he softly tugged the sleeve farther up my forearm to display the five-inch bruise just above my wrist.

I watched as he gazed at the stupid, stupid discoloration. "I got into an argument with my sister." Was there a point in not telling him who it was with? I only had to glance at the hard drawn line of his mouth to know he wasn't going to let this go. "Her husband was there and he got a little handsy, so I tried to knee him in the balls."

His nostrils flared and a muscle in his cheek visibly twitched. "Your sister's husband?"

"Yes."

His cheek spasmed again. "Why?"

"It was stupid. It doesn't matter."

Was that a grumble caught in his throat? "Of course it matters." His voice was deceptively soft. "Why did he do it?"

I knew that look on his face; it was his stubborn one. The one that said it was pointless to argue with him. While I wasn't crazy about spreading Susie's business around, much less share how rocky my relationship with my third oldest sister was, Susie and I could be on *Jerry Springer*. She made her choices years ago, and it was no one else's fault but her own what she had gotten out of them. We'd grown up under the same circumstances, neither one of us having something the other didn't. I couldn't feel any pity for her.

Rubbing my hands over my pant legs, I blew out a breath. "She didn't like the way I was looking at her and we got into a fight," I explained, leaving out a couple of details and colorful words, even though it wasn't much of an explanation. "Her husband overheard us arguing"—her calling me a bitch and me telling her she was an immature twat— "and he grabbed me."

You snobby bitch. What gives you the right to think you're better than me? She'd had the freaking nerve to yell in my face.

I'd responded in the only way all that pent-up anger in me was capable of. *Because I'm not a fucking asshole who loves to hurt everything in her life. That's why I think I'm better than you.*

Aiden's calloused fingertips suddenly brushed lightly over the bruising, lifting my wrist in the cradle of those hands that were an instrumental part of his multimillion dollar body. The tic in his cheek had gotten worse as I tipped my head farther back to look at that hard line his jaw made when he was gritting his teeth. His breath rattled out, and the thumb and index finger of one of his hands circled the middle of my forearm as he said, "Did he apologize?"

"No." I made myself clear my throat, uncomfortable, uncomfortable, uncomfortable.

I saw him gulp. The air filled with an unfamiliar tension. His swallow sounded loud in my ears. "Did he hit you?"

And just like that, I realized—I remembered why he might be so upset over the situation. I flashed back to that memory I'd shoved to the back of my brain, because I'd been worried about getting fired. How the hell could I have forgotten about it?

ALMOST IMMEDIATELY AFTER I first began working for the man known as the Wall of Winnipeg, I'd gotten dragged to Montreal for a charity event that he'd donated to. Afterward, Leslie—who had since moved from Winnipeg—invited me along to his house with Aiden for dinner with his family. Aiden had seemed distracted that day, but I thought maybe I'd been imagining it. I hadn't known him well then, hadn't learned the little nuances in his features or in his tone that gave away an idea of how he was feeling or what he was thinking.

We'd been having dinner with Leslie, his wife, two of his sons, and one of his grandkids, who happened to be the cutest little boy. The four-year-old boy had been climbing from lap to lap throughout our visit, and at some point, to my shock, ended up on the big guy's lap. The boy had reached up and started touching Aiden's face, tenderly and casually. His hand strayed to that heavy, thick, scar that stretched along his hairline. The boy asked him, "What happened?" in that blunt, cute way little kids were capable of.

The only reason I heard his answer was because I'd been sitting next to him. Otherwise, I was sure I would have missed the whispered, casual reply.

"I made my dad very mad."

The silence after his answer had been stifling, suffocating, and ir-repressible all in one. The little boy had blinked at him like he couldn't comprehend the answer he'd been given; why would he? It was obvious how much he was loved. Aiden's eyes slid over to my direction and I knew he realized I'd overheard him, because I couldn't look away fast enough and play dumb.

Aiden didn't say a word after that; he didn't remind me of the non-disclosure agreement that I'd been forced to sign my first day on the job, or threaten my life or future if I told anyone. So I sure as hell didn't bring it up either. Ever.

BLINKING AWAY THE memory and the sympathy that filled my chest, because Aiden was so touchy over an incident like this, I dropped my eyes to his beard. I didn't want him to see me, because I was sure he would know I was thinking about something he wouldn't want me to. "No, he didn't hit me. He's still alive." I cracked a little smile.

He didn't return it. "Did you tell anyone?"

I sighed and tried to pull my arm back. He didn't let go. "I didn't need to. Everyone heard."

"And they did nothing?" Was his cheek twitching?

I shrugged my shoulder. "I don't have that kind of relationship with my family."

That sounded about as fucked up as it was.

The betrayal that had pierced through me in that moment stabbed me again, fresh and painful. Tears pooled in my eyes as I relived the incident when I was eighteen that ruined what was left of the fractured bond I'd shared with them. Even my knee ached a little at the memory.

Those large fingers eased their grip on my hand just slightly, and in a smaller voice than he usually used, he asked, "She's your real sister?"

Real sister. I'd mentioned my foster parents, hadn't I? "Yes." I messed with my glasses. "We've never gotten along. She's about as far from what a sister should be as you can get."

"How many do you have?"

"Three."

"You're the youngest?"

"Youngest girl."

"They were there?"

"Yes."

"And none of them did anything? Said anything?"

Why did I feel so ashamed? My eyes started to sting, and that made me force my gaze upward. I wasn't going to feel bad. I wasn't going to hide. "No."

His gaze switched from one of my eyes to the other. "They live in El Paso?"

"I think."

His nostrils flared and he gently let go of my hand, my skin immediately missing the warm touch of his fingers. "Okay." He took a step back and turned his head over his shoulder. "Zac!"

What the hell? "What are you doing?"

He didn't look at me before yelling Zac's name again. "I need to borrow his car. If I fly, there will be proof I was there."

Holy shit.

"You—" I choked. "You—" I coughed that time, floundering. "What the hell are you planning on doing?"

"You kneeing him isn't doing it for me." Aiden didn't even grace me with a glance as he made his way toward my door. "*Zac!*"

Yeah, those tears pooling in my eyes decided *screw it*. They went for it. One, two, and three. "You've lost your mind, big guy."

"No. That asshole lost his mind. Your family lost their mind. I know what I'm doing."

This psycho was going to try and beat someone up, wasn't he? Holy shit. "You'd do that for me?"

Crap, my expectations were low if that made me teary.

The big guy stopped in front of the door and spun on his heel with a lot more grace than a man that large should be capable of. He blinked, piercing me with a glare. "We're partners. We're a team. You said it."

I nodded dumbly, earning me that "you're an idiot" look from him. His eyebrows went up just a little, his head just slightly forward enough to be confrontational. "If someone messes with you, they're going to mess with me, Van. I don't want to hurt your feelings. I might not be good with this friend crap, but I'm not about to let somebody get away with hurting you. Ever. Do you understand me?"

My heart. My poor, weak pathetic heart.

I swallowed and tried to nod away the clump of emotions plugging up every vein in my body. As much as I would love Aiden to go kick Susie's husband's ass . . . "The guard would see you driving his car, and there's a camera at the gate."

Aiden tilted his head and pinned me with another look that might have been a surprised one. "You've put some thought into this," he said slowly.

"Of course I have." He didn't need to know I'd been plotting *his* murder then. "That's why I know we have to wait."

"We?"

"Yeah. I'm not going to let you go beat him up alone. I'd like to get a couple stomps in too." I raised my eyebrows and smiled faintly, letting the tension slide off my shoulders. "I'm joking." Sort of. "It doesn't matter. I'll probably never see him again, and even if I do, their lives suck. Mine doesn't. That's enough vengeance for me. Trust me."

Well, at least most of the time it was enough.

"Vanessa . . ." He trailed off with a frown.

The next three sentences we shared between the two of us were going to be the last thing I thought about when I went to bed later that night.

"You've been with me for two years, but I figure I'm barely beginning to understand," the big guy claimed, his expression solemn.

"Understand what?"

"I should probably be scared of you."

SEVENTEEN

My eyes were crossing from staring at stock images for so long when my phone beeped with a text message. I yawned and picked up my smartphone.

Text Message
Miranda P.

Curious—more than curious because this was the first time I'd ever gotten a text from him—I pulled up the message and read it. Then I read it again. And again. And then I just stared blankly at my desktop computer screen.

They had found out.

Before I could panic, I made myself stretch my fingers wide and take a calming breath. *You already knew this was bound to happen.* At least that's what I told myself.

The more I thought about it, the more I should have been appreciative that the people at the chapel in Las Vegas hadn't recognized him. Or that people on the street had been oblivious and hadn't seen us going in and out of there. Or that the receptionist at the acupuncturist hadn't snapped a picture on her phone and posted it online.

Because I might not understand all people, much less most of them, but I understood nosey folks, and nosey folks would do something like that without a second thought. Yet, I reminded myself that there was nothing to be embarrassed about.

It would be fine. So one gossip site posted about us getting married. Whoop-de-do. There were probably a thousand sites just like it.

I briefly thought about Diana hearing about it, but I'd deal with that later. There was no use in getting scared now. She was the only one whose reaction I cared about. My mom's and sisters' opinions and feelings weren't exactly registering at the top of my list now . . . or ever. I made myself shove them to the back of my thoughts. I was tired of being mad and upset; it affected my work. Plus, they'd made me sad and mad enough times in my life. I wasn't going to let them ruin another day.

Picking my phone up again, I quickly texted Aiden back, swallowing my nausea at the same time.

Me: Who told you?

Not even two minutes passed before my phone dinged with a response.

Miranda: Trevor's blowing up my phone.

Eww. Trevor.

Me: We knew it was going to happen eventually, right?
Good luck with Trev. I'm glad he doesn't have my number.

And I was even gladder there wasn't a home phone; otherwise, I'm positive he would have been blowing it up too.

I managed to get back to looking at images on the screen for a few more minutes—a bit more distracted than usual—when the phone beeped again.

It was Aiden/Miranda. I should really change his contact name.

Miranda: Good luck? I'm not answering his calls.

What?

Me: That psycho will come visit if you don't.

Was that me being selfish? Yes. Did I care? No.

Aiden: I know.

Uh.

Me: You're always at practice . . .
Aiden: Have fun.

This asshole! I almost laughed, but before I could, he sent me another message.

Aiden: I'll get back to him in a couple days. Don't worry.

Snorting, I texted back.

Me: I'm not worried. If he drops by, I'll set him up in your room. 😊
Aiden: You genuinely scare me.
Me: You don't know how many times you barely made it through the day alive, for the record.

He didn't text me back after that.

I WAS IN the middle of eating lunch the next day when my phone beeped. So far, I hadn't gotten any threatening calls or texts from Diana, but I was still a little scared to look at the screen. I actually hadn't heard from her at all since I'd left her house. That wasn't unusual, but it still left me feeling a little anxious and a little mad. Luckily, it was Aiden's name that popped on to the display. I had finally gotten around to changing his contact information.

Aiden: Are you free this Sunday?

I was never free on any day, technically, but his question made me pause.

Me: It depends. Why?

Aiden: Come to my game.

Uh, was I imagining this? Was he really inviting me to one of his games for the first time in the history of the universe?

Me: I've gone to a few of your games.

Aiden: You've met me after a game five times.

He remembered that?

Me: I met you after a game five times, but I've gone to more than those, thank you.

Aiden: When?

Me: Last season I went to five. The season before that, I went to three. I haven't gone to any this year though.

Obviously.

Aiden: Why

Me: Because the guy who usually gets me tickets doesn't play for your team anymore . . .

Aiden: Zac got you tickets?

Me: Who else would?

Aiden: I could have.

The same person who couldn't tell me "good morning?" Riiiight. My phone beeped again.

Aiden: I could get you tickets now. All you have to do is tell me.

There was something about the fact he said "tell me" and not "ask" that made me grin.

Me: I didn't know that. You usually only get tickets for
Leslie and that's it. Zac always just gave them to me.
Aiden: Come this Sunday.
Me: I sort of had plans.

I lied. My plans were to get a little work done in the morning and
watch a couple of football games to make sure my fantasy football
quarterback and favorite wide receiver got the job done.

Aiden: Do you want Trevor or Rob to come visit?
Me: Is that a threat?
Aiden: It's a fact. I talked to both of them. They brought
up how you haven't been to my games.

I decided right then that I didn't want to know what they had talked
about. I didn't need to know either. If Aiden was threatening me with
visits from one or both of them, and they were aware that we'd signed
paperwork . . . that was enough for me. I could take one for Team
Graves if I had to, especially if it didn't involve those two jackasses.

Me: Fine. Get me two tickets, please.
Aiden: In the family box?

Hello no.

Me: In the bleachers, if you can, big guy. 😊

"I CAN'T BELIEVE I let you talk me into this," Zac whispered as we got
out of line at the concession stand located by the club level.

Honestly, I couldn't believe I had either. When I'd thought about
whom I could ask to go with me, I knew my options were limited.
There was Diana, who I hadn't talked to, was still frustrated with,
and didn't want to lie to again, especially since my marriage to Aiden
had been reported. There were a couple of people I'd met through

her who I hung out with every once in a while. Then there was Zac. I hadn't exactly had a whole bunch of time to make friends since moving to Dallas. So I'd gone out on a limb and asked Zac if he'd like to go.

What I hadn't been surprised about was his reluctance.

But I usually got what I wanted as long as I wanted it bad enough, and this was no different.

That didn't mean I had to be smug about it. Patting his arm, I steered him in the direction of the section our seats were in. He'd never been in the stadium as anything but a player before, and he'd been eyeing everything like it was new. There might have also been half a sneer on his face, but I was going to pretend to ignore it.

"Are you sure you're okay being here?"

"*Yes*," he insisted.

I wasn't sure if I entirely believed him, but he'd said the same thing to me all eight times I'd asked. Still, I felt a little guilty to be putting him through a game when he'd been released a little over a month ago. He'd come back with, "I guess I'm gonna watch a game at home anyway."

The more I thought about it, the guiltier I felt. He could have said no to coming, but he hadn't. "We can go have Mexican food afterward, how about that?" I nudged him.

His only answer was a grumble and something that resembled a nod.

Our seats were excellent. So excellent that I wasn't sure who the hell Aiden had to bribe to get them just days before the game. We were right at the fifty-yard line, third row. Surrounding the seats were a river of jerseys and Three Hundreds trademarked gear, and I could sense Zac's tension as we took our spots.

Setting our drinks down, the big Texan leaned into me. "Are you gonna tell me why we're sittin' here instead of in the box?"

I slid him a look. "I don't like the people there."

That had the nosey ass interested. "Who?" He even whispered the question, his eyes alight with interest. "Tell me."

Good grief. I couldn't help how much of an asshole I was about to sound like. "All of them."

Zac burst out laughing. "Why?"

I had to take a sip out of the beer I'd bought before I could muster enough mental strength to recollect that day. "Remember that time you got me tickets for there? The first time you invited me?" He didn't remember, but it didn't matter. "Well, I went . . . it was like *Mean Girls* with women who have been out of high school a long time. They were talking about each other nonstop: who had gained weight, who was using a purse from last season, who was cheating on who . . . It gave me a headache. Now I'm one of them."

"You're one of you, Van."

That made me feel nice. I might have preened as I took another sip of my beer and then touched my shoulder against his. "I like you, you know that, don't you?"

He snorted and grabbed his own beer bottle, taking a swig out of it. We settled in and watched the players come onto the field, the fans in the stadium getting to their feet and screaming all 80,000 of their lungs out. The Three Hundreds were playing one of their top competitors, the Houston White Oaks, and it was *packed*. I was planning on sending my foster dad a picture message later.

Unzipping my jacket so I could have free range of my arms and hands later in the game, I pulled my arms out of my sleeves and adjusted the bottom hem of the jersey I'd put on.

Beer shot out of Zac's mouth and right into his lap. "Van. *Van.* Why would you do that?" he cried, eyeing me like I'd lost my mind even as his hands wiped at his face.

I sat back in my seat and grinned. "Because you're my friend, and if anyone's watching, I don't want them to forget about you."

HOURS LATER, ZAC and I had gone to eat Mexican food—and squeezed in a margarita each—after the game, and were back at the house when Aiden finally showed up. Those huge legs dragged across the floor as he dropped his bag, looking every bit as tired and thoughtful as he usually did after a win. I didn't know why he got so thoughtful after a win instead of rejoicing, but I kind of liked it. When the team didn't win a game, he usually just looked revved up and downright pissed, in that quiet, brooding way of his. Like clockwork, he'd eat something then disappear into his room.

Stirring the boiling pot of quinoa noodles, I flashed him a grin over my shoulder. "Good game, big guy." He'd gotten three sacks, which wasn't a bad day at all.

"Thanks." He stopped in place. "What the hell are you wearing?"

With the spoon still in the pot, I shrugged. "Clothes."

"You know what I mean."

"A jersey?" I offered with a one-shoulder shrug.

Out of the corner of my eye, I saw him moving around. I felt him inspecting me. His voice was low and careful as he said, "You're wearing Zac's jersey."

"Yep."

"You . . . went to the game wearing Zac's jersey?" Still sober, still tiptoeing.

"Uh-huh." I glanced at him finally standing directly behind me, his back to the kitchen island. His arms crossed over that wide expanse of a chest. "I don't want anyone forgetting he's a quarterback," I explained before turning back around.

He moved then. He didn't say anything for so long, I thought maybe he'd walked out of the kitchen, but I found him sitting at the breakfast nook table with his elbows on his thighs. I realized his cheek was twitching, but he didn't necessarily look mad. He just looked . . . contemplative all over again.

"Are you okay?"

Only his eyes swept across the room before they landed on me and he tipped his chin down. "Fine."

"All right." The timer for the noodles went off, and I turned to the stove. Straining the noodles and placing them in a big bowl, I dumped the pecan seasoning and the vegetables I'd prepared earlier over them, giving them a stir. Setting the pot and the cutting board into the sink with one hand, I carried the bowl over to where Aiden was sitting and set it front of him. "I figured you'd be hungry. Just wash the dishes or put them in the washer, okay?"

That dark gaze tipped up to meet mine, surprise written all over those serious features.

I didn't know where the hell it came from, but I winked at him. "Thank you for the tickets, by the way. They were great."

"Thank you for the food," he said as he stood up, literally a foot and a half away from me.

The last time we'd been so close together had been when we were in Vegas and I gave him that peck on his mouth in the chapel, but I'd been so distracted at that point with everything going on, I hadn't been able to appreciate just how freaking huge he was up close. Because big, he was. Tall and broad at the shoulders and chest, and that trim waist only made everything else about him more imposing. He was radiating this insane amount of heat and the slight scent of coconut oil he put on his face every time he showered.

Good lord he was attractive.

I swallowed the saliva in my mouth and smiled up at him as if his presence wasn't a big deal. Like this lack of distance between us was an everyday occurrence. "Okay, well, enjoy your food. I'm going upstairs to watch some TV."

He thanked me again as he went to the cupboard for a glass.

What the hell had been up with that? I wondered once I was in my room, sitting on the edge of the bed.

What in the living hell had been up with me?

EIGHTEEN

I was in my room when the doorbell started going off like crazy. In all the time I'd spent at my new house, no one ever came over. Heck, even when I didn't live there, no one ever dropped by unexpectedly. The community's gate kept solicitors out, and his neighbors weren't exactly outgoing. If someone wanted a cup of sugar, they took themselves to the grocery store and bought it. I wasn't really sure who to expect, but when I checked the peephole, I was completely caught off guard.

Completely, totally, 200 percent caught off guard. *Damn it*.

It was Trevor. The guys' manager. The king of all asswipes.

"Who is it?" Zac yelled from somewhere upstairs, more than likely his bedroom. He had just gotten home about an hour ago, and we were planning on going for a run soon.

"It's Trevor!" I whisper-hissed, totally aware that he could hear me. The front door was sturdy but it wasn't soundproof.

There was a sound. A curse. Then Zac: "I'm not here!"

Double damn it. "Fine! You owe me!"

"Sure!" the traitor bellowed before his door slammed closed.

Grinding my teeth, I said a prayer under my breath and undid the lock.

"Hi . . . Trevor." I kind of sniffed with a frown, not even bothering to make myself smile and act as if I was happy to see him. The fact was, I wasn't. The wonderful fact was, I didn't have to pretend to be.

The emperor of jackasses didn't even waste the effort it would have taken to pretend to be civil. His expression went from exasperated to blank to shocked and finally into a scowl in the blink of an eye, and the scowl kept pulling down at his lips with each second that passed. "Where's Zac?" he practically spat.

What would happen if I closed the door on his face?

I knew Trevor had found out that we'd gotten married, and I was aware they'd "talked about it," whatever that meant. But I had no idea what had been said. No idea what Trevor knew or didn't know. And I suddenly wanted to cuss at myself for opening the door before finding out what I was supposed to say.

But if anyone could smell weakness in the air, it was this asshole. I couldn't falter. I couldn't bend. So I blinked at him, cool and distant. "Oh, hey. I'm doing great and you?"

The lines bracketing his mouth deepened, making his dark hairline pull forward. I wasn't imagining it when his eyelid twitched. "Don't get me started on you. Where's Zac?"

"Please, don't scare me." That time, I couldn't help but smirk at him, getting too much pleasure from the disdainful expression on his face. "Zac isn't here."

Trevor stared at me with those condescending eyes of his, that twitchy eyelid getting worse. "I know he's here."

"He's not."

"You were just yelling at him!" His shoulders hunched and everything. "I heard you."

I leveled an even glare at him and his three-piece suit in this weather. "First off, don't yell in my face. Secondly, you're imagining things because I'm home alone."

He didn't need to say it. I could tell word for word what he was thinking and that went along the lines of "I hate you."

I didn't like him either. I couldn't say I blamed him. I'd be thinking the same thing too, because I know he'd heard me.

"You're really going to tell me he isn't here?" he asked, cocking his head a half-inch and looking at me through narrowed eyes.

I nodded, busting out my best acting skills to smile brightly at him, even though I was aware there was nothing to brag about.

He simply stared at me.

And I smiled even wider. "I really need to get back to work. You should give him a call. I don't know when he'll be back."

That must have been enough to snap him out of whatever trance he was in because he shook his head. "That's why I'm here. He isn't answering my calls. He isn't answering anyone's calls or any fucking emails. He's turned into Aiden—"

That immediately made my ears go hot. "Hey."

"It's completely unacceptable."

I sucked in a breath and grinded my teeth, raising my hand up to stop him. "Stop it." Yeah, I went for it. What was he going to do? Fire me? "Calm down. Chill out. Don't yell in my face because I will slam the door shut in yours. I don't know why neither one of them returns your calls or your emails, so maybe think about that, huh? They'll call you back when they want to call you back, but I wouldn't call you back either if I was just going to get bitched at. And don't talk shit about your clients in front of me. I don't like it and it's unprofessional."

His face had progressively gotten redder with each word that came out of my mouth. A heavy vein in his neck had begun standing out at some point. "Do you understand how this works?" he asked carefully, crisply.

If he thought I was going to back down, he had another thing coming. Months ago, I would have kept my mouth shut and dealt with the fact he was technically my superior. He wasn't anymore though. "You work for them, right?" I asked in a smart-ass tone.

"You don't know anything," he hissed.

What was the point in wasting my breath?

Was he shaking? "I don't know what you did to get Aiden to marry you, but we should hash this out now," Trevor kept going.

"You think I did something to marry him?" I scoffed, slightly panicking. Trevor had seen us together when I worked for Aiden; he had to have witnessed the lack of fireworks between us.

The jerk nodded in that way that said how much of an idiot he genuinely thought I was. "Are you pregnant?"

The "no" was so sharp and ready on my tongue that I almost didn't catch it. It just about slipped from my lips from how pissed off I was at his ridiculous fucking assumption. What did he think I was?

Biting down hard on my molars, I flashed him a crazy-person smile. "Does it matter?"

"Yes, it matters!" he barked, pointing at me as his ears turned red. I'd swear on my life there should have been steam coming out of them to perfect the moment. "He told me you two don't have a prenup." He literally gasped in outrage. "That was the second thing I told him he needed to have when I signed him. Wear a condom and sign a prenup—"

I raised an eyebrow at him, just letting him vent by that point.

"—and of all the women in the world—*of all the women in the world*—he marries you. In Vegas. In secret, and he doesn't tell me. I'm trying to do what's best for him."

There's really only so much you can take from someone who's speaking so fast, whose voice turns so shrill it reminds you of a chalkboard. "Then do what's best for him. I'm not going anywhere, and you don't need to understand what there is between us. You aren't the only one who wants him to do well. So how about you worry about the things that really matter, like where he's going to play next year, if you really want to stress about something your little peanut brain can't understand."

Trevor stared at me for a second, his throat expanding, nostrils flaring. "*Peanut brain?*"

"I'm done talking to you. I'll definitely make sure to tell both of them you were here. Bye." Just like that, I calmly shut the heavy door in the middle of him speaking. I hadn't even slammed it. How was that for being a badass?

It took a second for me to realize just how draining that conversation had been. Sheesh. I honestly felt a little sick as I climbed the stairs back to my room.

I'd really never done anything to him. Not a single freaking thing besides be a smart-ass when he deserved it. Good grief.

Just as I was walking back to my bedroom, Zac's door swung open and his face peeked at me from the crack, all big eyes, nose, and mouth. "I'm sorry."

I waved him off. "You owe me. Get dressed so we can go on a run."

He wrinkled his nose. "You want to go out to eat instead?"

"No." I smiled at him brightly. "Get dressed and let's go. You need to get out of the house, darlin'."

"Van," he nearly whined as I disappeared into my room and closed the door behind me.

Before doing anything else, I picked up my phone and sent Aiden a quick message.

Me: The Angel of Shit paid a visit. Just warning you.

I'd taken off my clothes when my phone beeped with a message.

Aiden: Trevor?

Me: Yes ☹ If he shows up again, you might have to bail me out of jail was the last thing we messaged each other before I left.

THE FOLLOWING AFTERNOON, I heard the footsteps bounding up the steps before Zac burst into my room, his socks skidding across the floor. "Trevor's here," he hissed with raised, expectant eyebrows.

"Did you let him in?"

He shot me a look. "No, I don't want to see him. I heard someone park and checked the window. I told Aiden he was here before I came up."

"Huh." Thank God for small miracles. It was a Tuesday, which meant Aiden had the day off, since he'd just played a game in San Francisco. I narrowed my eyes at him and he squinted his right back before I raised a shoulder and cocked my head to the side. "So are we eavesdropping or what?"

"Duh." The man who hadn't smiled enough in recent days finally graced me with one. During our seven-mile jog yesterday, he'd frowned and pouted throughout the entire thing, probably cussing me out in his head. So I was glad we were back to being on speaking terms.

The sound of the front door opening and closing had me inching toward the doorway of my room. I'd stayed up the night before worrying about whether Trevor would dare come up the stairs to find that, while I was technically married to Aiden, we weren't exactly married-married. Obviously, it was a big flaw in our charade. It had only been the knowledge that Leslie was a gentleman and would never snoop or wander around upstairs that had worked in our favor. Otherwise, that would have been an awkward explanation.

Then I realized how dumb of a worry Trevor coming to the second floor was. Of course he wouldn't. Aiden wouldn't let him get anywhere near the stairs to begin with.

That didn't mean I wasn't curious as hell about what they were going to talk about.

And that was the excuse I was sticking to as Zac and I crept out of my room, and then crawled toward the top landing of the stairs, plopping on our butts, one ear aimed toward the stairs. I'd bet my savings account that Aiden wouldn't invite Trevor into his sanctuary—the kitchen and nook. I wasn't at all disappointed when their voices ended up in the living room, where I could hear their conversation almost clearly. I didn't bother reliving the last time I'd eavesdropped from this exact spot.

"What the hell, Aid? I've tried calling you a dozen times," Trevor's slightly higher tone started.

What did our household smart-ass respond with? "I know. I have caller ID."

Oh hell, it almost made me crack up when he talked to other people like that. Okay, really, it was me just getting a kick out of him talking to Trevor that way. I really didn't like that guy.

Silence. Then Aiden's low voice. "What are you doing here?"

"I came to see you and Zac since neither one of you will get back to me."

"We talked a week ago. What else is there for us to talk about?"

"Telling me 'Yes, I got married' and 'I'll make sure she goes to games,' then hanging up on me isn't considered us talking, Aiden. Jesus Christ. How could you not tell me beforehand?"

"It isn't your business."

"Everything about you is my business. You married your fucking assistant, man. I found out about it when the team's PR called me, asking me about a marriage certificate." Trevor was shouting.

"I married someone who I've known for two years and who no longer works for me. She's over age and so am I. I didn't get caught with drugs. I didn't get arrested at a strip club. I didn't get into a fight. Don't treat me like a child, Trevor. *I don't like it.*"

Zac and I shot each other impressed looks.

"Then don't act like a child. I told you. *I fucking told you from the beginning* you need to think with your head and not your dick, and you marry Vanessa during the season *without a goddamn prenup.* What the hell were you thinking? Is she pregnant?"

"You really believe I was thinking with my dick?" Aiden's voice was cool and crisp, remote and solitary.

Creepy. It was really creepy as hell.

"You weren't thinking with your head," was the stupid thing that came out of Trevor's mouth, giving me the urge to stick my tongue out at him.

"Don't presume you know anything, because you don't. You don't know anything about me, or Vanessa. And if she is pregnant, don't make that fucking face unless you're ready for the consequences."

Uh . . . he'd said the F-word, hadn't he? I hadn't been imagining it?

"She's my wife, and all she's ever done was watch out for me. Don't go there, Trevor. You don't want to go there, understand me?"

I was so freaking making him dinner. Maybe even lunch too.

"I didn't mean it in that way," the manager stuttered.

Aiden might have scoffed but the sound was too low for me to be sure.

His manager made a noise that sounded like a choke or a cough. "I didn't mean anything by it, man. Calm down. You dropped this bomb on me all of a sudden and it isn't a walk in the park trying to sort it out. Rob and I talked about it, and it would've been nice if we could have built up a story around it—"

"You really think I would have wanted to broadcast my marriage?"

"It would have been a good idea. You should have—"

"*I* don't need to do anything. You need to keep your mouth shut the next time you talk about her or us, and focus on doing your job instead. What the hell do you think I'm paying you for?"

"Nobody else would talk to me the way you do," was the brilliance Trevor came back with, sounding just as indignant as I'm sure he was feeling.

"Nobody else makes you as much money as I do. Did you forget that? It isn't anybody's business what I do when I'm off the field as long as it isn't negative. Deal with it."

"Fine," Trevor accepted with resignation and maybe some anger staining his voice. "Where's Zac?"

I eyed Zac and stuck my tongue out at him when his face took on an alarmed expression at Trevor's question.

"He went to visit his family," Aiden lied effortlessly, which surprised me, because I didn't think I'd ever heard him lie. He usually just resorted to hurting someone's feelings by speaking the truth instead of forming a fib.

"What is with you two—ugh. Okay. Forget it. Let him know I've left him about ten voicemails. He needs to call me back."

The big guy didn't make a verbal response of acceptance.

After that, I poked Zac in the ribs and hooked my thumb to point to my room. I crawled back then got to my feet. I took a seat at my computer table, going back to finish the last project I wanted to work on for the day. It didn't take long for the sound of the front door opening and closing to reach my room.

But I couldn't seem to shake off the idea bouncing around in my head. It wasn't like I was expecting Aiden to talk badly about me . . .

But, I was more than a little relieved he had stood up to Trevor in my honor. Finally. Maybe more than a *little* relieved, if I really wanted to let myself think about it.

When I went downstairs an hour later, I found Aiden sitting in the living room hunched over the big ottoman in front of the couch. Zac had let me know he was going to the grocery store, so I knew we were home alone. I made enough quinoa salad for four Aiden-sized meals and put three of the servings into containers for later. Serving myself a healthy portion, I made my way into the living room with my bowl.

He was in the same place he'd been when I started cooking. Two big feet were planted flat on the floor, his sweatpants hung low on his hips, and in his hands he held three small puzzle pieces. Spread out in front of him was what looked like a halfway completed one-thousand-piece puzzle of . . . a flying house? I'd barely crossed into the room when he glanced up and shot me a curious look.

"I made food. There's leftovers in the fridge if you want the rest of them," I offered, like he would say no to food.

I swore on my life he brightened up every time I ever told him there was food left over for him. It was cute and sad at the same time, and that idea only had me shuffling my socked feet on the floor even more. "Thanks for telling Trevor . . . what you told him," I blurted out, immediately making me want to smack myself in the face. What the hell was that?

His face was even and open, not at all embarrassed that I'd just admitted to eavesdropping on his conversation. "Don't thank me. I only said the truth."

I lifted up a shoulder and smiled down at him. "I appreciate it anyway."

He blinked those slumbering brown eyes, his nostrils flaring just enough for me to notice. "You have no idea how terrible you make me feel sometimes."

Wait. What? "Why?"

He sat forward, setting the puzzle pieces in his hands aside. "You're thanking me for defending you, Van. You shouldn't have to thank me for something like that."

I didn't have to tell him that, once upon a time, he hadn't and wouldn't have defended me. If I hadn't agreed to marry him, he wouldn't be in my debt. At this point, I had no house. He hadn't paid any of my student loans yet. The scale wasn't exactly balanced between the two of us. Yet I refused to believe he'd simply done it because of that reason.

Some part of me recognized that Aiden did care about me . . . now . . . in his own way. I just wasn't going to overanalyze why that was. It wasn't like I took it too seriously, just seriously enough to appreciate it. To know it meant something—just not everything.

"Well, I just want you to know I don't take it for granted. That's all."

He hummed, his face flat and expressionless, barely tethered and thoughtful.

"You can watch television down here if you want," he added suddenly.

What the hell? "You sure? You don't mind if I keep you company?" I asked, a little more shyly than I would have thought.

That had him rolling his eyes, blowing out a breath, and shaking his head. "Stop talking and sit down." He nodded, getting to his feet and heading into the kitchen without another word.

Suddenly uncomfortable, I cleared my throat and took a seat on the opposite end of the couch, crossing my heels as I placed my bowl in my lap. Grabbing the remote, I turned on the television and started flipping through the channels before settling on one of my favorite movies. If Aiden thought it was weird when he came back and found me watching WALL-E, he didn't say a word.

He also didn't get up and go sit in the kitchen.

NINETEEN

The next day, my phone rang in the late afternoon.

Aiden flashed across the screen.

I hit the "answer" button. "Hello?"

"Vanessa." He didn't ask if it was me; he just sort of said my name, as if demanding it to be.

"Yes?"

"My car won't start," he said in a tone that sounded accusatory, but couldn't have been. What did he think? That I went and booby-trapped his starter? If I hadn't done it when he used to piss me off, why would I do it now when he hadn't recently?

"Is your battery dead?" I asked, confused. He had leased it brand-new only a year ago; there was no way it needed a new battery so soon.

He muttered something under his breath, his tone abrupt. "I've already taken care of it. There's a tow truck on its way."

Uh. "Okay. What do you need then?"

"Can you pick me up?" he just went right out and asked.

I blinked, surprised that he was calling me and not taking a cab. "Oh. Sure. Where are you?"

"I'm at the main building. Where the team trains," he replied, fully aware that I knew what place he was referring to. I'd been there a few times in the past. "I need to go pick up some papers from the immigration lawyer's office today, too."

Eyeing the thunderstorm going on outside through one of the windows in my room, I sighed. I hated driving in the rain, but he rarely asked for any favors . . . unless they were major, life-changing ones. Whomp, whomp. "Sure. I'll be there as soon as I can."

He grunted out a "thank you" that was as forced as it sounded and hung up.

Some things never changed, did they? I smirked, saved my work, grabbed my purse, and headed downstairs to nab my keys. In a little more than no time, I made it to the facility I wasn't sure I'd ever come back to and showed the old pass Aiden had gotten me to get in through the security gate.

My phone's ringtone going off scared the hell out of me as I steered my car toward the correct building and parking lot. Half expecting it to be Aiden, I was surprised when Diana's name flashed across the screen.

"Her—"

"*How could you not tell me?*" the familiar voice on the other end of the line yelled.

Shit. "Hello to you too."

"Don't you 'hello to you too,' *cabrona.*"

Okay. She'd gone with *cabrona.* That was how pissed off she was. Fair enough.

"Do you want to know how I found out?" I didn't, but she didn't bother waiting for me to confirm an answer she should know. "*Rodrigo told me!*"

I winced.

As if I hadn't heard her the first time, she yelled again. "Rodrigo!"

I wasn't going to apologize. I knew it would just make it worse. I was aware of how things worked with her. At this point, the only thing to do that wouldn't piss her off more was to man-up to what I'd done and let her ream me.

"You got married and you didn't tell me!"

I stayed quiet and kept an eye out on the building to make sure Aiden wasn't appearing.

"It's because you think I'd tell everyone, isn't it?"

That was definitely the wrong question to answer. So I kept my mouth shut.

"You don't love me anymore? Is that it? Am I old news?"

Still, I kept my mouth closed.

"I can't believe you!" She let out a shriek that seemed to echo. Knowing her, she was more than likely in her car. "I'm going to punch you in the cooch."

At that, my silence ended. "I'd like to see you try." She hadn't grown up with my sisters. I knew how to fight a girl.

At least better than she did.

"No! Don't talk to me right now," she insisted. "You didn't tell me you got married. You're on probation, and I need to get back to work. I'm on my lunch break. If you want to get back on my good side this year, I'd like some of those chocolate-dipped strawberries."

That had me snorting. She was out of her damn mind.

"*You owe me.*" With that, she hung up as I pulled into the parking lot I was looking for. I let my forehead drop onto the steering wheel. That had gone better and worse than I'd imagined it would, but I was a little relieved it was out in the open, finally.

I drummed my fingers on the steering wheel as I looked around the empty lot. I wavered on getting out when a giant lightning bolt painted a jagged streak across the rainy lavender-gray sky. Minutes passed and still he didn't come out of the Three Hundreds' building.

Damn it. Before I could talk myself out of it, I jumped out of the car, cursing at myself for not carrying an umbrella for about the billionth time and for not having waterproof shoes, and ran through the parking lot, straight through the double doors. As I stomped my feet on the mat, I looked around the lobby for the big guy. A woman behind the front desk raised her eyebrows at me curiously. "Can I help you with something?" she asked.

"Have you seen Aiden?"

"Aiden?"

Were there really that many Aidens? "Graves."

"Can I ask what you need him for?"

I bit the inside of my cheek and smiled at the woman who didn't know me and, therefore, didn't have an idea that I knew Aiden. "I'm here to pick him up."

It was obvious she didn't know what to make of me. I didn't exactly look like pro-football player girlfriend material in that moment, much less anything else. I'd opted not to put on any makeup, since I hadn't planned on leaving the house. Or real pants. Or even a shirt with the sleeves intact. I had cut-off shorts and a baggy T-shirt with sleeves that I'd taken scissors to. Plus the rain outside hadn't done my hair any justice. It looked like a cloud of teal.

Then there was the whole we-don't-look-anything-alike thing going on, so there was no way we could pass as siblings. Just as I opened my mouth, the doors that connected the front area with the rest of the training facility swung open. The man I was looking for came out with his bag over his shoulder, imposing, massive, and sweaty. Definitely surly too, which really only meant he looked the way he always did.

I couldn't help but crack a little smile at his grumpiness. "Ready?"

He did his form of a nod, a tip of his chin.

I could feel the receptionist's eyes on us as he approached, but I was too busy taking in Grumpy Pants to bother looking at anyone else. Those brown eyes shifted to me for a second, and that time, I smirked uncontrollably.

He glared down at me. "What are you smiling at?"

I shrugged my shoulders and shook my head, trying to give him an innocent look. "Oh, nothing, sunshine."

He mouthed "sunshine" as his gaze strayed to the ceiling.

We ran out of the building side by side toward my car. Throwing the door open, I pretty much jumped inside and shivered, turning the car and the heater on. Aiden slid in a lot more gracefully than I had, wet but not nearly as soaked.

He eyed me as he buckled in, and I slanted him a look. "What?"

With a shake of his head, he unzipped his duffel, which was sitting on his lap, and pulled out that infamous off-black hoodie he always wore. Then he held it out.

All I could do was stare at it for a second. His beloved, no-name brand, extra-extra-large hoodie. He was offering it to me.

When I first started working for Aiden, I remembered him specifically giving me instructions on how he wanted it washed and dried. On gentle and hung to dry. He loved that thing. He could own a thousand just like it, but he didn't. He had one black hoodie that he wore all the time and a blue one he occasionally donned.

"For me?" I asked like an idiot.

He shook it, rolling his eyes. "Yes for you. Put it on before you get sick. I would rather not have to take care of you if you get pneumonia."

Yeah, I was going to ignore his put-out tone and focus on the "rather not" as I took it from him and slipped it on without another word. His hoodie was like holding a gold medal in my hands. Like being given something cherished, a family relic. Aiden's precious.

I couldn't help but glance at him out of the corner of my eye from time to time as I drove. The radio wasn't on, and it was one thing for us to eat at the counter together quietly but a totally different thing for us to be in the car not saying a word. "Did they tell you what was wrong with your car?" I made myself ask.

"The driver thought it was something with the computer."

That made sense. I gripped the steering wheel a little tighter as more lightning filled the horizon. "Has your training been going okay?"

"Fine."

"Please tell me more," I snickered. "At least you've won all your games so far."

"Barely," he said in a thin tone that seemed sandwiched between frustration and anger.

I'd seen a short segment just yesterday about this superstar the Three Hundreds had played against a few days ago, and I'd been amazed. "That guy from Green Bay was huge."

I could *feel* the insulted expression he was shooting my way, even though I was facing forward. "He isn't that big," he corrected me with a huff.

He was though. I'd seen pictures of the guy the Three Hundreds were playing against, and I'd seen him on television. The guy was six-foot-five and just shy of 300 pounds; he was definitely stockier than Aiden, and I could tell those extra pounds weren't pure muscle, but big was big. I kept my mouth shut though and didn't insist he was wrong. I could pretend his opponent hadn't been the size of Delaware. Sure.

"Well, your team won."

Aiden shifted around in his seat. "I could have played better."

What could I say to that? I'd sat through enough interviews with people fawning all over him to know that Aiden soaked up every single one of his imperfections and every mistake he'd ever committed. It was stupid and wonderful how much he expected of himself. Nothing was ever good enough. He had so much to improve on, according to him.

"Oh, Aiden."

"What?"

"You're the best in the country—and I'm not just saying that to be nice—and it means nothing to you."

He made a dismissive noise, those long fingers resting on his knee kind of flicked up in a dismissive gesture. "I want to be remembered years from now. I have to win a championship for that."

Something about his tone pecked at my brain, at that part of me that had stayed up for years to quit my day job one day. "Then you'll be happy?" I asked carefully.

"Maybe."

I wasn't sure what it was about his "maybe" that chewed up my insides. "You've won Defensive Player of the Year three years out of eight, big guy. I don't think anyone will ever forget you. I'm just saying. You should be proud of yourself. You've worked hard for it."

He didn't agree or disagree, but when I turned to look at the passenger side mirror, he was facing out the window with what amounted to about the most thoughtful expression I'd ever seen.

Maybe.

On the other hand, I might have been imagining it.

My phone started ringing loudly from its spot where I'd left it in the cup holder. I glanced at it, but the screen was faced down, and I couldn't get a good look without grabbing it, which I sure as hell wasn't going to do, especially when the rain started slapping the windshield more forcefully. As quickly as the ringing came on, it went out.

Then it started all over again.

"Are you going to answer that?" Aiden asked.

"I don't like to talk on the phone when I'm driving," I explained, just as the phone stopped ringing.

He hummed.

Then it started once more.

With a sigh, he grabbed it and looked at the screen. "It's your mom."

Oh shit. "Don't—"

"Hello?" the big guy answered, putting the phone to his face. "She's busy." I turned my head to see his lower lip slightly jutting out. "I'll make sure to let her know." By the amount of anger in his enunciation, that was the last thing he was planning on doing.

How about that? Before I could thank him for his phone-answering skills, he touched my phone's screen and set it back into the cup holder. Wariness wiggled around in my belly and I cleared my throat. "My best friend finally found out we got married."

"I thought you told her."

"She knew we were going to do it, but I didn't tell her we actually did. She said her brother told her, so I wonder how he found out."

"She didn't tell you?"

Thinking about how the conversation had gone again, I smirked at myself. "No. She was too busy yelling."

Aiden made a thoughtful yet absent sound.

"That might be why my mom called. I'm usually the one who calls her." Except for when she'd called in the wake of my failed trip to El Paso. Just thinking about it made me mad all over again. Maybe I'd wait to call her back . . . next month. I shook the bitter thought off. "Where's your lawyer's office at?"

Thirty minutes later, I pulled my Explorer into the multilevel covered parking lot adjacent to a tall professional office building.

"I'll wait here," I said, turning off the engine.

Aiden shook his head as he opened the car door. "Come with me."

I eyed my legs and then shook my own head. "I'm not really dressed . . ."

The big guy didn't even take in anything other than my face. "You always look fine. Come on."

He didn't wait for me to argue. He just shut the door on me.

I growled under my breath and got out, tugging my damp bottoms down and realizing that Aiden's hoodie was actually so long it went over my shorts. . . . Great.

With a resigned sigh, I found Aiden waiting for me off to the side. At least he had the decency not to mock me for how much of a mess I looked. Thunder shook the walking bridge we had to take to cross over from the lot to the building, and I might have walked a little faster than usual. Aiden had barely opened the door for me when the lights inside the building went in and out for a second.

The lights in the hallway flickered twice more as we walked to the elevator bank. Then they blinked again just as the big guy pressed the button to go up.

I paused, taking in the deserted hallway. "Should we take the stairs?"

He gave me a side look that said what he was thinking—*you're an idiot, Vanessa.* Instead, he verbally went with, "I'm too tired."

Oh. Huh. "Okay."

Before I could think too much more about the consequences of riding around in an elevator during a storm, the doors slid open. A couple was already inside, and they shuffled over into the corner to give us room when we entered. I didn't miss the way the man's eyes widened as Aiden backed against the opposite corner where they were, across from the doors. I put my back against the wall closest to him. "What floor, big guy?"

"Six."

Pressing the button, the lights blinked again as the doors shut. Wariness made my stomach churn as the elevator eased its way upward. The lights flashed one more time before the elevator jerked, stopping, plunging us into total darkness.

One, two, three, four—

Holy shit.

Holy freaking shit.

I tried to blink as the other woman in the elevator squealed, and her partner asked, "What the hell?"

There wasn't even an emergency light on.

It was pitch-black.

Shouldn't there have been a backup light?

Panic instantly seized my throat. Okay, it gripped my entire body, stringing every muscle so tight it hurt. In the time it took me to suck in a breath, my body began shaking. I made myself squeeze my eyes closed, ignoring the couple whispering in the corner.

Okay. Okay.

Everything was okay.

Everything would be okay, I told myself.

I was fine.

It was just a little outage because of the storm; big buildings like this had backup generators that would kick in in no time.

Didn't they?

I started patting the wall next to me to find the buttons on the panel, easing my touch around until I felt a small gap in the metal, feeling around the perimeter of it. It was rectangle-shaped, where I figured an emergency phone had to be. Elevators had emergency lines . . . I thought. The latch opened easily, and I grabbed the small phone from inside. I couldn't see a single thing, and as I touched around, there wasn't any pad of any sort to call out. There wasn't even a dial tone. The elevator wasn't moving. The lights weren't coming back on.

I held the phone against my ear, but there was no noise of any sort on the other end.

The power was completely out. The power had to be out.

My stomach seemed to drop to my knees.

It was so dark I couldn't see my fingers when I brought them up close to my face. I could hear my breathing getting louder by the second, feel my chest start to puff in quick, restless breaths that I hadn't experienced in a long time.

But the hum I was expecting, the one that signaled the power coming back on, didn't make its appearance after another minute. It didn't come back on after three or four minutes either, and the fear I'd been trying to ignore seized me in its rude, greedy grip even tighter.

"Vanessa?"

Oh shit, oh shit, oh shit.

I couldn't breathe. I couldn't breathe. I couldn't breathe. I couldn't think.

"Vanessa," came Aiden's voice again, whispered, strict and tight in the small space. "What the hell are you doing?"

I squeezed my eyes closed tighter, fighting it, fighting it, fighting it. "Nothing," I think I managed to wheeze out.

Stop, stop, stop, stop, stop. Chill out. Everything is fine. Everything is fine. You're just in an elevator. You're okay.

I wasn't okay. I wasn't anywhere near being okay.

I had asthma. Since when did I have asthma?

A hand touched my shoulder just as I blindly replaced the phone where it was and moved my hands down my stomach and thighs until I was hunched over, gripping my knees for dear life.

Think, Vanessa. Think.

"You're Aiden Graves, aren't you?" the male voice speaking sounded like a hum in the background.

"Yes," Aiden bit back in his familiar low grumble, his tone not inviting another remark. The hand on my shoulder tightened as I fought back a gasp for air. "Vanessa," he repeated my name.

Breathe, breathe, breathe.

But I couldn't. I was panicking. I squeezed my knees harder with my palms and somehow managed to suck in a rabid breath.

Think.

I was fine. The elevator wasn't that small. The lights were going to come back on eventually. I gasped sharply through my mouth.

"Sit down," Aiden hissed, the one hand on my shoulder putting enough pressure that I didn't bother picking a fight as I sank to my knees.

My keys! I slapped my hands around the pocket of Aiden's hoodie, and finally found the hard lump I was looking for in the right pocket. I yanked my keys out and latched onto the slick, metallic tube I'd had on my keychain forever. The small button on the back clicked into place . . . and nothing.

It wasn't working.

My phone! I started patting around my pockets when I remembered watching Aiden set my phone into the cup holder in my car. Cold dread sucked me in.

"Calm down," Aiden demanded in the dark.

You're okay. You're okay. You're okay. You're in an elevator. You're okay, I reminded myself.

"Vanessa." I sensed the radiant heat of his body against my knees. "You're fine," he stated over my wild pants.

I was too riled up to be embarrassed that I couldn't seem to breathe. I definitely couldn't open my mouth to talk either, much less get all bent out of shape for him bossing me around.

Another hand joined the first and curled big and consuming over my shoulders. "You're all right," Aiden's low, gravelly voice murmured in the dark elevator.

"What's wrong with her?" the unfamiliar male voice on the other side of the elevator asked. "Is she okay?"

"Take a deep breath." Thumbs kneaded my shoulders, ignoring the question from the stranger. "Breathe."

Breathe? I tried, but it came in and out as mostly a choke.

"Through your nose . . . come on. In. Out through your mouth. Calm down." Those big thumbs made small, almost angry circles over me. "Slow breath. Slow. In your nose, out of your mouth." If this had been any other situation, I would have been surprised by how calm and cool his tone was. How gentle and unrushed. How very unlike the person who had just been snapping at me when he first realized something was wrong.

"You're fine," Aiden commanded with a squeeze of the mitts he called hands. "Calm down. You got it," he coached me through the next ragged breath. "I'm right here." His breath washed over my cheek as his palms cupped my upper arms. "I'm not going anywhere without you." He squeezed, his words ringing through my ears. "You're not alone."

I was fine. I was fine.

It took a few wild inhales to really get a good breath in that didn't seem like I was struggling not to drown. As soon as I could, I shifted off my stinging knees to sit on my butt, dragging my legs up to my chest.

"Breathe, breathe, breathe," Aiden commanded.

I couldn't make myself open my eyes, but it was all right. I was still shaking, but I could live with that as long as I could get oxygen into my lungs. *In my nose, out my mouth* like the big guy had said. My breaths were sharper than they should have been, but there they were.

"You got it?" Aiden began moving around, his knee hitting my foot as I sensed him sit next to me.

"Yes," I puffed out, putting my forehead on my knees.

I was okay. I was okay.

My body gave a near-violent shake that said otherwise.

I was fine. I was fine. One breath in, one breath out. I clenched my eyes closed. I wasn't alone. As if to make sure, my hand crept over my lap and down my thigh until I brushed the side of Aiden's hip. My fingers touched the hem of his shirt, and I pinched the thin material between my fingertips.

I wasn't alone. I was fine. I shuddered out a breath as my biceps spasmed.

"Better?"

"Little bit," I muttered, rubbing my fingertips over the sewn hem of his shirt. *Stop being a baby. You're not dying. You're okay.* I made myself open my eyes and raised my head until it dropped back to the wall behind me. I couldn't see a single thing, but I was okay.

I was all right.

One deep exhale out, and I was breathing out of my mouth, calm, calm, calmer. By that point, the other couple in the elevator had resorted to whispering so low I couldn't bother to understand what was being said. Aiden, on the other hand, was familiarly silent, his deep, even breathing telling me he wasn't at all affected by whatever the hell was going on with the weather and the elevator.

Then again, if I weren't so terrified of the dark and small spaces, none of this crap would be a big deal either. It wasn't like we'd be stuck inside forever, and it wasn't like the elevator would suddenly plummet and we'd all die.

I hoped.

The elevator gave a sharp jerk and the woman screamed as the lights in the ceiling flashed bright for one precious second before going out once again.

Fuck this.

With skills I didn't even know I possessed, I was up, sliding over Aiden's knee and in his lap so fast I had no idea I'd even done it, because if I'd thought about it, there was no way in hell I would have done it. *No fucking way.* But the fact was, I had.

I was in Aiden's lap. He was cross-legged on either side of me, each of his muscular thighs cocooning my hips, his chin just behind my ear. I shivered.

Behind me, Aiden straightened; under my butt, his thighs tightened and strained.

It was then that I felt embarrassed. "I'm sorry," I apologized, already lifting up to lunge off him.

"Shut up," he said as his hands landed on my bare knees, shoving me back down onto him; my back hit the solid wall of his chest and it was right then I realized his shirt was soggy from the rain. I didn't care. Under me, his legs relaxed, my bottom settling on top of his feet.

It was like sitting on a beanbag. A big, firm, slightly wet beanbag that breathed . . . and had two hands cupping my naked kneecaps. Immediately and pathetically, I let out a long, deep breath and relaxed in the cocoon of Aiden. One of his thumbs rubbed the sensitive skin on the inside of my knee, just a quick circle-shaped brush that had me letting out another sigh.

The big guy hummed into the shell of my ear, his breath warm and way too comforting. "You want to tell me what that was about?" he asked in a whisper.

"Not really," I mumbled, clasping my hands in my lap.

He made a tiny scoffing sound but didn't say anything for a moment until . . . "You're sitting on me. I think you owe me."

I tried to lunge up again, even though I really didn't want to, but those huge hands clamped down even tighter, that time with his fingers spread wide, covering my kneecaps and part of my thighs.

"Stop it. I'm teasing you," he commented.

Teasing me? Aiden? Letting my head droop forward, I kept my eyes closed and let a rattled sigh out. "I'm scared of the dark." Like that wasn't completely obvious.

He didn't even let out a single breath. "Yeah, I got that. I would have given you my phone to use as a flashlight, but the battery went dead after I talked to you."

"Oh. Thanks anyway." I made myself let out another deep breath. "I'm really scared of the dark, like the dark in here, when I can't see anything. I have been since I was a kid," I explained tensely.

"Why?" he cut in.

"Why what?"

He made that exasperated noise of his. "Why are you scared of the dark?"

I wanted to ask if he really wanted to know, but of course he damn well did. I didn't necessarily want to tell him—nor had I ever wanted to tell anyone—but he had a point. I was a twenty-six-year-old sitting on his lap after I'd been on the verge of having a panic attack because the lights had gone out. I guess I sort of owed him.

"It's stupid. I know it's stupid. Okay? When I was five, my sisters"—though I'm pretty sure I would now blame Susie as being the main mastermind behind the incident—"locked me in a closet."

"That's why you're scared?" he had the nerve to scoff before I continued.

"With the lights off for two days," I finished up.

Aiden's voice didn't just react, it seemed like his entire body did too. Inch by inch, what felt like from his toes and up, went rock-solid. "Without food or water?"

The fact that he thought about that small detail didn't escape me. That was the shitty part. At least now, I thought that was the shitty part of the story. "They left me water and candy bars. Chips." Those bitches, even at seven, eight, and nine, had already been vicious by then. They had planned it. Planned on locking me in there because they didn't want to watch over me while our mom was gone. *They hadn't wanted to play with me*, for God's sake. They had taunted through the door before leaving me.

I shivered, even though I really would rather not have.

"Where was your mother?" he asked in that creepy, calm tone.

I wasn't sure what it was about all these memories I'd shoved aside for so long suddenly coming back that made me feel like a raw, open wound. I couldn't control the long breath I let out. "I think she was dating someone back then. It might have been my little brother's dad. I don't remember that well. He was in and out of our lives for a few years. All I know for sure was that she wasn't at home then." Sometimes she'd disappeared for a few days at a time, but that was my burden to bear.

"Who let you out?"

"They did." They unlocked the door and made fun of me for being a baby and peeing on myself. It had taken me an hour to get myself to crawl out of there.

"What happened after that?" He was still talking in that effortless, patient voice that screamed "wrong" at the top of its lungs.

Shame and anger made me shake. "Nothing."

"Nothing?"

"No."

"Did you tell your mom?"

"Of course I told my mom. It was her closet they put me in. I'd peed in there. She had to get the carpet replaced, because it smelled so bad." I'd smelled so bad. My hands had been so messed up from banging on the door, and my voice so hoarse from screaming at them to let me out . . . or to at least turn on the closet light . . . or if they couldn't turn on the closet light, to turn on the bedroom light . . . to no avail. I never knew for sure what they'd done in those two days I was in there, and frankly, I didn't care at all.

I didn't. Because kids that young shouldn't have been left alone to begin with.

His chest started puffing against my back as if his breathing was difficult. "She did nothing to your sisters?"

I wanted to crawl into myself. The tone he was using raked at my nerves, pulling the sides of the stab wound called my childhood wide open for inspection. It made me feel small. "No. She yelled at them, but that was it. I mean, she stayed home for a month or two afterward"—that was one of the times I remembered her being mostly sober—"and I slept with her every night. After that, I moved my things and shared a room with my little brother." I'd started locking the bedroom door after that as well.

The fingertips on my knees kneaded for a second, but I bet my life it was a subconscious gesture, mostly because his labored breathing hadn't gone anywhere.

"I have to sleep with a light on," I admitted to him, feeling his chest huff behind me. Dumb, dumb, dumb. "I don't know why I just told you that. Don't make fun of me."

There was a pause. A hesitation before, "I won't," he promised effortlessly. "I wondered why you had so many at your apartment and in your room."

I *knew* he'd noticed. "Please don't tell Zac. I wouldn't hold it past him to hide under the bed when I'm sleeping to try and scare the crap out of me."

"I won't." His palms shaped my knees. The insides of his arms seemed to frame my shoulders and arms. His breathing was low but not so steady against my ear. "It isn't stupid that you're scared. You shouldn't be embarrassed. It's everyone else who should be ashamed of themselves."

The only way I managed to answer was with a nod that I wasn't sure he knew of or not. Another rattling breath made its way out of my chest like a gust and I touched a patch of skin somewhere around his knee as I kept my eyes closed. "Thank you for helping me calm down, big guy. I haven't lost it like that in forever."

"Don't worry about it," was all he muttered in return.

I kept my hand on his leg, my fingertips against the coarse dark hairs that covered his legs. My breathing sounded too loud, my heart was still beating a little weird, while Aiden's was soft and barely audible. I focused on the in and the out of my lungs.

The other woman in the elevator mumbled, "This sucks."

It did. It really did.

The silence ate up the minutes, and I let my back loosen, the top of it touching Aiden's pectorals. The insides of his upper arms cradled me. His breathing was so even it made me sleepy.

The elevator gave a jerk that had me opening my eyes in reaction as the lighting flickered twice and stayed on. The woman on the other side squealed, but I couldn't even be remotely scared. I only cared about the lighting.

And it was right then, not being plunged in the dark, that I finally witnessed with my own two eyes the sight of me sitting on Aiden. Two long, muscular legs circled me, so long that the knees jutted out way past where mine ended. Two heavily muscled triceps popped on either side of my arms, playing my bodyguards. But it was the big hands on me, the wrists propped up so effortlessly on my thighs, that made something in me react.

He was hugging me. For all intents and purposes, Aiden was hugging me. Surrounding me.

Tilting my head back, I swallowed that thing making its way from my stomach to my throat, and prepared a nervous, slightly shy smile over my shoulder. Except when my gaze landed on Aiden's face, it was so serious . . . so damn serious. It wiped the expression right off my mouth.

The elevator gave another jerk, and almost immediately the phone on the wall began ringing.

With a light tap to my knee, Aiden picked me up and moved me off to the side, as if my weight was nothing to him—and it definitely wasn't nothing. He got to his feet and reached toward the wall, picking the phone off the cradle. His gaze drifted over me in the process, those ultra-sober features making me feel like I'd done something wrong all of a sudden. "Yes . . . It's about time . . . Yes." Just like that, he hung up, probably in the middle of the conversation. "It'll be about fifteen minutes."

Drawing my legs up to my chest, I wrapped my arms around them and nodded at his comment. He didn't sit back down; instead, Aiden leaned against the wall and crossed his arms over his chest. One ankle went over the other.

Not ten minutes later, a loud noise pierced through the elevator, and the next thing I knew, it began its ascent again. When the doors finally opened, two building employees were standing there, asking if we were fine, but Aiden walked right past them, as if they weren't there.

"Are you okay?" one of the employees asked.

Was I okay? I hadn't been, but I wasn't going to say anything. Mostly, I was a little bit embarrassed I'd freaked out and uncertain what the hell the look on Aiden's face had been about when the lights had come back on.

"Are you coming?" the big guy asked from where he was waiting.

There was the man I knew. "Hold your horses, sunshine. I'm coming."

His lips moved in a way that told me he wasn't particularly fond of "sunshine," but most importantly, he knew I didn't care that he hated it. "Let's go. He's paid by the hour and we're already late."

It didn't take long to find what we were looking for. A hardwood-framed glass door with etchings on the front and a plaque on the wall right next to it deemed that this was the lawyer's office.

Sleek, beautiful hardwood furniture in warm shades of brown and green welcomed us. It hit me again right then that I looked like a fifteen-year-old in a giant-sized sweater that made it seem as if I didn't have any clothes on underneath. Aiden didn't look much better; his T-shirt was clingy, he had on long, black shorts that went past his knees, and he was in running shoes. The difference was, he didn't give a single crap what he looked like.

Directly in front of the doors, an older woman behind a desk smiled over at us. "Can I help you?" she asked.

"Yes. We had an appointment with Jackson. I'm the one who called to say I was running late," Aiden explained.

That changed everything. "Oh, Mr. Graves. Right. One moment please. The lighting issue pushed his meeting late."

The lighting issue. Aiden and I looked at each other.

I couldn't freaking help it, especially now that we were out of the elevator of terror; I snickered and let the uncontrollable smile take over.

Those underused corners of his mouth tipped up just a little—just a freaking little—but it was what it was. He'd smiled. He'd fucking smiled at me. Again. And it was just as magnificent as it had been the first time.

When we took a seat to wait, he turned that big body to the side and pinned me in place. "What's that look on your face for?"

I reached up and touched the sides of my mouth and cheeks, finding that, yeah, I was mooning. Not smiling. I was mooning.

He'd smiled at me. Was there any other way in the world to react? "No reason."

His lids dropped low. "You look like you're on drugs."

That wiped my not-smile off my face. "I like your smile. That's all."

The big guy shot me a sour look. "You make me feel like a Grinch."

"I don't mean to. It's a nice smile. You should do it more often."

The grumpy expression on his face didn't assure me of anything. Eventually, when I sat up straight, he draped his arm over the back of my chair. Waiting until the woman at the desk was on the phone, I whispered, "What exactly are we doing here?"

"He wants to go over some information with me," he explained.

Couldn't the lawyer just have emailed it to us? I wondered, but kept my question to myself. "So I can't wait here?"

"No."

I fidgeted and lowered my voice even more. "The lawyer thinks this is real, doesn't he?"

"It's fraud otherwise."

Damn. I slunk in my seat, the bare heat of his forearm grazing the top of my neck. That damn word sent fear coursing through my spine. I didn't want to go to prison.

As if he was reading my mind, Aiden whispered, "Nothing is going to happen. No one's going to believe this isn't real."

I didn't know where he got his confidence from, but I needed to find some.

Luckily it didn't take too long for the door leading from the waiting room to the office to open. A couple came out, too busy speaking in a language that sounded like German to pay attention to us.

It was showtime apparently.

The second after we stood up, the receptionist waved us forward. I slipped my hand into Aiden's and gave it a faint squeeze.

He squeezed mine right back.

TWENTY

"Zac! Are you almost ready?" I yelled down the hall as I shoved my heel into my running shoe.

"I'm putting on my shoes, Mrs. Graves!"

Idiot. "I'll wait for you downstairs," I told him as I slipped my other one on.

"Okay," he yelled back just as I hit the stairs. Down them and into the kitchen, I found Aiden sitting in the breakfast nook, with a big glass of something brown and funky-looking in front of him that I'd bet a kidney had some kind of bean and vegetable in it.

Heading to the refrigerator to get a sip of water before the start of our jog, I asked over my shoulder, "Big guy, do you want anything from the fridge while I'm up?"

"No thanks."

It was Monday afternoon after the Three Hundreds played an away game the day before. The poor guy had gotten home from Maryland at four o'clock in the morning, and he'd had to drag himself out of bed at nine to meet up with the team's trainers, then sat through one meeting after another. His body language expressed just how exhausted he was. How could he not be?

I filled half my glass with water and chugged it down. Across the room, Aiden finally took his attention away from the current puzzle he was finishing, and asked, "Where are you two going?"

"For a run."

"Why is he going with you?" he plainly asked, a crease forming between his eyebrows. His long fingers seemed to swallow the puzzle piece in his hand.

"I talked him into doing the marathon with me." Was this really the first time he'd seen us leaving?

Something about what I said must have intrigued him, because his head jerked back and what looked like the beginning of a laugh took over his mouth. "*He's* going to run a marathon?"

Well that sounded insulting even to my ears. The fact that Zac walked into the kitchen the moment Aiden began his question didn't help the situation any. He scrunched up his nose as he cast his ex-teammate a long look. "*Yeah.*"

"You have the worst cardio I've ever seen," Mr. No Social Skills claimed, not at all embarrassed that he'd been overheard.

I couldn't disagree with him there. Considering Zac was an elite athlete, the first few times we'd gone running together was like going with a clone of myself during those initial two months after I'd decided I wanted to start training. I hadn't even been able to get two miles done without severe knee pain and panting, and I'd thought that was pretty good.

Zac, on the other hand, made it seem like I was leading him across the Mojave Desert barefoot and without water.

"I do not," he argued. "Why are you nodding, Van?"

I stopped what I was doing. "You do—oww! You didn't have to pinch me." I glared at who I thought was my friend, suddenly standing right next to me. "You do have terrible endurance. Your breathing has been worse than mine."

"I can do a marathon if I want to." Zac's cheeks turned slightly pink as I tried to back away from him to avoid getting pinched again.

"Of course you can. Your breathing just blows right now." I slapped him on the back, dodging out of his reach a second later. "Let's get this over with," I said, making sure I was at least five feet away from him at all times. "Let me pee first though, *Forrest Gump.*"

Zac laughed, half-assed lunging at me one more time.

I jumped back. I casually noticed Aiden out of my peripheral vision looking at me. Specifically, my legs. My tights were all dirty and I'd had to dig out a pair of shorts from my drawer that I hadn't worn in years. They were too tight and too short, and I'd had to put on a baggy T-shirt so the elastic band digging into my stomach and hips wouldn't be noticeable. I'd lost almost fifteen pounds since I'd started running, but I still didn't have anything close to a six-pack.

So I was a little surprised when those thick eyebrows knit together, his gaze focusing. "What happened to your leg, Van?"

I'd worn skirts and dresses around him on a few occasions when I worked for him. I had always figured he just hadn't cared to find out where I'd gotten the scarring that went from above my knee to below it. Hell, I'd been wearing cutoffs when we'd gotten stuck in the elevator together and sat in his lap afterward. His hand had been on my knee. How hadn't he noticed?

Now I realized he hadn't even looked at it.

I didn't care that it wasn't pretty, and I'd never tried to hide it. It was my badge of honor. My daily reminder of all the physical pain I'd gone through, of all the anger I'd had to get under control, and what I'd done with it. I'd finished school. I got back on my feet. I'd accomplished my goal of growing my business and venturing out on my own. No one else had done it for me but me. I'd saved. I'd worked. I'd persevered. Me. No one else.

And if I could do all that, when I was strong and when I was weak, I could remember it and let it lead me. My achy knee never let me forget what we'd been through in the last eight years.

I made my way out of the kitchen, because the truth wasn't a big deal. "I got hit by a car."

I just usually didn't tell people that it was my sister who'd been the driver.

By the time Zac and I made it out of the house, the sun had just started to hang low in the horizon. We jogged steadily for six miles one way before turning around to get back home. That last two miles on the way home we used as our cool down. After we'd caught our breaths, Big Texas abruptly snorted and asked, "How the hell hadn't Aiden noticed your knee 'til today?"

I let out a sharp snicker. "I was wondering the exact same thing."

"Jesus, Vanny, I think I noticed it the first week you started workin' for him." He shook his head. "He doesn't notice stuff that's not football-related unless it smacks him in the face."

It was true.

Then he said, "Like you."

And it was like something crashed down on my shoulders. Not necessarily a bad thing, but the truth was like a boa. It could be this heavy snake that could wrap around your neck and kill you, or it could be a feather boa, a nice, fun accessory to your life. In this case, I was going to force myself to take the truth in the form of the feather version. I'd already faced reality, and that reality was the one Aiden had admitted to me: he hadn't appreciated me until I left.

It was what it was. You couldn't force someone to care about you or love you. I knew that way too well.

But Aiden was a man who only loved one thing, and if you weren't that one thing, too bad. It was all he'd known for so long, he hadn't looked in his peripherals at everything else surrounding him. I could accept that nothing else was anywhere near as important as football. What I wasn't able to do was wrap my head around what Leslie had said regarding Aiden's grandparents and the grief he'd gone through when he lost them. He'd never even mentioned them in front of me. But I guess that was just the way he was.

Now though, in his own way, I knew he cared about me. That said something, didn't it? I didn't think I was trying to pull at straws or make something bigger than it needed to be. I was simply taking what I could get and not making it out to be something it wasn't.

I could live with that.

So I shrugged at Zac. "Yeah, exactly like that. He's just so focused he doesn't care about anything else. I get it." I did.

With a big sigh, Zac sniffed. "It's workin' for him. He's the only one on the team that's an All-Pro." The shape his mouth took after he finished talking made a bittersweet sensation go through my heart. I couldn't help but think: poor Zac.

So I smacked him in the arm. "Quit pouting. You're only twenty-eight. That one quarterback played until he was almost forty, didn't he?"

"Well . . . yeah. He did."

"See?" That was enough for now, wasn't it? I went with changing the subject. "Are you doing anything for Halloween?"

"WHERE ARE YOU going?"

I stopped at the door and held out the jack-o'-lantern-shaped bucket I'd bought the day before, so he could see the three bags of candy I'd torn open and dumped inside. "Nowhere. I was going to sit outside."

Sitting in what I'd began to consider calling his throne—the breakfast nook—the big guy had a puzzle spread out in front of him. I didn't know why I thought it was so cute but it was. It really, really was. Those big shoulders were always hunched over while he worked on them, and I didn't need to catch him unawares to know he sometimes stuck his tongue out of the corner of his mouth when he was really into it. Now though, on Halloween Day, his entire body was turned to the side as he caught me on my way out.

Aiden's eyes dropped to my body in what I might have thought was the third time since we'd met, and he cocked a thick eyebrow, his face a plain, stony mask. "You're all dressed up."

"It's a costume," I said a little self-consciously. "For Halloween." For the record, I loved Halloween. Other than Christmas, it was my favorite holiday. The costumes, the decorations, the little kids, and the candy . . . it had been love from the first October 31st I could remember.

Aiden tilted his head just slightly to the side. "What are you supposed to be?"

Was he serious? I looked down at my costume, thinking I'd done a pretty good job putting it together three years ago, when I'd last worn it to a friend's party. The overalls, the yellow shirt, the one-eyed goggle pressing into my forehead. It was obvious. "A minion."

The Wall of Winnipeg blinked. "What the hell is a minion?"

"A minion. *Despicable Me.*" I blinked when he stayed silent. "Nothing?"

"Never seen it."

Blasphemy. I'd ask if he was serious, but I knew he was. I stared right at him. "It's one of the cutest movies in the entire universe," I explained slowly, hoping he was joking.

He shook his head, his eyes flicking low again. "Never heard of it."

"I don't even know what to say to you, and at the same time, I'm not sure why I'm surprised you haven't heard of it," I said. "You have no idea what you've been missing out on, big guy. It's probably the cutest animated movie after *Finding Nemo*."

"I highly doubt that." But he didn't say he hadn't heard of *Finding Nemo*. That was something.

"I have the DVD in my room, borrow it."

Before he could respond, a knock sounded at the door and a bolt of giddiness shot through my chest as I clutched the bucket of candy in my hand and prepared myself for the trick-or-treaters on the other side.

Two small kids who couldn't have been more than six years old stood on the doorstep with really elaborate cloth sacks extended.

"Trick or treat!" they pretty much shouted.

"Happy Halloween," I said, taking in the petite Power Ranger and Captain America as I dropped a few pieces of candy into each bag.

"Thank you!" they shouted back simultaneously before running to the adult standing at the end of the sidewalk waiting for them. The adult figure waved at me and I waved back before sticking my head back into the house. "I'll be outside," I called out to Aiden, grabbing the collapsible chair that I'd left right by the door earlier for this occasion.

I'd barely settled into the seat on the small patio outside when the front door opened and the legs of a chair just like mine peeked out, the big six-foot-almost-five man I was legally married to following after it.

"What are you doing?" I asked as he dropped his chair next to mine, farther away from the door.

"Nothing." He eyed me as he pretty much fell into the canvas. Honestly, a small part of me was worried it was going to rip at the seams when he plopped down, but by some miracle it didn't. Leaning back, he crossed his arms over his chest and stared forward across the street.

And I stared at him.

He never sat outside. Ever. When would he have time? And why would he?

"Okay," I mumbled to myself, moving my attention back to the street to spot a pair of kids three houses down. It was still early, only six, so I didn't think much of the absence of little ones crowding the streets. In my neighborhood growing up, it would be five o'clock and the streets would be lined with the smallest children first, and by eight o'clock, the older ones would be busy making their rounds. Most of the houses in that neighborhood had been decorated to the best of their abilities—never ours though—but it had been *awesome*. Everyone had been into it.

My mom never really went out of her way to buy us costumes, but that didn't stop my little brother or me from dressing up. I'd gotten really good about making something out of nothing. Every year, hell or high water, we dressed up and went out with Diana, chaperoned by her parents.

Even at my apartment complex, there were quite a few kids who had dropped by in the two years I'd been there. This, on the other hand, was a bit of a disappointment, but maybe it was just too early?

"You like all this stuff?" that gruff voice peeped up.

I sat back in the chair and plucked a small Kit Kat from the jack-o'-lantern on my lap. "Yes." I shoved half of it into my mouth, letting it hang out like a cigarette. "I like the costumes and the imagination. The candy. But I love the costumes the most."

He eyeballed me briefly. "I can't tell."

I crossed my eyes and angled myself slightly toward him. "What? It's not like I'm dressed up as a sexy rabbit or nurse at the Playboy mansion or something."

His gaze stayed forward. "Isn't that what most girls aim for?"

"Some . . . *if you have no imagination.* Pssh. Last year, I dressed up as Goku." Diana and I had gone to one of her friends' Halloween party. I'd gotten her to dress up as Trunks.

That had him glancing at me. "What's a Goku?"

Yeah, I had to clutch the sides of the canvas seat below me as I leveled my gaze at his bearded face. "He's only the second single greatest fighter in anime history. He was a character on a show called *Dragon Ball*." I realized I was whispering and ranting at the same time, and coughed. "It's a Japanese cartoon that I love. You've never heard of it?"

Those thick eyebrows knit together and one big foot crossed over the other as he stretched out in the poor, poor chair. "It's a cartoon . . . with fighters?"

"Intergalactic fighters." I tried to draw him in, raising an eyebrow. "Like *Streetfighter* but with a plot. It's epic."

Adding the intergalactic part must have been too much, because he just shook his big head. "What the hell is an intergalactic fighter?"

"A fighter . . ." I stared at him and grabbed two pieces of candy, handing him an Airhead because I knew it was vegan. "Here. This might take a while."

"HE HAS A tail the entire time?" Aiden held the same Blow Pop up against his lip that he'd taken from the jack-o'-lantern bucket after polishing off the Airhead. I may or may not have had to force myself not to look at his mouth for more than a second or two at a time. "That seems stupid. Someone could grab it and use it against him."

The fact that he was thinking strategy over an anime that I was so fond of got me pretty damn excited; I just had to be careful not to let it show on my face. "No, he lost his tail when he grew up," I explained.

We'd been going on about *Dragon Ball* for the last hour. In that time, exactly four kids had come up to the house for candy, but I was too busy explaining one of my favorite shows in the world to Mr. I-didn't-have-a-childhood to really focus in on that.

He blinked as he thought about my explanation. "He lost his tail when he hit puberty?"

"Yes."

"Why?"

"Why does it matter? It's genetic. Guys grow hair in places when they hit puberty; he can lose his tail if he wants to lose his tail. You just have to watch it to understand."

He didn't look particularly convinced.

"After that, there's *Dragon Ball* Z and *GT*, and those are even better in my opinion."

"What's that?"

"The series when they get older. They have kids, and then their kids grow up to become better than them."

His eyebrow twitched and I was fairly certain his mouth did too. "Do you have that on DVD too?"

I smiled. "Maybe."

He gave me a side-glance, reaching up to scratch at his bearded cheek with his last three fingers. "Maybe I'll have to watch it."

"Whenever you want, big guy. My video collection is your video collection."

I swear he nodded as if he'd actually take me up on my offer.

With a victorious sigh, I turned my attention back to the street to see that it was completely empty. Not a single soul roamed our block or any other block within visual distance. Something tickled at the back of my head, really making me think about the evening, about Aiden coming out to sit with me.

I bit my lips and asked slowly, "That's probably it for kids today, huh?"

He lifted a shoulder, pulling the lollipop out of his mouth. "Seems like it."

I got up with the nearly full container of candy and made sure to keep my face down as I collapsed the legs of the chair together. Something clogged my throat. "Kids don't really go trick-or-treating in this neighborhood, do they?"

Aiden hummed the most obnoxious nonanswer in the world.

And I had my answer.

I couldn't believe it had taken me so long to figure it out.

He had known kids didn't come out to trick-or-treat in his neighborhood—his freaking gated neighborhood. So he'd come out to keep me company. How about that. *How about that.*

"Aiden?"

"Huh?"

"Why didn't you tell me there weren't little kids here?"

He didn't bother looking at me as he headed into the house with his chair tucked under an arm. "You looked excited. I didn't want to ruin it for you," he admitted without a shy note in his voice.

Bah-freaking-humbug.

If there was something I could have said after that that would have been appropriate, I had no idea what it could have been. I thought about the tiny kindness he'd done me as I took the chair from him and set both of them back into the garage while he went to the bathroom.

My stomach growled and I went about rinsing some chickpeas and drying them while my mind wandered to Aiden. He appeared in the kitchen and sat at the breakfast table, his broad back curling over it as he worked on his puzzle in peace. I made dinner—quadrupling what I usually would have made for just me alone—and told myself that I was only doing it because he'd been nice to me.

I wasn't even going to bother asking if he was hungry. He was always hungry.

When the food was ready thirty minutes later, I served up two bowls and held the one with three times as much as the other out to him. Aiden's eyes caught mine as he took it.

"Thank you."

I just nodded at him. "You're welcome. I'm going to go watch TV while I eat." I made it all the way to where the living room met up with the hallway that went straight down the middle of the house.

"You want to watch that *Dragon Balls* show?"

I stopped in my tracks when he spoke.

"I'm curious now what a little kid with a monkey tail who can supposedly 'kick ass' looks like."

Glancing back to make sure he wasn't pulling my tail, I spotted Aiden sitting on the edge of his seat, ready to get up if I gave him the notice. I was dumbstruck for a second before reacting. I had to force myself not to smile like a lunatic. "It's *Dragon Ball*, big guy, and you don't have to ask me twice."

TWENTY-ONE

was sitting at my computer when the first massive lightning bolt hit. The house shook. The windows rattled. Wind howled, slapping the house's siding. The height of the storm I'd seen the meteorologist on TV forecasting had finally come.

And I panicked, saving my work as quickly as I could so I could turn off my computer.

Then the next bolt hit, the light so bright right outside my window it seemed unreal, closer to a nuclear blast than an act of nature. The lights had no hope. Just like a candle going out, they were there one second and gone the next.

"Fuck!" I muttered to myself, already diving from my desk toward the bed, blind, slapping my hands around so I could find the nightstand. My knee found it first, and I cursed, grabbing the spot that I was sure was already turning into a bruise with one hand and finding the top drawer with the other. It didn't take me long to find the small LED flashlight inside. I made sure it was always in the left corner, and sure enough, it was right there.

Flicking it on, I sucked in a deep breath before jumping back on the bed and sliding under the covers. The flashlight was the best thing money could buy; 500 lumens for a contraption three inches long. I moved the bright beam around the ceiling and toward the open doorway, listening as the screaming winds outside got louder. I shivered.

It wasn't like I hadn't gotten a warning that a storm was coming in advance. It had been raining steadily for some time, but instead of the storm moving away, it had just gotten heavier and heavier. Great.

This was so stupid. I hated being so scared of the dark. I really did. It made me feel like a dumb little kid. But no matter how much I tried to tell myself it was okay, that I was fine . . .

That didn't do anything.

I still shook. My breathing still got bottled up in my throat. I still wanted the lights to come back on.

"Vanessa? Where are you?" Aiden's rough voice carried its way from down the hall. I could barely hear his footsteps as they got lost mixed in with the noise outside.

"In my room," I called out, weaker than I ever would have wanted. "What are you doing awake?" Sleepy Pants had gone to bed at his usual time: nine. Three hours ago.

"The thunder woke me up." Another big flash of lightning illuminated the body filling the doorway a moment later, and I flicked my flashlight at his legs.

His bare legs.

He was only wearing boxer briefs. There wasn't a shirt over his chest. Aiden was standing in my doorway in just boxer briefs, his medallion around his neck, and muscles.

So many muscles.

Stop it. I needed to stop it right away.

"Jesus. How bright is that thing? Point it at the floor, would you?" he said in a voice that confirmed he'd been dead asleep just minutes ago. I flicked the light toward the ceiling instead. "You all right?"

"I'm okay," I said, even as an unnecessary shiver racked my spine. "Just pissing my pants. No big deal." The laugh that came out of my mouth sounded just as fake and awkward as it felt. I sounded like a crazy person.

The sigh he let out made it seem like he was completely putting himself out as he strode forward, around the side of the mattress before stopping, towering. "Scoot over."

Scoot?

I wasn't going to ask. I should, but I didn't as my heart seemed to climb into my throat and take a seat.

I scooted. Neither one of us said a word as he climbed onto my bed and under the covers as if it was no big freaking deal, like this wasn't the first time he'd done it. I didn't let myself get all shy and prudish, or anywhere near it. Desperate times called for desperate measures, and I wasn't going to say no to the other half of my paperwork getting into my bed when I'd rather not be by myself.

Lightning flashed brighter than bright through the two windows in my room once more before plunging the house into that eerie darkness that creeped me the hell out, despite the beam of light aimed at the ceiling.

Without a shameful bone in my body, I wiggled over the foot between us until his elbow touched mine.

"Are you shaking?" he asked in a strange tone.

"Only a little bit." I scooted an inch closer, soaking in the heat his body was throwing off.

Aiden sighed like I was torturing him, while all I'd done was mind my own business in bed. "You're fine."

I moved the light in the shape of a circle across the ceiling. "I know."

Another great big sigh only possible from a man his size made its way out of his throat. "Come here." His voice seemed to rumble across the sheets.

"Where?" I was already next to him. I rolled onto my side.

"Closer, Van," he ordered, exasperated.

I wasn't anywhere near being worried about how weird it was to be in bed with someone who hadn't even given me a real hug once in the entirety of the time we'd known each other. I definitely wasn't thinking about how he was mostly naked and how I only had underwear and a tank top on.

So I moved over, right on over until I realized he wasn't on his back any longer. He was on his side. I practically pressed up against him, my face right between his pecs, my arms between my chest and the middle of his.

He was warm, and he smelled wonderful, like the expensive coconut oil and herbal soap he used. The same stuff I used to order him from online once upon a time when things between us had been so different. I couldn't begin to imagine that Aiden—that same man who had spent a minimum of five days a week keeping me at arm's length five months ago—was in my bed right then because he knew about my phobia.

Later when I was capable of it, I'd think about him waking up and coming to my room, but right then wasn't the time.

He shifted a little, just a little. The bristles covering his chin brushed my forehead for a split second. He made a noise, a soft one, a relaxed one, and his facial hair touched me again, lingering just a moment longer on my skin. "How have you survived the last twenty years being terrified of the dark?" His question was so cottony, so pliable, I opened my mouth to answer before I thought twice about it.

"I always have a flashlight," I explained. "And except for these last two years, I've always lived with someone. Plus, it's rare that I'm ever in complete darkness. You learn how to avoid it."

"You lived with a boyfriend?" he asked casually, his breath warm on my hair. If his tone was a little too casual, I didn't pick up on it.

"Uh, no. I've never 'lived' with one. I've only had three and it never came up." I locked my gaze on that shiny gold medal draped high over his left pectoral. "Have you ever lived with a girlfriend?"

The scoff that came out of Aiden made me jump just because it was so unexpected. "*No.*" His tone sounded either disgusted or disbelieving that *he* would do something so stupid. "I've never been in a relationship."

"Never?"

"Never."

"Ever?"

"Ever," the smug-ass responded.

"Not even in high school?"

"Definitely not in high school."

"Why?"

"Because every relationship will end up one of two ways: you'll end up breaking up, or you'll end up marrying the person. And I don't like wasting my time."

That had me tipping my head back so I could meet his eyes. His expression said he thought I'd lost my damn mind, but my mind was too busy to be lost. He had a point about the outcome of relationships, but the rest of it . . . his lack of dates. The religious medallion around his neck. It all suddenly made sense.

"Are you . . ." I couldn't get it out. "Are you saving yourself for marriage?"

He didn't throw his head back and laugh. He didn't flick me on the forehead and call me an idiot. Aiden Graves simply stared at me in the shadowy room, his face inches from mine. When he was done staring at me, he blinked. Then he blinked some more. "I'm not a virgin, Vanessa. I had sex a few times in high school."

My eyes bulged. High school? He hadn't been with anyone since freaking high school? "In high school?" My tone was as disbelieving as it should have been.

He picked up on what I was trying to hint at. "Yes. Sex is complicated. People lie. I don't have time for any of it."

Holy. Shit. I watched his face. He wasn't lying. Not even a little bit. That suddenly explained what the hell he did in his room for hours by himself. He masturbated. He masturbated all the time. I felt my face get hot as I asked, "Are you a born-again virgin?"

"No." Those lashes lowered over his eyeballs again. "What would make you think I was?"

"You've never had a girlfriend. You don't ever go on dates." You jerk off all the time. Crap, I needed to stop thinking about him and his hand and all the time he hung out in his room.

Aiden was definitely giving me a "you're an idiot" face. "I don't have time to bother trying to have a relationship, and I don't like most people. Women included."

I wrung my hands, which were still between our two bodies. "You like me a little."

"A little," he repeated with only a small curve to the corners of his mouth.

I let his comment go and reached forward with one of my index fingers to point at the St. Luke's medallion around his neck. "Isn't this a Catholic saint? Maybe you're religious."

His big hand immediately went up to touch the quarter-sized object he carried around with him always. "I'm not religious."

I raised my eyebrows, and he gave me an exasperated expression.

"You can ask whatever you want."

"But will you answer?"

He huffed as he settled that massive, mostly nude body in front of me. "Ask your damn question," he quipped brusquely.

I held the tip of my index finger directly above his medal before drawing my hand back toward my chest, feeling über shy. I'd wanted to ask him for years, but I'd never been confident enough to. What better moment than when he was commanding me to ask? "Why do you always wear it?"

Without a hint of reservation, Aiden answered. "It was my grand-father's."

Was that my heart making a racket?

"He gave it to me when I was fifteen," he went on to explain.

"For your birthday?"

"No. After I went to go live with him."

His voice was smooth and comforting. Everything about it had me closing my eyes, sucking up his words, and giving me this sense of openness. "Why did you go live with him?"

"Them. I lived with my grandparents." The bristles of his beard touched my forehead again. "My parents didn't want to deal with me anymore."

That was definitely my heart making all kinds of horrendous noises. This all felt too familiar, too painful even for me.

Possibly too painful even for Aiden.

What Aiden was saying didn't add up with the man across from me. The one who rarely raised his voice in anger, hardly ever cursed, rarely fought with any of his opponents much less his teammates. Aiden was a low-level charge—determined, focused, disciplined.

And I knew way too well what it was like to be unimportant.

I wasn't going to cry.

I kept my eyes closed and Aiden kept his secrets close to his heart.

His breath touched my forehead. "Did you ever go to therapy?" he asked. "After what your sisters did?"

Maybe this wasn't a conversation I wanted to have after all. "No. Well, I went to a psychologist when I left my mom's house. Well, when CPS took custody. They only asked questions about what things were like where my mom was concerned. Not about . . . anything else really." In hindsight, I figure they wanted to be sure I hadn't been abused by her or anyone else she could have brought into her kids' lives. The psychologist must have seen something in my older sisters that he didn't like because we got split up into different houses. Honestly, I'd never been happier than I was after that.

How messed up was that? I couldn't even bother feeling that guilty about it, especially not when we'd gone to a good family with strict but caring adults. Not like what I'd had before. "I don't like being scared. I wish I wasn't, and I've tried not to be," I blabbered on mindlessly, feeling defensive all of a sudden.

He reared back, and I could tell he was looking at me with an uncertain expression. "It was only a question. Everyone is scared of something."

"Even you?" I made myself meet his eyes, easily batting away the defensiveness I'd felt a moment ago and clinging on to the subject change.

"Everyone but me," came his smooth, effortless response.

That had me groaning. The bright beam of light between us was throwing shadows over parts of his face. "No. You said it. Everyone's been scared of something. What about when you were a little kid?"

The silence went thoughtful just as thunder made the windows rattle. I subconsciously touched him right between the pecs with my fingertips.

"Clowns."

Clowns? "Really?" I tried to imagine a tiny Aiden crying over men and women with overly painted faces and red noses, but I couldn't.

The big guy was still facing me. His expression clear and even, as he dipped his chin. "Eh."

God help me, he'd gone Canadian on me. I had to will my face not to react at the fact he'd gone with the one word he usually used only when he was super relaxed around other people. "I thought they were going to eat me."

Now imagining *that* had me cracking a little smile. I slid my palm under my cheek. "How old were you? Nineteen?"

Those big chocolate-colored eyes blinked, slow, slow, slow. His dark pink lips parted just slightly. "Are you making fun of me?" he drawled.

"Yes." The fractures of my grin cracked into bigger pieces.

"Because I was scared of clowns?" It was like he couldn't understand why that was amusing.

But it was. "I just can't imagine you scared of anything, much less clowns. Come on. Even I've never been scared of clowns."

"I was four."

I couldn't help but snicker. "Four . . . fourteen, same difference."

Based on the mule-ish expression on his face, he wasn't amused. "This is the last time that I come over to save you from the boogeyman."

Shocked out of my mind for a split second, I tried to pretend like I wasn't, but . . . I was. He was joking with me. Aiden was in bed joking around. With me. "I'm sorry. I'm sorry, I was just messing with you." I scooted one more millimeter closer to him, drawing my knees up so that they hit his thighs. "Please don't leave yet."

"I won't," he said, settling on his pillow with his hands under his cheek, his eyes already drifting to a close.

I didn't need to ask him to promise not to leave me; I knew he wouldn't if he said so. That was just the kind of man he was.

"Aiden?" I whispered.

"Hmm?" he murmured.

"Thank you for coming in here with me."

"Uh-huh." That big body adjusted itself just slightly before he let out a long, deep exhale.

Without turning around, I laid the flashlight down behind me and aimed the beam toward the wall. He didn't ask if I was really going to leave the flashlight on all night—or at least however long the battery lasted. I just smiled at him as I took my glasses off and set them on the unused nightstand behind me. Then I tucked my hands under my cheek and watched him.

"Good night. Thank you again for staying with me."

Peeking one eye open, just a narrow slit, he hummed. "Shh."

That "shh" was about as close to a "you're welcome" as I was going to get.

I closed my eyes with a little grin on my face.

Maybe five seconds later, Aiden spoke up. "Vanessa?"

"Hmm?"

"Why was I saved on your work phone as 'Miranda P.'?"

That had my eyes snapping open. I hadn't deleted that entry off the contacts when I quit, had I? "It's a long, boring story, and you should go to sleep. Okay?"

The "uh-huh" out of him sounded as disbelieving as it should have. He knew I was full of shit, but somehow, knowing he knew, wasn't enough to keep me from falling asleep soon after.

And when I woke up when it was still dark outside, rain pattering the windows, it took me a moment to realize where I was: on my bed, and I was doing my best to imitate a blanket.

Aiden's personal human blanket.

One of my legs was thrown over his thigh, a forearm was flopped across his bellybutton, and the top of my head was literally nestled onto his bicep. My freaking mouth was an inch from his nipple.

What in the hell was I doing?

Moving my head slightly back, I found Aiden on his back with his palm acting as his pillow—where his pillow was, I had no idea—and his other arm, the one whose biceps I was using as a pillow, was wrapped around my neck.

Pulling my leg and arm back so that I wasn't acting like a massive octopus, I slowly rolled over, keeping my head where it was. I tried to imagine what Aiden would have thought if he'd woken up and found me in that position, and I didn't want to know.

What he didn't know wouldn't hurt him.

"I WOKE UP in the middle of the night to get a drink of water," Zac said over a bowl of oatmeal and bananas.

I took my glasses off and let out a big yawn. Aiden had accidentally woken me up that morning at six when he'd rolled out of bed. My bed. The one he'd slept in with me all night. Well, for six hours. I'd tried going back to sleep, but I hadn't been able to. Instead, I'd lain in bed and watched television until I figured I was awake enough to get some work done before eating breakfast.

"And your door was wide open," he continued.

I slammed my mouth closed.

"Noticed you weren't alone, darlin'." The idiot didn't even bother hiding the shit-eating grin on his face. He was enjoying this way too much.

Now I could have handled the situation in a few different ways. I could have played dumb. I could have freaked out. Or I could have made it seem like it wasn't a big deal. When you're dealing with one of the nosiest men in the world, option three was really the only choice. Tapping the fork tines against the plate, I leveled an even look at the dark blond across from me. "The lights went out last night during the storm."

"Uh-huh."

He was eating this up. "He knows I'm scared of the dark," I continued.

"Scared of the dark." Those tawny eyelashes fluttered. "Uh-huh."

"That's all that happened. Stop looking at me like that."

Zac chuckled before spooning oatmeal into his mouth. "Whatever you want, Mrs. Graves."

That had me groaning. "It wasn't even like that."

"I'm not arguin' with ya, darlin'." He *said* that, but I wasn't remotely convinced he was going to let it go.

"It really wasn't like that at all," I added anyway. "He's just . . . trying to be my friend."

A friend who climbed into bed with you? I wondered to myself. Maybe next time he would just get me a lantern for emergencies.

I could easily believe he'd woken up from the lightning and the crazy thunder and the crazier wind. But what had made him think about coming to my room once the lights had gone out? Because he'd seen how it was for me, right? Because he cared at least a little, and that's what friends did. Or maybe it was because if I had a heart attack in bed, everyone would see that this thing between us wasn't real, and he wanted to protect his reputation.

I didn't have the energy or the will to think about it too much.

Zac raised an eyebrow before digging back into his food once more. "You're more than likely the first person he's ever tried to be friends with, Van."

I eyed him, suddenly feeling a little uncomfortable. I just shrugged and went back to eating my food. After all, what would be my argument? "You're his friend."

"Not so much, sugar."

I couldn't totally disagree with him; all the components I thought made up friendship were seriously missing between Aiden and Zac. They didn't do anything together. As far as I saw, they never really talked to each other, especially since Zac had gotten kicked off the team. That bond between them had become even thinner. They were just, well, roommates.

Then again, this was Aiden. Did we expect him to give hugs and write love letters? "You know, that day we went out and you got hammered? He came downstairs and helped me get you on the couch. He was worried about you. That says something, I think."

It was obvious he brushed off my words, and I didn't push. I didn't get male friendships and I probably never would. "Are you spending Thanksgiving with Diana?" he asked.

I shook my head. "No." I'd texted her a couple days ago and her response had been **TOO SOON TRAITOR**. I'd give her another week to chill out unless she contacted me first. It wasn't a big deal. After all, it was just Thanksgiving. How many years had I settled for macaroni and cheese in a box for it? "My little brother has a game on Friday. I'm just going to stay here. What about you?

Zac scrunched up his nose. "I gotta head home. I wouldn't hold it past my ma to come get me and drag me back by the ear if I don't." He chuffed. "It wouldn't be the first time."

I snickered, thinking of Mrs. Travis and agreeing with him. She was intimidating and outrageous, and a southern belle down to the tips of her French-manicured nails. I'd met her on several occasions when she'd come up to Dallas for games. "I could see her doing that."

"She would. I think she thinks she's been givin' me enough slack since I got released. '*My baby needs to come home and let his mama help him get sorted out*,' her last voicemail said." He shot me a look. "You wanna come with me?"

For a moment, I contemplated tagging along but shook my head. "I should probably just stay here. Thank you though."

He shrugged, only looking slightly disappointed. "If you change your mind, you know you're welcome."

"I do. Thanks, Zac. I'd tell you to stay, but honestly, I'm a little scared of your mom. I'd probably drive you myself if I had to."

"Chicken."

I grinned. "You're the one who doesn't want to go home. Just make sure you keep up with running. I don't need you slacking off. Your smoker's lung is bad enough and we're on a tight schedule."

He moaned but grudgingly nodded. "I will," he assured me with a smile that came and went as quickly as it had appeared. "Before I forget again—what the hell is up with you and Christian?"

The grin I had on my face disappeared. "Nothing."

"Don't *nothin'* me. You said that thing about not likin' him for a reason, and I kept fuckin' forgettin' to ask you about it. What happened?"

When the hell had I acquired an older brother? I wondered before the tall blond, who looked nothing like me, waved his fingers in a "come on" gesture that had me scowling. "It isn't a big deal."

He simply moved his fingers again, and I realized in that moment, he wasn't going to let this go. He'd put his Aiden britches on, apparently.

I figured the sigh that came out of me was well deserved. I dropped my head back, slowly lifted it, and peeked at him with one eye.

"He's a douche bag. You know that," I went with, opening my other eye. "And he tried coming on to me once."

Zac blinked those baby blue eyes. "When?"

"Maybe a year and a half ago." It was definitely a year and a half ago, but who needed to be specific? "I was out with Diana at a bar and he was there. He was drunk. He recognized me . . . and then he just started being obnoxious, trying to kiss me and be sneaky and touch my butt. Just douche-bag stuff."

Reaching up, my friend tugged at his earlobe and shot me the fakest smile someone as genuine as Zac was capable of. That didn't put me at ease. At all. "No shit, sugar."

I waved him off. "It isn't a big deal. I just try to stay away from him now. I shouldn't have even brought it up."

His eyes had kind of glazed over and he seemed to daze off, looking at something over my shoulder.

"Yoo-hoo. Zac?"

His eyes strayed back to look at me, focusing, a real smile finally reappearing on his mouth. "Sorry."

This guy didn't have a rude bone in his body; the fact he'd zoned out didn't sit well with me. I narrowed my eyes at him. "What were you thinking about?"

He threw my words back at me. "Nothing, Mrs. Graves."

"Stop it."

THE NEXT WEEK went by pretty quickly. I had a lot of work to do, and when I was called and requested for an emergency babysitting job by Diana's brother, Rodrigo, because she couldn't get out of her appointments, I didn't say no. I couldn't say no. I really liked his boys, and even if Rodrigo was an idiot who refused to believe his sister could lie to him, he was still a great guy. It just so happened that I found a little toy his kids had that made me laugh, and paid the oldest five dollars for it.

My mom had called once to ask if I was planning on coming for Thanksgiving dinner, and I gave her the same response I had every

Thanksgiving since I was eighteen. "No." I'd stopped bothering to make excuses why I couldn't make it. My little brother wasn't going to be there, and him begging would have been the only reason I'd show up, but he'd never do that to me. She didn't say a word about Susie or the other two demons I shared genetics with.

Before I knew it, it was Wednesday and the house was empty. With a Thanksgiving Day game against the Three Hundreds' top rivals, the only roommate I had who was still in town was gone all the time.

So I was surprised on Wednesday afternoon when my phone beeped from its spot next to me on the desk.

It was Aiden.

> **Aiden:** Game tomorrow?
> **Me:** Sign me up, but just one ticket this time. Please 😳
> **Aiden:** Only one?
> **Me:** Yes . . .

Zac was gone and Diana had let me know via text message that she was going to see her parents in San Antonio for Thanksgiving and that if I wanted to come along she wouldn't purposely wreck her car on the drive there. I texted her back, letting her know I appreciated her generous offer but was fine with staying in Dallas, because I was planning on seeing my little brother who was playing a game nearby on Friday. I figured on Thanksgiving Day, I could get ahead on some T-shirt designs I'd been inspired to do instead.

> **Aiden:** There's no one to go with you?
> **Me:** < -- Forever Alone -- >
> **Aiden:** < Forever Annoying >
> **Me:** You'd miss me if I was gone, sunshine.

I'd barely hit "send" when I cursed, then sent him another message.

> **Me:** Thanks for the ticket.

He didn't respond, but when I got out of the shower that night and found something in the team's colors wrapped in clear plastic on my bed, I stared at it. And when I ripped off the packaging and shook it out to see that it was a brand-new Three Hundreds jersey with GRAVES written on the back, I smiled so hard my cheeks hurt.

Taking a peek at the clock next to my bed, I saw it wasn't nine yet and made my way to Aiden's room, the master bedroom down the hall. His door was closed when I got there, but I knocked, listening for him on the other side.

Sure enough, "Vanessa?"

"It's Muffin."

He made a noise I couldn't distinguish. "Come in."

I turned the knob and slipped inside, leaving it open behind me. Sitting on the edge of his California king–sized bed, Aiden was busy rubbing a towel over his head. The first thing I noticed was how smooth his jaw was. Without the beard, he looked younger . . . nicer. I'd only seen him freshly shaved a handful of times in the past, since he usually did it at night and it all grew back in while he slept.

"Did the light go out in your room?" The smug-ass dragged a towel over the back of his neck as he asked.

"You're so funny." I rolled my eyes so he knew how irritating I thought he was. "Dummy."

The corner of his full mouth perked up a bit as he tossed his towel into the hamper in the corner of the room.

And it was right then that I realized he was only wearing that little piece of gold resting right by his collarbones and boxer briefs. Gray, form-fitting, made with some kind of spandex, boxer briefs.

My mouth went dry and I averted my eyes to look somewhere else—anywhere else—instead . . . instead of at those huge thighs I used to see all the time in compression shorts when I would take pictures of him. Or instead of that thick, shadowy bulge tucked along to the left against his leg. I locked my eyes on his dresser. "I, ah, saw the present you left me on my bed," I noted, grasping for words.

"Uh-huh," he muttered as I saw him stand up in my peripheral vision and make his way toward the same dresser I was trying to focus on.

What was he doing? I swallowed and peeked at the greatest butt I'd ever seen for one second before looking away again. "I just wanted to say thank you."

The two bulky muscles lining either side of his neck went up and down. You'd never seen trapezius muscles until you'd seen Aiden's. "I got it for free, and you needed a new one."

I glanced at his butt one more time for a second. I was weak. Then I glanced again. *So freaking weak.* "They gave it to you for free?" My voice sounded strained, and why wouldn't it? I couldn't stop staring at the greatest bubble butt and pair of thighs in the universe. I wanted to bite them. I honestly wanted to bite them.

"It's the only one I've ever asked for. They had to give it to me," he explained over his shoulder.

His comment warmed me way more than it should have, and it had me focusing on the gold chain around his neck. I wanted to ask him about his parents and why they weren't figures in his life. I wanted to know if he'd been a pain in the ass when he was a kid. More than anything though, I wanted to find out what his favorite thing about his grandparents was. But I didn't. Instead, I asked his back, "Can I ask you something?"

"I said you could."

We might get along better, but I still wanted to shank him from time to time. Something told me that would never change. "I've always wondered, why didn't you play hockey instead of football?"

He turned that big, damp body around to face me as he slipped heather-gray pajama pants up his legs. Those long, size 13 feet peeked out from beneath the baggy hems of his pants. And that upper body . . .

It hadn't gotten old, and I hadn't become desensitized to those hard, square pecs covered with a sprinkling of dark chest hair. Or those hard slabs of stacked abdominal muscles. Those wide shoulders, trim waist, and bulging biceps only made him look that much more spectacular. He'd turned down a magazine cover photo shoot for some stupid reason the year before, and I hadn't understood why. Even when he was at a higher weight, he still looked amazing. If he sold a calendar filled with pictures of himself in it, he could make so much money.

That was something to think about later when Aiden wasn't busy telling me I was stereotyping the rest of his countrymen. "Not every Canadian is good at hockey," he explained, tying the cord of his pajama pants.

I glanced at his calm face and raised my eyebrows. "Are you saying you sucked at it?"

He gave me that smug look I usually hated as he planted his hands at his waist. "I didn't 'suck at it.' I'm good at most sports. I didn't enjoy playing it, is all."

Arrogant much?

"You've sat through all those interviews with me. You know everything," he added in a way that struck a chord with me, like he was trying to tell me something I couldn't piece together.

"You've always just talked about how you liked playing lacrosse, but that's it." For some reason, no one had ever outright asked him why he didn't play the more popular Canadian sport than one that was predominantly American, at least as far as I could remember.

The big guy leaned his bottom against the dresser. "My grandfather enrolled me in it for a few seasons when I was younger, but it didn't click for me; you didn't know that?" I shook my head. "My high school's hockey coach tried recruiting me to play for him in Grade 10. I was already six feet tall. I weighed 200 pounds, but I told him I wasn't interested."

While I recognized the differences between football and hockey were vast, I still couldn't comprehend what he was trying to hint at. "What didn't you like about it?"

"I didn't like it. It's that simple." His tongue poked at the inside of his cheek and the big guy didn't make any theatrics about what he said next. "My dad used to beat the shit out of me because he could, once a week at least until I hit puberty. I've gotten into enough fights in my life; I'll fight somebody if there's a good reason, but not for a game."

I never tried to throw myself too much of a pity party over what I'd grown up with. Over not being loved enough by my mom. Over not being important enough for whoever my dad was to stick around or at least attempt to meet me. While I definitely wasn't as messed up as my sisters, I had a temper. I got angry easily. But I had made myself learn how to control it. I had decided early on that I wasn't going to let that emotion define me.

I wanted to be better. I wanted to be a good person. I wanted to be someone—not necessarily someone great or someone important—but *someone* I could live with.

My little brother didn't drink at all, and I knew it was because of our mom's drinking problem. While he was four years younger than me and had spent less time in that household than I had, he remembered enough. How could he not? But I didn't want to avoid alcohol because I was scared of what it could do to me. I didn't want to demonize it. I wanted to prove to myself that it wasn't a monster that destroyed lives unless you let it.

Life was all about choices. You chose what to make out of what you had. And I wasn't going to let it make me its bitch. I could be a mature adult who knew her limits. I could be a good person. Maybe not all the time, but enough.

So Aiden's explanation, and the fact that his motherfucking asshole dad used to pick on him, pricked at the soft, tender pieces of this place that went deeper than my heart. I knew what it was like to not want to fall into a hole that had been dug for you before you even had a chance to fill it up. It made my eyes sting.

I made myself look down so he wouldn't see what had to be eighty different unwanted emotions written all over my face.

And maybe Aiden felt as unbalanced as I did, because he set the subject back into place and moved on to a safer one. "I was playing lacrosse before that anyway."

The rest of the story I was familiar with, and I told it while my gaze was still on the muted beige carpet. "Then Leslie talked you into trying football," I relayed back to him the information he'd shared with others a hundred times before. According to the story, he'd never played football before and he'd been interested. The rest was history. Except now I knew a fragment of the story I didn't before — he'd known Leslie for a long time; he'd been his grandfather's best friend. Leslie believed he'd asked him at the right moment. It had been a split-second decision that had changed the entire course of Aiden's life.

That summer between grades 10 and 11, he gained twenty pounds of muscle and practiced with Leslie several times a week. By the middle of his last year of high school, several schools in Canada and the U.S. had already begun trying to get in on the Aiden Graves pie. He was a phenomenon. A natural. His talent and hard work were etched so deeply into him, it was impossible to ignore the diamond in the rough.

"Leslie asked me to play for him the day after my grandfather caught me with a girl in his backseat, and told me I needed to find something more productive to do with my time or he would."

How about that. He really wasn't a virgin. Huh. My mouth twitched and I raised my gaze up to meet his. "Well, I think it's really admirable that you only get into fights with people who deserve to get the shit kicked out of them. If no one else ever tells you, it's really noble. Very superhero-y."

My comment had the big guy rolling his eyes, uncomfortable with my compliment. Well, he was uncomfortable with every compliment ever hurled his way. I didn't know why I found it so attractive, and I didn't really want to, but it was impossible to feel otherwise. How could someone be so arrogant but so humble at the same time?

"I'm not even close to being some kind of hero," he argued.

A burst of affection filled my chest. "You came to save me last week when I needed you. You can be an off-white knight in shining armor," I told him before I could think twice about what I was saying.

His chin seemed to jerk back and those irises focused on me. His jaw went tight.

I'd already said enough, and I didn't want to push too much. At the rate I was going, I'd end up complimenting his butt next. "Okay, I know it's close to your bedtime, and I just wanted to say thank you for my gift. I'll wear it with pride, but just don't tell Zac I left his at home."

The big guy nodded, standing straight. He shook out his hands at his sides. "Good night, Van."

I took a step back and grabbed the doorknob, smiling as I closed the door on my way out. "Night, night."

MEET ME IN the family room, the note, written in neat print on the back of a grocery store receipt, read; I'd only been expecting my ticket, not the pass to get me through security that had been inside along with it.

The pass burned as a constant reminder inside my pocket the entire game — a game they lost. I'd kept touching it to make sure it hadn't fallen out, trying to wrap my head around why he would ask me to meet him afterward. I mean, I'd met him afterward a few times, but it had always been because he needed something from me when I worked for him.

I had to ask a few of the stadium's employees where to go, because when I used to meet up with Aiden in the past, I would usually drive straight over and go through the entrance allocated for family members.

I wasn't looking forward to going to the family room, mainly because it would be the first time I'd see everyone since last season. I wouldn't call any of the wives I'd been friendly with "friends," but I didn't think they'd forgotten about me in a year. Back then, I'd been the only woman in Aiden's life, and for a little while, I'd been "the new girl," because most of them hadn't been convinced I was his assistant and our relationship was solely a business one.

And now . . .

Well, now I looked like a lying schmuck when there really hadn't been anything going on between Aiden and me in the past. But it wasn't like anyone was going to believe that now, even if I hadn't seen them since his injury last October.

If I wanted to be honest with myself, I was dreading it a little.

Okay, more than a little.

I had to really reach down into my spine and pump some steel into it, reminding myself that I knew I hadn't lied to anyone. As long as I knew that, it was all I would need. I was there for Aiden, not anyone else. In my head, I kept repeating those words as I marched through security checkpoint after security checkpoint with my pass and ID in my back pocket ready to get put to good use.

The "family room" was really just a glorified area on the way toward the players' parking lot, with a few couches and circular tables, clear away from the media. I took my time walking over, but it came too quickly anyway. With one last security check, I raised my chin up high and walked into the room like it was no big deal, like I had nothing to feel bad about.

The room was packed. Packed with kids and women and men of all ages. It was stuffed full of Three Hundreds apparel. The first "Oh, honey, congratulations!" smacked me right between the shoulder blades, and while I wasn't any sort of actress, I didn't like being a rude asshole when it was me being deceptive.

So I turned around and tried to give the woman talking a bright expression.

What followed was probably one of the most painful thirty minutes I'd ever spent, and that was saying a lot considering my last trip to El Paso had sucked complete ass.

"I am so happy for you!"

"You two are meant for each other!"

"Are you expecting?"

"You have to make sure to always support your man."

"Make sure to plan the baby for the off-season!"

Meant for each other? My man? A fucking *baby*?

I wasn't sure how I didn't throw up. Honestly. Then there were all the subtle comments about how an NFO player's wife, especially a player for the Three Hundreds, was supposed to act. The players were supposed to be the center of the universe. Families were preferably not seen and not heard. "We" were the invisible support systems.

I didn't know a lot about the women, but I knew enough about the guys from the bits and pieces that Zac occasionally shared with me, and only a few of them were impressive. And if a guy was a piece of crap, what was his girlfriend or significant other like?

It was when I was in the middle of thinking about things like that, that I remembered I was married to the person who was considered by many to be the biggest asshole on the team. At least according to what Zac had told me in the past. He wasn't friendly, much less open, and he put zero effort into establishing friendships with anyone, much less the spouses and families of the people he played alongside with. He'd said it time and time again, he didn't have time for friendships or relationships.

What did that say about me? I was a lying asshole, depending on how you analyzed the facts.

I was in the middle of trying to lie to one of the vets' wives that I'd already had a Thanksgiving meal when players began trickling into the room. Apparently, her husband was one of them, because she patted my arm almost immediately after peeking over my shoulder. "I'll have to get your phone number next game. We should get together, babe."

On top of being an asshole, I was an imposter. Here were these women who were trying to be nice and include me—though a portion of them were those who had turned me off from hanging out in the family box—and here was I. A fake wife. I was a person who would be out of their lives in a few years, if not sooner depending on whatever Aiden decided in the near future.

Maybe this whole hanging-out-in-the-family-room thing hadn't been a good idea.

The good thing was, the regular season was already more than halfway over.

With a loose one-armed hug, she left me standing there alone for the first time since I'd walked into the room. I watched as the players approached their families in varying moods. Some of them had acceptant smiles, some of them had reluctant ones, and others wore sad smiles. A few looked pissed and didn't bother trying to hide it; it was obvious they would have rather been anywhere else than where they were.

Where was Aiden?

Had he forgotten about me or—

That familiar, big head suddenly appeared in a group of men just slightly smaller than him. Those brown eyes set deep into that broadly painted bone structure scanned the room quickly before they landed on me.

I waved.

His features weren't molded into any kind of particular emotion as he tipped his chin down. Those fine, full lips mouthed, "Ready?"

I smiled and nodded. Making my way through the crowded room, I kept my gaze on Aiden's face for the most part. I passed by two of the guys I'd done some work for in the past and stopped briefly when one of them shook my hand; the other player, the super-sexy one every female Three Hundreds fan was in love with, gave me a hug.

I was going to have to tell Diana about it. She'd lost it when I'd told her I was doing some work for him.

Apparently, I must have had a look on my face that said exactly how attractive I found his teammate, because Aiden was frowning when I reached him. I could feel the eerie sensation of multiple eyes on me, on us, looking and judging, and I knew what we needed to do. I made my eyes go wide and I flashed him a fake, toothy smile he would definitely realize was a sign to mentally prepare himself.

In hindsight, I should have kissed him.

Instead, I hugged him, my arms going around his waist for the first time ever.

The fact that we'd—literally—slept together but hadn't even officially hugged was beyond me. This had been two and a half years in the making.

If I had ever taken the time to imagine what it would be like to hug Aiden, the reality of it wouldn't have been disappointing in the least. Despite the fact that his broad shoulders tapered down to a trim waist, it wasn't that small. It was an illusion based on how muscular and oversized his upper body was.

My hands found each other around the small of his back. My chest met with his abs, and they were just as hard and unyielding as they looked. I pressed the side of my face to the spot right between his pecs, cheek first. His body was warm from the shower he'd taken and he smelled like the clean, gentle scent of his soap.

In the middle of me taking in the soft fragrance coming off him, he put his arms around me. Gently, gently, gently. One arm went around the top of my shoulders and the other one directly below it. He tightened his embrace and brought me in an inch closer into the cocoon of his massive body.

I tried not to freeze. He was hugging me. *He was hugging me.*

Something settled at the top of my head and I knew, I just freaking knew, it was his chin.

It was probably the second best hug I'd ever gotten in my life; only beat by the one my foster dad had given me when he visited me in the hospital right after Susie had hit me with her car. He'd been the first person to show up, the first person to come into my room after I'd woken up, and I'd lost it. And he'd given me a hug and let me grieve for the death of the rocky relationship I'd had with her.

But this was a completely different kind of hug.

While Zac wasn't a small man by any means and my little brother was six-foot-four, I'd never been hugged by someone as large as Aiden. I liked it. I liked it a whole lot. His bicep, pressed over my ear, seemed to muffle the noise of the people talking in the background. It was like being swallowed up by a tornado. A big, muscular, warm tornado with an amazing body that was going to watch out for you for the next few years of your life, even when you weren't on the best terms.

A big, muscular, warm tornado with an amazing body that was finally my friend.

That thought had me smiling into the beloved hoodie he had on. "This is nice," I admitted in a whisper.

The chest under my face tightened as much as those refined muscles could possibly get.

The hug only lasted possibly five seconds total before I drew back, but I was grinning like a total idiot, and I might have even been blushing, because the moment was so monumentally epic, it felt like I'd won a gold medal. Then I remembered the team had lost their game, and I dug into my front pocket for one of the slightly melted peppermint patties I'd snuck into the stadium. I had planned on eating it, but when I found the pass with my ticket, I ate one, saving the other for the big guy.

Holding the small plastic wrapped candy out, I raised my eyebrows.

He raised his eyebrows right back and plucked the chocolate from my palm, tearing it open, and sticking it in his mouth, the wrapper disappearing into the pocket of his jacket.

I watched him as he chewed it slowly and asked, "Do you have to do anything else?"

The Wall of Winnipeg shook his head, his attention totally focused on me, instead of the people around us.

My face went a little warm, unsure of how I felt with him and being the center of that intense stare. "You want to go home?"

"Yes."

"Will you drive me to get my car? I parked in the normal people's lot—"

"I'll give you a ride."

"I don't know if they'll let you drive into the parking lot . . ." I trailed off when he gave me that "you're an idiot, Van" look. I really wanted to stick my finger in his nose. "Right. Of course they'll let you in. Give me a ride then."

Aiden silently agreed, steering me with a tilt of his head toward the exit.

We'd taken maybe two steps when I spotted a familiar face standing at the entrance to the family room. I rolled back my shoulders as we approached the Three Hundreds' wide receiver. I saw the moment he spotted Aiden and then happened to glance to see me next to him. The smile that came over his face was downright unsettling, and it pissed me off.

"Good game, man," Christian Delgado said to Aiden, even as his gaze stayed locked on me. "Hi, Vanessa."

"Hi, Christian," I greeted him back, my voice flat, totally unenthusiastic.

"How you doing?"

"Fine, thank you, and you?" I seriously sounded like Lurch from *The Addams Family*.

The handsy fucker winked. He freaking winked at me, even as Aiden played my oversize shadow. "Great, honey."

Honey? Really?

A weight landed on my shoulder. Out of my peripheral vision, a wrist was draped there, long fingers hanging loosely. I kept the look on my face blank as we passed him and headed toward the tunnel.

I finally glanced up at Aiden once we were far enough away from the family room and Christian. "Sorry about springing that hug on you, but I knew people were watching and it would have looked strange if we didn't."

He kept his attention forward with a dismissive shake of his head. "How'd it go in there?"

"I had five women I'd never talked to in my life ask how many months along I was. Then three other people told me I'd better plan to have a baby during the off-season unless I wanted the powers that be upset with me." I raised my eyebrows thinking about those conversations again. I didn't like people telling me what to do, especially people I didn't know who were butting into something that wasn't their business.

"Ignore them."

"I should," I sighed, still torn between feeling bad for being a liar and annoyed with the other women for being so damn nosey.

He frowned down at me. "What is it?"

"Nothing."

Aiden squeezed my shoulder. "What is it?"

I shot him a look that was the closest imitation of his possible. "I feel bad being super friendly with them when this isn't what they think it is." I caught the crease between his eyebrows as they deepened. "And who knows what'll happen in a few months, right?" I lowered my voice, knowing how confidential this information was.

His nod was slow, not necessarily wary but something else completely; something I couldn't identify. "You couldn't live in a different state than me," he said out loud like this wasn't something he should stay quiet about.

I glanced around the walkway we were going down, just to make sure no one had popped up out of nowhere with a recording device in hand. "You want to talk about this now?"

"Why not?" the man who lied only every blue moon asked with a hunch of his shoulders.

Seeing no one around, I shrugged under his wrist. "Because maybe you don't want everyone to know?"

"I don't care, Van. I'm always going to do what's best for me. If anyone's surprised by that, it's their fault."

The fact that I'd kept my plan to quit a secret for two months didn't make me feel guilty. At all. I always knew Aiden of all people would understand what I'd done if he put some thought into it.

"You're fine moving?" he asked.

"I knew what I was getting myself into with you, big guy. I'm not going to suddenly back out on you. You told me you weren't totally happy here. This is your dream." I knew his contract was almost over. I knew even after he signed with a team, there was always the chance he could be traded. I was prepared for that reality; I'd made sure of it. Sure there was Diana, but continents could separate my best friend and me, and we'd still find a way to talk. Distance wouldn't do anything to our friendship. I'd survived not being her neighbor since I was fourteen. Plus, I was never moving back to El Paso. Ever.

On the other hand, my brother had his own life. We saw each other as much as we could, but with him in school and playing basketball, it wasn't often enough. After his game in Denton, it would more than likely be another month or two until I saw him again.

I was okay with that, because I knew he was fine. He was doing what he loved. It was with that thought, standing next to this man who clung on to his dream with every finger and toe, that I stopped walking. So did he.

Aiden's expression was carefully muted, but I wanted to make sure he understood. "I can work anywhere, and anyway, I'm here for you, not the team. Do whatever you need to do."

The expression on his face turned a little funny.

"We'll figure it out, but don't worry about me," I tried my best to reassure him. I wasn't sure why he thought I would change my mind or back out on him or do whatever it was that he thought I would. I'd thought about this long and hard before I'd agreed to marry him. An athletic career wasn't a guaranteed thing, even if he was in the best shape of his life.

Something so bright could be blown out in no time.

I smiled up at him and asked, "Are you hungry?" I blinked. "Stupid question. You're always hungry. I'll make something at the house."

"You haven't eaten?"

"I ate before I came to the game, but that was hours ago."

"You need to make sure you're eating enough with all the running," he threw in, making me almost trip. "What did you do today?"

"Nothing. I stayed at home."

"What about your friend you're always talking to? She lives here, doesn't she?"

"Diana? She went to her parents' house yesterday."

"In El Paso?"

"No. They moved to San Antonio a few years ago."

"You didn't want to go with her?"

"I'm not used to making a big stink about Thanksgiving. I'd rather get some work done and make some money."

Was that a half smile that came over Aiden's mouth? I'm pretty sure it was.

"I like Halloween and Christmas. That's all," I explained a little more in detail. Eyeing that fraction of a smile, I made myself ask the question I'd been thinking of the last few days since the nearby grocery store had begun carrying Christmas trees. "Hey, would it bother you if I put up a tree for the holidays?" And decorations, but I kept that to myself.

I had prepared myself for him to say no.

But he didn't say no as he guided me through the parking lot toward his Range Rover, parked in the closest spot in the lot, because he was one of the first people to get to the stadium. "If it makes you happy, it wouldn't bother me."

I snapped my head up to look at him. "Really?"

"Yeah." He snuck me a glance. "Stop acting like you're shocked. You really think I would tell you no?"

And suddenly, I felt like an asshole. "Maybe."

Those brown eyes rolled. "I don't care about Christmas, but if you want to do something, go for it. You don't have to ask. It's your house too."

Looking up at him, I didn't know where the knot in my throat came from, but it took a long time for it to go away.

didn't know who he was trying to fool, because he wasn't fooling anyone.

The black knit beanie he had pulled down to nearly his eyebrows wasn't hiding anything. Neither were the sunglasses he'd left on even after we got out of the car. Sure his hoodie mostly hid just how developed those big muscles underneath it were, but a nearly 300-hundred-pound man wasn't exactly inconspicuous.

It was like dressing an elephant in camouflage.

In this case, it was a sports superstar going into a college-level basketball game trying to be as inconspicuous as possible with the most minimal effort. That was the thing about Aiden, he never really went out of his way to go incognito. He just preferred being a hermit at home to avoid being spotted. Hence, why I'd been hired. I understood. I really did. He valued his privacy, and in my heart, I knew he would be the exact same way if he weren't famous.

Yet here he was, walking into a basketball stadium with me in Denton, Texas, where there was going to be at least a few hundred people in attendance, all to watch my little brother play.

When I'd gotten up early that morning, the day after Thanksgiving, the last thing I expected was to find Aiden awake at the breakfast nook. Usually the day after a game, he slept like the dead and even went as crazy as to get an extra two or three hours more of snooze time. With the Three Hundreds' game falling on Thanksgiving Thursday, the team gave the staff and players the rest of the weekend off.

But there he'd been at nine in the morning, in the kitchen, eating an apple, looking just as surprised to see me awake as I was to see him.

After dinner the night before, we'd watched two episodes of *Dragon Ball Z*, and then Aiden had tromped upstairs to hit the sack.

"Where are you going?" he had asked that morning.

"My little brother has a game," I answered him as I made my way toward the fridge to make breakfast.

Holding the apple up to his face, his features went pensive. "What kind of a game?"

It was then that I realized I had never told him. "He plays college basketball for Louisiana."

The Wall of Winnipeg blinked. "What position?"

"Point guard." I wasn't sure why, but I suddenly asked, "Do you want to come? It's only an hour away."

"I was planning on resting today . . ." He kind of trailed off and shrugged. "What time do you want to leave?"

Yeah, I'd been dumbstruck for a second.

It had only taken me the entire drive to decide that maybe I should have left him home. It wasn't like I cared if fans came up to him or anything—he was what he was—but I hadn't taken into consideration that he might not enjoy being gawked at for hours if anyone recognized him.

And why wouldn't anyone recognize him? He was the face of a professional NFO team in Texas. Even people who didn't watch football knew who he was with the big-name endorsements he had.

I then reminded myself that Aiden was always well aware of the pros and cons of the decisions he made. Always. He was a big boy and he made his own choices, so screw it. If he wanted to tag along, who was I to say no? I kept my mouth closed and my advice to myself.

And so, hours after my invitation, we were at the coliseum where the university held its games. Finally getting a chance to watch my little brother play for the first time this season, I was pretty excited both to see the team's starting point guard and to have the Wall of Winnipeg tagging along when he was usually content to stay home.

After picking up the tickets I'd bought on the way from will-call—I had originally only purchased one—we made it through security without any issues. In no time at all, we found our section, and Aiden gestured me to go ahead of him down the stairs.

The stadium wasn't anywhere near being packed. Considering it was the day after Thanksgiving, most of the North Texas's students were probably with their families, doing things other than going to a basketball game. There were only a couple handfuls of Louisiana colors in the stands. It suddenly explained why we'd gotten such good seats at the last minute.

By the time we sat down, the game hadn't started yet, but it was almost time for the players to come out. I smiled over at Aiden when he was seated next to me, the side of his denim-clad knee touching mine. I reached over and patted his thigh. I mean, I'd sat on his lap. He'd slept in the same bed as me. I'd given him a hug. What was a little pat in comparison? "Thank you for coming."

His careful expression slowly melted into a flat one. His words were clear-cut. "Shut up."

I stared at him for all of two seconds before grinning and touching his thigh again with a snort. "What? I can tell you thank you as much as I want."

"Don't."

I ignored his comment. "I'm glad you came. Doing things with someone else is a lot more fun than being alone, even if you're telling me to shut up. I appreciate it. So sue me."

Aiden made an exasperated sound. "I'm going to find the bathroom. I'll be back."

I gave him a thumbs-up before he got to his feet, which earned me an annoyed look, and then he disappeared up the stairs. I sat there drumming my fingers on my kneecaps waiting for the players to come out of the locker rooms. Someone tapped on my shoulder from behind, and I glanced back to see three guys in their early twenties sitting forward, eager expressions splashed all over their faces.

"Hi," I said a little uncertainly, wondering what was going on.

One guy elbowed the other one, and the third cleared his throat as he scratched behind his ear. If there was one thing I knew, it was people who felt awkward, and these guys were it.

"Is that Graves?" the one in the middle who had gotten the elbow asked.

Shit.

"Who?" I smiled sweetly, using my best dumb-girl eyes along with it.

"Aiden Graves," the friend said, like that would help if I really had no idea who that was.

Was I supposed to admit it was him? Or continue playing like I'd never heard of Aiden? A part of me wanted to go with the latter, but if someone caught a really good look of him and confirmed that it *was* him . . .

Well, Aiden wasn't the type to run away from anything.

So I dropped the doe eyes and nodded. "Yeah. Our secret."

From the way they reeled back, they were either shocked or they didn't believe me. All three of them blinked for a second before suddenly snapping out of it.

"It's really him?" one of them whispered.

The one in the middle muttered, "Holy fuck," before going a little pale.

"He's even bigger in person," the one on the right muttered, turning in his seat to look around like Aiden would have magically reappeared in just a couple of minutes.

The guy was right though. Pictures didn't do him justice. Hell, I was used to seeing Aiden up close and personal all the time, and I still hadn't become desensitized to him.

"*What is he doing here?*" the one on the left asked.

It was a fair question. Aiden had gone to college in Wisconsin. "My brother plays for Louisiana," I explained, deciding to go with the truth again. I mean, I couldn't really pull off a lie well anyway.

"Are you his girlfriend?"

The guy in the middle hit his friend on the right with his forearm. "Don't be a fucking idiot. Obviously she's his girlfriend, dumbass."

"You're both dumbasses," Lefty stated. "He got married. I saw it on-line." A hesitant look came over his face as he glanced at me. "Didn't you?"

Shit. Well, I did this to myself. In for a penny, in for a pound. My face got all red and hot even though I was trying to will it not to. "Yep."

"I'm not surprised. I love your hair." Righty smiled.

Yeah, my face went a little hotter and I shifted in my seat, conscious that I was two weeks past when I needed to do something with the fading teal color in my hair or just color over it. "Oh, thanks."

"Dude, would you shut the fuck up? Graves can eat you if he doesn't kill you," his friend, the guy in the middle, whisper-hissed.

I took that as my cue to turn around and face forward. They kept arguing behind me in whispers. Should I have played dumb?

Sometime later, in the middle of a little girl singing the national anthem, Aiden's big-ass butt plopped down into the seat next to mine. I tucked my elbows in to give him more room just as he handed over a souvenir cup filled with what I had a feeling was going to be Dr. Pepper. He had a bottle of water in his other hand.

I leaned over and patted the top of his hand. "Thank you, big guy."

He made sure to meet my eyes before leaning into me in return; his tongue poking at the inside of his cheek. "You don't have to thank me all the time."

"Shut up." I used his line on him, earning me a head shake and a flash of a tiny grin in return from the man whose face was about four inches away from mine. Just as he started to pull away, I tugged on his hoodie sleeve so he could come closer.

He did. Aiden was so close the side of his bristly jaw brushed the tip of my nose. I didn't jerk back, but I stayed in place, letting that wonderful clean scent coming off his skin fill my nostrils. "Those guys sitting behind us recognized you," I whispered.

Aiden shifted his face just enough so that his mouth brushed my earlobe. "Did they say anything to you?" That gritty, deep voice seemed to go straight to the center of my chest.

It took everything in me not to shiver as his breath hit the sensitive spot on my neck. "They asked if you were you and I said yes." I had to swallow as another soft puff of breath hit my neck. "And they know we're . . . you know . . . *together*."

He didn't react.

"I didn't know what to say. Sorry," I whispered.

That had him pulling back just enough to give me a dry look. "Vanessa—"

I beat him to it. "Shut up."

"I was going to tell you to stop saying sorry, but that works too."

Did he just smile at me? Did he just smile *smugly* at me? I wasn't sure. I wasn't sure, but I was going to take it as a yes. Yes, he had just smiled at me playfully.

And that had me blinking once. My heart beating twice. "In that case . . ."

"Shut up," he finished for me.

I burst out laughing as I reached into my purse and pulled out a red apple I had hidden under my scarf to get it through security and handed it over. "What a good boy. If you behave, I might have a smashed up Vega bar in my pocket for you."

I didn't know what it said about me that I carried snacks around for him, but whatever. He was like my puppy I had to make sure ate enough. You know, a massive puppy that made my insides feel discombobulated from time to time. Yeah, *discombobulated*. It was that bad.

He took the apple from me and reclined into his seat just as the teams' centers approached the middle of the court for tip-off. How the hell had I missed the players getting on the court? I took off my jacket, rolled back my shoulders, and prepared to cheer on my brother.

"Which one is he?"

I pointed at the pale-skinned idiot who I used to put on dresses for fun when we were younger. "Number thirty."

"He's taller than I thought he'd be," Aiden noted absently.

"I think his dad was tall."

Aiden glanced at me briefly. "You don't have the same one?"

"No. At least, I'm pretty sure we don't. I've never met mine as far as I know." And by that I meant, I'd never had any man pick me up and tell me I was his as a kid. My little brother's dad hadn't paid much attention to me when he'd been around. When I saw Aiden out of the corner of my eye, I noticed his face was tight. His jaw jutting. "What is it?"

His Adam's apple bobbed. "You've never met your father?"

My neck went a little hot and for some reason I got embarrassed. "No."

"Do you look like your mom?"

I reached up to mess with the leg of my glasses. "No." My mom was a blonde, somewhat pale, and she was only five-five. I was more peach-skinned, my hair a natural brown with a little red, and I was taller than the rest of the women in my family. "My friend Diana's mom used to tell me she thought my dad must have been Hispanic or maybe Mediterranean or something, but I don't know for sure."

"Have you always been tall?"

If I really strained and stood up straight, I was almost, *almost* five eight. "My sisters used to call me the Blind Giraffe." *Where's the Blind Giraffe at?* Bitches. "I was all legs and glasses—ooh look. They're about to play."

From the first time I jumped to my feet to cheer on my brother, I could tell Aiden wasn't prepared for what kind of fan I was. At least, what kind of fan I was for my little brother. By the beginning of the second half, he had started leaning away from me, fussing and whispering, "You're scaring me," after I got to my feet and started yelling at the ref for a shitty call made against Oscar, my little brother.

But it was the way he made his eyes go wide during halftime and pretend to shrink even farther away from me that made me laugh.

"Who are you?" he deadpanned, which made me snicker.

"What? I was the same way at your game yesterday."

Those black eyelashes hung low over his eyes. "Zac's seen you?"

I nodded.

Aiden blinked. "I think I want my jersey back."

I blinked back. "Tough shit, sunshine. It's mine now."

The corners of his mouth had barely started to pull up when someone yelled, *"The Three Hundreds suck! You suck, Toronto!"*

What in the hell?

Just as I started to glance around to see what idiot was yelling, Aiden's index finger touched my chin. I stopped. "Don't bother."

"Why?" I tried turning my head, but apparently his finger had Hulk-like strength, because it didn't go anywhere.

"Because I don't care what he thinks," he said in a tone so serious I quit trying to look elsewhere and focused in on that handsome, grave face.

"But it's rude." His hand moved from my chin around to the back of my head, that big palm cupping my neck. His thumb to the tip of his middle finger seemed to stretch nearly all the way around my throat.

"Do you think I suck?" he asked me, seriously, in a voice low enough for only me to hear.

I snorted, about to open my mouth and say something really smart-ass, but his thumb dug deep, the pressure making me groan out a hoarse noise of *holy shit, do it again.* But somehow I managed to say, "No," instead.

"Then why would I care what someone else thinks?" he murmured, steady and confident.

I didn't lower my face as I told him the truth. "I can't help it. I didn't like people talking about you when I worked for you, and I like it even less now."

Those dark brown eyes bore into mine. "Even when you used to flip me off?"

"Just because you've made me mad doesn't mean I ever stopped caring about you, dummy," I whispered in a frown, totally conscious of the guys sitting behind us. "I would have done just about anything for you back then, even when you got on my nerves. I might have just waited until the last minute to push you out of oncoming traffic, but I'd still push you out of the way."

I tipped my head in the direction of where the idiot had yelled from a minute ago. "Now it's definitely going to bother me that you're just minding your own business, living your life, and someone you don't know is yelling that kind of stuff. That guy doesn't know you. Who is he to talk shit to you?"

Damn it, just thinking about it had me craning my neck to try and turn around, but the hand on my nape kept me in place. All that intense Aiden-focus burned through the flesh of my skin, through the calcium of my bones, and straight into the very root of me. His nostrils flared at the same time as his thumb did that circle-massage thing that made my leg go numb.

"The only people in the world who can hurt you are those you let have that ability, Van. You said it—that guy doesn't know me. In my entire life, I've only cared what four people thought about me. I'm not worried about that nobody back there, understand me?" His hand moved, one finger, dry and callused, slipping behind my ear to rub around the shell where it met my head. It was probably the most intimate thing anyone had ever done to me.

Words—breathing—life seemed to catch in my throat as I took in those incredibly long lashes framing such potent eyes. The line of his shoulders was imposing and endless. His face was so severe and thoughtful, it plucked at my heart, but somehow, somehow I got myself to nod, the world in my throat. "I get it."

I did. I got it.

Did he care what I thought? He explained himself, his decisions, and his thoughts. But what did it mean?

He'd said he had four people in his life, and I now figured three of those had been his grandparents and Leslie. Who was the other person whose opinion mattered to him? I wondered.

I bit the inside of my cheek and let out a shaky breath. "I know you don't care what that asshole thinks, but that doesn't mean I'm not willing to pretend he punched me in the arm. You'd just have to be my 'witness.'" I smiled weakly at my joke. "Team Graves, right?"

Aiden didn't smile back.

His forehead tipped forward, and before I could react, before he said another word to me, he leaned forward, forward, forward and pressed his mouth just to the side of my mouth. A peck. A shot better than tequila, made up of friendship and affection and organic sugar.

When he pulled back, just a few inches, just enough for our eyes to meet, my heart pounded this crazy rhythm that might have been a borderline heart attack. I couldn't help but smile. Nervous and confused and overwhelmed and completely caught off guard, I had to gulp.

"GO BACK TO DALLAS!" the man sitting somewhere behind us yelled again, and the hold Aiden still had on the back of my neck tightened nearly imperceptibly.

"Don't bother, Van," he demanded, pokerfaced.

"I'm not going to say anything," I said, even as I reached up with the hand farthest away from him and put it behind my head, extending my middle finger in hopes that the idiot yelling would see it.

Those brown eyes blinked. "You just flipped him off, didn't you?"

Yeah, my mouth dropped open. "How do you know when I do that?" My tone was just as astonished as it should be.

"I know everything." He said it like he really believed it.

I groaned and cast him a long look. "You really want to play this game?"

"I play games for a living, Van."

I couldn't stand him sometimes. My eyes crossed in annoyance. "When is my birthday?"

He stared at me.

"See?"

"March third, Muffin."

What in the hell?

"See?" he mocked me.

Who was this man and where was the Aiden I knew?

"How old am I?" I kept going hesitantly.

"Twenty-six."

"How do you know this?" I asked him slowly.

"I pay attention," the Wall of Winnipeg stated.

I was starting to think he was right.

Then, as if to really seal the deal I didn't know was resting between us, he said, "You like waffles, root beer, and Dr. Pepper. You only drink light beer. You put cinnamon in your coffee. You eat too much cheese. Your left knee always aches. You have three sisters I hope I never meet and one brother. You were born in El Paso. You're obsessed with your work. You start picking at the corner of your eye or fool around with your glasses when you feel uncomfortable. You can't see things up close, and you're terrified of the dark." He raised those thick eyebrows. "Anything else?"

Yeah, I only managed to say one word. "No." How did he know all this stuff? How? Unsure of how I was feeling, I coughed and started to reach up to mess with my glasses before I realized what I was doing and snuck my hand under my thigh, ignoring the knowing look on Aiden's dumb face. "I know a lot about you too. Don't think you're cool or special."

"I know, Van." His thumb massaged me again for all of about three seconds. "You know more about me than anyone else does."

A sudden memory of the night in my bed where he'd admitted his fear as a kid pecked at my brain, relaxing me, making me smile. "I really do, don't I?"

The expression on his face was like he was torn between being okay with the idea and being completely against it.

Leaning in close to him again, I winked. "I'm taking your love of MILF porn to the grave with me, don't worry."

He stared at me, unblinking, unflinching. And then: "I'll cut the power at the house when you're in the shower," he said so evenly, so crisply, it took me a second to realize he was threatening me . . .

And when it finally did hit me, I burst out laughing, smacking his inner thigh without thinking twice about it. *Who does that?*

Aiden Graves, husband of mine, said it: "Me."

Then the words were out of my mouth before I could control them. "And you know what I'll do? I'll go sneak into bed with you, so ha."

What the hell had I just said? *What in the ever-loving hell had I just said?*

"If you think I'm supposed to be scared . . ." He leaned forward so our faces were only a couple of inches away. The hand on my neck and the finger pads lining the back of my ear stayed where they were. "I'm not."

As if the peck he'd given me hadn't done enough damage, the way he said that sent my heart pounding again. My chest flushing hot. Everything I thought I knew seemed to spiral out of control.

He was messing with me. Flirting with me. Aiden Graves. What was this?

It didn't help that, before I managed to get my heart back in shape or get my head on straight, my phone started vibrating. When I saw the incoming message as a picture from Diana, I didn't think much of it.

But when I unlocked the screen and saw the picture, it only sent me reeling all over again.

She had attached a shot of her television. On the screen was a picture of Aiden and me sitting in the stands just minutes before, his face so close to mine, his arm around my back. It looked . . . well, I didn't know what exactly it looked like, but Aiden and I were laughing. I could see what it didn't look like.

It didn't look like this thing between us was fake.

But then it got me thinking. Had Aiden just been extra friendly and flirty because he suspected this would happen?

"LOOK, HE'S RIGHT there." I smacked Aiden with the back of my hand before pointing at the brown-haired booger standing just outside, surrounded by teammates and other people not affiliated with the university. "Oscar!"

My brother didn't turn around.

"Oscar Meyer Weiner!" I yelled again.

That had him swinging his head around with a big grin on his face. Raising one hand, I waved, and tugged on Aiden's hand briefly with the other, urging him forward. After away games, he usually didn't have much time to hang around, so I wanted to take advantage of the few minutes we had together.

As we walked closer, I spotted my brother cutting a path through the crowd, only to stop abruptly for a second and look back and forth between Aiden and me, before he continued walking toward us. Behind Oscar, more than a few of the crowd were looking in our direction too.

My brother was smiling, but his gaze kept trailing to Aiden in confusion. "Why didn't you tell me you were coming?" he demanded as I took a step forward and let my brother give me a big hug, pulling me up off my feet. He'd been taller than me for nearly the last ten years and never let me forget it.

"I texted you on the way here, but I figured your phone was off when you didn't write me back," I said as he lowered me. I grinned at him, putting my hands on each side of his face to squish his cheeks together. We weren't super close anymore, but I loved the hell out of him. He'd been the only one in my family to never disappoint me.

He stuck his tongue out and tried to lick my hand.

I gave his cheek a pinch before I dropped my hands and took a step back so that my shoulder brushed the side of Aiden's arm. "Oscar, Aiden. Aiden, Oscar."

It was Aiden who extended his hand first.

"It's nice to meet you," Oscar said, his tone a little surprised as he shook Aiden's hand.

"Same." The big guy pulled back. "You played a good game."

I eyed him a little out of the corner of my eye. Had he just paid him a compliment?

My brother's face turned a little pink as he nodded. The big idiot was like a younger version of me—words weren't our strength in life. "Oh, ah, thanks. Everybody's been talking about how you were at our game," he stammered before his gaze swung over to me as his face kept that nice rosy shade. "I didn't think you'd be here together."

I shrugged, not knowing how to respond. "How was your Thanksgiving?"

Oscar shot me that face that said it meant about as much to him as it meant to me. "We had practice, most of us went to the coach's house for dinner. You?"

"I worked and then went to his game afterward." I elbowed Aiden's forearm.

"Hey . . ." His eyes darted behind me for a second; an uncomfortable look crawled over his long face. Oscar blew out a long, shaky breath. "Damn it, Vanny. I'm sorry, okay? You caught me off guard and I forgot . . ."

I didn't like where this was going. We never apologized to each other. If anything, Oscar and I had always understood what we needed to do to survive. He'd given me his blessing to go to school far away from him, and I never gave him shit for going weeks between contacting me.

But I had this terrible feeling . . .

"Susie is here. At least, she said she was going to be here."

Motherfucker. *Motherfucking fucker.* My teeth clenched down, one row aligned on top of the other, and I had to will my face from reacting. It took nearly everything in me to play off the anger filling me up. Of all the times to come see Oscar, Susie had to come now? Since when had she given a shit about him? While they'd always been nicer to him than they'd been to me, none of my sisters had ever really paid that much attention to him.

"I came to see you. It's fine," I lied. It wasn't fine. I didn't want to see my sister, and I didn't want him to feel bad either. As if I wasn't about three seconds away from screaming, I asked, "Are you heading back to Shreveport now?"

He nodded, the discomfort brutally apparent on his face. I guess he did know me well enough to not be fooled. "Yeah." Oscar stopped talking, his eyes going pained in a way that said "I'm so sorry" and raised his hand to wave at someone behind me. "Vanny, I'm sorry. I'm so sorry. If I knew you were coming, I would have told her . . ."

Not to come? I could be a better person for Oscar. "Don't worry about it. I'm not going to make you choose between us." That had him making a croaking noise that I waved off. "Don't be dumb. Give me a hug."

The clean, young lines of his face twisted and strained, but he nodded and quickly wrapped his arms around me. He whispered into my ear, "We have a game against San Antonio in a couple weeks. Come please. Both of you."

I pulled back and nodded a little more tightly than I would have liked. I really didn't want to make him feel bad, but just knowing Susie was in my general vicinity made me go to ten. Having Susie around when I'd driven an hour to come see Oscar pissed me off that much more. "I will. I'm not sure about the Hulk here with his schedule, but I'll go." I smiled at him. "I'll see you soon then. Love you."

"Love you, too, Vanny." Teeth locked, he glanced at Aiden and extended his hand again. "It was nice meeting you. Good luck the rest of your season."

The big guy nodded and shook his hand. "Thanks. You too."

I sensed the evil almost immediately. I spotted my sister and her idiot husband within seconds of turning around. It was like my body was tuned in to know where she was at; it always had been. It was a protective instinct, it had to be.

Apparently, she found me in the crowd immediately too. She was glowering, her mouth twisting as her gaze bounced from me to Aiden and back again. Almost four inches shorter than me and only two years older, Susie looked so much older than her actual age, but that was the consequences of drugs, heavy drinking, and just being a miserable bitch in general. Unhappiness prematurely aged a person, my foster mom had told me once. She was right.

But I still couldn't summon up any sympathy for my older sister. I believed in choices. We'd grown up in the same environment, went to the same schools, and had about the same intelligence, I figured. She'd always been a ruthless, angry, mean person, but at thirteen, she'd started doing stupid crap that led to more stupid crap and more stupid crap and more stupid crap until she was buried under so much crap, she could never find her way out of it.

You couldn't expect anyone to take care of you better than you could take care of you.

Summoning up every inch of adult in me, I told myself not to be petty. I wouldn't be petty no matter how much I wanted to. So I forced out a "Hi, Susie. Hi, Ricky" at both her and her significant other, the same one who had given me a bruise and had gotten damn near kicked in the balls for it.

Just as suddenly as the thought entered my head, the big body next to me suddenly froze in place. I didn't need to look at him to know his entire frame went rigid; I could feel it. Feel him. "Is that him?" he asked in a low voice that made the hairs on the back of my neck rise.

"Who?" I was dumb enough to ask.

"The guy who gave you the bruise on your arm."

The *oh shit* on my face must have been enough for him, because the instant I thought the answer—the *"yes* it's that bastard"—a muscle in Aiden's cheek popped. And he was gone. Those long legs ate up the few feet of concrete between us and Susie. Before I could say a word, stop him, tell him that guy wasn't worth the energy it took Aiden to get riled up, the Wall of Winnipeg had walked directly into the path of my sister's husband, effectively stopping the five-foot-ten-ish man in place. Considering he was never close enough to most human beings to really illustrate how large he really was, in that moment, with the two of them mere feet apart from each other, the difference was striking. Aiden dwarfed him in every way.

But it wasn't the obvious size difference that shocked me. It was the way Aiden, a professional athlete at the peak of his career, was reacting. I had never seen him so still. He was breathing out of his nose like a goddamn dragon. His biceps were so bunched and strained—I could tell from even under his hoodie—and he had the single cockiest expression on his face that I had ever seen, and that was saying something, because I thought I'd witnessed the most annoying of all his expressions. But the one he had on right then put all the rest to shame.

Aiden was pissed. *Pissed.* The king of control looked like he wanted to rip apart my sister's boyfriend/husband/whatever the hell he was.

And it was what he said next that tore me in half.

The Wall of Winnipeg stared down at the much smaller man, and in a voice that was as close to a cool, unattached statement as possible, he said, "Touch my wife again and I'll break every bone in your goddamn body."

My wife. Not Vanessa. He'd gone with *my wife*.

He'd cussed. For me. For my honor. He'd said the G-word, and it was just about the most romantic thing I'd ever heard in my life, because Aiden didn't do that.

Then he steered that acid-like gaze to my sister, who suddenly looked more uncomfortable than anyone in the world had ever been. He didn't say a word, but I could feel the disgust. I could feel words bouncing around in his head, shaping his tongue. I was sure Susie could sense them too.

It was right then, in that instant, that I realized I might be a little in love with Aiden. Not in a way that was anything like the easy crush I had on him in the past, but different. So, so different.

Shit.

Shit, shit, *shit*.

Seriously? I asked myself. *Are you fucking serious, Vanessa?*

TWENTY-THREE

I t was the garage door opening and closing at noon the following Monday that had me saving my work.

Neither one of the guys should have been home that early.

Zac had just gotten back from south Texas the night before, and he typically hadn't been getting back from training until three or four. On Mondays, Aiden didn't get home earlier than three. It was the shortest day for him out of the week, and after having the weekend off following their Thanksgiving Day game, there was no way he'd get home earlier. Mondays usually just consisted of a visit with the trainers, a workout, lunch, and a couple of different meetings that included watching the last game's film.

So who the hell was home, and why?

I got up and called out, "Who's home?" When there wasn't a response, I jogged down the steps to make my way toward the kitchen and paused when I spotted Aiden drinking a glass of water. "*What the hell happened to your face?*" I just about shouted the second I caught sight of the red and purple along his jaw.

He set the glass of water down on the countertop and gave me a flat look. "I'm fine."

He was so full of shit. I made my way around the island anyway. "I didn't ask if you were fine. What the hell happened?"

He didn't reply as he stuck his hands under the sink's fountain sensor and splashed water on his face. *What the hell did he do?* Aiden rarely got into fights. Hell, he'd told me why they were so few and far between, and I'd never heard a better reason for it. He didn't have an explosive temper; he usually just bumbled around at being irritated all day.

As he dried his face, I grabbed an ice pack from the freezer, wincing when he set the towel aside, giving me an up close look at the bruises that were going to take up a good portion of his face in a few hours.

Did I realize he was trying to avoid talking about whatever happened? Of course. I just didn't care.

Handing over the ice pack the instant he'd thrown away the paper towels, I took a step back and took in his features again in disbelief. "Did you get jumped?"

"What?" His gaze swung over to me as he frowned just a little bit. He was insulted. He was genuinely insulted. "No," he snapped, not in a mean way.

"Are you sure?" I asked hesitantly. Sure, he was huge, and sure, in raw strength he definitely had 99 percent of other men beat, but if there were multiple larger-than-average guys trying to beat him up, it could happen. Right? Just thinking about that possibility suddenly pissed me right off.

Pressing the ice pack against the line of his jaw, he shook his head just the tiniest bit, his eyes doing this dismissive flutter. "I didn't get jumped."

His assurance wasn't doing it for me, damn it, and I was getting angrier by the second. I touched his arm. "Tell me what happened, Aiden."

"Nothing."

Nothing. The right side of my mouth went tight. "You beat yourself up then?"

That scoff said more than the word "No" did.

"Then . . ." I trailed off, not giving this up.

"I don't want to talk about it." I'd already known that from the beginning. But as stubborn as he was, I was too. And I wasn't going to let it go, because this right here, the clear signs of him getting into a fight with someone on his team was a sign of the apocalypse. Aiden didn't give enough of a shit about his teammates to care what they said about him or to him.

He'd said it at the game, there were only a few people he'd ever met whose opinions mattered to him. And I knew that wasn't something he said for the heck of it. He meant it.

I'd been trying my best since Friday not to think about the basketball game we'd gone to. Or at least, I'd attempted not to think about what he'd said to my sister's husband or how he'd looked at Susie like he wanted to kill her. The memory of him grabbing my hand and walking with me to the car in silence as anger marred that handsome face had drilled a hole straight into my heart. Then, as we'd sat in my car, he'd said, "I'm sorry I didn't go with you."

All I'd managed to do was sit there and frown. "To where? El Paso?" His response had been a nod. "It's fine, big guy. It's all water under the bridge now." I couldn't help but reach over and put my hand over the top of his. "That was nice of you to stand up for me, by the way."

Well, I thought it had been more than nice, but the realization of what I thought I felt was something I never wanted to voice.

Then Aiden had gone and done it as he faced forward, staring out of the windshield, teeth gritted, jaw tight. "I've let you down too many times. I won't do it again."

Just like that, this feeling of dread poured through my stomach, making me antsy. He'd spent the rest of the weekend more remote than normal. While he hadn't become outgoing since we'd begun getting along a lot better, Aiden had retreated into himself a little more. He'd worked out and finished and started another puzzle, which was his telltale sign that he was trying to work something out in his head or relax.

It all suddenly made me nervous, and a little, tiny, baby bit worried. Pulling one of the stools at the island back, I plopped into it and simply stared at that discolored, harsh face in unease. "I just want to know whether I need to steal a bat or make a phone call."

His mouth had been open and poised to argue with me . . . until he heard the last thing I said. "What?"

"I need to know—"

"What do you need to steal a bat for?"

"Well, no one I know owns one, and I can't go buy one at the store and have it caught on videotape."

"Videotape?"

Did he know nothing?

"Aiden, come on, if you beat the shit out of someone with a bat, they're going to look for suspects. Once they have suspects, they'll look through their things or their purchases. They'll see I bought one recently and know it was premeditated. Why are you looking at me like that?"

His mauve-colored eyelids went heavy over the bright whites of his eyes, and the expression on his face was filled such a vast range of emotions, one after another after another, that I wasn't sure which one I was supposed to hold on to. He switched the ice pack to the other side of his bruised jaw and shook his head. "The amount you know about committing crimes is terrifying, Van." His mouth twitched under the rainbow of whatever he was thinking. "It scares the hell out of me, and I don't get scared easily."

I snorted, pretty pleased with myself. "Calm down. I went through this phase when I was into watching a lot of crime TV shows. I've never even stolen a pen in my life."

Aiden's careful expression didn't go anywhere.

"I'm not trying to kill anyone . . . unless we had to," I joked weakly.

His nostrils flared so slightly I almost missed it. But what I didn't miss was the way the corners of his mouth tipped up into a tiny smile.

I smiled at him as innocently as possible. "So do you want to tell me who's going to get the fists of fury?" I hoped I sounded as harmless as I intended, even though I felt the exact opposite as every second passed.

"Fists of fury?"

"Yep." I held up my hands just a little so he could see them. He had no idea the number of fights I'd gotten into with my sisters over the years. I didn't always win—I rarely won, if I was going to be honest—but I never gave up.

The sigh that came out of him was so long and drawn out, I kind of prepped myself for the half-assed answer that was going to come out of his mouth.

"It's nothing." There it was. "Delgado—"

The brakes in my head came to a screeching halt. "You got into it *with Christian?*"

He glanced at me through those incredibly long eyelashes, moving the ice pack a little lower on his jaw. "Yes."

That dreaded feeling in my stomach got worse. "Why?" I hopefully asked as calmly as I could, but I was pretty sure it came out relatively strangled.

Please, please, please. Don't let it be why I think it might be. Christian had been a creep on Thanksgiving, but it wasn't like he'd made grabby hands at me.

Aiden's face said it all. His mouth opened slightly and the tip of his tongue touched the corner of it. That brief silence was cold. "You could have told me," he accused.

I gulped. "Told you what?"

His gaze was through the thick row of his eyelashes, and I caught his hand flexing over the ice pack. "What he did to you. How he acts around you."

Zac. I was going to wring his neck. "I'll tell you what I told Zac: it isn't a big deal."

The big guy went stone-cold still. A muscle in his jaw popped and a vein in his neck throbbed.

"It is a big deal, Vanessa. Zac mentioned it to me right before he left, but I thought if it was a big deal, you would have said or done something about it. *You didn't.*" He leveled that dark, angry gaze at me, his jaw tightening. "I saw the way he looked at you after the game. I heard the way he talked to you while I was right there. He knows we're married, and he still did that shit."

Did he just cuss for the second time in a week?

"I am not okay with that," he claimed in that incredibly deep voice, his spine straight and shoulders back. "I'm not fine with you always thinking you have to deal with things on your own."

Remorse filled me, but only for a second. I straightened my own back and glared right back at him. "You didn't have to get into a fight with him over it, Aiden. I don't want that guilt on my head. The last thing I want is for you to get angry with yourself later."

Plus, what would I have done back then? Told Aiden his teammate had tried coming on to me? He wouldn't have done anything. I knew that. The Aiden from a few months ago knew that too.

"I did have to, and I would do it again."

I blinked. Then I blinked a little more, having to look up at the ceiling so that I could collect my words. A touch at the side of my jaw had me tipping my head to look into those deep brown eyes.

Everything about him was serious and intent. "I know you think I wouldn't care," he said in that whisper voice that bled solemnness, "but I would. I do. We're in this together."

My mouth suddenly dry, I nodded. "Yes."

"*Trust me*, Van. Tell me. I won't let you down."

Yeah, my throat and tongue thought they were the Sahara. My eyes on the other hand wanted to be the Amazon. I didn't even realize I needed to sniffle until I did it. As much as I'd been telling myself over the last two days that I'd imagined being a wee bit in love with him, my heart held on to the truth. I was. I hated it, but I was. I recognized it, sensing that stir in my chest. I was falling, if not more than a little, in love with Aiden. My husband of convenience.

And it was terrible. I had no right. No business to do so. This was an agreement between two people who barely spoke to each other. How could I do this for the next five years? What the hell was I going to do with it?

I had no idea.

"You believe me, don't you?" he asked, tearing me out of my thoughts.

I made myself focus on the face that was as familiar to me as the rest of my loved ones' were; that tight mouth, the hard lines of his cheekbones, the thick slashes of his eyebrows. Control and discipline in flesh and bone.

I nodded, forcing myself to give him my best easygoing, total-liar smile. "I do. Of course I do." I touched his forearm. "Thank you again for standing up for me."

He grumbled, "Stop it."

I smiled a little more genuinely. "I have this cream for bruises; let me go grab it."

Aiden jerked his head back like I was about to try to shove a hot dog in his mouth. "You know I don't care about bruises."

"Too bad. I do. He can be black and purple tomorrow—and I freaking hope he is—but I'd rather you weren't." I winced at the small crack in his lip. "What did he have to do? Take a running start to reach your face?"

Aiden burst out laughing, not even grimacing as his cut split wide.

"Seriously, Aiden." I reached up to touch his bruised jaw gently with my fingertips. "Did he sucker punch you?"

The big guy shook his head.

"He actually managed to get a fair shot in?" I wasn't going to lie. I was a little disappointed. Aiden getting punched was almost like finding out Santa Claus wasn't real. He'd gotten into a handful of fights in his career before—I'd seen footage of it online when I shared it on his fan page, because people were vicious and loved that kind of thing—and while he wasn't this hotheaded asshole who liked to get into it for no reason, each time it happened, he beat the shit out of whoever tried to start something with him.

It was impressive. What could I say?

Then he gave me that dumb look that drove me nuts and I frowned. "No. I made sure he hit me first, and I let him do it twice before I hit him back," he explained.

This sneaky son of a bitch. I didn't think I'd ever been so attracted to him before, and that included all the times I'd seen him in compression shorts. "So he'd get blamed for it?"

One corner of his mouth pulled back in a smug half-smile.

"Are you going to get into big trouble?"

He raised a big shoulder. "They might just dock my game check. They won't sit me out. We're too deep into the season."

That had me choking. "A game check?" That was thousands. Hundreds of thousands. A stupid amount of money. Everyone in the world could look up his annual salary online. All that money was split up into seventeen total payments deposited throughout the regular season. *All that money.* I had to bend over and slap my hands against my knees, already on the verge of gagging. "I'm going to throw up."

The sigh he let out went in one of my ears and out the other. "Stop. You're not going to throw up. Let me shower, and then I'll put that cream on," he said, patting me on the back lightly.

He was wrong. I was going to throw up. How the hell had he just upped and thrown away that much money? And for *what*? All because Christian was an idiot who thought common rules of society didn't apply to him?

I knew Aiden. I knew he had the self-control of a saint. He thought his decisions through. He didn't even enjoy beating someone up, or something like that. He had thought enough about what he was going to do, to know that he wanted Christian to get the first punch in. I wasn't going to think he hadn't taken the repercussions of getting into a fight into consideration.

And he'd done it for me.

What a fucking idiot. He could have just given me the money, and that would have been enough to make me forgot about that weasel trying to shove his tongue down my throat while attempting to grab my butt over a year ago.

But as much as I thought of how dumb it was to lose a game check, this burst of something special and warm filled my heart before quickly being replaced by guilt.

I ran upstairs, grabbed the stinky bruise salve that worked like a miracle, and headed back down, knowing what I needed to do to help ease the responsibility I felt for what happened. I grabbed a few things out of the freezer and the pantry and turned on the oven to make a quick meal for my off-white knight in shining armor.

When he came down the stairs a little later, the quinoa had just finished cooking and I'd turned off the stove.

"Smells good," he commented, going around to grab a glass from the cabinet and filling it up with water. "What are you making?"

"Chana masala," I told him, knowing he'd be well aware of what it was.

I wasn't surprised when he made a hungry noise as he leaned a hip against the counter and watched as I lined one of the big mixing bowls I used to always put his meals in with bagged spinach. I peeped at him out of the corner of my eye and took in the coloring along the solid lines of his face.

It pissed me off.

"What's that face for?" the man I'd once assumed didn't know much about me asked as I measured two cups of the grain and dumped it into the bowl.

Shrugging a shoulder, I put three cups of the chickpea mixture over everything. "Your face is making me mad."

He snickered and I groaned, realizing just how that came out. "I didn't mean it like that. You have a fine face. Very good-looking." *Shut up, stupid. Just shut the hell up.* "It's your bruises. I feel bad. I should have done something about it when it happened instead of making you deal with it."

Passing the giant bowl over, he held it between us, catching my eyes. His face was pensive and as open as it got, but what I realized was there wasn't a trace of residual anger left on him. He really wasn't bothered by what happened, not at all. "Don't worry about it. I did what I wanted to do."

He always did what he wanted to do. What was new? "Yeah, but it happened a long time ago."

"And that makes me feel even more responsible, Van."

I frowned. "For what?"

"For everything. For not noticing. For not caring. For not making you feel like you could tell me things." His voice was hoarse and just a little ragged.

My heart hurt.

I really hurt in that split second following his admission.

Realistically, it wasn't like I hadn't known that we hadn't been BFFs when I worked for him. I'd known, damn it. *I'd known.* But to hear him say it . . .

It felt like an ultra-fresh burn to a delicately skinned place. That place being right between my breasts. The most important place of all.

It took every single ounce of emotional maturity I had in me not to . . . well, I wasn't sure how I could have reacted. But I did realize, the more I suppressed the hurt, that I couldn't—shouldn't—hold him being honest against him. It wasn't news. He hadn't cared about me, and he'd taken me for granted. At least he realized it now, right?

Yeah, telling myself that wasn't helping much. My eyes really wanted to get teary, and I wasn't going to let them. It wasn't his fault.

I made sure to meet his eyes. "It's all right. You did something now." I took a step back. "Enjoy your food. I started putting up the tree this morning, but I stopped to return some emails. I'm going to go ahead and finish it."

Those chocolate-colored eyes roamed my face for a second and I knew, though he didn't say anything, that I'd been caught.

Whether he didn't want to deal with me being a softie or he understood my need to lick my wounds in private, he kept his words to himself and let me walk out of the kitchen with my heart a little burned around the edges.

I'd left a huge mess in the living room that morning. A bomb seemed to have gone off in a pile of tissues, and boxes were strewn everywhere. I'd gone shopping the day before to buy Christmas ornaments and decorations, and spent so much money, but I hadn't minded, because this was the first year I'd really have a tree of my own. I hadn't bothered putting one up at my apartment, because I was gone so much and there really hadn't been room. Instead, I'd put up a three-foot pre-lit tree with glued-on ornaments. This year though, that little tree was now in my bedroom.

Here, at Aiden and Zac's, I scored a seven-foot Douglas pine that Zac had helped me carry and set up the night before. In a house full of tall men, there wasn't a single step ladder in the vicinity, so I'd resorted to dragging a stool into the living room to help me reach the places I couldn't on my own. The lights had gone on this morning, and I'd squeezed in some ornaments too.

I usually loved putting up a Christmas tree. We'd had one at my mom's house a few times, but it wasn't until I was with my foster parents that putting up a tree and decorating became a big deal. It had started to mean something to me. Climbing onto the stool, I couldn't ignore the thought circling back around in my head.

He hadn't given a shit about me.

Or at least, he hadn't appreciated me.

That second idea was just as bitter as the first one.

I worked in silence for a little while, wrapping a beautiful red ribbon around the branches then stepping back to adjust it. I had just started opening up more boxes of ornaments when I sensed the other presence in the room.

Aiden was standing between the hallway and the living room, and his gaze was sweeping through the room, taking in the rest of the decorations I'd put up. The reindeer candles, a sparkly red Christmas tree made of wires, the wreath on the mantel, and finally, the three hanging stockings.

The three hanging stockings that I'd stitched sequins onto the night before, spelling out the first letters of each of our names. Black for Aiden, green for Zac, and gold for me.

Eventually, he tore his gaze away from the stockings and asked, "Need help?"

I'm not going to take this personally, I told myself. "Sure." I held out the box I'd just opened in his direction.

Aiden took it, glancing from the decorations to the tree and back at me. "Where do you want them to go?"

"Wherever."

Taking a step closer to the object of our decorative talents, he shot me a look. "Where do you want them to go, Van? I'm sure you had it planned out."

I did, but I wasn't going to give my help any shit. "Anywhere as long as they aren't too close together. . . . Really. I just don't want them close together. . . . And maybe keep them toward the top since those are small. Big ornaments go closer to the bottom."

The sides of his mouth twitched, but he nodded seriously and went to work.

We stood there in front of the tree for the next hour, side by side. His arm brushed mine, my hip brushed his, and more than a couple of times, he caught me trying to climb up on the stool before he plucked whatever ornament I had in my hand and put it up himself. Neither one of us said much.

But once we were done, we took a couple steps back and took the seven feet of gloriousness all in.

I had to say, it was beautiful, even if it looked a lot smaller with Aiden next to it. Red and gold with hints of green here and there, glass ornaments hanging from long branches, ribbon circling it—it was the kind of tree I'd dreamed about as a kid. I glanced at Aiden. His face was clean and thoughtful, and I wondered what he was thinking about. Instead though, I went with a safer question. "What do you think?"

His nostrils flared just a little and a soft, soft, soft smile perked up the corners of his mouth. "It looks like something from a department store."

I rubbed at my arm and smiled. "I'm going to take that as a compliment."

The firm man nodded. "It's nice."

It's nice? From Aiden? I'd take it as "it's amazing" from just about anyone else. The more I looked at it, the more I liked it, the happier it made me, and the more grateful I was for all I had to be thankful for.

Thanks to Aiden, I was living in a wonderful house. Thanks to Aiden, I had money to buy the decorations, the ornaments, and the tree. And thanks to Aiden, I had managed to save up enough money to pursue my dreams.

Maybe we hadn't been soul mates, and maybe he really hadn't cared about what I added to his life until I was gone, but I had so much because of him. And I would continue to have so much because of him too. That knowledge softened the hurt from an hour ago enough for me to clear my throat and say, "Ai—"

He interrupted me. "Are you putting up lights outside?"

"YOU DID IT all today?"

"Yep." We'd done it all in a matter of hours.

After having to visit two different stores to buy enough Christmas lights to decorate the house, the trips had definitely ended up being worth it. Round, blue LED lights outlined the roof and garage. Two different individual packages of lights had to be used to wrap around the pillar by the front door. Another box was used to go around the big window, and I'd twined more lights through the branches of the tree in the front yard.

"You and Aiden did this?" Zac then asked, his arms crossed over his chest. I'd been outside putting up the last of the lights when he'd pulled his truck into the garage.

"Uh-huh. He even got on the roof with me, even though I kept telling him to get back in the house before he fell off or one of the neighbors called the team and told them what he was doing." There were specific things in his contract he was prohibited from doing: riding anything with wheels, including but not limited to motorcycles, scooters, mopeds, Segways, hoverboards, and skateboards. He couldn't do anything that required a waiver, like skydiving. And there was also a specific note in his contract that said he wasn't allowed anywhere near fireworks.

I'd read his contract one day when I found it in a saved folder on his computer and I'd been bored.

Aiden's exact response to me trying to shoo him off had been, "Don't tell me what to do."

Sometimes, I really wanted to choke him out for being so stubborn. Then again, he'd been the one to bring up putting Christmas lights up when I hadn't prepared for it, simply because I didn't want to do it all alone.

Zac snickered, his hands in his pockets. "I'm not surprised. How long did it take?"

"Three hours."

He glanced at his watch and frowned. "How early did he get home?"

Aaaaand that reminded me what he'd done, what he'd said. I frowned and muttered, "Right after twelve," knowing that was going to reel him in.

Hook, line, and sinker. "How come? Those Monday mornin' defense meetings usually last 'til two."

I punched him in the arm. "You tell me, big mouth."

Nosey McNoserson immediately perked up. "What I do?" He'd barely asked the question when his eyes went a little wide and that chin went right back down, his ears seeming to perk up.

"You told him about Christian, you snitch. You know what happens to snitches?"

"They get stitches?"

I punched him again. "Yes! He got into a fight with him today."

Zac's lip dropped, and he gaped. Honestly, I loved Zac. I really did. "No!"

Okay, he got on my nerves for telling Aiden what had happened, but he was still so funny it was unreal. "Yes! He got into a fight with him!" Zac's mouth went even wider, his blue eyes darting from one side to the other like he couldn't handle what I was telling him. "He got—"

"Aiden?"

"Yes."

"Our Aiden?"

I nodded solemnly.

Zac still didn't believe me. "You sure?"

"He told me. He has the bruises to prove it."

"No. He wouldn't." He looked away and then looked back at me. "*Aiden?*"

"*Yes.*"

He opened his mouth and then closed it. "I don't know . . ." His lips moved but nothing came out. "He doesn't . . ."

"I know. I *know* he doesn't."

"What the hell took him so long? I told him a week ago," he suddenly noted in exasperation.

Good gracious. He was making faces because Aiden had taken too long. Uh. "Because when I went to the Thanksgiving Day game, Christian called me honey or something, and was just being a creeper in general—wait. It doesn't matter. Why did you say anything to him anyway? I told you that as friends. Circle of trust."

Zac huffed and gave me a look that resembled one of Aiden's a little too closely. "Why wouldn't I tell him?"

"Because it didn't matter."

Yeah, he was definitely giving me one of Aiden's faces. "If I was the one you were married to, I'd want him to tell me."

"Traitor." That made sense, but I wasn't going to admit it.

The blond snorted. "Van, think about it for a second. Aiden's not— he's not going to give you a hug, tell you you're pretty, and call you his best friend, but I know him, and he cares about you."

Now he does, I thought. "If I die, he can't get his papers fixed so easily."

His blue eyes narrowed and he gestured toward the front door. "If you die, who else would he have that gives a shit about him?"

What was that supposed to mean?

"C'mon. Let's go inside. I'm starvin'," he finished up.

I took one more peek at the bright blue lights and followed him in. We had barely opened the door when the persistent beeping of Aiden's ringtone started going off from somewhere in the kitchen. I ignored it and headed toward the fridge, pulling out leftovers from the day before.

"What do you have?" Zac asked, peeking over my shoulder as I scooped food onto a plate.

"Pasta." I just handed it over. There wasn't a point in asking him if he wanted it. Of course he'd want it.

"Yum," he said, without even tasting it.

Aiden's phone began to ring again just as I set my plate into the microwave to warm up. By the time it was done, the phone had stopped ringing and started up all over again. I sat down to eat, and it started beeping. *Again.*

"Who the hell is calling him?" Zac asked as he stood in front of the microwave watching his food heat up.

Leaning to the side, I dragged Aiden's phone over and glanced at the screen. **TREVOR MCMANN** flashed across the screen. Ugh.

"Trevor," I said.

Zac made an impolite noise. "I bet he's callin' about today."

I winced. He was probably right. "Have you talked to him?"

"I talked to him on Thanksgivin'. I figured if he started talkin' a whole buncha nonsense, I could pass the phone over to my mama," he admitted with a laugh.

The phone started ringing one more time. Good gracious. I picked up his phone and hesitated. This was my fault. Wasn't it? "I'm going to answer. Should I answer?"

"Take one for Team Graves."

Damn it. I answered. "Hello?"

"Aiden what the—"

"This is Vanessa." I made a face at Zac mouthing, "Why did I do this?"

"Put Aiden on the phone," he demanded without any pretense.

"Ah, I don't think so," I said quickly.

"What do you mean you don't think so? Put him on the goddamn phone."

"How about you hold your horses. He's napping. I'm not going to go wake him up, buddy. If you have a message, pass it along. If you don't have a message, I'll make sure to tell him you called." Either way, I wasn't going to tell Aiden shit. Trevor just didn't need to know that.

"Goddammit, Vanessa. *I need to talk to him.*"

"And he needs his sleep."

Trevor made a noise that was more than a huff and less than what? A growl. I could tell how pissed off he was right then, how important he felt the conversation he wanted to have with Aiden seemed to be. The thing was, I didn't care. "You and I haven't had a chance to chat lately, but don't think I've forgotten about you. This shit today is your fault. I know it is."

"I don't know what you're talking about, and I'm pretty sure Aiden pays you to support him, not call and nag. I know I sure as hell don't want to listen to you right now. So, I'll make sure to let him know you called."

"Vanessa!" the son of an asshole had the nerve to shout.

"Yell at me again, and I'm going to make sure you regret it, do you hear me? I think you have enough to worry about without adding me to your list," I growled into the phone, getting more pissed by the second. "And calm your asshole talking to Aiden too while you're at it. I don't appreciate you treating him like a little kid."

"You're a pain in—"

I pulled the phone away from my face, and with my other hand gave the phone my middle finger. Putting it back against my face, I said, "Your ass, I know. I'll let him know you called, but I'm just letting you know you should calm down before you talk to him."

"He got into it with Christian because of you, didn't he?"

"If you knew anything about him, you'd know he doesn't do anything without a reason, so think about that."

Trevor made a noise over the line that I quickly ignored.

"I'll let him know you called. Bye."

Yeah, I might have shoved my finger against the screen again a lot more aggressively than what was really necessary, but it felt like I needed to, since I didn't have a phone to slam into its cradle.

"He's such a fucking asshole—" I started to say as I looked up, only to find Zac with a hand over his eyes.

I felt it right then.

Slowly turning on my stool, I found Aiden standing just inside the kitchen with his eyebrows raised.

"I hate him." I held his phone out toward him. "And you should probably turn off your phone before he calls again."

I WAS IN my room hours later when Zac slipped in through the door, his eyes bright, his expression that little-boy one that put me in a good mood. "Guess what?"

I paused the show I was watching and raised my eyebrows, sitting up straight on the mattress. "I don't know. What?"

"I found it," he said even as he skid across the floor in his pajamas, his cell phone clutched in his hand.

That had me perking up. "What did you find?"

Zac sat on the edge of my bed right next to me. His back was to the headboard as he held the screen between the small space between us. "Look."

I did just that.

Maximized on the screen was an image of two men in Three Hundreds practice jerseys without pads. I didn't have to look at the number on the bigger man's shirt to know it was Aiden; I knew that body. I knew that body like the back of my hand. Plus, his helmet was off and hanging off the fingers of his right hand. I had to think for a moment about the guy standing a few feet away from him though. Number eighty-eight. Christian.

They were the only people on camera. With about five feet separating them, they were both facing the field where one could only assume was the rest of the team. There wasn't any sound unfortunately.

On the screen, Christian happened to turn just as Aiden's hands went to his hips, his body language deceptively casual if it wasn't for the set to his shoulders.

It only took a few moments before Christian threw his arms out to the sides and took two steps toward the man I was married to. His stance became confrontational even before he pulled his helmet off and threw it, his feet taking him the two other steps between him and Aiden.

The big guy stood tall, his hands minutely flexing at his hips. Maybe no one else would notice the movement, but I did. Christian's face was visible on the screen, his cheeks turning red, his mouth getting wider, as one could only assume he was yelling.

And then it happened.

Christian's fist flew forward and Aiden's head jerked back just slightly. The big guy took a step backward as his hands fell to his sides.

Christian hit him again.

The man known as the Wall of Winnipeg dropped his helmet on the ground almost casually. His big hands flexed and stretched wide at his sides shortly before he lunged. That huge fist went up and connected; Christian's head flew back. Aiden hit him again with that dominant left hand, his big body up and towering over the smaller man's by that point so that the only thing visible after the second hit was Christian on the ground just as players ran up to them.

Aiden let them push him away as he backed up, his attention staying focused on the wide receiver on the ground as they became surrounded by other players and staff.

Zac tapped his thumb against the screen, turning his head to give me a wide-eyed look.

I could only stare at him with my mouth just slightly open. We both only managed to blink at each other.

And the two of us said the same thing at the same time: "Holy shit."

TWENTY-FOUR

Diana's horrified face warned me about what she was going to say before she actually vocalized it. "Get inside before anyone sees you," she practically hissed.

I made sure she watched me roll my eyes as I brushed past her into her apartment. Yeah, I knew I had about an inch of my natural hair color peeking out from my roots, but I didn't really care. The only reason why I hadn't dyed it back to its normal reddish brown was because I'd texted her for the first time since Thanksgiving to ask what box of dye at the pharmacy she recommended, and gotten, You're already on my last nerve. Buy it and I'll kill you.

Which was why I found myself driving an hour to go visit her on her day off a few weeks after Thanksgiving, putting up with the sneer on her face as her gaze roamed over my hair again. I swear she might have even shuddered a little.

Her repulsion wasn't enough to keep me from kissing her on the cheek and giving her butt a slap in "hello." It had been way too long since we'd last seen each other. She'd pretended to be mad long enough.

She gave me a smack in return as her eyes wandered over me briefly. "Besides your hair, you look really good."

I felt really good. "I've been running four days a week and riding a stationary bike once a week."

Diana eyeballed me again. "You should probably buy new clothes soon."

"Maybe." I shrugged and looked her over, not so subconsciously looking for finger-shaped bruises on any of her exposed skin. I didn't find any, but I did notice the bags under her eyes. "You look tired."

The fact she didn't flip me off when that would have been her normal reaction didn't hit me until much later. "I am tired. I'm glad you noticed." She knew better than to wait for me to apologize. "I've been working doubles, I'm not getting enough sleep. I'm turning into you."

"A successful, hardworking woman. I think I'm going to shed a tear."

"Oh, fuck off. Go into the kitchen and take your shirt off," she ordered, cracking up. I didn't even get a chance to make a joke about her wanting me to strip before she stopped me with a hand. "This isn't *Striptease*. I'm not giving you a dollar or taking you out to dinner first."

"Fair enough," I muttered and made my way into the kitchen where I peeled my T-shirt over my head.

"So . . . how have you been?" she asked slow and purposely awkward.

I used the same dull tone. "I'm fine. And you?"

"Good," my robot-voiced best friend replied.

Our eyes met and we both smiled. She shoved at my shoulder and I tried to pinch her stomach. "Are we fine now?" I asked with a laugh.

"Yeah, we're fine. Now tell me everything I've missed."

We spent the next hour talking. I told her about Thanksgiving and going to Aiden's game. Twenty of those minutes consisted of us going over the day of my little brother's game, how Susie had shown up, what Aiden had said to her husband, and then explaining the hatred on the big guy's face as he'd stared at my sister. I told her about him helping me with the Christmas tree and lights. How he got into a fight with Christian, whom she remembered clearly from that night at the bar, because she'd threatened to kick his ass after I told her what had happened.

By the end of it, she had me under a helmet that looked like something out of the NASA space program, and she looked dazed.

"Jesus," she said twice.

"I thought I was over this stage in my life."

"No shit. It's like something out of those novelas my mom watches."

"The same ones we used to watch with her," I pointed out. It was how I'd learned Spanish.

Diana laughed from the spot she'd taken in front of me, sitting with her legs crossed. "We would run home after school and watch them, wouldn't we?" She made a wistful noise. "It seems like forever ago, huh?"

It really did. I nodded. They were some of my fondest memories before I'd been moved across town and never experienced them again. While living with my mom had left me with a handful of good memories and a dozen terrible ones, it had still been every-thing I'd known.

Di seemed to brush off whatever distant memory she was thinking of and asked, "What are you gonna do then?"

"With what?"

"With your husband. Who else?"

She could have been talking about my sister. Smart-ass. "Nothing."

Diana gave me this expression that said, *Who do you think you're talking to?* "Don't 'nothing' me. You're still goo-goo with him. I can see it."

I opened my mouth to tell her I wasn't goo-goo over anybody, but she did her hand thing again, stopping me.

"You're really gonna try and lie to me? I can see it, Vanny. Hello. You can't sneak anything by the master." I'd snuck my marriage by her, but why bring that up? "Seems to me like he likes you too. I don't think he'd spend so much time with you if he didn't."

All I could do was let out a restrained grunt.

"You're gonna be together for the next five years. Why not make the best out of it?" she brought up.

I wanted to mess with my glasses, but I kept my hand lowered. "We made a deal, Di. This was supposed to be business. It isn't his fault I'm an idiot."

"Why are you an idiot? Because you want someone to love you?"

"Because he doesn't love anything. He doesn't want to. How awk-ward would it be if I did or said anything? I'm not going to back out on our deal now. He cares about me, but that's all."

If there was anyone in the world who knew me almost as well as I knew myself, it was her. And what she said next confirmed that. "Vanny, I love the hell out of you. You're my sister from another mister, you know that, but you have a messed up conception of what you're willing to work for and risk. I don't know if he's capable of loving you or not, but what's the worst that will happen? You guys are married. He isn't going to divorce you now."

What was the worst that would happen?

I'd lose my friend.

Diana reached forward and tugged at the hem of my jeans. "Do whatever you want. I only want you to be happy. You deserve it."

I scrunched up my nose, not willing to talk about Aiden any longer; every time I did, especially when it was with the L-word in the subject, it made my entire body hurt. I'd loved enough people in my life who didn't love me back and didn't bother hiding it. So I guess Diana was right—there was only so much risk I was willing to take.

That was depressing.

Clearing my throat, I pointed at the Christmas tree behind her, ready to talk about something else. I couldn't believe the holidays were less than a week away now. When I'd worked for Aiden, time had gone by fast, but since I'd quit, it went by even faster than before. "When are you leaving for your parents?"

"I'm leaving Christmas Eve. I have to be back at work on the twenty-sixth," she explained. "Are you staying here?"

Where else would I go?

"I'M TAKIN' OFF," Zac said from my doorway a few days later.

Spinning in my chair, I blinked over at him before coming to my feet. "Okay. I'll walk you down."

"Aww, you don't have to."

I rolled my eyes and pushed at his shoulders when I was right in front of him. "I want to give you your Christmas present."

"In that case, lead the way, darlin'," he said even as he took a step back and let me walk ahead.

The Christmas tree lights were turned off when we got downstairs, and I pushed the gifts underneath it aside to find Zac's. Picking the two perfectly wrapped boxes out from the corner where I'd stashed them, I handed them over. "Merry Christmas."

"Can I open them now?" he asked like a little boy.

"Go for it."

Zac ripped the paper off each box and opened them with a grin on his face. Inside were sleep pants and slippers. What do you get a man who had everything? Things he really liked, even if he had a dozen other of the same stuff.

"Vanny," he gurgled, holding his arm wide with one gift in each hand.

"You're welcome," I said, stepping into his embrace.

He squeezed me and rocked me from side to side. "Thank you."

"Sure."

He took a step back and put his things into his bag before shoving half his arm in and yanking out what looked like a card. "For you, my girl."

I took the card from him with a big smile on my face, touched that he'd gotten me one. I tore it open and pulled the card out, opening it to find a gift card inside for one of the local sporting goods stores. But it was the horrible scrawl inside that really caught my eye.

> To my closest friend,
>   Merry Christmas, Vanny. I don't know what I
> would've done w/o you the last few months.
>   Love you.
> —Z

"I'm not good at buyin' presents, so buy yourself some new shoes for the marathon, ya hear? You better have 'em by the time I come home. Don't go buyin' somebody else somethin'," he prattled.

"Thank you," I muttered, giving him another hug. "I promise I'll buy myself something. When are you getting back?"

"I'm gonna stay through New Year's. My PawPaw hasn't been doin' so well, so I wanna spend some time with him." He winked. "And this real sweetheart I used to date in high school messaged me a few days ago to see if Big Texas was gonna be in town."

I snickered. *Big Texas.* There was no way she was referring to him as a person. "What happened to that girl you were talking to here?"

Zac made a noise. "She was cuckoo."

"Have fun back home then."

"I will." He leaned down and gave me a peck on the cheek. "Go visit Diana if you get lonely, hear me?"

"I'll be fine." This wouldn't be my first Christmas spent without a big group. I knew I would survive. I slapped him on the butt when he turned to head to the door. "Drive careful and tell your mom I said hi."

Zac grinned at me over his shoulder, and just like that, he was gone and I was home alone.

I SHUT THE garage door with a slight smile on my face, Aiden's Christmas present in hand, torn between feeling pretty lousy and slightly excited about the little treasure waiting for tomorrow morning.

Going for a ten-mile run earlier had exhausted me, but not enough. I'd baked sugar cookies shaped into trees, candy canes, and stars, which took my mind off everything for a couple of hours, and then the doorbell had rung and the post office delivery person had presented me with four different boxes labeled to me. I'd opened them up like a little kid.

My foster parents, Diana, her parents, and my little brother had all sent me gifts in different levels of wrapping. I'd gotten a pack of watercolors, colored pencils, several pairs of new underwear—from the only person who would buy me that—a pretty watch, and pajamas.

Miss u, a card in my little brother's gift said. He was spending the holidays with one of his teammate's family in Florida.

I'd sent them all gifts two weeks before, even sending my mom and her husband a gift basket. Luckily, I hadn't been expecting a present from them; otherwise, I would have been sorely disappointed. The gifts served to make me feel loved and lonely, and I wasn't sure how the hell it was possible to feel two such conflicting emotions.

Aiden had been home since noon, and I could tell he was in a strange mood. He'd been awfully quiet, spending his time working out and also working on a puzzle in the breakfast nook while I'd made cookies, and then he'd headed upstairs, saying he was going to take a nap. I stayed downstairs only long enough to make sure Aiden was asleep; then I'd taken off to pick up his present. Luckily, he'd still been asleep when I got home, and I set his gift up in the garage, confident that Aiden wouldn't be leaving anywhere and spoil his surprise. Inside, I turned on the television to drown out any possible noises that came from the garage, then sat on the floor and used the watercolors my foster parents had sent me.

I kept checking the garage every hour since then. Nearly all the lights in the house were turned off when I made my way through the house with the package in my hand, my back aching from so much time hunched over. At the bottom of the stairs, I listened for Aiden, but there wasn't a peep. Why would there be? Despite it being Christmas Eve, he'd had to wake up early and report to team headquarters to check in with the trainers, because his lower back had been giving him trouble the last couple of weeks.

In the laundry room, I set the carrier down. I'd already put two blankets inside, refilled the water bottle mounted to the door, and put food into the small bowl that attached to the door too. I'd let the little rascal out on the front lawn and waited until he pooped and peed. The cute face peeked out at me through the grate and I stuck my fingers in there to give his nose a rub.

While the garage was well insulated, and I knew it wouldn't be cold, I hated the idea of leaving him in there. Taking him up to my room was out of the question, because I had a feeling he would bark. I left the light on for him and made my way back to the kitchen, where I cracked open the container of sugar cookies I made and inhaled two of them.

I turned off all the lights except the set under the kitchen cabinets, filled a glass with water, and headed upstairs. In my room, I grabbed clothes to take a shower, feeling downright off. I stayed under the stream longer than I usually would have, and climbed out of the tub, telling myself to quit being such a party pooper.

I had just opened the bathroom door when I heard, "Van?"

"Aiden?" Okay, that was a stupid question. Who else would it be? With my dirty clothes under my arm, I walked down the hall. His door was open. Usually when he went to sleep, he closed it, and I guess I hadn't glanced over when I'd come upstairs.

He sat with his back propped up against the headboard, a bedside lamp illuminating part of the room. Half of his body was under the covers and the other half was unfortunately covered in a T-shirt by one of his endorsers. Aiden gave me a speculative look.

"Are you okay?" I asked, resting my shoulder against the doorframe.

"Yes," he answered in such an earnest, easy way that I didn't know what to do with myself.

Huh. "What are you doing?" The television wasn't on and a book was set on his nightstand.

"I was thinking about the game last week, and what I could have done differently."

Of all the things in the world, why did that just happen to reach straight into my ribs and grab my heart? "Of course you were."

Aiden lifted one of those big, brawny shoulders, his eyes going to the super-sexy, long-sleeved, button-up flannel pajamas I had on. "Are you going to sleep?" he asked, even as his gaze raked its way back up to my face.

"I'm not that tired. I'll probably watch some more TV or something."

Even in the dark light, I could tell his cheek twitched. "Watch it with me," he suggested easily.

Wait. What?

"You're not tired?"

"I took a long nap. There's no chance I'm going to sleep soon," he explained.

I smiled and rubbed my foot along the edge of where the hardwood floor hallway met the carpet of his bedroom. "Are you sure you don't have more plays to think about?"

Aiden gave me a sour look.

He was inviting me to watch television with him. What other answer was there besides "Okay"?

By the time I got back to his room after depositing my dirty clothes in the hamper in my room, the big guy had scooted over to one side of the bed and turned on the television propped on one of his dressers. With his hands linked behind his head, he watched me as I came in, feeling just slightly awkward.

I gave him a tiny smile and kept eye contact as I pulled the comforter up and slipped under it, waiting to see if he'd complain. He didn't. There was about two feet of space between us on the California king. I moved the pillow against the headboard and settled in with a sigh.

"Van?"

"Hmm?"

"What's wrong?"

Tugging the sheets up to my neck, I blinked at the ceiling. "Nothing."

"Don't make me ask you again."

And that only made me feel bad. It was easy to forget how much he knew about me. "I'm fine. I've just been feeling pretty mopey to-day for some reason; maybe it's hormones or something. That's all." I wrung my hands. "It's dumb. I love Christmas."

There was a pause before he asked, "You don't visit your mom?"

"No." I realized after I said it how dismissive I sounded. "My sisters spend it with her. She's married now and has step-kids who go over there. She's not alone." And even if she were all by herself, I would still not go. I could be honest with myself.

"Where's your brother?"

"With his friend."

"Your friend? Diana?"

With how busy he'd been, we hadn't spent much time together other than saying hi and bye and catching some TV at the same time. "She's with her family." After I said it, I realized how it sounded. "I swear, I'm usually okay. I just feel off, I guess. What about you? Are you fine?"

"I've spent most of my Christmases alone for the last decade. It isn't a big deal."

Of all the people to spend the holidays with, it was with the one whose history was a little too similar to mine. "I guess the good thing is, you don't have to spend it alone anymore if you don't want to." I'm not sure why I said what I said next, but I did. "At least while you're stuck with me."

Could I sound any more pathetic?

"I am stuck with you, aren't I?" he asked in a deceptively soft voice.

He was trying to make me feel better, wasn't he? "For the next four years and eight months." I smiled over at him, even as this incredible sense of sadness filled my belly like sand in an hourglass.

His head jerked back. The action was tiny, tiny, tiny, but it had been there.

Or had I imagined it?

Before I could wonder too much about whether he'd reacted or not, the big guy who seemed to swallow up his bed bluntly asked, "Are you finally going to tell me what your sister did to piss you off?"

Of course he would ask. Why wouldn't he? It wasn't like I considered it a secret. I just didn't like talking about it. On the other hand, if there were someone in the world I could talk about Susie with, it would be Aiden. Who would he tell? The thing was, even if he did have someone to, if I really thought about it, he was more than likely the most trustworthy person I knew.

I wasn't sure when that had happened, but I wasn't going to wonder about it too much, especially not on Christmas Eve when he'd invited me to his bed, and I was feeling lonelier than I had in a long time.

Shifting a little on the mattress, I propped my head up on my hand and just went for it. "She hit me with a car when I was eighteen."

Those incredibly long, black eyelashes hovered low over his eyes. Were his ears going red? "The car accident," his voice was hoarse, "the person that you told me ran you over . . ." His blink was so slow I might have thought there was something wrong with him if I hadn't known otherwise. "It was your sister?"

"Yes."

Aiden stared straight at me, the confusion apparent in the slight lines that crept out from the corners of his eyes. "What happened?" he ground the question out.

"It's a long story."

"I have time for you."

"It's a really long story," I insisted.

"Okay."

This guy. I had to stretch my neck as if warming up for this crap storm. "All of my sisters have issues, but Susie's always been something else. I have anger problems, I know. Surprising right? The only one of us who I think doesn't have problems is my little brother. I think my mom was boozing it up while she was pregnant with us, or maybe our dads were just different levels of assholes, I'm not sure."

Why was I telling him that? "Anyway, things have always been bad between us. I don't have a single decent memory of her. Not one, Aiden. There was the closet thing, her coming up and smacking me in the face for no reason, yelling at me, pulling my hair, breaking my things for no reason . . . I mean, all kinds of crap. I didn't fight back for the longest until I got tired of her shit, right around when I grew to be bigger than she was, and I finally had enough. She had already been drinking and doing drugs by then. I knew she had been for a while. But I didn't care. I was tired of being her punching bag.

"Well, this one time, she really kicked my ass. She pushed me down the stairs and I broke my arm. My mom was . . . I don't know where she was. My little brother freaked out and called 911. The ambulance came and took me to the hospital. The doctors or the nurses or someone called my mom. She didn't answer. I didn't know where she was and neither did any of my siblings. The hospital finally called CPS and they took me, and then they took them. I don't know how long it took my mom to figure out we were all gone, but she lost custody.

"I spent the next almost four years with my foster parents and little brother. I saw my mom a few times, but that was it. Right after I went away to school, she started calling me asking what I was going to do during the summer, telling me how she'd love to see me. I don't know what the hell I was thinking back then. She had a steady job, so I went . . . and it wasn't until I got there that I realized she wasn't living alone. Susie and my oldest sister were living with her. I hadn't seen either one of them in years.

"I should have known then that it would have been better for me to go somewhere else. My friend Diana's parents were still living next door, but she was doing something that weekend, so she wasn't going to be home, and I didn't want to stay there without her; my foster parents had told me I always had a home with them—I mean, my little brother was still with them. But for some stupid reason, I wanted to give my mom a chance. We—Susie and I—started fighting the moment I got there, and I should have fucking known. The moment I saw her, I could tell she was on something. I tried to talk to my mom about it, but she blew me off and said Susie had changed, blah, blah, blah.

"Seriously, it was my second night back, and I had walked by my mom's room and found her going through my mom's drawers. We started arguing. She called me a bunch of ugly stuff, started throwing things at me, and nailed me with a vase. I barely saw her grab my purse off the kitchen counter when she ran out of the house with whatever else she had grabbed before I caught her. I was so pissed off, Aiden.

"It's so dumb when I think about it now, and what's even dumber is that I still would have chased after her even knowing what would happen. She got into her car, and I started yelling at her through the window when she backed out of the driveway. I didn't want to get my toes run over, so I went to stand in front of her car when she suddenly put it into drive and hit the gas pedal."

Anxiety and grief kind of grabbed my lungs as I kept telling him what happened. "I remember her face when she did it. I remember everything. I didn't black out until the ambulance showed up, which was after she peeled out of the driveway and left me there. Diana had gotten home early and she was in her room when it happened, and overheard us shouting. She came out right before Susie hit me and called 911, thankfully. The doctor told me later on that I was lucky I had my body turned just right and that she only hit one of my knees and not both."

How many times had I told myself that I was over this? A thousand? But the betrayal still stung me in a million different sensitive places. "*Lucky*. Lucky that my sister hit me with a car and only hurt one of my knees. Can you believe that?"

Something bubbled up in my throat and then made its way up to the back of my eyes. Some people would call them tears, but I wouldn't. I wasn't going to cry over what happened. And my voice definitely wasn't cracking with emotion. "My tendon was ruptured. I had to miss an entire semester of school to recover."

The big guy stared at me. His nostrils flared just slightly. "What happened after she hit you?"

"She disappeared for a couple months. Not everyone believed me when I told them she'd done it, even though I had a witness. I was pretty sure she'd been sober when she did it—that's probably why she was stealing money, to go get whatever it was she wanted. My mom wanted me to forgive her and move on, but . . . how could she ask me to do that? She knew what she'd been doing. Susie had stolen money from her too. She'd chosen to do it, you know? And even if she'd been high, it would still have been her choice to get high and steal shit from the people she was supposed to love. Her choices led her to that moment. I can't feel bad for that."

I couldn't. Could I? Forgiveness was a virtue, or at least that's what someone had told me, but I wasn't feeling very virtuous.

"I went and stayed with my foster parents afterward. There was no way I was going to stay at Diana's right next door. My foster dad had me do his accounting work, be his secretary, all kinds of things so I could at least earn my room and board, because I didn't want to free-load off them. Then I went back to school once I was better."

"What happened with your sister?" he asked.

"After she hit me, I didn't see her again for years. You know what kills me the most though? She never apologized to me." I shrugged. "Maybe it makes me a little cold-blooded, but—"

"It doesn't make you cold-blooded, Van," the Wall of Winnipeg interjected with a crisp tone. "Someone you should have been able to trust hurt you. No one can blame you for not wanting to give her a hug after that. I haven't been able to forgive people for less."

That made me snort bitterly. "You'd be surprised, Aiden. It's still a sore subject. No one besides my little brother understands why I'm mad. Why I don't just get over it. I get that they've never liked me, for whatever reason, but it still feels like a betrayal that they'd be behind Susie instead of me. I don't understand why. Or what I did to make them feel like I'm their enemy. What am I supposed to do?"

Aiden frowned. "You're a good person and you're talented, Vanessa. Look at you. I don't know what your sisters are like, but I can't believe they're half of what you are."

He listed the attributes so breezily they didn't feel like compliments. They felt like statements, and I didn't know what to do with it, especially because in the back of my head, I knew Aiden wouldn't say those things to make me feel better. He just wasn't the type to nurture, even if he felt obligated, unless he genuinely, really wanted to.

But before I could think about it anymore, he admitted something so out of the blue, I wasn't remotely prepared for it. "I might not be the best person to give you family advice. I haven't talked to my parents in twelve years."

I jumped on that wagon the second I could, preferring to talk about him than me. "I thought you went to go live with your grandparents when you were fifteen?"

"I did, but my grandfather died when I was a senior in high school. They came to the funeral, found out he had left everything to my grandmother, and my mom told me to take care of myself. I've never seen them since then," Aiden recounted.

"Your dad didn't say anything?"

Aiden shifted in bed, almost as if he was lowering himself to be flatter on the mattress. "No. I was four inches taller than him by then, sixty pounds heavier. The only time he talked to me when I lived with them was when he wanted to yell at someone."

"I'm sorry to talk about your dad, but he sounds like an asshole."

"He *was* an asshole. I'm sure he still is."

I wondered . . . "Is he why you don't cuss?"

No-bullshit Aiden answered. "Yes."

It was in that moment that I realized how similar Aiden and I were. This intense sense of affection, okay maybe it was more than affection—I could be an adult and admit it—squeezed my heart.

Looking at Aiden, I held back the sympathy I felt and just kept a grip on the simmering anger as I eyed his scar. "How did he do that to you?"

"I was fourteen, right before I hit my big growth spurt." He cleared his throat, his face aimed at the ceiling, confirming he knew that I knew. "He'd been drinking too much and he was mad at me for eating the last lamb chop . . . he shoved me into the fireplace."

I was going to kill his dad. "Did you go to the hospital?"

Aiden's scoff caught me totally off guard. "No. We didn't—he wouldn't have let me go. That's why it healed so badly."

Yeah, I slid lower into the bed, unable to look at him. Was this what he was feeling? Shame and anger?

What were you supposed to say after something like that? Was there anything? I lay there, choking on uncertain words for what felt like forever, telling myself I had no reason to cry when he wasn't.

He shifted around on the bed for a second before abruptly saying, "I'm pretty sure he wasn't my real dad. My mom's a blonde, so is he. They're both average. My grandparents were blonds. My mom used to work with this guy who was always really nice to me when I went to her job. My parents fought a lot, but I thought it was normal since my dad was always trying to fight somebody. It didn't matter who." The similarity to Diana's boyfriend didn't escape me. "My grandmother was the one who admitted to me that my mom used to cheat on my dad."

I wondered if they were still together or not. "That sounds like a miserable experience for both of them."

He nodded, his breathing slow and even as his gaze stuck itself on the television. "Yeah, but now I see that they were both so unhappy with each other that they could never be happy with me, no matter what I did, and it makes it a lot easier to go on with my life. The best thing they ever did was relinquish their rights and take me to my grandparents. I didn't do anything to them, and I'm better off with the way things turned out than I would have been otherwise. Everything I have, I have because of my grandma and grandpa." He turned his head and made sure to make eye contact with me. "I wasn't about to waste my life away, upset, because I was raised by people who couldn't commit to anything in their lives. All they did was show me the kind of person I didn't want to be."

Why did it feel like he was talking about my mom?

We both lay there for a while, neither one of us saying a word. I was thinking about my mom and all of the mistakes I'd taken upon myself in all these years. "Sometimes, I wonder why the hell I bother still trying to have a relationship with my mom. If I didn't call her, she'd call me twice a year unless there was something she needed or wanted, or she was feeling bad about something she remembered doing—or not doing. I know it's shitty to think that, but I do."

"Did you tell her we got married?"

That had me snickering. "Remember that day we went to your lawyer's office and you'd answered her call? She was calling because someone had told her; they recognized my name." The next snicker that came out of me was even angrier. "When I called her back, the first thing she asked was when I was going to get her tickets to one of your games. I told her never to ask me that again and she got so defensive . . . I swear to God, even now, I think about how I never ever want to be anything like her."

My hands had started clenching and I forced them to relax. I made myself calm down, trying to let go of that anger that seemed to pop up every so often.

"Like I said. I don't know your mom and I really don't want to ever know her, but you're doing all right, Van. Better than all right most of the time."

All right. Most of the time. The word choice had me smiling up at the ceiling as I calmed down even more. "Thanks, big guy."

"Uh-huh," he replied before going right for it. "I'd say all the time, but I know how much money you owe in student loans."

I rolled onto my side to look at him. Finally. "I was wondering if you were ever going to bring that up," I mumbled.

The big guy rolled over to face me as well, his expression wiped clean of any residual anger at his memories. "What the hell were you thinking?"

I sighed. "Not everyone gets a scholarship, hot shot."

"There's cheaper schools you could have gone to."

Ugh. "Yeah, but I didn't want to go to any of them." I said it and realized how stupid that sounded. "And yeah, I regret it a little now, but what can I do? It's done. I was just stubborn and stupid. And I'd never gotten to do what I wanted to do, I guess, you know? I just wanted to get away."

Aiden seemed to consider that a moment before propping his head up on his fist. "Does anyone know about them?"

"Are you kidding me? No way. If anyone asked, I told them I got a scholarship," I finally admitted to someone. "You're the first person I've ever admitted that to."

"You haven't even told Zac?"

I gave him a weird look. "No. I don't like telling everyone that I'm an idiot."

"Just me?"

I stuck my tongue out. "Shut up."

IT DIDN'T MATTER how old I got, the first thing that came to mind every morning on December twenty-fifth was, *It's Christmas.* There hadn't always been presents under the tree, but after I'd learned not to expect anything, it hadn't taken away from the magic of it.

The fact I woke up the next morning in a room that wasn't mine didn't curb my excitement. The sheets were up to my neck and I was on my side. In front of me was Aiden. The only thing visible other than the top of his head were sleepy brown eyes. I gave him a little smile.

"Merry Christmas," I whispered, making sure my morning breath wasn't blowing directly into his face.

Tugging the sheet and comforter down from where he had it up to his nose, he opened his mouth in a deep yawn. "Merry Christmas."

I was going to ask when he'd woken up, but it was obvious it hadn't been long. He brought up a hand to scrub at his eyes before making another soundless yawn. He punched his hands up toward the head-board in a long stretch. Those miles of tan, taut skin reached up past the headboard, his biceps elongating as his fingers stretched far, like a big, lazy cat.

And I couldn't stop myself from taking it all in, at least until he caught me.

Then we stared at each other, and I knew we were both thinking about the same exact thing: the night before. Not the long talk we'd had about our families—and that raw honesty we'd given each other—but about what happened after that.

The movie. The damn movie.

I didn't know what the hell I'd been thinking, fully fucking aware I was already mopey, when I asked if he wanted to watch my favorite movie as a kid. I'd watched it hundreds of times. *Hundreds of times.* It felt like love and hope.

And I was an idiot.

And Aiden, being a nice person who apparently let me get away with most of the things I wanted, said, "Sure. I might fall asleep during it."

He hadn't fallen asleep.

If there was one thing I learned that night was that no one was impervious to Littlefoot losing his mom. Nobody. He'd only slightly rolled his eyes when the cartoon started, but when I glanced over at him, he'd been watching faithfully.

When that awful, terrible, why-would-you-do-that-to-children-and-to-humanity-in-general part came on in *The Land Before Time*, my heart still hadn't learned how to cope, and I was feeling so low, the hiccups coming out were worse than usual. My vision got cloudy. I got choked up. Tears were coming out of my eyes like the powerful Mississippi. Time and dozens of viewings hadn't toughened me up at all.

And as I'd wiped at my face and tried to remind myself it was just a movie and a young dinosaur hadn't lost his beloved mom, I heard a sniffle. A sniffle that wasn't my own. I turned not-so-discreetly and saw him.

I saw the starry eyes and the way his throat bobbed with a gulp. Then I saw the sideways look he shot me as I sat there dealing with my own emotions, and we stared at each other. In silence.

The big guy wasn't handling it, and if there were ever a time in any universe, watching any movie, this would be the cause of it.

All I could do was nod at him, get up to my knees, and lean over so I could wrap my arms around his neck and tell him in as soothing of a voice as I could get together, "I know, big guy. I know," even as another round of tears came out of my eyes and possibly some snot out of my nose.

The miraculous part was that he let me. Aiden sat there and let me hug him, let me put my cheek over the top of his head and let him know it was okay. Maybe it happened because we'd just been talking about the faulty relationships we had with our families, or maybe it was because a child losing its mother was just about the saddest thing in the world, especially when it was an innocent animal, I don't know. But it was sad as shit.

He sniffed—on any other person smaller than him it would have been considered a sniffle—and I squeezed my arms around him a little tighter before going back to my side of the bed, where we finished watching the movie. Then he turned to look at me with those endless brown eyes. "Stay here tonight," he'd murmured, and that was that.

Had I wanted to go to my room? Not when I was lying in the most comfortable bed I'd ever slept on, snuggled under warm sheets. What was I going to do? Play hard to get? I wasn't that dumb. So I stayed, and Aiden eventually turned off the lights, save for the one in the en suite, and we finally shared a brief "good night."

If I didn't know Aiden any better, I would have figured he'd been embarrassed to have gotten so sad over a cartoon, but I knew him. He didn't get shy.

But he hadn't said a word about needing a moment or asking me to get out of his bed.

Now, we were facing each other and we both knew what the other was thinking about. Neither one of us was going to say anything about it though.

I gave him a gradual smile, trying to play it off. "Thanks for letting me sleep in here with you."

He did something that looked like a shrug, but since his arms were still up past his head, I couldn't be sure. "You don't take up any room." He yawned again. "You don't snore. You didn't bother me."

I'm not sure what it said about me that I felt clearheaded and way too well rested. Mostly though, I felt antsy like a little kid.

"Do you want your present now? Or later?" I asked, knowing that I damn well wanted to give him his present now. I was so giddy, and the reality that I was probably more excited than he was going to be was a real predicament, but . . .

Who cared? If he didn't want it, I would keep it. I'd love the hell out of the eight-week-old puppy downstairs if he didn't. It was a golden retriever, because I knew it was going to need to be the sweetest thing in the universe to put up with Aiden's bullshit.

"Later is fine," he said like a true adult instead of like a little kid eager to open his presents on Christmas morning.

For a split second, I felt totally disappointed. But only for a split second before I made a decision. "Too bad. Don't leave the room. I'll be back in a second."

I hopped out of bed and practically ran toward the laundry room downstairs. I fished the little yellow guy out of his crate and cursed when I realized he'd pooped and lain on it. Actually, it looked like he'd rolled around in it. "Damn it."

I gave him a kiss on the head anyway and then ran up the stairs to give him a bath, only stopping by my room to pick up the bow I'd bought for him that had been sitting in my nightstand drawer for the last week, since I'd put down a deposit on him. I couldn't give Aiden a poopy puppy, could I?

Just as I made it to the bathroom, I yelled, "Give me fifteen minutes, big guy!"

Rolling up my sleeves, I gave the little guy a few more kisses on his soft head and waited for the water to warm up enough. The second it was ready, I grabbed the bottle of honey almond puppy shampoo and began lathering him up. Considering I hadn't given a dog a bath ever, it was a lot harder than it seemed. He had too much energy. He peed inside the tub. He kept jumping up on the edge, trying to get out, or get on me, I couldn't be sure.

The soap went everywhere; I could feel it on my face. My top was soaked, and it was still one of the happiest moments of my life. That face just killed me a little.

Why hadn't I gotten a dog before? For me?

"What are you doing?" the voice asked from behind me.

I froze there with my arms in the bathtub; one was busy holding the puppy who had his paws on the edge while his head peeked over the rim, and the other was on the tap in the middle of turning it off. Looking over my shoulder, I frowned over at him, grabbing the towel I'd left on top of the toilet seat.

"I told you to wait in your room," I muttered, only slightly disappointed he'd ruined the surprise in a way. I only had to look at those expressive, big, brown eyes on that beautiful puppy face to get over it.

I was in love.

And a huge part of me didn't want to give the puppy over, but I knew I had to.

"What is that?" Aiden's grumbling voice grew just the slightest hint louder, curious, so curious.

Wrapping the towel around the wet, almost scraggly-looking ball of innocence, I pulled him to me as I got to my feet and snuggled him one last time before glancing up at the man standing in the doorway. Aiden's eyes were wider than I'd ever seen and might ever see them. Down at his sides, his fingers twitched. Those dark orbs went from the bundle against my chest to my face and back again. Pink rose up on the tips of his ears and he asked once more, "What is that?"

I thrust the little guy forward. "Merry Christmas, big guy."

The man known as the Wall of Winnipeg took the towel-wrapped bundle from me and simply stared at it.

Should I have gotten him something else? There were a couple of other small presents I bought him, but this was the big one. The one I'd been shaking in excitement over.

"If you hate him . . ."

The dog let out a sharp, playful bark that sliced through the air. I got to watch as four emotions flashed across Aiden's features. Confusion, recognition, surprise, and elation.

He brought the baby up to his face.

Aiden stared at the retriever for so long, I started to think I'd imagined the elation that had been on his face a moment before. But I knew he liked animals, and he'd mentioned once in an interview how much he wanted a dog but wanted to wait until he had more time to be a good owner.

But the longer I waited, watching, not sure what to expect, the more surprised I was when he tucked the soft yellow buddy under his chin and moved his arm to cradle it to his chest *like a baby*.

Ah hell. I hadn't been prepared. My body wasn't ready for Aiden holding a puppy like a baby.

Shit, shit, shit.

"Vanessa . . ." he kind of choked out, making the situation worse for me.

"Merry Christmas," I repeated hoarsely, torn between smiling and crying.

He blinked, and then he blinked some more as his free hand touched the small, perfect features on the young, innocent face. "I don't know what to say," he kind of mumbled, his eyes glued to his puppy. His chin tipped down, and I swear he cuddled the dog closer to him. "I've never . . ." He swallowed and glanced up at me, our eyes meeting. "Thank you. *Thank you*."

Was I crying? Was I seriously crying?

"You're welcome." I might have, kind of, smiled at the blurry vision of these two. "I know you said you don't have time for relationships, but there's no way you can't make time for him. Look at him. I loved him the moment I saw him. I was almost about to play it off like I bought him for myself when you walked in."

He nodded quickly, too quickly for my heart to handle appropriately. "Yeah, you're right. I can make time." Aiden licked his lips and pierced me with a brief look that had me frozen in place once again. It was the single sweetest, most eye-opening expression I'd ever had anyone direct at me. "I'm starting to understand that you can always make time for the things that matter."

HOURS LATER, WE were sitting on the floor in the living room with the new love of Aiden's life, and I was thinking that this had turned out to be the best Christmas ever. We'd spent the day with the puppy, which surprised me. I guess a part of me had expected Aiden to take off with him and disappear so he could enjoy his new child alone, but that hadn't been the case at all.

As soon as he'd realized the puppy was still soaking wet, he'd looked at me and said, "What now?"

For the next hour, we dried the unnamed puppy and took him out to pee, while Aiden sprayed out his dirty kennel and I supervised. Then he set up the food bowls I'd brought along with some kibbles and water. What followed that was breakfast in the kitchen together with the puppy running around, then taking him outside again after he peed in the kitchen. Aiden hadn't even thought twice about wiping it up.

Since then, I'd showered and gone downstairs to watch some television, and that's where Aiden had found me after he'd apparently showered . . . with his little guy in his arms.

It was seriously killing me. This gigantic guy carrying an eight-pound dog around in his huge arms. God help us. I needed to find some puppies and pay some ripped models to pose with them. I could make a killing if I put them on calendars.

Or maybe it was just Aiden who I found so attractive holding a puppy that he was clearly enamored with.

I wasn't going to overanalyze it too much, I decided pretty quickly.

With the gas fireplace going, the Christmas tree lights on, and everything just so peaceful, the day just felt right. I'd called my extended family—my brother, Diana, and my foster parents—after I'd showered to wish them a happy holiday.

I stretched my legs out in front of me, keeping an eye on the blondie curled up on the floor right between my feet, when Aiden, who was sitting next to me, suddenly turned and said, "I still haven't given you your presents."

I blinked. He what? I hadn't been expecting anything, but I'd feel like an ass saying that out loud.

"Oh." I blinked again. "You got me something?"

He narrowed his eyes a little, like he was thinking the same thing I had just been. "Yes." Getting to his big feet a lot more effortlessly than someone that large should have been capable of, he tipped his head in the direction of the stairs. "Follow me."

Follow him I did, up the stairs, down the hall, and toward . . . his office.

His office?

Ahead of me, he pushed open the door and tilted his head for me to go forward.

I hesitated at the doorway, watching him watch me as I did. Aiden's hand reached in front of my face and flipped on the switch. Stacked on top of his big hardwood desk were two presents carefully wrapped in peppermint striped paper. I didn't have to ask to know that those big, careful hands had done the wrapping, not some stranger.

That alone made my nose tickle.

"Open the first one," he instructed.

I shot him a glance over my shoulder before walking inside the office and taking the gift off the top. Slowly, I undid the wrapping and peeled the slim box out. I knew what it was the instant I saw the name of the company. It was a brand-new, top-of-the-line tablet. It was the one most graphic designers would salivate over but never actually buy, because you could talk yourself into spending less money on something *almost* as good, pretty easily.

Holding it to my chest, I turned around to face him with my mouth wide open. "Aiden—"

He held up his hand and rolled his eyes. "Thank me after you open the next one."

About ready to ignore him and give him a hug right then, I decided to be a good sport and open the next gift first, since he'd asked so nicely.

The next present was in a bigger box, like the fancy scarf case I'd seen my roommate in college collect things in. Just like the last present, I opened it up slowly and pulled out the perfectly cube-shaped box.

Peeling off the top, I couldn't help but crack up at the pile of nightlights and flashlights inside. There were two small ones with keychains looped through the base of them, and three different plug-ins: one shaped like Jupiter, another of a star, and the third was a plain column-shaped one that promised to be the best on the market. Apart from those were four flashlights in various sizes and colors: pink, red, teal, and black. I picked up the metallic pink one.

"They reminded me of your hair colors."

Oh no. "Aiden—"

"I know it isn't much compared to what you gave me, but I thought it was good enough at first. I haven't bought anyone a present in years—"

"It is enough, dummy," I said, looking at him over my shoulder, holding what was the most thoughtful gift anyone had ever given me.

The big guy cleared his throat. "No. It isn't. I owe you."

He owed me? "You don't owe me anything. This is . . . this is perfect. More than perfect. Thank you." Fucking nightlights. Who would have thought?

Two big hands landed on my shoulders. "I owe you, Van. Trust me." Just as quickly as they'd gotten on me, his hands retreated and he added, "This isn't a present, but hold out your hand."

I did, cupping it high above my shoulder, curious as to what he was going to give me. Chewed up gum?

Something cool and small fell into my palm. It was pretty heavy.

When I lowered my hand, all the saliva in my mouth went just about everywhere else in my body.

"It isn't a gift. The jeweler called yesterday and said it was ready. I was going to give it to you, but . . ."

At first, I honestly thought it was a rock. A big, light blue rock. But I must have been so confused I didn't see the white-gold band that lay against my hand. Then it hit me: it was a ring. Holding it up closer to my face, years of shopping at vintage thrift stores came back to me.

An emerald cut, slightly bluish-green stone—aquamarine to be exact, my birthstone—was mounted on the thin band. On each side of the stone were three accent diamonds. Just below the plain white gold was a simple diamond-encrusted band that fit around the bigger ring like a set, very subtle.

It looked like one of those cocktail rings people in the 1950s wore . . . except I could tell, *my heart could freaking tell*, this wasn't some cheap knockoff from a catalog.

"I figured you needed an engagement ring. I didn't think you'd like a diamond. This seemed more you."

"Shut up." I gaped at the ring a second more, my breathing getting heavier.

"No," he snapped back. "If you don't like it—"

"Stop talking, Aiden. It's the most amazing ring I've ever seen." I held my hand up closer to my face and shook my head in a daze, looking up at his eyes with my heart on my tongue. "It's for me?"

"Who else would it be for? My other wife?" the annoying ass asked.

He'd gotten me a ring.

And it was—

Damn it. Damn. It. I couldn't love him. I couldn't. I couldn't, especially not because he'd chosen me something perfect. Something *me*.

I tried to beat back the emotion just enough. "You could have just given me a band. I don't care what everyone else thinks," I kind of whispered as I slipped the wedding set onto the appropriate hand and finger.

"I don't care either, but I got it for you anyway."

TWENTY-FIVE

"I'm in love."

Watching Leo zoom from side to side across the tile floor, a vision of everything wonderful in the universe, I couldn't help but agree with Zac. All three of us loved the little yellow ball of fur, and it had only been two full weeks. In that time, between Aiden and me, we'd potty trained the little turkey and set up a schedule. When the big guy was gone, I kept him with me and made sure to take him outside every couple of hours.

Leo was brilliant, and I completely regretted giving him to Aiden instead of keeping him. Not that it really made much of a difference whom he belonged to, since he technically spent more time with me anyway with his daddy gone all the time. With the Three Hundreds moving through the postseason, advancing through the wild card bracket, they were entering the divisional playoffs. Their game was the next day, and needless to say, the man who insisted on carrying the weight of the world on his shoulders was feeling every inch of stress.

Needless to say, I was giving him a wide berth and trying to be as supportive as I could, which meant I'd been making enough dinner to feed everyone in the household. Aiden was Jedi-level focused, and when he was home, he spent all the time he could with his new kiddo, while also resting as much as possible.

"I love him," I said as the little guy trotted over to where we were sitting at the nook, draping his body over my sock-covered foot. "He sleeps on my lap for hours while I'm working. It's so hard not to want to keep him on me all day."

Zac leaned down to give him a rub with the tips of his fingers, but Leo was out cold. We had gone for a twelve-mile run at the gym where Zac was training, and immediately afterward took Leo out of his crate, which Aiden kept in his room, and let him run around in the back-yard. Sitting straight, Zac took a big drink of the lime green Gatorade bottle sitting in front of him. "Are you goin' to the game tomorrow?"

"I was planning on it. Did you want to go?"

He went back to peeking under the table. "You have anybody else to go with you?"

Since that first game, Zac hadn't gone with me to any of the rest. I'd been going alone. "I can go by myself. It isn't a big deal."

"I know you can go by yourself, but it's a division game. It'll be nuts."

I crossed my eyes. "I grew up with three psychos. I can handle nuts."

Zac raised his eyebrows and I realized what the hell I said. *I could handle nuts.* Idiot.

I groaned. "You know what I mean."

He grinned big, wide, and so not innocent. "Just for you, I won't say nothin'." The doofus winked. "Look, I'll go with you tomorrow. Just make sure Aiden gets us good seats since you think you're too good to sit in the box."

"Too good to sit in the box?" I squawked. "I just don't want to get friendly with the other players' wives. That's all."

That had Zac sitting back with a frown. "Why?"

"I told you." Or was it Aiden I told? I couldn't remember. "I feel like a phony."

"You're not a phony."

I lifted up a shoulder. "I feel like one. Plus the season is almost over. Who knows what's going to happen? He hasn't kept me in the loop at all about what's going on with Trevor or even brought up when he's leaving for Colorado this year." Honestly, I hadn't thought too much about him leaving for the off-season, because I didn't want to. The one and only time I had, it had made me sad to think about not seeing him for months at a time. I'd rather live ignorantly than with this weight of missing someone who wasn't gone around my shoulders. Plus, he would tell me when he was leaving . . . wouldn't he?

"He hasn't told me a single thing, Vanny, and the last time I talked to Trevor, it was just to go over what my goal for the off-season was," Zac explained.

That gave me an excuse to forget about Colorado for the moment and remember that what Aiden decided to do with the rest of his career didn't just affect me; it affected Zac too. If he went to a different team, it wasn't like Zac would go. Things had been so strained between them the last couple of months that I had no idea where they stood. "Have you decided what you're going to do?"

"My old Texas coach gave me a call a few weeks ago. Said he was plannin' on retiring this year, and he's from a town real close to Ma's. I think I might end up heading back to Austin to work with him."

Austin? I gulped selfishly. "Really?"

"Yeah. It wouldn't hurt to go home. I told you how guilty PawPaw made me feel during Christmas," he explained. Zac said his grandpa kept reminding him he wasn't getting any younger.

Then the second step of the future hit me. Sure we'd only been living together for five months, but . . . we might end up in different states. Forever. I'd be essentially losing Zac, one of my closest friends. What kind of messed up, self-absorbed dimension had I been living in to not contemplate these outcomes?

He must have seen the despair on my face, because he let out a sharp laugh of disbelief. "Why you gettin' upset, sugar?"

"Because I won't be seeing you anymore," I said with every ounce of horror I felt. "You're basically my second best friend."

"Aah shit, Van. You're basically my best friend too." Those blue eyes widened for a moment. "I don't know what I would've done without you these last few months."

I had to reach up to swipe at my eyes with the back of my hand. I'd been the biggest crybaby since Christmas, and I had no reason for it. "Why am I getting so upset? We'll still text message each other, right?"

"Of course we will. *Of course we will.* Come on." Were his eyes getting shiny? "Gimme a hug. You're gonna make my mascara run."

I laughed even as I threw my arms around him. "You're an idiot, but I love you."

With two arms slung over my shoulders, his chest gurgled beneath mine in what sounded like a watery chuckle.

"You don't have to do the marathon if you don't want to," I let his shirt know.

"You haven't put me through hell for me to back out on you now, darlin'. We're doin' it."

"But if you'd rather go to Austin sooner than later . . ."

"We're doin' this," he insisted. He pulled back, his hands going to my upper arms so he could peer down at me. "You know you're gonna be all right, don't you?"

"Doing the marathon or if I have to move with Aiden?"

Those light blue eyes narrowed down at me. "I'm not worried about you doin' the marathon. You got that thing in check. I meant movin'."

"Oh, yeah." I shrugged. "I'm not that worried about it. I don't do much here in Dallas anyway, and Aiden's been keeping me company a lot more."

Part of me expected him to say something like "I'd noticed," because he'd been teasing me mercilessly from the moment he came home after the New Year and seen the ring Aiden had bought me. The fact I only took it off when we went running didn't help. Instead though, Zac nodded, his smile easy. "He'll make sure you're fine."

That had me snorting. I wanted to tell him about Aiden and how I'd been feeling but . . . I couldn't. I just couldn't. Every day this thing with him just got stronger. Worse. How do you fall in love with the man you're supposed to divorce in a few years? I was an idiot, and sometimes I didn't want to face the facts of just how stupid I was.

I wasn't really convinced of the idea that Aiden would make the effort to make sure I settled in okay in a new city. I knew what his main focus in life was, and it definitely wasn't me. "How are things going with both of you anyway? Has it gotten any better?" I hadn't really seen them talk much in the last few weeks, not that they ever talked much to begin with, period.

"All right." His answer was as innocent as I expected. "Why?"

"I haven't really seen you two talk. I was just wondering if something had happened."

Zac shook his head. "No. Things are different now. That's all. He doesn't know what to say to me, and I don't know what to say to him either. The last time I tried to talk to him he lectured me on how it was my fault I got cut from my team. I know it's my fault, but I don't wanna hear him say that. Look, don't worry about him and me; I'm not the one who's got his ring on my finger. You two are gonna be fine."

Wait a second. . . . "What's that supposed to mean?"

"You know what." He winked.

"No. I don't know." I didn't like where this was going, and I definitely disliked the intelligence in his eyes even less.

When Zac put a hand on the top of my head and gave me a pat, I crossed my eyes. "Don't be a dunce. He got into bed with you—"

"Because I was scared!"

"He got into a fight for you, Van. If that doesn't say it all, I don't know what does."

"Because—"

He apparently didn't care what I had to say. "I've seen the way you look at him. I know how you've always looked at him."

No.

"You'll never meet anybody more loyal than him, Van, and I don't know anybody better that Aiden could have ended up with. You might be the only person in the world who can put up with his ass. I just hope you two do something about it and not waste time."

I could only stare at him blankly.

It was the garage door opening that snapped us both out of the stare down we were having. By the time we separated, with Zac thinking he knew some dirty little secret and me not sure what the hell was going on, Aiden had opened the door to the garage. Leo shot up from beneath the table, bounding toward his daddy.

Immediately crouching down, Aiden scooped up his blond ball and hoisted him up into those brawny arms that seemed so at odds with the now ten-pound puppy. His eyes swung from Leo to Zac then to me. I was sure we looked pretty suspicious just standing there like deer caught in the headlights, but oh well.

I smiled at him, hoping I didn't look as flustered as I felt. "Hey, big guy."

"Hi." With the arm that wasn't holding Leo up, he reached up to stroke down the length of Leo's spine, his irises bouncing back and forth between Zac and me once more. Walking toward us, he tipped his chin down to nuzzle the puppy before stopping in front of me and dipping his mouth to plant a soft, dry kiss on my cheek that had me rooted in place.

What the hell was happening?

What in the hell was happening?

"I'm going to shower," Zac said, shooting me a smirk that said "See?" With a smack to my lower spine, he left the kitchen, leaving me there alone, confused and wondering if this was a dream I hadn't woken up from.

Restraining the urge to pinch myself, I gulped and glanced at Aiden as my insides went haywire. "How was your day?" I pretty much croaked out.

The big guy shot me a funny look as he rubbed the other side of his cheek against Leo's fur. "Fine. Meetings and practice." Aiden had Leo so high up, the puppy's body hid everything below his eyes. "How was your run?"

"Tiring. We did twelve miles on the hill setting at the gym." He kissed Leo's nose and something in me died. "Your kid's already run around outside, and he's pooped and peed."

At "your kid" a small smile curled the corners of Aiden's mouth. Those brown eyes switched back to me and asked, "You're still coming to the game tomorrow?"

"Oh. Yeah. Of course. Is that fine?"

Aiden made a noise on his way toward the refrigerator. "Don't ask me stupid questions, Vanessa."

"Well. I don't want to just assume, thank you."

He huffed and said over his shoulder, "You know I would tell you if I didn't want you there."

"I figure, but you never know."

Aiden's attention was forward when he replied with something that had me wondering if he was dying. Or delusional. Or maybe this entire moment was just a dream. "You don't ever have to worry about me not wanting you somewhere. Got it?"

And like the idiot I was, the one who didn't know how to process hints, or roll with things in a clever, cute way, I said the dumbest thing I could have said, "Oh. Okay."

Idiot. Idiot, idiot, idiot.

It haunted me the rest of the day.

THE BOOING WAS overwhelming.

More than overwhelming. It was so deafening even my soul could feel it.

Three Hundreds fans in the stands were roaring with disapproval and disappointment. To say that they were pissed would not adequately describe the situation at all. The game had been awful. In the first quarter, Zac's enemy, the team's quarterback, was sacked—or tackled—and had his arm broken. In the third quarter, Christian Delgado was tackled so hard his helmet flew off and he sustained a concussion. I didn't cheer.

And that had just been the tip of the iceberg for bad luck. Zac, who was my bodyguard for the game, had been gripping his heart from the very beginning, and that was saying something from the man who hadn't rooted for the Three Hundreds once since he'd been let go.

The offense played terribly and Denver had taken advantage of how rattled and distracted the Three Hundreds' defense was. Well, every other player on defense other than Aiden. Every time the camera landed on him, and every time I managed to catch a glimpse of his face, thanks to how close my seats were, he had that stone-cold expression, like his role alone would be enough to get the team through.

Unfortunately, it hadn't been.

The booing had started before the game had even finished, and when the players for the Three Hundreds walked off the field and in the direction of the sidelines, the third-biggest player on the team had stopped before making his way toward the tunnel that led to the locker rooms. Aiden stood there at the fifty-yard line, just shy of crossing over with his hands on his hips facing me. I knew those tendons along his neck well, I could see the tightness in his shoulders that no one else would be able to pick up on, even the angle in which he held his wrists told me a story.

Disappointment flowed deep in that big body.

I lifted my hand up and gave him a wave.

He didn't wave back, and I wasn't totally surprised. A male broken heart was a difficult thing to come back from.

So I did the only thing I could think of that he would understand; I lowered my waving hand, placed it in front of my belly, and raised up my middle finger like I had all the other hundreds of times I'd done it in the past when I thought he wasn't looking.

And with his helmet still on, the Wall of Winnipeg shook his head, and I knew that was pretty much a laugh.

"Hey, you don't fucking flip off Aiden Graves!" an angry male voice yelled at me from down my row.

I looked over, ignoring Zac's closely looming body, more than likely preparing himself to defend my honor, and gave the man defending Aiden a calm smile. "He's my husband."

In the blink of an eye, the rough, older man who had yelled completely cooled down. I caught him taking a peek at my hand, where sure enough, my brand-new ring was. I found myself looking at it at least twenty times a day and touching it another twenty times. I still couldn't believe he'd given it to me. "You shitting me?" he barked.

"No." I had a Graves jersey on.

"Oh." Just like that, it was fine. "Carry on." The man paused and seemed to think for a moment. "Would you tell him Gary from Denton hopes he doesn't leave this shitty team? Excuse my French, but we're fucked without him."

What else was I supposed to say? "Okay. I will." But by the time I glanced back at the field, the big guy had disappeared.

"That was awful," Zac deadpanned.

The scoreboard was still lit up, mocking fans and the players who had by that point also disappeared.

14-31.

Sheesh.

"I think we need to get the hell out of here," Zac said from behind me as two people in the stands about five rows up started yelling at each other.

Yeah we did. "Come on," I said, pointing toward where we needed to go. He put his hand on my shoulder and followed after me.

I squirmed my way through the masses walking up the stairs en route to the exit. The fans were so loud my ears ached. Fully conscious of the two passes in my pocket, I turned around by the concession stands as I found a small area that was out of the way of the human traffic trying to exit.

"Are you going to the family room?" he yelled so I could hear him.

The score loomed in my head and I shrugged. "I don't know. Do you want to go?"

Zac shot me a look that reminded me of Aiden's favorite one. "No." That had been a stupid question, but he was kind enough not to point it out. "But you should."

Going up to my tippy-toes, I said into his ear, "I don't think he'd want to see me right now."

He stepped back and clearly mouthed, "Go."

I took a step toward him again. "I don't like the idea of just dumping you and making you drive home alone," I explained. "Plus, what if he doesn't want to take me home?"

"Get outta here, Van. You're not dumpin' me, and we both know how Aiden's takin' this right now. Go. I might getta drink before I get home, but call if you need me."

Yeah, I wasn't feeling very optimistic or hopeful. I knew Aiden. I knew how he got after losses, especially a playoff loss that tanked so badly. Sure, maybe I'd slightly amused him by flipping him off, but I was pretty worried about going to see him.

Well shit. What was he going to do? Yell at me?

I didn't consider myself a coward. Screw it.

With a hug and a promise that he wouldn't drive drunk, I took the long way toward the family room. Security was tighter than usual, but I finally made it to my destination to find the family room overflowing with people. Small groups bundled together, faces grim, some forcefully bright, but mostly, it was a bunch of "aww shit."

I wasn't the only one sort of dreading seeing the person they were there for.

My thing was, I just wasn't sure if Aiden would even want me around despite giving me a pass. He'd hinted that he wanted me to go to the game, but now that they'd lost . . . I palmed the peppermint patty I'd stuck in my pocket just in case. The man he used to be would have wanted to be alone, but this Aiden, the one I knew now . . . well, I wasn't sure.

On the other hand, if he didn't want to talk to me, if he would rather be by himself, I would understand. I wouldn't hold it against him. I wasn't going to let it hurt my feelings or bother me.

This was a business deal. We were friends.

That sounded about as hollow in my head as it felt in my heart. The season was over. What was he going to do now?

So it was that uncertainty that kept me in the corner by the hallway so I could keep an eye out and catch Aiden before he left.

Not long after I settled into my spot on the far side of the room, and after I'd waved at a few of the women who had been friendly with me in the past, a couple of players started trickling out of the locker room. More minutes passed and more men came out. But none of them was Aiden.

Rubbing my hands over my pants, I started messing with my phone, checking to see nothing really. I just hated standing there by myself. Shuffling from foot to foot, my thumb rubbed at the side of my wedding ring set, the slightly rounded edge of the stone an easy distraction as more guys came out, some of them glancing in my corner, but most of them heading straight toward their loved ones. As the minutes passed, the room emptied out, and I was left trying to decide how long to wait until I called a cab. Ten more minutes maybe? Zac had to be long gone by then, and I definitely wasn't going to call Diana to come pick me up. According to her last text message two hours ago, she was spending time with her boyfriend. Yuck.

Rubbing my hands on my jeans again, I swallowed and waited. Then I started messing with the zipper of my jacket. Up and down. Up and down.

Ten minutes and still no Aiden. Three-fourths of the room had to have cleared out by that point.

I pulled out my phone and searched for the number to the taxi company. With a sigh, I glanced up just as I was about to hit the call icon on the screen, and spotted the big, dark-haired man coming down the hallway. His face was a cool mask that said, "Get out of my fucking way and don't talk to me." The way he held his shoulders and the stern purse of his mouth said the same thing.

Well, shit.

For a second, I thought about keeping my mouth shut and hitting that call button but . . . I was there, wasn't I? And I trusted him not to embarrass me.

I thought.

"Aiden?" I called out, a lot softer than I expected, and wanted.

Those dark eyes flicked from the floor to eye level before his even stride faltered and he paused in the hallway. He'd worn a suit to the game that day and the two-piece charcoal gray looked great. It was only the duffel hanging off his shoulder making him look like the Aiden Graves I knew—the one who didn't feel comfortable in anything other than his favorite ten-year-old hoodie, shorts, and runners. A crease formed between those thick slashes called his eyebrows for only a second, before I could think twice about what I was doing, I waved.

More waving. Help me.

The corner of his mouth twitched, and I knew I'd made a mistake. I shouldn't have come. I should have left with Zac.

His nostrils flared at the same time he took another step forward, and another, no words coming out of his mouth.

I was so dumb. So damn dumb. What had I done thinking that

all those little things he'd been saying and doing actually might have meant something? Just because we'd told each other things that I was sure we hadn't told anyone else didn't mean we were more than friends. You could trust someone and not be their friend . . . couldn't you?

At the last second, he stopped in front of me. A foot taller than me, so much wider, Aiden was . . . he was huge. His presence was overpowering.

His body radiated heat and that wonderful clean scent of his skin; I swallowed as he stood in front of me. The swallow turned into a shaky, uncertain smile. "Hi, big guy. I wasn't sure if you wanted me to come back or not, but—"

"Stop." Aiden ducked his face at the same time those massive hands came up. One went to my cheek, the other went to cup the back of my neck. He kissed me.

Aiden kissed me.

His bottom lip went to my top one, his grip reassuring and un-yielding as he dragged his mouth to kiss me fully. And I did what any sane person would have done: I let him, and I pressed my lips to his instinctively. Our mouths met in a peck that was followed by a big, guttural sigh fanning over my neck for a moment, his forehead pressing against mine.

Okay. All right.

Okay.

I didn't know what the hell had just happened, but I wasn't about to let myself overthink it.

My heart beating, I tipped my mouth up to kiss him the same way he had me, my hand reaching to touch the side of his neck. Dropping back to my heels, his forehead followed mine down. I drew my hand over to knead his thick trapezius muscles, copping a feel for what may or may not be the first and last time I would ever be able to.

I wanted to ask him if he was okay, but I knew the answer.

The deep sigh coming out of his chest told me what I needed to know. So I reached up with my other hand and began kneading the other side of his neck. Sure, he had trainers who did this, and he had enough money to pay a professional, but I massaged the tops of his traps anyway. The people surrounding us seemed so insignificant and small in that moment, in life in general, that I didn't care they were around.

"That's nice," Aiden kind of whispered.

I only dug in harder with my thumbs, earning a small smile from the man who passed them out like they were golden tickets to Willy Wonka's Chocolate Factory. I swore he was grumbling with pleasure like a big bear. "Better?" I asked once my fingers began to get tired, drawing my palms across his shoulders.

He nodded. "Much."

"I'll make you dinner when we get home. What do you say?"

"I'll say okay."

"Are you ready to go?"

He nodded once more, the small amount of pleasure on his face slowly draining.

Stepping back, I hesitated. Had I done too much? Was he already regretting kissing me? Which was stupid because if I gave myself the chance to think about it, I'd know Aiden didn't do things he would regret. . . . Unless it was what he'd done to me before I quit. But I didn't let myself think about it. "Do you mind giving me a ride, big guy? Zac took off."

"He brought you?" he asked as he raised his chin, his gaze meeting my face.

I nodded.

"I'll take you." I smiled distractedly and let him lead me through the hallway, blatantly ignoring the teammates we passed, and nodding only at the venue's employees who greeted him or wished him a good night.

Reaching his SUV, he unlocked the doors and opened the front passenger door, waving me in and closing the door behind me. By some miracle, I managed to keep my level of dumb-face to a minimum. Afterward, he threw his bag into the back and got inside. The silence wasn't necessarily heavy on the drive home. I knew he must have had a hundred different things going on in his head, and I wanted to let him have his space.

Leaning my head against the window, I yawned and thought about all the things I needed to do when I got home, so that I wouldn't think about the things I had no business putting too much thought into. Like that kiss in front of his teammates' families and the Three Hundreds' staff.

"What are you thinking about?" Aiden asked out of the blue.

"I was just thinking about everything I need to pack for my trip to Toronto. Remember I told you I was going to that convention?" I explained. "What about you? What are you thinking of?" I asked before I could think twice about why I would ask him something I didn't actually expect him to answer.

But he did.

"How ready I am to move on with my life."

"You mean switch teams?" I grasped on to that with two hands. I could easily imagine how hard it was for him to be such a good player on such an inconsistent team. How could it not be discouraging?

He made a noise deep in his throat, his attention focused on the road ahead of him.

"Have you talked to Trevor about it any more?"

"No. Last time we talked, he said there wasn't a point in making plans until the season was over. He knows what I want to do. I don't want to keep repeating myself. If he wants to pay attention, he can; if he doesn't want to, he knows my contract with him is going to end right before I'm eligible to sign with another team."

Huh. "Do you . . . know where you want to go?" I realized why we hadn't talked about this topic before. He wanted to focus on the season, not on the what-ifs that would all take place afterward. But suddenly, there seemed to be so much pressure and focus on all the possibilities. The moving. The future.

Casually, casually, casually, he raised a shoulder. "How do you feel about heading up north?"

North? "How far north are we talking about?"

Those coffee-colored eyes peered at me over his shoulder. "Indiana . . . Wisconsin . . ." he threw out.

"Ah." I looked forward to collect my words and put them in an order I wouldn't regret. "I can live just about anywhere. I'll just have to buy better winter clothes."

"You think so?" Why did his voice sound so amused all of a sudden?

I snorted. "Yeah. Some winter boots, a scarf, and some gloves, and I'll be fine. I think."

"I'll buy you a dozen jackets and winter boots, if that's what you need," he threw out there in a tone that was getting more amused by the second.

It made me perk up a little bit. "You don't need to do that. You do enough for me as it is, big guy."

His fingers drummed the steering wheel and he seemed to shake his head. "Van, I'll buy you a jacket or ten if I want. We're in this together."

Ovaries. Where were my ovaries?

"Aren't we?" Aiden suddenly asked in a hesitant voice.

I lifted my head off the window and really turned to look at him. There was something so devastating about his profile it was annoying. There was something about *him* that was so great it was annoying. He was so dumb sometimes I couldn't handle it. "Yeah. Of course. We're Team Graves."

He made an amused sound and I suddenly remembered what I'd kept making myself put off asking him. "Hey, are you . . . when are you going to Colorado?" I mean, the season was over. The last two years, he'd left as soon as he was able to, yet this year, he hadn't said a word to me. Then again, why would he? I wasn't the one leasing out a house or making plans to rent a car or anything.

Just like that, his body language completely changed. He went rigid. His fingers curled over the steering wheel. His tongue poked at his cheek. "I'm supposed to leave the second week of February."

"Oh." That was about three weeks away. "Are you still going for two months?"

He didn't vocalize his answer; he simply nodded.

But the response still hit my heart like a sledgehammer. He'd be gone for two months. Sure we didn't have in-depth talks every day, but at least in the last month and a half, I couldn't remember a day where I hadn't spent some time with him, even if all we did was watch television quietly or sit on the floor with Leo between us.

"Cool," I kind of mumbled, but it wasn't cool at all.

TWENTY-SIX

Tossing the fifth shirt over my shoulder, I groaned. It wasn't until I had to pack that I ever thought I didn't have enough clothes. It was like a ninja snuck into my closet and drawers and stole everything that fit me well and looked good.

"What are you doing?" Aiden's low, grumbling voice asked from behind me.

I turned around to spot him leaning against the doorframe, hands in the pockets of his gray sweatpants, one ankle over the other. I blew a lock of pink hair that had fallen into my eyes away in frustration. "I'm trying to pack for my trip tomorrow."

"What's the problem?"

Damn it. I sighed. He really did know me, and that only made me feel sheepish. "I can't find anything I want to wear." That was mostly the truth. The other half of the truth was that I'd been pretty grumpy since his last game when he'd admitted he was going to Colorado after kissing me like it was no big deal. He was leaving in two weeks. For two months.

He raised his eyebrows as if telling me to continue, only egging on my nerves.

"I feel like I'm going to the first day of school tomorrow. I'm so nervous," I admitted the other tiny part of it.

Aiden frowned as he uncrossed his legs and took a step inside my room. "About what?" he asked, bending down to pick up two of the shirts that had landed on the floor. Setting them on the bed, he took a spot right next to them on the mattress facing me.

"The convention." This was exactly how I'd get before the first day of school. The nerves. The nausea. The dread. The worry about who I would sit with. If anyone would actually come by my table. What the hell had I been thinking registering? It wasn't like I was starving for business. I got a steady flow of new customers, on top of my returning, loyal clientele.

"It's a book convention. What are you worried about?" He picked up the last shirt I'd tossed on the bed and held it up, looking over the long sleeves and royal blue color. "What's wrong with this one?"

Nerves were eating up my chest and my soul, and he had no idea or any way to comprehend what I was going through. I didn't think Aiden knew what insecurity was. I ignored his comment about the shirt. "What if everyone hates me and no one talks to me? What if someone throws something at me?"

Aiden snorted, setting the shirt he'd been holding aside and picking up the next one on the pile. "What are they going to throw? Bookmarks?"

That had me groaning. "You don't understand . . ."

Aiden peeked at me from over the collar of the blouse, and from the wrinkles around his eyes, I could tell he was smiling just a little bit before he put it on the other side from where he'd left the blue one. "No one is going to throw anything at you. Relax."

I swallowed and went to take a seat on the bed next to him, his thigh touching mine. "Okay, probably not, but what if . . . no one comes by my booth? Can you imagine how awkward that would be? Me sitting there all alone?" Just thinking about it was making me anxious.

Shifting on the mattress, he reached over and touched my thigh with his fingertips. The smile on his face melted completely off and he stared at me with that hard, serious face. "If no one goes by your booth, it's because they're stupid—"

I couldn't help but crack a little smile.

"—and they don't have any taste," he added, giving me a squeeze.

My smile might have grown a little more.

"I looked at your website. I saw the before and after images of what you've done. You're good, Van."

"I know I'm good—"

His chuckle cut me off. "And people think *I'm* cocky."

I elbowed him in the arm with a laugh. "What? I am. There's not a lot of things I'm really good at, but this is the one thing no one can take away from me. I've worked hard at it."

The expression on Aiden's face hinted at amusement as he held up the blue shirt he'd previously set aside. "Then you know you have nothing to worry about. Take this one with you."

I grabbed the shirt he held with a huff and nodded, quietly folding it. I moved around the room and collected the other things I wanted to take with me. I was only spending two nights, I didn't need a whole bunch, but I was still taking more than enough just in case. I'd rather have too many shirts than not enough.

I kneeled down to grab my carry-on luggage from beneath the bed, casting a glance at him as he folded the shirts I'd set aside that I wasn't taking.

He caught me looking at him and only slightly raised his eyebrows. "Stop looking like you're going to be sick, Van. You'll be fine."

"You keep saying that, but then again you're not intimidated by anything, big guy. You run at guys the same size as you or bigger for a living."

His eyebrows crawled up even higher on his forehead. "Fear is all in your head."

"I hate it when people say that."

"It's true. What's the worst that will happen? People won't talk to you? They won't like you? People who really know you like you."

"Trevor doesn't."

Aiden gave me that flat, exasperated look of his. "Since when do you care what he thinks? Trevor is an idiot when it comes to anything that won't make him money. So what if there's a chance some people that you don't know don't like you? Their opinion shouldn't matter. At the end of the day, you're still going to be you—the you I know who would flip me off in the middle of a stadium—and no one's opinion will change that."

Oh brother.

This huge knot filled my throat and I couldn't do a thing but kneel there awkwardly and look at him. To a certain extent, he was right. I didn't usually care what other people thought. Of course, I didn't like to be embarrassed, who did? But for Aiden "the Wall of Winnipeg" Graves, the hardest working, most dedicated person I had ever met, to think so highly of me? Well, it meant more to me than it should have.

Way more.

He finished folding the rest of my clothes and patted the stack next to him. "Am I driving you to the airport?"

I REALLY SHOULD have stayed home.

Two days later, I'd been at the convention behind my table for almost three hours. My table, which I had reserved at the last minute, was located in the farthest corner away from the entrance. My banners were set up; I had a few paperbacks propped up, and bookmarks, pins, and pens with my logo scattered across an electric-pink tablecloth I had dyed over and over again in the garage until it reached the perfect shade. I'd even brought a light-up sign that Zac, who was apparently extremely handy, had helped me build over the course of the last week after we had our training runs.

I'd sent him, Aiden, and Diana all a picture text of my booth when I'd set it up that morning. Only Zac and Di had responded, which wasn't entirely surprising I guess. But I wasn't going to let myself worry about it too much.

I knew I wasn't delusional thinking that my table looked pretty damn neat. Everything popped and the jewel tones of the books I'd brought and the giveaways all fit really well together. It was nice, but nice didn't do anything when everyone seemed to smile at it and then walked right on by to get in line to get their books signed.

Even the author next to me, who had told me she only had one novel out, had people stopping by to talk to her. I thought the fact she had a semi-attractive man, who was apparently the cover model for her novel, definitely helped bring people over.

Why hadn't I thought to ask Zac to come along?

Women loved him before he opened his mouth, but as soon as they found out he was a pro football player—well, at this point, a temporary ex-NFO player—it made them flock to him like locusts. He would have definitely pretended to be a cover model if I'd asked.

Damn it. A group of three walked by me and cast an interested glance my way before continuing onward.

I'd leave if I wouldn't feel like such a damn wuss doing so. I'd paid a lot of money on my flight, hotel room, and all the things I'd bought for my table, on top of the fees to set up. Hell, just thinking about how much I spent made my throat dry. But you had to invest money to make money. My foster dad, who had his own successful exterminating business, used to tell me that.

I was about to reach under my table to grab a bottle of water when a movement in the crowd on the near opposite wall caught my attention. One author whose table was perpendicular to mine had a line of people about thirty people long, filling the wide aisle. But there on the other side of the line, women of all ages and colors started to shift; all of them slowly turned and twisted their heads at something.

It was the head above and behind the crowd I noticed first. Walking forward, in a faded-black hoodie I'd washed and folded countless times, was a man. A man I could have recognized even if he'd dyed his hair blond and worn a cassock. I'd recognize Aiden anywhere.

It was the way he held his broad shoulders, those long legs that carried that confident stride, and the cocky way he held his head that said more than enough. The way his arms rested at his sides and that thick neck confirmed the Wall of Winnipeg was really here.

Aiden was here.

I didn't know why, and honestly, I wasn't even wondering why. I couldn't have cared.

Aiden had come.

I sucked in a breath and got to my feet, the biggest smile I'd ever made making my cheeks instantly ache.

Those brown irises raked across the room. Some part of me was fully aware that everyone within a twenty-foot parameter was focused in on him. Sure, there were a good number of male models around the convention hall, but none of them were Aiden, or anywhere even remotely close to him. I hadn't bothered giving any of the models more than a quick, curious glance, which said everything there was to know about my feelings for the big guy. Men with great bodies were awesome, sure. Friendly guys who knew how attractive they were and liked flaunting it and flirting with their fans were a magical thing.

But Aiden wasn't smiles and coyness. He didn't know or care that he was unforgettable. He had a confidence that went deeper than that of a man who liked what he saw in the mirror; Aiden valued the skills he'd developed through hard work. He believed in every inch of himself. He cared about what he could do and pushed himself to be better than he was the day before, not any of the external crap so many other people valued so much.

And all that manliness, that self-confident swagger, and the mentality that good was never enough had just settled its attention on me, standing there with a grin that more than likely made me look like a lunatic.

I'd swear on my life, my heart was on the verge of exploding with joy and surprise. I was probably trembling a little bit too in restrained energy and downright shock. Here was this man who valued his time, who hadn't taken anything close to a vacation, or allowed himself to be distracted from his ultimate goal in all the time I'd known him.

Yet he was here.

"Holy mother . . ." I barely heard the woman at the booth next to mine stutter loudly before I dropped to my hands and knees, crawled under the table, and popped back up on the other side to find those large, size thirteen feet heading in my direction.

He raised his eyebrows at me, the corners of his mouth pulling up when we finally stood feet apart. "Hi."

I was going to burst. I was going to freaking burst inside. "I'm about to hug you," I warned him in what sounded like a gasp, clenching my hands at my sides. "I'm about to hug the shit out of you, and I'm sorry I'm not sorry."

Those thick eyebrows seemed to climb up his forehead an inch higher, his cheek ticking in this strange way that made him seem a little embarrassed. "Why are you saying that like I should be scared?"

The "scared" was barely out of his mouth when I threw my arms around his neck. Screw a friendly body hug. I went for that thick neck I had a feeling I could dangle off without making him pull a single one of his thousand muscles. My face went straight to between his pecs, burying itself there, cradling my face like the hardest and best-looking boobs in the universe.

The joy made me shiver. "You came," I muttered into the soft material of his hoodie. About eighteen different emotions clogged my throat. "I don't know why you're here, and why it's freezing outside and you're only wearing this jacket instead of a coat like a normal human being, but I'm so happy to see you, you have no idea."

I had goose bumps, freaking goose bumps, as I squeezed my arms around him, burying my face a little deeper into the crevice between his pectorals.

"Stop talking," Aiden muttered as two big arms swallowed my back whole. And then, he was hugging me. His biceps cradled my ribs as he pulled me into him, up to the tips of my toes. Our fronts seared together.

Tears clouded my eyes, but I closed them and gave Aiden one more squeeze before slowly sinking back to my heels. Gazing up at that handsome, severe face, I had to bite the insides of my lips to keep from grinning like a total lovesick idiot, which was exactly what I was.

In that moment, I don't think I had ever loved anything half as much as I loved Aiden.

Sliding my hands from his neck over to his shoulders and finally down to those biceps I knew were perfectly sculpted from gawking at them so often, I patted him. Then I grabbed him and tried to shake him.

And then I started grinning all over again. So what if I looked like an airhead who was in love with a man she had married as part of a business relationship? I was, and I'd never been totally good at being anything other than me.

Of all the people I would ever want in my corner for moral support, here was the most unexpected one . . . and the biggest one. My friend. The keeper of my secrets. My moral support. My paperwork.

Plus, with reflexes like his, if anyone threw something at me, he could deflect it. Not that that would happen, since hardly anyone even noticed I was there.

Thinking about having him in my corner didn't help anything. It just made me want to cry, and now wasn't the time. Hell, the next decade wasn't the right time. I had to remember that, even as my heart gave a little beat at the acknowledgment Aiden had shown up.

I slid my hands down his biceps to his elbows and finally to his wrists. "Are you going to stay for a little while?" I asked, trying not to build up too much hope. Maybe he had some kind of . . . something he'd come for besides me.

Turning his wrists, he slid his hands down until we were palm to palm. "I just flew four hours to get here. Who else would I be here for?"

I loved this man.

That was what I thought. What I said though was a completely different thing. "Okay, smart-ass. Let me grab a chair for you then," I said, taking a step away before blinking at him. He really was standing there in the middle of a convention in his hoodie with a backpack on. He was here. *Here.*

With a squeak I hadn't made since I was probably twelve, I threw my arms around Aiden's arm and hugged him once more for a split second.

"Okay, I'll be right back," I said, loosening my hold and taking a step back to find him looking down at me with the strangest expression on his face.

"I'll get one," he muttered, tipping his head toward mine. A small smile creased the corners of that ultraserious mouth. He dropped his chin. "Has anybody thrown anything at you?"

I crossed my eyes. "Not yet."

Aiden blew out a breath and gave me that look that got on my nerves. "Told you." He reached forward and tapped my elbow with his fingertips. "I'll be right back."

I wasn't sure where he planned on getting a chair from, but if anyone got what he wanted, it was Aiden. He'd figure it out. With that thought, I crawled back under the table and took my seat again, suddenly feeling way more optimistic—and about 800 times happier—than I had minutes ago.

I'd barely plopped down and shuffled my seat forward when I realized that both of the authors on either side of me were staring. Literally staring. One of them even had her mouth open.

"Please tell me that's not your brother," the one whose mouth was actually closed stammered out, her gaze zoomed in on the direction Aiden had disappeared to.

"That's not my brother," I said a little more smugly than what was necessary, my thumb rubbing over the top of my ring.

"Is that a model?" The one who was gaping practically panted. "Because he's never hugged me like that before." She hooked her thumb at the man sitting next to her, who was frowning while also facing where Aiden had gone.

I bit my cheek and tried to hold back my smile even as my soul rejoiced with *Aiden! He's here!* "No."

Both women just looked at me blankly for so long I reached up to fiddle with the leg of my glasses, feeling a little awkward.

The male model finally leaned around the author he was sitting with. "That's Aiden Graves, isn't it?"

And, of course, someone was going to immediately recognize him. I'd seen an ad of him at the airport the night before.

"Who's that?" the author on my left asked.

"The Wall of Winnipeg. The best defensive player in the NFO," the guy answered, his gaze bouncing between the spot Aiden had gone and me, his expression more than a little curious. "Are you writing a book about him?" he asked, and I swear I almost rolled my eyes. The sign behind me with my name on it clearly said I did graphic design. Plus, we were at a romance convention. I didn't know I wrote biographies.

"No," the familiar, deep voice answered unexpectedly, right before he dropped a metal chair into place right next to me. "She's mine."

And he went for it.

My heart went for it too—over the cliff that is.

I thought—

Well it didn't matter what I thought. Or why he'd gone with that instead of going with any other answer except the slightly painful truth. Painful because my insides clung onto the M-word even though it shouldn't have. Somehow, with Aiden wielding it, it felt like a weapon of mass destruction intent on destroying my heart.

I should have known better. I knew how stupid it was to feel something for him other than friendship. I really did. This between us was business—he'd made that point abundantly clear before we'd signed paperwork. We both got something out of it. But friendship had blossomed between us—a genuine one that had tugged on my head and heart so much that it had turned into more. For me at least.

I loved Aiden, and hearing him claim me as his bypassed every instinct in my body that had pushed me to succeed on my own. It didn't make me feel like I was worth more, but it gave me a turbo boost regardless of how stupid it was for me to take his statement out of context. It was useless to hope. Useless to love him. Care about him, sure. I'd cared about him for years. Had a massive crush on him during that time too.

But this . . .

It made me want to hope, and that was the last fucking thing I needed.

Now, these people who I may or may not see again in my life would know for sure we were together. I knew how things like this worked. Each person would tell another person and most people in my industry—and in the profession that I wanted to work with, which included potential customers in this room—they would all know Aiden Graves and I had married, and in five years, they'd know what I lost. Everyone would know we'd gotten divorced, if they even remembered.

Which they probably wouldn't. Would they?

For the price of paying off my student loans, I was going to have to live with it. I'd have to, and that knowledge made my chest give this unnatural squeeze that made my entire body ache. How could I miss something I still had?

A big, sturdy elbow nudged me. "What's the matter?" Aiden asked in a slightly quieter voice, uselessly trying to keep the conversation between the two of us. I wasn't fooled. Everyone around us was probably trying to listen in.

I made myself blink my depressing, unnecessary thoughts away and turned my chair enough to face him, wiping my expression off. At least that's what I hoped. "I was just . . . I'm fine. I can't believe you're here."

"A happy surprise?" He watched me with those dark eyes before the side of his kneecap kissed the side of mine.

Did he sound hesitant or was I imagining it? I thought about playing it off, but then again, all signs pointed at the fact that the big guy actually knew me. He would recognize if I were lying. "Duh," I whispered. "It just got me thinking about how the next four-ish years are going to pass in no time, and how much I'll probably miss you afterward." I gave him a frown that was trying to be a smile. "It's dumb. I'm so happy to see you, and I'm already getting upset thinking about not having you around."

Why was I telling him these things? And why were my eyes tearing up all of a sudden? I blinked up at Aiden, uselessly wiping at them with the back of my hand, and let out that horrible laugh when you're crying but you want to think something is funny. "I'm so happy you're here and I'm crying," I cry-laughed bitterly, suddenly aware that all these people I didn't know who were busy checking out Aiden could probably see me getting upset.

When I raised my gaze to make sure Aiden thought I was being as crazy as I imagined I was being, I realized he wasn't smiling. Not at all. The unimpressionable look on his face didn't say that he thought I was being nuts, and he wasn't going to tell me I was getting worked up for no reason. Instead, his Adam's apple bobbed and he stared at me as if he was at a loss for words.

Which only made me feel awkward. Wiping at my eyes again, I sniffled and made myself smile at him, not earning even a fraction of one in return. I wasn't going to worry about it. "Sorry. I don't know why I got so worked up. My hormones must be all out of whack." I swallowed and licked my lips, still all too aware that he was burning my face with his gaze. "I'm so happy you're here. I really am. This was the best surprise ever."

His bearded cheek dimpled, and I knew he was biting down on the inside of it, his nostrils flaring in the process. A deep, deep, deep sigh slowly expelled from his lungs, and I swore, it was almost like his chest deflated. His entire body language changed in such small details I would have missed it if I didn't know him as well as I did. But the fact was, I knew Aiden. I knew almost everything about him, and I saw the signs.

I just didn't know what to do with them. The only thing I was aware of was that I wanted him to have an idea of how much it meant to me that he was here. With me.

In that moment, I knew this unrequited love I felt for Aiden was going to end up in heartbreak. The real problem was that my head didn't seem to care about the consequences. I leaned forward, putting my hand on the solid bulk of the middle of his thigh, and kissed his bristly cheek, maybe not imagining the background noise of the women around me reacting to me touching and getting so close to him. "I really can't believe you're here."

"You said that already," he murmured as his eyes dropped from mine to somewhere slightly below.

"Too bad. I'm in shock." I gave his leg a squeeze before straightening in my chair and grinning at him. "Yay," I whispered.

His eyelids hooded low over those clear, dark orbs. "You're going to give me diabetes."

That had me bursting out laughing, lifting the stress off me for a moment, earning me that tiny little curl on the corners of his mouth.

He reached up and touched a lock of the pale pink color Diana had dyed my hair weeks ago. "I'm going to get a green tea. Do you want that sugar with a side of coffee crap you like?" he asked, already getting to his big feet.

"Yeah, but I don't know if they'll let you in with a drink or not."

He gave me one of his looks. "They'll let me in." One hand going to my shoulder, he squeezed it and then picked up my table on one edge, moved it aside, and sidestepped through the gap he'd made. Then he put it back where it had been without moving any of my things over.

It definitely wasn't my imagination that 90 percent of the women he walked by in line—and behind their tables—watched him and his tight, round butt make their way to the exit.

I was so screwed.

A hand moved in my peripheral vision. "You married that?" the lady next to me asked, even though her face was glued on that fabulous butt.

This huge knot formed in my chest as I watched Aiden's broad back disappear into the crowd. I had to suppress what I was sure was going to be a sigh. "Yep."

"I TRIED TO get here earlier, but I couldn't get a flight," he explained a few hours later when we were lying on my bed in my hotel room with eight boxes of take-out scattered between us. Two dishes had some variety of tofu inside, three boxes were steamed rice, two were all sautéed veggies, and one had sweet and sour chicken. The three apples, four bananas, two fruit cups, and large green tea he'd had at the convention hadn't satisfied the big guy at all.

Dipping my chicken in extra sauce, I eyed him, still on a high from him surprising the hell out of me by showing up. It was unreal. The fact that I'd had person after person approach my table, after he came back with drinks and snacks, hadn't escaped me at all. To give him credit, Aiden had handled the attention as well as could be expected. He went as far as to say "thank you" and "nice to meet you" to the people who asked him for autographs once word got around he was there.

Sure, everyone who had dropped by came for him or used me as an excuse to approach the table, but by the end of the convention, all of my business cards had been taken and so had most of my bookmarks and pins. I'd been tagged in at least fifty pages online, more than one including some kind of picture of the big guy and me.

I wasn't dumb; I would take what I could get, even if it was for the wrong reasons, and I'd capitalize on it. So what if everyone in the future knew our relationship hadn't worked out and then wondered what had happened to cause us to split. So what if the first thing they assumed was that he cheated on me. That was what everyone usually guessed when couples broke up.

Telling myself I didn't care what anyone thought didn't make it any easier to swallow.

I would know we hadn't split up for that reason. It would have to be enough.

"When did you start looking?" I asked him, shoving the thoughts of cheating and divorce aside again and focusing on him being here.

He hummed, his mouth full. "Yesterday."

Aah, hell. I knew I might have laid it on too thick when he'd driven me to the airport. It might have been me telling him, "Stick my hard drive in the microwave if I don't come back," that did him in.

"There weren't any flights last night, and I had to wait to talk to Zac so he could watch Leo; otherwise, I would have gotten here sooner," he added.

"I really didn't mean to guilt-trip you into coming."

He shrugged. "You would never ask me to come, and I wouldn't have if I didn't want to."

While I knew that was the truth, I still felt just a tiny, little, baby bit bad. Just a little. "Yeah, I know, but still. I shouldn't have cried so much about it or made you think—"

"—you were going to have things thrown at you." He let out a low chuckle that was all playful and totally unexpected. Aiden reached over and set his palm on my knee, careful not to touch me with fingers that had sauce on them. "I went to bed worried."

He was worried about me?

"Everyone seemed nice," he ended.

Of course everyone had been nice to him. Okay, they'd been nice to me too, but it was different. Everyone had been checking him out, before and even some after they realized I caught them in the act.

I wasn't going to lie. This unfamiliar and territorial feeling took over every time I saw women take on expressions that made it seem as if they were two seconds away from jumping his bones while he'd sat there, completely oblivious to the world around him, with a book in those million-dollar hands. And I thought then, of course they checked him out. Here was this massive, incredibly attractive man in a romance novel convention . . . reading a damn book.

But that part of my brain hadn't been fond of the ogling, even though I logically couldn't blame them. I wasn't going to be surprised if pictures of him showed up on the internet tomorrow—if they hadn't already been posted—with ridiculous memes or captions beneath them.

And just thinking about it filled me with smugness that he was legally my husband, so all these jealous women could eat shit. . . . I knew what my chest was telling me, what it was feeling. Possessiveness. Horrible possessiveness.

I didn't like it. I didn't like it at all. This was Aiden. My friend. The man I was married to so he could become a resident. The guy who watched television with me. Sure, I was in love with him, but I knew there was nothing I could or would do about it. I knew what we were to each other for the most part.

Possessiveness had nowhere to live in our complication.

"They were all nice because you were there," I explained, giving him a side-glance to take in his reaction. "No one came by before you got there."

He blinked, not caring at all that I was telling him his looks were the reason why I had people drop by. "If they didn't walk by, it was because they're blind and dumb, I told you, Van. You had the best-looking promo stuff out of everyone. I took your bookmarks."

"You really took my bookmarks?"

He raised his eyebrows. "Two."

He was killing me. He was slowly killing me. "You sneaky ass." I smiled even wider and patted the hand he had on me. "I really can't believe you're here. In the Motherland."

"I'm from Winnipeg."

"I know what city you're from, dummy. I just thought you would never come to Canada again."

Aiden paused. "I don't hate it here."

"But you never want to visit and you don't want to live here. Isn't that why you . . . got me? Because you don't want to move back here?"

"I don't *want* to live here."

"Because of your parents?" I had the nerve to ask.

His head kind of tilted, that full mouth forming a thoughtful line. "They'll never be the reason I make a decision ever again, Van. I don't want to live here anymore. I don't have anyone here except Leslie." The fork in his hand jerked. "Everything I care about is in the States."

I gave him a wary look and nodded as if I understood, but I didn't. Not really.

The big guy just touched me again and I smiled that time.

"I owe you big time."

That had him groaning before he dug back into the tofu he had on his lap. "You don't owe me anything," he said into the container.

"I do. You have no clue how much this all meant to me."

Aiden rolled his eyes, even though he was glancing down.

"I'm serious. You have no idea. I can't thank you enough."

"I don't need your thanks."

"Yeah, you do. I want you to know how much it means to me. My own mom didn't even show up to my college graduation, and you caught a flight to come sit with me and be bored out of your mind for hours. You have no idea how much you've made my day—my month."

He shook his head and raised his gaze, his long eyelashes sweeping low as he leveled that ring of warm brown on mine. "You haven't left me when I needed you. Why wouldn't I do the same for you?"

TWENTY-SEVEN

"**M**y friends are coming to visit after I get back from the All Star Bowl."

Leaning against the counter two days after we got back from Toronto, I gulped down the rest of the water in my glass and narrowed my eyes in Aiden's direction. Sitting at the breakfast table, he'd greeted Zac and me when we'd dragged our feet inside following our run a few minutes ago.

I was exhausted, beyond exhausted, and with only three weeks left until the marathon, I was seriously beginning to doubt I'd be able to finish it. I'd been struggling to finish eighteen miles a week ago, so a little over twenty-six? Eighteen miles was more than I ever imagined I could do, so I realized I wasn't appreciating the long strides I'd taken over the last few months. Needless to say, I was busy worrying about how the hell I was going to tackle eight more miles when Aiden made his comment.

I blinked at him. "What?"

"My friends are coming to visit . . ." He trailed off as if making sure I was listening. "After the All Star Bowl."

I was listening, but I didn't get why he was giving me a strange, expectant look. He'd learned he was voted into the All Star Bowl when we'd flown back to Dallas from Toronto. He was set to leave tomorrow. "Okay . . ."

"They're coming to visit us."

Slowly backing up toward one of the stools at the island, I slid onto it, forcing my sluggish, distracted brain to focus. *Us.* He'd said us. They were coming to visit—

Oh shit. "*Us.*"

He nodded solemnly, watching me closely.

Okay. "And they want to stay here?" I asked, even though it was a stupid question that I already knew the answer to. Every time his friends had come by in the past, they had always stayed with him.

Why would this time be any different?

Oh right, because I lived with him and stayed in the room that had always been used as a guest room.

And because we were legally married and had agreed to pull this charade off so neither one of us would get in trouble with the law.

Oh hell.

Realistically, it wasn't the end of the world, and we could figure something out. We could. We would. It wasn't a big deal. This was bound to happen at one point or another. "Okay. Do you . . . I can stay with my friend while they're here if you want. You can pretend I went to visit someone." Or maybe I could find a last-minute getaway somewhere warm. It wouldn't be the first time I'd gotten Diana to pretend to be sick so we could go somewhere.

Apparently, my comment irritated him. "This is your house too. I'm not asking you to leave because they're coming. We knew this was going to happen. They want to see you too. It isn't a big deal."

Why did that seem to be his life's motto when it was something that mostly only affected me? And why wasn't I telling him that I'd met his friends in the past before and that it really wasn't necessary for us to see each other now? It didn't *really* matter if I was home or not, did it?

"I already told them you were going to be here," he concluded.

There went my argument.

He scratched his jaw, and my gaze stuck to the white-gold wedding band he'd started wearing right after Toronto. I wanted to ask him about it, but I was too much of a coward. "You'll have to stay in my room," he explained.

With him obviously. Where the hell else would I sleep? One of the guys usually took the bed and the other crashed out on the couch downstairs.

The problem wasn't that I would just *stay in his room*.

The problem was that I would have to stay in his room with him, on his bed, was what he wasn't telling him, but knew he was implying. It wasn't like you could exactly hide a blow-up mattress, and I knew this diva sure as hell wasn't going to sleep on the floor, because neither was I.

It's not a big deal, I told myself. *It'll just be like a sleepover.* I'd done sleepovers a thousand times. Aiden and I were adults, sharing a bed didn't mean anything. We'd already done it the night the lights went out. We'd done it again in Toronto when he surprised me. We would just be, literally, sleeping on opposite sides of a California king–sized bed. Doing it again shouldn't cause me to lose any sleep over it.

Except for the small fact that I'd been carrying this love I felt for him around my neck since the book convention, and it had only gained weight each day we were together.

"Okay," I found myself agreeing as my heart warned me I was asking for it. "That's fine."

He nodded. "Yeah, I know, Van. They're coming the day after I get back. It'll work out," he assured me.

I HEARD THE two loud, male voices before I saw them. Chris and Drew, the only friends Aiden had, other than Zac, who had mostly become an acquaintance, and me, his sort-of-fake wife. Saving my work, I closed my laptop and grabbed my tablet with my free hand. I'd already taken everything else I would need for the next few days and moved it into the big guy's room.

While Aiden wasn't a shopaholic—his "fancy" wardrobe consisted of three suits, four dress shirts, two dress pants, and a black and brown belt—the rest of his closet was filled with boxes of trophies, shoes, and other free clothing that hadn't been opened, and it was packed. His dresser had the rest of the stuff he typically wore: sweatpants, workout shorts, enough T-shirts to clothe an entire basketball team, and tons of underwear and socks.

The point was, there wasn't space for my clothes, so it didn't seem like a stretch for us to say I kept my clothes in the other room if the guys opened my drawers and saw my things inside, which I doubted.

What did worry me was this façade we were going to try and pull off. Why had we agreed not to tell anyone else the truth? Couldn't we have made some exceptions?

No. I knew we couldn't. If you told one person something, they told another, and then that person told another, and finally, everyone found out. That's why we'd both jumped into agreeing to keep it a secret as much as possible.

We could do this. We could play it off, I promised myself as I put my laptop and tablet on the desk in the office. I'd left my desktop computer in my room.

I crept down the stairs listening to . . . four male voices? I'd barely cleared the landing when I spotted Aiden standing in the living room, circled by three men nearly all in the general vicinity of his size, give or take twenty or thirty pounds. I recognized Chris's close-cropped hair and Drew's long, black dreadlocked hair, but it was the back of a blond head I wasn't familiar with that caught my eye.

"Vanessa," Aiden called my name. "Come here."

I swerved my attention over to find him standing there with his hand extended in my direction. I hesitated maybe half a second, not long enough for his friends to turn around and notice, but long enough for Aiden to raise his hand an inch from where it was up-turned. His face was so . . . expectant, so fucking expectant, like he didn't doubt I could play this off, that I realized how badly I needed to, how much my terrible-lying ass was willing to do to make sure he was happy.

I walked forward and took his hand, steeling myself for this massive lie sitting on my soul.

"You know Drew and Chris," Aiden said as he gestured toward the men in front of him. Drew was carrying Leo in his arm, letting the little guy go to town nibbling at one of his dreads.

Squeezing Aiden's hand, I smiled at the two friends I'd met before and reached forward to shake their hands as the blond-headed man took a step forward out of the corner of my eye. "Vanessa?"

It took me a second to recognize the handsome blond-haired, green-eyed man standing in the living room. His hair was a lot shorter than it had been the last time I'd seen him more than six years ago. The fact he'd filled out even more and gotten older only made him look so much more different than the nineteen-year-old I used to know.

"Cain?" I took a step forward, grinning wide.

"No fucking way." He blinked for a minute, shook his head, and grinned so wide I wasn't paying attention when he cut the distance between us and hugged the hell out of me, pretty much crushing me against his chest for a moment before pulling back and shaking his head some more. "I can't believe it." He hugged me again. "What a small world."

"I know." I smiled, so shocked to see him I really couldn't think of anything else to say.

"I'm gonna guess you know each other," Drew said.

I glanced at him and nodded, looking back at Cain in surprise. "We went to school together." Then the pieces all clicked together.

But Cain explained it anyway. "Before I transferred to Wisconsin, I was at Vandy." Those green eyes flicked back in my direction as he smiled. "We had what? Three classes together?"

I nodded. "Yeah, and you tried copying off my quizzes for the first two weeks until you talked me into helping you study." What he hadn't known was that I didn't give away my hard work for free, but he'd learned that quickly after I shot him down time after time.

"I can't believe you're Aiden's Vanessa." Cain glanced at the big guy, who was standing just slightly behind me and to the right.

I wished.

"That's me," I said, taking a step back, the side of my hip and butt bumping into Aiden. Almost instinctively, a wrist and then an elbow climbed over my shoulder and the heavy weight of his arm draped over me. I had to tip my head back to find his gaze. Why did he look so serious?

"Where's Zac?" Drew asked.

The big guy seemed to shift next to me, his side pressing into mine. "He's at the gym, isn't he?"

He was, and I was so happy he was taking it seriously enough to keep training even though the season was over and most players were taking a small break—hence, the four of them standing in the living room. Well, at least I knew Chris and Drew played professionally; I wasn't sure what Cain did now. "Yeah. He's usually back by four." We always went for a run afterward, but I wasn't sure if we were going to go, since Aiden's friends were in town. Then again, they were Aiden's friends; Zac just happened to get along with them. He got along with everyone.

"Well, I'm hungry, who wants to go out to eat?" Drew asked.

"Me," the other two that didn't live with me replied.

The arm around me tightened. On the rare occasion he went out to eat, there were only a couple places he liked. "I'll choose the place."

I snorted. "I need to finish two covers by tonight, so I'm going to get back to work. You want me to keep Leo?"

Aiden shook his head. "It isn't that cold. We'll take him. I want him to get used to riding around in a car more."

"Well, you guys have fun. I'll see you later."

With a wave to all of them and an extra smile thrown in Cain's direction, I ran back upstairs. The two covers I was working on were going to be hand-drawn designs, so I set up my brand-new tablet and quickly got to work. I'd already jotted down ideas I had, so I quickly set forth drawing the bones for one of them so I could send it off before going any further.

One hour bled into two, and at some point, I heard the door open and a handful of male voices float up the stairs. The low hum of the television reached the office, but I kept on working.

It wasn't until the garage door opened once more and the voices got louder that I sat up and listened. Sure enough, a few minutes later, someone pounded up the stairs and "Van!" reached me.

"In the office," I yelled back, already saving my work.

Zac peeked his head into the doorway and grinned. "We goin'?"

"Sure. Let me get dressed."

He nodded, disappearing in the direction of his room. Sneaking into my bedroom, I grabbed my running clothes—leggings, a long-sleeved thermal shirt, sports bra, socks, and shoes—and darted into Aiden's room to change. I had just finished pulling up my leggings when the door to the bedroom opened and Aiden came in, shutting it behind him.

I smiled as I sat on the edge of the bed, my heel on the mattress. "How was lunch?"

He lifted a shoulder and eyed me, leaning against the door. "Good."

"What restaurant did you go to? The Chinese place, that café you like, or Thai?" I asked playfully, slipping my sock on.

"We went to eat Chinese."

"Where's Leo?" I asked.

"Downstairs," was his curt reply before going with, "Did you and Cain date?"

My sock fell out of my hand. "*What?*"

Aiden straightened his upper back as he pushed off the door he'd been leaning against. His face was so remote, I had no idea what the hell that was supposed to mean. "Were you and Cain together?" he repeated himself.

I kept my gaze on him as I reached down and picked up the sock. "Aah, no."

His cheek twitched.

"No." I blinked. "The only reason he started talking to me back then was because he wanted to copy off my work."

Why was he making that face?

"I'm serious. That was the only reason we became friends."

He was still making that damn face.

"What? Okay, maybe I thought he was cute, but that's all." I shrugged. "Guys like that don't like girls like me, big guy." Honestly, while it was the truth, I had no idea why the hell I'd said it.

His nostrils flared and his shoulders drew back. "Guys like what?"

Damn it. There went me feeling awkward as hell. "You know . . ." I made myself look down as I chewed on the inside of my cheek. "Like that."

"Like me?" he asked in a low voice.

"Not you-you, necessarily. I just mean . . . look, it doesn't matter. I know what I have to work with." I was all right-looking. Every so often, I got hit on. But I wasn't a major bitch, I worked hard, my crazy was usually under control, and I thought that mattered more than a face that would eventually get wrinkled. "When you can pretty much date whoever you want, and most of you guys can, I'm not going to be at the top of anybody's list—"

"Shut up, Vanessa," he snapped.

I scoffed. "You shut up."

"Van!" Zac exclaimed, banging on the bedroom door. "Chop, chop!"

Getting to my feet, I quickly slipped my shoes on and shot Aiden a frown. "Look, we never did anything more than eat dinner a few times and study for tests together. I never had any dreams of being his girl-friend or any crap like that, and he never gave me the impression he was interested. I'm not going to do or say anything to jeopardize this between us, okay? You're the guy I signed paperwork with."

He didn't move away from the door, even as I approached it. What did happen was that he seemed to be grinding his teeth together.

I touched the middle of his chest; the big, perfectly developed slabs of his six-pack hardened under my fingers. "I promise, big guy. I would never break my promise to you. You know that." When he didn't say anything, I used my chin to gesture toward the door. "I need to go. When I get back, I'll make a few casseroles or something so you don't have to go out to eat again. Okay?"

Grudgingly, Aiden nodded and moved aside to let me open the door. Zac stood at the bottom of the stairs. "Come on, darlin'. We're on a tight schedule."

FIVE HOURS LATER, my legs were all noodle-like and I felt sick. It went past exhaustion and dehydration—we'd started carrying water reservoirs on packs around our back. I felt like I had the flu. We had taken it easy after our long run two days ago, and our day off had been yesterday. But a puny seven miles with a negative split had damn near killed me. My knees. My ankles. My shoulders. Every single thing ached. Pounding back water hadn't made me feel any better, drinking coconut water hadn't helped, sitting down to rest didn't make a difference, and neither did taking a shower and putting on pajamas.

I'd had to pull up a chair in front of the stove to cook dinner for goodness sakes.

Even Zac wasn't faring too much better. He'd gone straight upstairs to shower after we got back and had taken his food to his room to eat. It was only through sheer will that I sat in the living room with the guys and ate dinner while watching a basketball game, since we didn't have a dining room table.

What the hell had I been thinking trying to do a marathon? Why hadn't I gone with a half one to start off with and work up from there?

"You need some help?" a slightly familiar voice asked from somewhere behind me.

Glancing over my shoulder as I rinsed the dishes so I could set them in the dishwasher, I spotted Cain standing in the kitchen with a few glasses in hand. The guys had all headed outside a little while ago, wanting to break in the fire pit. Chris had offered to do the dishes, but Aiden never got to see his friends, so I told him I could do it.

Even if I ended up passed out in the middle of it.

"If you want," I replied.

"Scoot over."

I did, and let him take the spot closest to the dishwasher. I rinsed off a dish and passed it over to him, smiling tiredly. "Thanks for helping."

"No problem." His forearm brushed mine as I handed him another plate. "When's the marathon you're doing?" he asked, pointing out that he'd been paying attention when Chris had asked me about it during the commercials over dinner.

"In about two weeks." Just saying the number out loud made me want to throw up. I barely survived running twenty miles days ago. How was I going to add six point two more?

"That's cool."

I was too tired to try and make a joke about how not cool it was while I was on the verge of dying. "What have you been up to since school?"

We hadn't seen each other since the end of the spring semester of our freshman year. Cain had transferred schools the next fall, and even though I didn't remember whether he'd ever called or text messaged me afterward, he might have. I'd been in the middle of recuperating from my accident, and those next six months had gone by hazily, a mix of pain medicine and anger. I hadn't been anyone's friend then other than Diana's, and that was mostly because she wouldn't let it be any other way, and truthfully, I hadn't given Cain much thought after that.

"I'm in Philadelphia now. I was in San Diego before that for a few years, but everything is great," he said as he bent over to set the dish in the lower rack of the dishwasher. "How long have you and Graves been together?"

Considering I wasn't sure how much Chris and Drew had told Cain, much less what Aiden told them, I was going to wing it. "Well, I worked for him for two years. We've been living together for five months now." That way I didn't have to get too specific.

"For real?"

"For real."

"Huh," he kind of muttered under his breath. "That's . . . surprising."

A faint reminder of what I had told Aiden in the bedroom earlier flicked through my brain, and I had to keep from snickering.

His elbow touched mine again as he took another plate from me, his green-eyed gaze reaching mine for a moment. "You look fucking great by the way."

Everyone telling me I looked great recently only made me really self-conscious about what they used to think of me before. Did I look like shit? "Oh, thanks." My weight had always yo-yoed depending on how much exercise I was doing. I gained it really easily and lost it really easily, but I couldn't remember freshman year where I was, but it might have been at one of my heaviest periods.

Yeah, the silence after that was just plain weird. Luckily, it didn't take long to finish rinsing everything off and setting the dishwasher to clean. Cain headed out while I wiped the counters off. I was so tired, but it was only nine o'clock at night. I grabbed a glass of water and chugged half of it down before trudging outside to see the guys for a little bit longer.

Pushing open the French doors leading to the patio with the last little bit of strength I had left, the heat from the stone fire pit hit me in the face immediately. In the second it took for my eyes to adjust, I found all four of the guys sitting around it in various stages of wide-open legs and slouches, hanging out.

"You finally made it," Drew, the nicer of his friends, exclaimed. On his lap was the blond ball of fur, completely passed out. Apparently, Leo had won someone else over in no time at all.

"Yeah," I said pretty weakly, dead on my feet and realizing there were only four seats and they were all taken up.

"Here, take my seat," Drew said quickly.

"Oh, that's okay."

"Sit with me," Aiden suggested, or maybe demanded, without hesitation.

I stared at him, squeezing the cool glass lightly between my hands, debating whether to excuse myself or take a seat because there wasn't another option. What was I going to do? Offer to take the floor when there was a perfectly good leg I could sit on? A leg that belonged to the man his friends believed I'd married out of love. Okay, come on.

For a moment, I thought about dragging out one of the dining room chairs, but it would just seem weird. And I really didn't want to walk any more than I needed to.

I mean, it wasn't like this was the first time I'd sat on someone's leg. Friends did that kind of stuff. Married people snuggled, at least that's what I reasoned with myself. Not because I wanted to sit on his lap or anything. Nope.

I dodged around the only set of long legs in my way and stopped right by Aiden's knees, watching as he spread them. I let myself glance at his face, shadowed by the fire, and took a deep breath. It was his idea, wasn't it? Turning my body so my back was to him, I slowly lowered myself onto the middle of his thigh, forever conscious that I wasn't exactly ninety-eight pounds. My butt hit the middle of that intensely muscular leg, and just as I started to get comfortable so my back was straight, he lifted his foot. With one big palm to the side of my waist, he pulled me in so that I slid all the way up to where his hip met his leg, off to one side of the cradle of his groin. My entire side pressed into his chest.

My face didn't go hot or anything, but my pulse went nuts in reaction as I took in our positions. I appreciated the arm that happened to sling low across my back, his palm resting on my hip, cupping it over the flannel material of my pajamas. His other hand was busy, the thumb wrapped around the inside of my knee while the four other fingers framed the outer side of it.

My entire body lit up, aware of the sweet smell of Aiden. How big the muscles under my bottom were. How warm and well developed the muscles searing into my arm and chest were. And how close his face was to mine.

He was looking at me, that subtle side inspection that I could feel into the deepest part of my belly. The corner of his mouth was tilted just slightly up in what was half a smirk and half a smile, all Aiden.

I smiled at him nervously and maybe a little shyly as I slowly pulled my arm up from its space between our bodies and slipped it around those wide shoulders I noticed at least five times a day every day.

"Good?" he whispered, the arm warming my lower back flexing.

"Yes. Am I crushing you?" I whispered.

"You and your questions." He seemed to peer at me closely. "You're not feeling good?"

Was it that noticeable? "No," I said loud enough for only him to hear. "I feel sick and everything hurts."

"How many miles did you run?"

"Only seven."

He murmured something under his breath, his body stirring under mine. "You should elevate your legs. Is your knee bothering you?"

"Everything is bothering me," I whined, and I didn't even feel bad about it.

A low, soft snicker puffed against my ear and that big hand shifted over my knee. Before I could react, Aiden moved me so I was sitting across him. One of his hands was on one thigh and the other landed on my shin.

He cupped my calf with that big hand and began to knead.

Seriously, a tingle shot up the back of my thigh and lower back. There was no way to stop the sound of pleasure and pain that came out of me. "Oh my God," I muttered under my breath, sounding more like a pant.

A small chuckle nudged at the side of my cheek as he massaged my calf, then worked his way up to my quadriceps. Of course his hands were strong; I seriously felt my leg go numb with how good and bad it felt at the same time.

"I should tell you that you don't have to do that." I had to suppress another gurgle when he hit a tender spot high on my calf. "I'm not. That feels amazing. Thank you."

An almost indecipherable grunt came out of Aiden's throat, but I was way too gone to pay attention. The arm around my back tightened, clutching me closer. His fingers worked slow and steady, from the muscles right above my ankle to even higher, so high if I was any less tired than I was, I would have realized it was too close to the seam of my underwear.

The soft lull of conversation from Aiden's friends went in one ear and out the other, and I only caught brief words here and there. Aiden didn't talk much as we sat there around the chiminea, and he rubbed one of my legs and then the other as best as he could, which was the same way he did everything. The best. I couldn't help but focus more on his steady breaths and the pressure of his hands than what the guys were actually talking about.

That was the strange part. I usually couldn't sit somewhere doing nothing without getting bored, but I found myself doing just that, minus the bored part. With a big, warm body surrounding me, and a small fire going strong feet away, I just let myself relax.

And I kept relaxing as I listened to his friends argue about some football player, I thought. The occasional rumble of Aiden piping in with his low voice so close to my ear kept me company. I didn't even notice when my head landed on his chest, or when my forehead hit the side of his throat.

His palm slid to the meatiest side of my thigh, four fingers on my hamstrings, one finger on the top. His other forearm draped over both of my knees. I definitely didn't notice when I put my hand on his stomach, much less when I snuck it under the Henley he had on and palmed the square-shaped muscles covered by soft, hair-freckled skin under my fingers.

I was barely aware of Aiden shifting his grip, after who knew how long, to practically cradle me. I was dozing, more asleep than awake. More comfortable than I should have been in a man's arms. A man who I was in love with, but didn't love me back, and more than likely never would. His heart already belonged somewhere else.

I was only half aware when, at some point later, Aiden got to his feet with me in his arms and said in a voice quiet enough so that it wouldn't wake me, "I'm putting her to bed."

And Drew asked, "You coming back?"

With Aiden answering, "No. I'm tired. You want to give me the little guy?"

"Nah. I'll keep him tonight. I promise I won't crush him."

I was yawning, fighting the sleep that had pulled me and my bones under, wanting but not really wanting to open my eyes and walk to his bedroom on my own two feet. When he swung me up higher as he headed into the house, I yawned again, nosing the side of his neck with my fingers along his collarbone, absently feeling how smooth the skin there was.

"I got you," he whispered in that quiet, grumbling voice.

Who was I to tell him no?

I fell back asleep. Unaware of him laying me on the bed and taking my slippers and socks off.

And I definitely missed the rough way he pressed his mouth against my temple before he turned off the light, plugged in a nightlight I had no idea he'd bought, and got undressed himself.

TWENTY-EIGHT

"Why are you staring at me?"

Could I have tried to play off the fact that I'd been lying in bed with my head propped up on my palm, staring at him? Absolutely not. What the hell else could I have been looking at? I'd been doing it for so long that, knowing Aiden, he'd waited to make sure I was doing what he thought I was doing.

Which I had been.

I'd woken up maybe ten minutes before and lay there, appreciating how cozy it was under the heavy covers and on the perfectly comfortable mattress. But when I finally forced myself to open my eyes, the first thing I saw was the big guy. Aiden was on his side, his hand pillowing his head. That normally harsh face was . . . well, it was still pretty rough. It wasn't soft and dreamy; he honestly looked like he was thinking about bad plays in his sleep. His mouth was slightly open with the softest, even breathing coming out of it. With the covers pulled up to his chin, he looked too damn cute.

I hated it.

Why? Why him?

Of all the people in the world I could have chosen to think the world of, it had to be this one. The one who didn't want a real relationship because he didn't want to put time into it. The guy who only loved one thing in his life and everything else came trailing after it.

Then again . . .

He'd been making a serious effort to spend time with me. He'd done things for me that I still couldn't completely wrap my head around. He'd been more than just friendly with me.

What did it mean though? Weren't those part of the requirements in a real relationship? Wasn't it enough to be with each other when you could, or was I just trying to convince myself there was something there? He'd kissed me. That couldn't mean nothing, could it?

That was exactly what I was in the middle of thinking about—and eyeing those great lips—when he caught me. So all I could do was give him a closed mouth smile. "Why not?"

Cracking both eyes open, Aiden rolled to his back and stretched his arms high behind his head, rolling his wrists in the process as he yawned.

"Thanks for putting me in bed last night," I said, watching the swift line of his throat as he yawned again.

He grumbled, "Uh–huh," as he rolled his shoulders before slipping his arms beneath the covers again.

"And for giving me a massage." I had already tried moving my legs, and sure they were sore, but I knew how much worse they could be. I'd done everything I was supposed to do to help prevent the stiffness, but there was only so much a body that wasn't 100 percent to begin with could handle.

"There wasn't much to massage."

Uh. "What's that supposed to mean?"

"I have more muscles in my glutes than you have in your thighs."

Anyone who had seen Aiden's ass would know that was a fact, so I wasn't going to take it personally. Maybe because I was still so sleepy, I raised my eyebrows at him and said, "Have you seen your butt? That's not an insult. It has more muscles in it than most people have all over their bodies."

His own thick eyebrows rose about a millimeter, just slightly, but enough for me to notice. "I didn't know you paid that much attention to it."

"Why do you think you have so many female fans?"

Aiden let out another low groan, but he didn't tell me to stop.

"You could raise a small fortune if you ever auctioned off the chance for a person to take a—"

"Vanessa!" Mr. Proper reached over to throw a hand over my mouth, like he was shocked.

That big hand literally covered me from ear to ear, and I burst out laughing, though it was muffled.

"You make me feel cheap," he said as he slowly pulled his hand away, but the shine in his eyes said he didn't really mind it that much.

I stretched my own limbs with a yawn. "I'm just telling you what anyone else would."

"No, no one else would ever say that to me."

So he had a point. "Well, I'll tell you the truth then."

He made this noise that had me rolling to face him again. "You always have."

Why did it feel like he was trying to tell me something? "I'll always try to be honest with you," I lied, hesitantly. Unless it was something I was scared to tell him, like my feelings for him, or me quitting.

"You can tell me anything."

How was I supposed to live my life after that? Especially when I was lying on his bed and he was sitting up next to me, sharing the same covers. I wished I had the guts to tell him anything, but the truth was, I didn't.

There was only so far I was willing to jump on my own.

I SENSED THE weight of a stare before I glanced up. Directly in front of me and his desk was the big guy. Literally right in front of me. I'd been completely hunched over, so focused on what I was doing that I had zoned out.

"Jesus Christ. *How do you not make any noise?*" He was stealthy like an overweight mutant cat, damn it.

"Skills." I swear to God I almost choked. He took a step forward, his hands planting themselves on the edge of the desk as he leaned over to look at what I was working on. "What is that?"

I lowered my pencil to the desk and slid the piece toward him. "It's a diptych tattoo design." I pointed at the images on the two separate panes I was still in the middle of outlining. "It's supposed to be one for each leg, you see? One part is Medusa's face and the other is her hair—the snakes."

When he didn't say anything, I held back a frown. "You don't like it?" I thought it was coming along well.

"Van, that's . . ." He lowered his face closer to the design. "It's amazing. Someone's paying you to do that for them?"

"Yep." I looked back at the Medusa and had to agree with him. It was pretty damn awesome. "I know a guy in Austin who does tattoo work. Sometimes someone will ask for a certain style he's not good at, and if no one else he works with can do it, he'll reach out to me. My line drawing is pretty good." I glanced back up at him and grinned. "My watercolors aren't too shabby either. I'm a woman of many talents."

Unless someone wanted a portrait, then I'd pretend to be asleep so I wouldn't have to admit how bad at them I was.

"I've never really thought about tattoos much, but I might have to think about having you make me one," he answered in a distracted voice.

"I could whip you up a nice clown. All you'd have to do it ask," I joked, sliding the design toward me.

Yeah, that big, beautiful grin crawled up with full force over his mouth, cracking my soul open in half. "The five of us are going out for dinner. Take a break and come."

I didn't need to eye the sketch to know that I'd worked on it almost as long as I could. When I drew, I'd learned the hard way that I needed to pay attention to my limit; otherwise, things started to go downhill. And I'd probably gotten there about fifteen minutes ago when my fingers began cramping.

"All right." I reached across the desk to grab the case where I usually put my box of pencils. "Give me ten minutes to get dressed."

Aiden nodded.

Fully aware that Aiden wasn't dressed up and he wouldn't go anywhere that would require him to put on anything dressier than jeans, I settled for a pair of skintight jeans that I'd resorted to sticking in the dryer on high heat so they would still fit me, a V-neck red elbow-length shirt, and black heels I hadn't worn since the last time I'd gone out, months and months ago.

Not surprisingly, all of the guys were downstairs waiting. I knew they were planning on leaving the next day. I had to take one stair at a time, and I winced every single step, muscles I didn't even know I had responded to the achiness from my run yesterday. I'd briefly thought I was coming down with something but shoved the possibility aside.

It was Zac who spotted me first, a big, dumb smile coming over his face.

"Don't say anything," I muttered to him before he could make a crack.

That only made him laugh.

I should have thought about putting on tennis shoes instead.

"I'd give you a piggyback ride, but I can barely walk myself," he apologized as I groaned at the bottom of the staircase.

Jokingly, I smiled at Aiden, who was standing next to Zac, and batted my eyelashes.

The Wall of Winnipeg did what the Wall of Winnipeg would do and simply shook his head. "You can't baby it. You'll only feel worse tomorrow."

This son of a bitch. I snickered, and then I snorted, watching as his features took on an uncertain expression before I lost it, slapping a hand on Zac's shoulder so I'd have something to lean on.

Did I know he was telling the truth? Of course I did. I'd stretched earlier and cried. No shame in my game.

But . . . Wasn't he supposed to be my cream-colored knight? My knight in shining armor who would carry me around to prevent me from being in pain?

Of course not. Aiden was going to tell me to do whatever the best thing for me was, even if it hurt like hell.

And I seriously couldn't love him any more. Not a single bit more. And I couldn't tell him.

"Why are you laughing?" he asked.

I had to take my glasses off to palm one eyeball at a time, wiping my tears away, not caring that the little makeup I'd put on earlier in the day was more than likely coming off.

"Man, you're supposed to take care of your woman." That was Drew who said it. "Help her out."

That only made me laugh even more.

"Oh, Aiden." I looked up at the man in question and grinned. "I'm fine. I can walk. I promise. You're right."

"I know I am." He held out his hand. "Come on."

I WOKE UP with my hand in Aiden's pants.

In his boxer briefs to be specific.

The back of my hand was pressed against a warm butt cheek. I had one knee against his hamstring. His back was about three inches from my mouth. My other hand was numb under my face.

But it was the hand I had in his underwear that alarmed me the most.

The sheets and comforter thrown over us didn't let me see much, but what did you really need to see when you knew exactly what you were touching? Nothing.

Slowly, I tried pulling my hand out. I got most of my thumb out and was in the process of getting the rest of my fingers to safety too when Aiden tipped his head over his shoulder and gave me a sleepy look.

"Are you done groping me?" he asked, his voice sand-scratched.

With a sound I didn't necessarily want to consider a hiss, I pulled my hand out of its warm cocoon of male flesh and underwear and held it to my chest.

"I wasn't groping you," I whispered. "I was just . . . making sure none of the guys sneaked in and tried to get you."

His sleepy gaze widened. "That's why you grabbed it all night?"

"No I didn't!"

"Yes, you did," the man who never lied claimed.

And that had me shutting my mouth. "Really?"

He nodded, rolling onto his back and stretching those brawny arms over his head, a siren's song for my eyes.

"In that case, I'm sorry." I eyed the tuft of black hair in his under-arm, which for some reason I found so attractive. "Not."

Aiden drew his arms back down, that handsome bearded face clearly amused.

That old, familiar painful knot filled my throat as I took in those features I enjoyed looking at so much—that scar along his hairline that defined him and that gold chain peeking out from beneath his T-shirt and what it meant.

I really did love him, and he was leaving for two months. I wasn't sure if it was everything that had happened to me with my family in the past, or if I was secretly just a possessive person with the right—or in this case wrong—person, but I didn't want him to leave. And there was no way I could ask him to stay.

Reaching forward, I touched the bump under his shirt where his medallion was and I said as much as I was willing to say. "I'm going to miss you," I admitted.

That big hand reached up to brush my hair away from my face, gentle, gentle, gentle, those long fingers catching on a few soft pink tangles. Slowly, he moved across the bed, leaning toward me, pressing his forehead against mine, and all I could do was close my eyes, taking in the warmth of his body and the tenderness of his gesture.

I couldn't breathe. I couldn't move. I couldn't do a single thing but lie there taking the moment in.

"I'm going to miss you a lot," I told him, just so he'd know it wasn't going to be some casual thing, like missing him when I'd first stopped working for him.

That hand in my hair dug deeper, reaching my scalp, holding more hair in those strong fingers. He exhaled, his breath washing over my chin.

He didn't say he was going to miss me back. Instead, his lips went to my chin, then to that nook between there and my lips. His breath was hot, his mouth moist as he trailed it an inch higher. It was me who cut the distance between us. Me who nipped at his lip.

But it was him who went for it. Aiden turned his mouth to the side and sealed our lips together, going from chaste to hungry in one second flat. He went one direction and I went the other, our tongues clashing instinctively. Dueling, dipping. Aiden ate at my mouth and

I let him. We kissed and we kissed. My tongue brushed his over and over again, and it wasn't enough.

My hands had gone to his head, keeping him there as he rose above me, never losing the lock he had on my lips. He was so swift I didn't even realize he had spread my legs wide and settled his hips and body between them. Aiden kissed me like he never wanted to stop. His hand gripped my hair a little tighter, as if I was planning on going somewhere when my death grip was just as vicious and demanding as his.

And then he settled his groin against mine. The rigid, hard, so-long erection nestled right between my legs as he went down to his forearms. Aiden rocked his hips, rubbing the seam of my body through the thin material of both of our bottoms, and I lifted my butt to get more of him.

This was a terrible idea, and I wasn't going to stop it. I wasn't ever going to tell him to stop. It didn't make a lick of sense, and I didn't even remotely care.

Tearing my mouth away from his, I sucked in a breath when he gave a rough roll of his lower body, a pump, a jerk that said he wanted in. And I wanted him in.

"Van," Aiden growled.

It was right then that the house alarm started beeping like crazy. Going off and off and off, like when the code hadn't been pressed in time. Then Leo, who was in his crate and hadn't made a single peep all night, began barking.

With a curse that sounded like "fuck," Aiden stopped what he was doing. He was panting. His forehead went to mine, and I could hear him swallow hard. "*Damn it*," he hissed, shifting back to sit on his haunches, those brown eyes nailed to me lying there in front of him with my feet planted flat on his bed, my knees at his sides while I tried to catch my breath. "It's probably the guys, but I should make sure." He swallowed again and blinked, even as his hand, which had been on the bed, reached over to squeeze the giant hard-on tenting his sleeping pants.

I couldn't look away. I absolutely could not look away from the bell-shaped tip that was pulling the elastic of his sleep bottoms away from his waist. Every instinct in me screamed that I should reach forward and give his thick shaft a squeeze. I wanted to beg him to come back.

But the stupid alarm wasn't stopping.

"The guys?" I reached over blindly and snagged my glasses and cell phone off the nightstand almost immediately. I slipped my glasses on to peek at my phone, finding the time and a notice that I had three missed calls from Diana. That was weird. "It's nine in the morning," I said absently. It had been years since she'd drunk dialed me.

"They didn't come home last night," he said, throwing one leg over mine, his big hand squeezing my calf before he jumped off the bed with a grace I didn't miss, even as I tried to wrap my head around what had just happened. At the door, Aiden stood there for a minute before slipping a hand inside his pants and adjusting himself. "I'll be right back."

I nodded.

His mouth opened for a moment, but he closed it. "I'm sorry, Van." That stupid beeping got even louder and he shook his head. "Let me check."

Then he was gone.

We had just been making out, on the verge of doing something we couldn't come back from, and he was out of the room.

Seriously? Of all the times they could have come in, they had to do it right then? They couldn't have waited a few more minutes?

I didn't doubt it was them, but what the hell were they out doing until nine? Didn't clubs close at three? I sat up in bed as I yawned, thinking more about why Zac wouldn't put in the code, and then thinking back about what the hell they had just interrupted.

With a sigh, I redialed Diana's number, promising Leo, who was crying in his crate, that I'd let him out in a minute as I put the phone to my face and crossed my legs, the dampness between them making me feel really uncomfortable now. The phone rang three times before she finally picked up.

"Hey," I said.

I'd known Diana what seemed like my entire life. I'd been there with her when her first serious boyfriend broke her heart, and I'd been there when her dog died. I'd thought I'd heard every emotion possible in her voice over such a long time period. So I wasn't prepared at the wrecked, distraught, "Van," that crackled out of her mouth.

"Di, what's wrong?" I immediately freaked out.

She was sobbing. I could tell she'd been doing it for a while. Through the tears and the distraught tone in her voice, she told me what happened. By the time we hung up, my entire body was numb. I forgot about Leo as I sat there for a moment, trying to collect myself.

I couldn't even find it in me to cry.

Getting to my feet, I attempted to swallow the pain in my throat. Nearly blind and going almost on instinct, I forced myself down the stairs. My ears were ringing. When had they started ringing? I wondered distractedly, trying to process my thoughts and finding myself completely unable of thinking about anything.

It was amazing how quickly things could change; that possibility never ceased to amaze me.

The tears had just started catching up to me by the time I found all of the guys in the living room. It wasn't until I spotted Zac on the couch with what was a very visible cast on the foot he had propped up on the ottoman that I lost it. Guilt and anger finally wrapped their spiny fingers around my heart, wringing the words right out of me. My voice broke as I asked, "Aiden, can you drive me to the hospital?"

TWENTY-NINE

stared at the screen of my phone until the **MOM** flashing across it finally bleeped out, replaced by **MISSED CALL**.

Not a single bit of me felt guilty for letting her call go to voice-mail. Not one single freaking little bit. I'd call her back. Eventually. I was too tired after my run.

"Darlin', you want somethin' to eat?" Zac's voice piped up un-expectedly from his spot across the kitchen.

I hadn't even realized I'd zoned out so completely when my phone started buzzing. I raised my eyes to find my roommate with one hip against the counter, a spatula in his other hand. But it was the crutch he had shoved under his armpit that caught my gaze. I didn't need to look around to know he'd left his other crutch propped up by the refrigerator. I'd found it there at least ten other times over the course of the last two weeks.

Yeah, crutches. The first time I'd seen them was when he and Aiden's friends had shown up to the house, after spending hours at the emer-gency room thanks to a hairline fracture in his foot. Every time I saw them, they made me want to cry. Not because he'd broken some bones, which was terrible in itself, but because of what it reminded me of.

They reminded me of Diana's face when Aiden and I picked her up. Aiden had driven me to the hospital the minute I got myself together enough to explain what happened. How Diana had gone out with her coworkers and stayed out late. How her boyfriend had shown up to her apartment in the middle of the night, angry that she'd stayed out so late. Had she cheated on him? How many dicks had she sucked? Why hadn't she invited him? She told me about how he'd then hit her and kept hitting her before storming out, enough so that she knocked on her neighbor's door and had him drive her to the hospital. How she filed a police report against him.

I'd spent the next two days at her apartment so she wouldn't be alone, listening to her tell me how wrong things had gone. How embarrassed she was. How stupid she felt.

I couldn't remember much after that. I felt like I was in a dream. The guilt I felt for not making her tell me something was going on was suffocating, debilitating. Why hadn't I said more? Done more? This was my best friend. I knew better. Hadn't I lived with the lies of what was secretly going on at home for half my life?

Her black eye, busted lip, and the bruises I saw all over her wrists and neck when I sat in the bathroom with her while she showered were seared into my eyelids. I wasn't surprised at all when, on the second day, she said she wanted to go stay with her parents in San Antonio for a while. She wasn't sure how long; she just knew she wanted to go be with them. I helped her pack two suitcases.

I knew Aiden's friends were gone by the time the taxi dropped me off at home; there weren't any cars other than mine in the driveway or on the street. Aiden had been in the nook when I first came inside. He'd walked up to me and hugged me without a word, letting me bury myself into that great big chest.

I'd been helpless countless times in my life—too many times really—and once more, as an adult, it was nearly too much to bear. Because there was nothing you could do when someone you cared about had something like that happen.

And the anger and the regrets ate you up.

In the days that followed, I couldn't shake off the guilt or the disappointment in myself for not doing something or making Rodrigo, Diana's brother, confront her. When I went to Aiden's bed that night, and every night afterward, because being with him made me feel better, he welcomed me without a word or expression of complaint. I didn't feel like talking, and I'd gone to the only person in the world who would understand better than anyone what had happened to someone I loved.

Then the day came that he was set to leave for Colorado. He'd stood in front of me in his room, given me a hug, kissed my cheek, kissed my mouth gently, slipped something over my head and he left.

My friend was gone. My puppy with him.

I couldn't remember ever feeling so alone.

It wasn't until he was out of the house that I looked down and saw what he had left me with. His medallion. The St. Luke's medallion his grandfather had given him. It made me cry.

Zac, who I didn't think knew how to handle the mood I was wrapped in, didn't do much more than make sure I ate, and checked on me from time to time.

But nothing changed the biggest truth resting on my soul in the aftermath of Diana leaving: I missed the hell out of the big guy. *Missed the shit out of him.*

Good things in life were precious, and I'd been too much of a coward to do anything about the gift I'd been given, and it seemed like I was reminded of it every day.

From the moment he'd landed in Durango, Aiden had begun texting me. First with Made it. Then he'd attached a picture of Leo sitting on the floor of the rental car he had for the next two months. Then a picture of him running through the snow at the house in Colorado.

A week passed in the blink of an eye. He sent me at least four text messages a day. Two of which were always of Leo; and the other two were usually something random.

Took your entire Dragon Balls collection in case you're wondering where it is, he'd let me know. I hadn't even noticed the DVDs were missing.

> Leo ate the toe of my runner while I was showering.
> How's your knee?

He sent me bits and pieces every day that tugged at me, only making me miss him more through the haze of sorrow surrounding my thoughts and heart.

After a couple of days of missing just about everyone I loved, I accidentally found the toy I'd bought from Rodrigo's kids months ago. The small plastic clown had been hidden beneath a stack of papers I'd put in my nightstand. I'd bought it with the intention of putting it in Aiden's shower as a joke, but I'd forgotten all about it.

It made me cry, these deep belly tears that had me on the floor with my back to the bed. I cried for Diana, who had looked beyond devastated at her boyfriend's betrayal. I cried for my mom, who I couldn't find it in me to call back. And I cried because I loved someone who might not love me back no matter how badly I might want him to.

At the end of it, I got up to my feet, set that clown on the corner of my desk, and resolved myself to keep going. Because doing otherwise was not an option.

I dug into work with a vengeance; I got back to training, even though my motivation had hitched a ride to a different continent. I'd retreated into myself more with this hole left in my heart, focusing on these things to distract me as I waited for the people I loved the most to come back to me.

Unfortunately in the process, I hadn't been a good friend to Zac. I knew he'd been worried about me; it would have been the same if our shoes had been on opposite feet. I realized he still *was* worried about me.

Zoning out in the kitchen didn't help anything, and I really had to dig in to manage to smile for him. "I'm not hungry yet, but thanks, Zac."

He nodded a little reluctantly, but didn't press the issue as he faced the stove again. "What'd you do today? Eight miles?"

Planting my elbows on the table, I eyeballed his cast. "Yeah, and I did three at marathon pace," I bragged. He'd run with me enough and cussed alongside me when we'd started adding marathon pacing to our runs. Zac knew it was hell.

As selfish as it made me, my disappointment had reached a level I didn't know what to do with; the reality harsh and bitter. After everything that Zac and I had been through together, all the times we'd taken turns throwing up after we'd started hitting the seventeen-mile-long slow distance runs, the times one of us had had to help partially carry the other once we'd run out of steam thanks to training five days a week, all the aches and pains we'd shared . . . I was going to have to go on this journey on my own, without my closest companion.

The guy who had lost his favorite thing in the world and had let me force him into training for a marathon.

If that wasn't friendship, I don't know what was. It just made me feel more terrible about disappearing on him, even if it had just been because I didn't want to drag him into the pit I'd fallen into, when now he had something else to contend with on his road to recovery and the rest of his career.

From the choppy sigh that came out of him, I already knew what he was going to say before it actually came out of his mouth.

"I'm so sorry, Vanny."

And just like the other time he'd apologized for slipping off an icy curb by accident, I said the same thing. "It's *okay*. I promise." Was I slightly brokenhearted? More than slightly. Would I ever tell him that? No.

"It was *stupid*."

The urge to rub right between my breasts was overwhelming. "It was an accident. I'm not upset with you." My voice cracked and I had to swallow. "It's just been everything. I'm fine, I promise."

The expression on his face when he turned around said what his mouth didn't: *You're not okay.*

Was anyone ever totally okay though?

I found myself lowering my head to rub the back of my still sweaty neck. "You know you don't have to stay here with me if you'd rather go back home, right?"

The original plan had been for him to go home right after the marathon, spend some time with his family, and then begin working out with his old college coach. Now? Well, I wasn't positive, but I did know he was supposed to be moving out and he hadn't yet.

Zac slanted me a look.

"What?"

"I'm not leavin' until you do your damn marathon, all right?" he insisted.

"But you don't have to, okay? I promise you have nothing to feel sorry for. If you change your mind and you want to go—"

"I'm not."

Since when did we have three stubborn asses living at the house?

"But if you do—"

"I'm not. PawPaw can wait a week. He'll probably outlive me," Zac argued.

"If you want to stay, stay, but if you don't want to, it's all right. Okay?" I insisted too, trying my best to give him a reassuring smile.

He simply shook his head.

Just as he opened his mouth to say something, the doorbell rang and we shot each other a frown. "Did you order pizza?"

"No."

I'd ordered a couple of my books that had gone to print a few days ago, but chose the free shipping option, so there was no way it was them. I shrugged at him and got up, walking slowly toward the door, trying to get myself to relax. When I glanced through the peephole, I took a step back and stared at the door blankly.

"Who is it?" Zac called out.

"Trevor."

"What did you just say?"

"It's Trevor," I answered coolly, knowing he was already screwed by yelling. "Have you been ignoring his calls?"

"Maybe."

That was a *yes*.

"I just won't open the door then," I said before there was a loud knock on the door.

"I can hear you!" Trevor bellowed.

I didn't feel like dealing with this, now or a decade from now. "What do you want me to do?" I ignored the man on the other side of the door, all of a sudden not caring if he'd heard us or not.

Zac cursed from the kitchen, and a moment later his crutches hit the tile as he hobbled his way toward the front door. With a resigned sigh, he said, "I can get the door."

"Are you sure?" I asked, even if inside I was kissing his feet for not making me have to put up with Trevor.

"Yeah."

I took a step away. "Do you want me to stay down here?"

He hesitated for a moment before nodding. "I'll take him into the living room so you can eat something."

Nodding, I walked pretty damn quickly into the kitchen and busied myself pulling things out of the fridge to eat, despite still not being hungry, as Zac opened the door. I really tried to ignore them, but it was hard. Bits and pieces of conversation floated from the living room to the kitchen way too easily.

"What the hell were you thinking?"

"What's going on with you?"

"What am I supposed to do with you when there's shit floating around the internet about you falling outside of a club and breaking your foot?

"You think anyone's going to want to take you now?"

Now that comment had me taking a step away from the stove and toward the hallway that led into the living room, ready to tell Trevor he needed to shut the hell up. But Zac didn't need me defending him. He'd been avoiding Trevor for a long time anyway, and even if he knew what he wanted to do, and I knew, he needed someone else in his corner.

I just didn't necessarily want it to be Trevor the douche, but it was his career, not mine.

Almost an hour later, the sound of someone clearing their throat had me looking up from where I was sitting at the breakfast table, with my feet propped up on one chair, a movie playing on my propped up phone, and a plate I'd just finished scraping the last bit of rice off.

"I'm surprised you didn't go with Aiden to Colorado," the manager commented from his spot leaning against the framing between the hallway and the kitchen.

I raised my tired gaze to his and shook my head. "I couldn't. I have something I have to do here in a couple of days," I explained, purposely leaving out what happened to Diana and my run. He didn't need to know, and what would he do anyway? Give me some half-assed apology I didn't believe? "There's no point in my flying back and forth," my dry, monotone voice added on. Plus, it wasn't like Aiden had invited me. He'd barely wanted to talk about it each time I'd brought it up.

The snicker that came out of him made me straighten my back. "He could afford it."

And there it was. I blinked at him. "I make my own money, and I'm not going to waste mine or his."

"You sure about that?" He had the nerve to raise an eyebrow.

Could he not tell this was the last thing I wanted to do? "Yes, I'm sure. You want to check my bank account?" I'd already had to send in copies of my bank account information to the government to prove I could support Aiden and me—in a much less lavish lifestyle, but I *could* if push came to shove, at least the government thought so.

Trevor made a small noise in the back of his throat that had me leveling my gaze at him.

I didn't want to talk to him; now he was just downright pissing me off. "Is that what this is about? Do you think I'm here to blow all of Aiden's money? Did you think I was trying to win him over or something?" I asked slowly, carefully trying to finally understand what it might be about my personality that had made him so hostile from the moment I'd started working for him.

From the way he pulled at his ear, in that nervous tic I'd picked up on years ago when he was frustrated, I'd hit the nail perfectly on the head.

"*Really?* You interviewed and hired me. I didn't even know who he was until you told me." Yeah, I was getting just as defensive as I thought I sounded. "You could have fired me if you had that much of a problem with it."

"Fired you?" His hand went to the back of his trimmed salt-and-pepper head. "I tried firing you at least four times."

What?

Trevor's lip snarled. "You didn't know?"

"When?" I coughed out.

"Does it matter?"

It shouldn't but . . . "It does to me."

The angry, bitter man simply gazed at me like I was dumb. "He wouldn't let me."

You know nothing, Vanessa Mazur.

I didn't understand. I didn't understand at all.

"The last time I suggested we find him someone else, he said the first person that would go between the two of us would be me. *Me.*"

Some things just sort of clicked together. Why Trevor had always been such an asshole to me—prima ballerinas didn't like dancing in anyone else's limelight. Why he had fought so much to try to keep me from quitting—to save his own hide. Why he'd been so on edge since we got married and didn't tell him—because it seemed like we were ganging up on him, which was a partial truth.

But the news made me reel.

It felt like the rug had been pulled out from under my feet.

He'd liked me. Aiden had fucking liked me. He hadn't been joking so many months ago.

The way Trevor cleared his throat was rough, catching, like he was trying to compose himself after losing his shit. "Anyway, tell Aiden I'll be calling him soon. You two might be packing your bags and moving to colder pastures," he noted. "See you."

I didn't say another word to him. What the hell else was there to say?

With shaking hands, I picked up my phone and typed out a message to the big guy.

Me: I didn't know Trevor wanted to fire me.

An hour later, I got my response.

Aiden: Did he go by the house?

He wasn't even trying to bullshit me.

Me: Yeah.

Aiden: Yes, he wanted to get rid of you. I didn't let him.

Was he on crack?

Me: You didn't say anything when I left. I just
thought . . . you didn't care.

Aiden: I wasn't going to force you to stay if you wanted
to go.

Me: But you could have said something. I would have
stayed longer if you'd just asked.

I'd barely typed that out when I realized how stupid of an argument that was. If he'd asked. Aiden was like me, he wouldn't have
asked. Ever.

Aiden: I got you for longer, didn't I?

CHAPTER THIRTY

Why was I still doing this?

Why?

Why hadn't I just said, "Van, who gives a shit whether you can run a marathon or not? You did more than you ever imagined you could. Who do you have to impress?"

As much as I hadn't wanted it to, life had taken its toll on my head and confidence. Since everything happened, I'd barely been able to add another mile and a half to my distance, and that was pushing it. I walked and bitched while I did it, and afterward, I was so tired and my knee ached so badly, I crashed out on the bed after my shower and refused to get up.

Every sign said doing the marathon was a terrible idea.

Nothing changed the fact that I missed Zac's company, and the way he motivated me to keep going even when we were both cussing about how stupid doing this was.

I had to do it. I'd trained for months. Not finishing wasn't an option.

I could do it.

I wasn't freaking the fuck out. Nerves weren't making my hands shake. I wasn't subconsciously rubbing over my ring finger every few minutes, searching for that token of Aiden he'd given me that I'd left at home because I was too scared to lose it. Aiden's necklace was tucked under my shirt for good luck. Surrounded by so many people who were smiling and just seemed so fucking stoked to participate, it honestly disheartened me a little.

Twenty miles. I could run twenty miles. That was something to be proud of, wasn't it?

I had barely thought that when I mentally smacked myself. Of course twenty miles was something, but I'd put my body through hell for these last few months for what? For this.

If I didn't do this, I needed to get my ass kicked. Even if I came in fucking last, I had to finish it. Screw it.

I shook out my hands. I could do this.

"Are you Vanessa Mazur?" a voice to my right asked.

Finding a woman wearing a T-shirt that said she was volunteering at the marathon, I forced a smile on my face and nodded. "Yes."

She thrust out a cell phone in my direction. "You have a call."

A call? Gingerly taking the basic flip phone, I watched as she backed away before raising it up to my ear. "Hello?"

"Muffin," the deep voice answered.

I pulled the phone away from my face and took in the screen, recognizing the number. "How the hell did you get this number?"

"I didn't. Trevor did. I tried calling your cell, but it went straight to voicemail," Aiden explained.

"Yeah, I left it in my pile of stuff," I pretty much stammered, still trying to process that he'd somehow, some way, gotten in contact with me. He hadn't called me since he'd left. We'd only communicated via text message, and the sound of his voice went straight to my heart.

In what had become a typical Aiden way, he asked, "Are you all right?"

"No." I looked around to make sure the woman who handed me the phone wasn't listening. There were too many people around, all living their own lives, worrying about themselves. "I'm trying to talk myself into doing this even if I come in last," I admitted.

"You're about to run a marathon. Do you think it matters if you come in last as long as you finish it?" he asked.

I blinked and let the anxious tears pool in my eyes for the first time. "But what if I can't finish it?"

The voice on the other end let out a sigh. "You can finish the marathon. Graveses aren't quitters."

Graveses. Graveses weren't quitters. I didn't want to cry. I wasn't going to let myself lose it now of all times. At least not completely.

"But I'm not really a Graves, and I haven't even been able to finish twenty-six miles, much less twenty-six point two. Not once. I'm dying by twenty."

"Vanessa," he rumbled my name in a way that felt like a caress to my spine. "You're a Graves where it matters. I don't know anybody else who could do what you've done. Come out on top of what you have. You can do this. You can do anything, do you understand me? Even if you limp your way through the last sixteen miles, you're going to finish it because that's just who you are."

This weird hiccup thing crept up my throat, and the next thing I knew, I dropped my hand away from my face to control myself. It didn't take long, but it was the most difficult control I'd ever tried to get ahold of. With a few deep breaths, I put the phone back to my ear, emotion overwhelming my nostrils. "In case I die on my run, I want to tell you something." I wanted to tell him I loved him. Fuck it. What the hell had I been waiting for?

He was a good man. The best type of man—for me at least. The more I thought about what was between us, the more I picked up on the breadcrumbs he'd been leaving for me for some time now. He cared about me. He more than cared about me. I knew it from the bottom of my soul.

"Tell me afterward. You're not going to die," he replied, smoothly with conviction.

"No, I need to tell you now just in case," I insisted.

Aiden let out a sigh. "You're not going to die. Tell me afterward."

"But what if—?"

"Vanessa, you can do this. I'm not doubting you for a second, and you shouldn't be doubting yourself either," he demanded. "I know you're hurting right now, but I'm willing to bet none of your sisters would be able to do what you're about to do."

He'd gone for the killing blow. The one thing in the world to resuscitate me. Aiden got me and he got me good. "I've got this," I said in a muffled voice. I had to have this. There wasn't a choice, was there?

"You've got this," he repeated with more conviction. "You can do this."

Now or never right? "I've got this."

He made a light noise, a tender one. "That's my girl."

His girl? "I am?" I just outright asked him, hoping more than a little he wasn't just . . . that was stupid, Aiden wouldn't just say that.

"The only one," he said it like there was no other choice in the world.

How could I not tackle universes with that kind of possessiveness from the most driven man I'd ever meet? "I might not be able to walk after I cross the finish line, but I'm going to do it. Can I call you after I'm done when I'm lying on a hospital bed?"

"You'd better."

I HAVE BEEN through some shit in my life. I knew what pain was, I'd dealt with it on and off for years, sometimes more *on* than other years. I understood the basics of working hard and succeeding. And I liked to do my best at everything I attempted. I always had, and I wasn't going to worry or wonder why that was.

But the marathon . . .

I'd prepared as much as I could to run it, considering everything. I knew my limits and my body.

But after that fifteenth mile marker . . .

Everything began to shut down.

I wanted to die.

Each step began to feel like hell incarnate. My shins were crying invisible tears. All my important tendons and ligaments thought they were being punished for something they'd done in another lifetime.

And I wondered why the hell I'd ever thought doing this would be my crowning achievement after my long road. Couldn't I have just raised money for a charity or something? Was I too young to be a foster parent?

If I lived through this, I could do anything, I convinced myself. I'd do an Iron Man competition, damn it.

Okay, maybe I'd prepare for a triathlon if I finished this prison sentence.

If I finished it.

If.

If I didn't die. Because it sure as hell felt like I was on the cusp.

I was thirsty, hungry, and every step sent a streak of pain straight up my spine and into my head since I'd begun to lose my stride and run sloppier. I might have had a migraine too, but my pain receptors were too focused on everything else to notice.

But I thought about Aiden, my brother, and Diana. I thought about Zac.

And I closed my eyes and pushed. Each mile got harder; hell, each foot became more difficult to move. I was slowing down because I was crossing into the Underworld.

But I could die after I crossed the finish line, because I hadn't trained and busted my ass for months not to. If anything, I became more and more determined to drag myself across the finish line if it came down to it. By the time I made it to the last mile, I was more limping and lurching than even walking. My calves had locked up on me. My shin splints were going to be a serious pain in the ass for weeks to come, and my quads were shredded.

Honestly, I felt like I had the flu, Ebola, and strep throat combined.

Thinking back on it, I wasn't sure how the hell I managed to cross the finish line. Sheer will and determination, I guess. I'd never been so proud of myself or pissed off at myself than right then.

I thought I started crying, mostly because every bone and muscle in me was crying, and because I couldn't believe I'd actually made it.

But when I spotted that giant, brown-haired man beelining through people like a runaway train, I definitely started damn near bawling. People cheered me on, but I couldn't find it in me to thank them because I wanted only one thing and it wasn't close enough.

I wanted the big-headed mirage coming toward me, and I wanted it three hours ago. I wanted it two weeks ago.

Even from the forty feet that separated us, I could see him through my blurry eyes, frowning as he found me mixed up in the crowd. I dropped to my knees, ignoring the personnel that surrounded me, making sure I was okay. Realistically, I knew I wasn't dying. Not really.

It was just . . . traumatic. And all I wanted was a hug, a shower, food, and a nap.

Mostly though, I wanted that human-sized steamroller barreling through the people who separated us with even more urgency. He was like Moses parting a sea of people. The second he stopped in front of me, I held my arms out and let him grab me under the armpits, dead-lifting me before engaging those giant biceps and pulling me up to be eye to eye with him. I didn't appreciate that incredible feat of strength, because what he did afterward . . .

I threw my arms around his neck and he hugged me. In front of everyone, he hugged the living shit out of me as if he hadn't walked out on me and left me alone when all I wanted was him. I wrapped my legs high above his hips like a spider monkey, not giving a crap about the wedgie my shorts were giving me, much less that there were photographers, who were supposed to be busy taking pictures of the marathon runners, circling the Wall of Winnipeg and me in our moment.

Yeah, I cried into his neck and he pressed his face against my hair. His words were low, reassuring, and whispered.

"That's my girl. That's my fucking girl."

"What are you doing here?" I practically bawled into him.

"I missed you."

"You what?"

His arms tightened around me. "I missed you very much."

Oh hell.

"I had to come see you," he continued on.

"You were here, and you didn't tell me?"

"I didn't want to distract you," that low voice explained, his hand cupping the back of my neck. "I knew you were going to do it."

His words only made me want to cry more, but not necessarily just tears of joy. "I'm dying. I need you to get me a Segway. I'm never walking ever again," I blubbered.

"You're not dying, and I'm not buying you that," he said.

"Everything hurts."

Was he laughing? "I'm sure."

I realized I didn't care if he was laughing at my expense. "Can you carry me?"

"You're insulting me, Van. Of course I can." I thought he kissed my cheek, but I couldn't be sure, because my eyes were closed and I was scared to open them and find that I was dreaming and imagining this all happening. "But will I?" he asked.

I only embraced him tighter and squeezed my exhausted thighs around him as much as I could, which probably only lasted three seconds total. It was a miracle I managed to do that, honestly.

I was pretty sure his mouth grazed my temple and I sniffled, pausing. "Are you kissing me?"

"Yes. I'm so proud of you."

"Okay," I whined with a sniffle. Yeah, I hugged that big neck even tighter. "Will you take me home, big guy?"

My no-nonsense, no-bullshit Aiden said it. "After you walk around for ten minutes to cool down."

"YOU NEED TO replenish your carbs," Aiden said as he came into my room with a plate in his hand. On it was brown rice, black-eyed peas, an entire avocado, what looked like roasted and sliced squash, and perched on the edge was an entire apple. He had a glass of water in his other hand and a small bottle of coconut water tucked under his arm.

I sat up in bed with a yawn, tossing the throw I'd slept wrapped in to the side. "You're an angel." I still couldn't believe he'd come back. It didn't seem real.

He walked over to the side of the bed, dropped his hip on the edge, and passed over the glass of water first. "Did you have a good nap?"

Considering I'd gone straight from the car to the bathroom, where I'd sat in the tub cross-legged and showered, and then dragged my way back to my room and passed the hell out, I felt pretty well. The muscles in my legs were incredibly tight and even my shoulders felt extremely tense. I felt ill, but I figured that was only because I should have eaten more than the two bananas Aiden had shoved into my hand on the car ride back and the bag of mixed nuts Zac, who had been waiting on a bench after the marathon, shared with me.

"Yeah," I told him, chugging down half the water before taking the plate from his hand and digging in without another word.

I caught Aiden watching me when I took the time to look at him, but I was so busy inhaling the food, I didn't do it much. About three-fourths of the way through my plate, I finally wiped at my chin with the back of my hand and shot him a grateful smile. "Thank you so much for making that for me."

"Uh-huh." He pointed at the corner of his mouth. "You have rice right there."

Wiping at the spot he was pointing out, I asked, "How long was I asleep?"

"About three hours."

Three hours? Shit, I didn't think I'd slept that long.

"Van." Aiden's face swam into my groggy vision. "What were you going to tell me before your run?"

Aww shit. Shit, shit, shit. Had I completely forgotten about it? No. I'd thought about what I'd told him at least a thousand times in the four hours it took me to run. I'd wanted to kick myself in the ass for saying anything at least half the time. The other half of the time, when I was reminding myself I was amazing and I was running a marathon so I could tackle the world and Iron Man competitions, I felt like I'd done the right thing.

With a plate of food he'd cooked for me on my lap and a bottle of coconut water between his massive thighs and an empty glass on my nightstand, I was going to tell Aiden I loved him.

I loved him. I loved him so much I would do just about anything for him. I loved him enough to risk spending the next four and a half years of my life with a man who would more than likely divorce me and move on with his career.

Because fuck it, what was life if you didn't live it and make the most out of it? What was life without loving someone who cared about you a lot more than he cared about anyone else? That was my truth. Aiden had hugged me and told me he was proud of me in front of reporters and strangers alike, when he held on to his privacy with both hands.

And it hadn't been fake.

I could do this.

I would.

Because I would rather tell him than spend the rest of my life wondering about *what would have happened* if I'd told him he meant the world to me. That he was the first new person in my life I completely trusted. That I could settle for being number two in his life until he had more time.

So I said it, even though my fingers were gripping the plate so hard I was worried it would break. I made myself look him in the eye as I did it. "I was going to tell you . . . I was going to tell you that I love you. I know you said you don't want a relationship, and I know things between us are super complicated—"

The plate in my hands was taken away.

"—but I love you. I'm sorry I'm not sorry. I didn't *want* to be—"

"Vanessa."

"I don't want to be someone's number two or number three priority because sometimes I like to be greedy—"

"Van."

"—but I can't help how I feel. I've tried to stop, I swear. But I couldn't."

Then it came. "Shut up."

I closed my mouth and frowned at the bearded face frowning down at me.

"Did you listen to anything I told you when you finished your run? I've missed you. I've missed you so much you can't begin to comprehend how much. I didn't want to leave you. I kept trying to talk myself out of going. Why do you think I never brought it up?"

Now that had me thinking. "But . . . you didn't say anything when you left. You took Leo."

"You didn't ask me to stay." He squeezed my hands. "I took Leo because I couldn't take you. I assumed you wanted to stay with Diana and do your marathon because you didn't feel the same. I was going to ask you to come with me."

"You were?"

That handsome, wonderful face leaned closer to mine. "How do you not know that you mean the world to me? I haven't made it clear enough?"

"I don't know," I stuttered. "Do you love me?"

His gaze was so intent the entire world seemed to stop. "You tell me. I never stop thinking about you. I worry about you all the time. Every beautiful thing I see reminds me of you. I can't finish my practices in Colorado without wishing you were around," he said in a steady tone. "You tell me what I feel."

With a burst of strength I didn't think I had in me, I made myself get up to my knees, and leaned over to press my mouth against his.

And I wasn't surprised when Aiden instantly wrapped an arm around my lower back and pulled me into him, his mouth tilting to the side and opening. With a swipe of his tongue across my bottom lip, I opened my mouth and let it brush against mine, slow and hesitant, exploratory.

Aiden kissed me like . . . good lord, like we were having slow, intense sex. At least the kind of slow, intense sex I'd seen in porns before.

Our chests were sealed against each other's, his arms were around me and my hands were in his hair, and we just kissed. We kissed and we kissed and we kissed the shit out of each other like we did that day in his room before everything.

It could have lasted for five minutes or it could have been for twenty, but when he finally pulled his mouth away, I let out a cry right onto his mouth.

Aiden's sigh wafted over my chin as he planted that sexy, full mouth on one side of my jaw and then the other, his palms cradling the sides of my ribs possessively. "Your door is open and Zac is here," he said into my skin.

"Damn it," I whispered.

He chuckled. "Later. I promise."

"You do?"

He hummed and kissed my cheek. "Finish eating."

—

I WOKE UP on my side hours later. So many hours later it took me a second to remember where I was. Why I was where I was—Aiden's bed. After I ate another small meal, I'd gone to his room and laid down, asking if Leo was fine with Leslie, who had stayed on babysitting duty with the precious blond prince in Colorado. I remembered getting really tired and beginning to doze off.

Apparently, he hadn't kicked me out of his bed and had instead tucked me in, and at some point in the night—or maybe he'd done it from the beginning—Aiden had come up behind me and wrapped an arm around my waist.

Which was exactly where and how I found myself in that moment.

I was awake, on my side with Aiden directly behind me, grinding his erection into my bottom as his hand snuck between my legs; those fingers were touching me low. Low. Right where my entire body centered. Right where I could tell how wet and anxious I was after so long.

How long has this been going on? I asked myself before I accepted that it didn't matter.

I was squirming, moving my hips at the sensation behind me and in front of me. The long pipe under his clothes pressed hot against my butt; strong fingertips rubbed over the thin cotton of my panties and pajama pants. That big chest I admired on a daily basis was aligned with my back, molded to it.

He rolled his lower body and I rolled against him. The feel of him big and hard behind me was seriously the most amazing thing in the world. His mouth latched onto the nape of my neck, kissing, then biting where it met my shoulder. I panted. Aiden rubbed me lightly where I wanted him the most and I choked on the sensation, reaching behind me blindly to sneak my hand between our bodies. I cupped him, or as much of him as I could, and stroked up and down over that thick ridge that seemed to go on forever from the base.

"Aiden, please," I whispered when his fingers circled over the too-damp material covering the seam between my thighs.

He answered by nipping my earlobe before sucking it between his lips.

"*Aiden*," I repeated, gripping him hard in my hand before adjusting my position and slipping between the elastic of his boxer briefs and the hot skin of his lower abs. The short, bristly hairs at his root tickled my palm for a moment before I wrapped my palm and fingers around his base. My palm slid over from the tip of his erection all the way to the firm sack just below his base. I gave his balls a squeeze before doing the motion all over again. All that silky, hot skin brushing over my hand, his slick, damp tip painting a line over my fingers, palm, and inner wrist.

Without a warning, he yanked the hem of my pants down to my knees, and while I was still reacting to that, the fingers he'd been using to rub over my panties hooked onto one side of the scrap covering me, and he tugged the material over. "Yes?" he asked, brushing a big, blunt finger over my exposed sex.

"Yes." What else was there to say? To beg for?

His hips withdrew from my backside before he returned, the mushroomed tip I'd been rubbing a second before prodded at me from behind.

Drawing my knees up to my chest as much as I could without doing anything to the pants knotting my legs together, I stayed on my side. He nudged his penis a little more at my opening, prodding with the not-so-small head below his waist before I opened my leg a little . . . and he surged. In. Inside of me. Hot, long, and so fucking hard I might have choked a little.

Slowly, he stroked his way inside, channeling his way into me.

Slowly, I pushed back and sucked in a breath when he bottomed out.

The swift intake of air Aiden took turned into a growl.

Each thrust gained momentum, all the way in, all the way out. Flesh parting around hard muscles, clinging and squeezing. His hand snuck up inside the front of my shirt, over my belly button, up and up until his fingertips pinched a nipple between them. His other hand made its way over my head to grab my hand, holding it in front of me against the bed.

He pumped and pumped his hips, the sound making a slapping noise against my bottom. He hit a spot inside me that was too much, making me squeeze my legs tighter together, only making it that much better.

I tipped my head back and his lips caught mine, kissing me. Ruthlessly, his tongue dove in against mine, consuming everything I had in me. Aiden rolled his hips and pounded. His kissing was relentless. His fingers going from one breast to another, rolling and pinching the small nubs that wanted him more and more every second.

"I want to come inside you," he whispered into my ear.

That was all it took. I cried out. Coming. Coming.

Then Aiden groaned, low and sexy, he thrust faster, more relentless and offbeat. His hips slapped mine, the noise wet and almost sloppy. With one more solid push, he thrust in completely and made this hoarse sound as he came, holding me to him so close and warm. The place where we met was wet as his erection twitched and pulsed inside of me.

I kissed him, swallowing his groans, enjoying the way he involuntarily moved inside of me. With a gasp, he pulled his mouth away, his hand letting go of mine to latch around my chest, pulling me into his frame, letting me love the feel of him warm and a little sweaty around me. He was panting. Hugging me. That big body wrapped around me, his penis only slightly softening.

I couldn't find a single word to say that would be appropriate for what I was feeling right then, much less come up with a sentence that would do the moment justice. Settling my head under his chin, I let out a rattled exhale of exhaustion. Aiden's hand cupped my breast, his mouth lingering at the space below my ear. I was boneless, painless, ecstatic, and relieved. When his palm squeezed my breast, I tipped my head back and searched for his mouth. Aiden, in that way of his that always knew everything, found my lips. His tongue met mine, tasting, exploring, savoring.

As the minutes dragged on, Aiden hardened. I felt that thick muscle inside of me lengthen, and continue getting longer, driving me instinctively back toward his hips, driving him deeper. Filling, so damn filling. But it was more than that elemental need for an orgasm that turned me on. It was Aiden's body, his warmth, his mouth, the way every part of him was big and how perfectly in control of himself he was.

I loved Aiden. I more than loved him, and that made all the difference.

When he pulled out of me at the same time he ripped his mouth away, this noise that sounded like a whine came out of me for only a split second as his hand trailed down the front of my thigh. "Come here," he said in that rocky, rough voice that was lower and huskier than normal. He ran his hot palm up my hamstring before palming one of my butt cheeks. "I want you on top of me," he whispered. "I need you," he used the same words he'd used on me so many months ago.

I didn't need to be told twice. Getting to my knees, I went to his side, a little nervous, a little shy despite what we'd just done. Aiden was sprawled on his back, his boxer briefs were caught on his massive thighs just below the pink sac I'd been fondling minutes ago. Nestled into the base of rich brown pubic hairs, his swollen penis bobbed shiny and wet with his come and mine down to the root, the shaft mauve-colored against the trail of dark hair starting at his belly button.

"You are the sexiest man I've ever seen," I blurted out, shaking my head as I took his lower body in again.

The small smile that crossed his face sent a shiver down my spine. He reached forward and brushed the pads of his index and middle fingers along my two lower lips. "You have no idea what you do to me, Van. No. Idea." He repeated the motion. "Do you want to know how many times I've jerked off to you in this bed? In the shower? Every day I wanted a little more from you and a little more, and it hasn't been enough."

Good grief.

The only thing I knew for sure I wanted in that moment was his shirt off. He must have been thinking something along the same lines, because his fingers went to my shirt. Before I knew it, it had been thrown to the floor, my underwear tugged off and flying in the same direction. As Aiden pulled his shirt over his head, I pulled his boxers down those muscular legs, taking my time to touch those impressive muscles, my thumbs streaking up the inside of his thighs on the way back up.

Without a word, with those eyes burning a path all over my breasts and face, Aiden sat up reaching for my hips. His lips caught my nipple in the process. I was on my hands and knees straddling him a moment later, dragging the seam between my legs over the straining erection at the center of that endless body.

And then I was reaching back, aligning that broad tip against me, fully aware of how wet I was from him coming in me and loving the idea he didn't care. His moan got lost in mine as I slowly sank onto him, his mouth hovering over the nipple he'd been sucking on. Aiden's hands guided me to move over him. His lips urged me on, catching one breast and then the other, moving to the space between them with peppered kisses.

When I rocked back, sheathing him in me completely, Aiden lay flat on his back. His chin went high, the tendons along his neck straining. I swallowed up the sight of him naked, those wide shoulders against the pale gray of his covers, his sculpted pectorals rising and falling with his choppy breathing. My two favorite things to take in were the ridged muscles of his six-pack flexing on and off, and seeing my thighs along his hips and sides.

I couldn't stop myself from leaning forward, planting one hand on the mattress beside his head, the other going to the center of his chest, his skin hot, his muscles hard. One of his hands went up to cup the back of my head, bringing my face down for him to catch me in an open mouth kiss. We were in that position, still linked with our lips when he started drilling his hips up. We were still making out when I came, my inner muscles rippling, lost in my orgasm, when his penis twitched and he let out a hoarse groan, coming again.

I pretty much collapsed on him at that point, breathing harder than after I'd finished the marathon, more euphoric than ever in my life. Our bodies being aligned was overwhelming. His heart beating under my chin was more than I ever could have imagined.

His arms wrapped around my back, keeping my breasts against his slightly sweaty chest. Aiden hummed above my head, "I love you."

And I hummed right back, my entire soul swelling. "I know." Because I did. "I love you, too."

"I know," he said in return. The closeness between our bodies more apparent than ever in that moment.

"You really want me to go to Colorado with you?"

"What have I told you about stupid questions?" he asked. "Yes, I want you to."

I smiled. "Sheesh. I just wanted to make sure. I want to go. I want to be where you are." Before I thought twice about it, I told him what I would realize later was the most significant absolute truth in my life. "Home is where you are. I would go anywhere for you if you wanted me to be there."

One of Aiden's palms slid down the length of my spine, ending at the small of my back. He seemed to talk into my hair. "I don't know anything about relationships, Van, but I know I love you. I know I've waited my entire life to love you, and I'll do whatever I have to, to make this work."

Maybe that was the thing about love I never understood before Aiden. Like football and art, like anything that anyone in the world has ever wanted, love was a dream. And just like a dream, there were no assurances behind it. It didn't grow on its own. It didn't blossom without food to feed it.

It was the greatest in its subtleties.

It was the strongest in its selflessness.

And it could be forever with someone who wasn't afraid to never give up on the possibilities it presented.

EPILOGUE

"I T'S OVER. THE SAN DIEGO GUARDS HAVE MADE THE COMEBACK OF A LIFETIME. THEY'RE GOING TO THE SUPER—"

I smiled, and bounced the two butts on each of my thighs as the television anchors went over the game that had finished an hour ago. Most of the game hadn't gone the way anyone in the box wanted it to. Hell, I thought at least 70 percent of the audience hadn't wanted things to go the way they had.

Because the Guards had been losing by fifteen up until the last quarter. The disappointment in the team's family box had been tangible. Heavy and sedated, I thought we were all some degree of numb up through the beginning of the fourth quarter.

We all wanted them to win, but for me, I probably wanted it at a little more than everyone else in the room besides the worried mothers.

This was Aiden's last season, and I'd known how badly he wanted to win. How much he wanted to go to the biggest game of them all. For once.

He was arguably the best defensive end in the league and had been his entire career. He'd won Player of the Year three more times since we'd gotten married, been to every All Star Bowl, and won achievements on television award shows . . . But he still hadn't gotten a ring. The Ring. He had made it to the playoffs but the teams he was on had never made it to the championship before the big game—until now.

And in this last season, the team had been doing so well, everyone had assumed this would finally be it. Then, it had all started to go terribly wrong, and the dream began to slip away. One of the linebackers had dislocated his shoulder. A cornerback had limped off the field after a play. The team's defense had been in shambles. But by some sort of miracle, the Guards' offense staged the comeback of the century, the defense got it together, and they won.

Seeing it with my own eyes hadn't helped make it more believable.

They had won. *They'd fucking won.* I felt like *I'd* won. As if I'd be the one going to the big game in two weeks.

"You want me to take one of them?" one of the wide receivers' girlfriends asked from her spot in the seat next to me as we hung out in the room that had been assigned for team members' families.

I gave her an appreciative smile and shook my head. "I got it, thanks. I'm sure they'll be out in a minute."

The younger woman nodded, wringing her hands as she smiled wide. "Yeah. I can't wait." She bit her lip and looked around, her knees bobbing under the table. The energy coming off her was infectious.

"It's amazing, isn't it?" I asked.

"Yeah, yeah." She smiled. An early-twenties brunette, I knew she hadn't been with her boyfriend for long. Last season, there had been a different woman who showed up to the family room for number eighty. "I want to scream. I can't believe they did it." Her voice had started to rise in volume before her eyes strayed to the two little monsters on my knees. "Matt said Aiden was planning on retiring after this season."

There it went.

"Yep." It was a bittersweet thing. For one, I was relieved. I'd read too many articles about the long-term effects football had on players' brains and bodies over the last few years, and I knew Aiden had been more than relatively lucky in his career. He'd never really had any injuries that weren't minor since that incident with his Achilles tendon so many years ago, and that was better than most other people had it. On the other hand, no one knew how much he loved playing better than I did. Football had been everything he worked hard for, and he was hanging up his cleats and jersey, and retiring at thirty-five years old.

A huge chapter of his life was closing, and I was just slightly worried about how the transition would go in the months to come. Over the years, we'd found a balance in our relationship that worked, that thrived more and more every day despite his schedule and my workaholic tendencies, but . . . well, he was quitting football. His great love.

"Oh! Look! They're coming," the girl said, already pushing back and getting to her feet.

All of the guys who began trickling inside the family room had ecstatic expressions on their faces.

On the other side of the room, I spotted Trevor standing there with arms across his chest, talking on his phone. He must have sensed me glaring at him, because his eyes moved across the crowd of people to land on me. I gave him the middle finger behind Sammy's back and he simply stared, shaking his head in disbelief but not doing anything else.

Asshole.

Just because he was a ruthless bastard who made sure Aiden got what he wanted didn't mean I had to like him. At this point, after so many years, I think my hatred for him was more for fun than anything, but he was still a shark without a heart.

A shark who had gotten Zac a really good deal with a new expansion team in Oklahoma a year after he'd gotten cut from the Three Hundreds. They hadn't gone very far this year, but Zac was playing better than ever, a starter for the third year in his career. He was actually my quarterback on fantasy football and had been since he'd been signed on. He was still single, still dumb. Still one of my closest friends, and already referring to himself as Uncle Zac any and every time he came by to see the boys.

Some days I couldn't wrap my head around how much I loved the two greatest things I would ever have a part in creating. There wasn't a single thing I wouldn't do for them, and that knowledge was only slightly painful once in a blue moon when it made me think about my own mom and her failings. Nothing between us had really improved, and I was well aware that was my fault. There was too much I was unwilling to let go of, but at least at this point in my life, I couldn't regret the decisions I'd made. I was happy, happier than happy, and I wouldn't feel bad about it.

I sat on the chair and waited, watching as the players filtered in and headed straight for their families. People cheered and hugged, overjoyed. It didn't take long for Aiden to lurch his way over, his face with that same blank, careful expression on it as he looked around the room. The big guy was finally going to the big game and he wasn't even smiling. Why did that not surprise me?

Then he spotted us in the back corner.

Sammy saw him at the same time. His hands thrust forward. "Mommy! Look! Daddy!"

And the smile that came over the love of my life's face made me grin like an idiot. The honesty, openness, and genuine joy in Aiden's expression still reached this part of me that hadn't existed before him.

It was my smile. Our smile. The one he saved up for moments when it was only our little team together. And it didn't hold a trace of anything football-related in it, as he gazed from me to the two small ones at my sides, wearing matching jerseys in sizes much larger than someone their ages should wear. Little chubby asses. I'd honestly been relieved to have to go through C-sections to give birth to them. Those big heads, just like their dad's, would have done some serious, serious damage.

I could remember Diana holding Sammy after he'd been born, shaking her head. "This head would have ripped your ass wide open, Vanny."

When I'd started having contractions while pregnant with Gray, a little over a year later, that had been the mental picture I'd gone into the hospital with. It was just what I didn't need to worry about. Fortunately, everything had worked out fine.

The big guy looking at us as he crossed the room in the wake of a tremendous win confirmed that. Aiden didn't hesitate to drop to his knees in front of us, his gaze going from Sammy to me and then to Gray. He always did that, like he couldn't choose what to focus on. Some days he looked at me longer, some days it was Sammy, other days it was the tiny guy. Every day was Leo, the last member of our group, who was waiting patiently at home.

This would have been year five in our agreement, but Aiden had gotten his conditional green card, and then his residency years ago and had passed his citizenship exam already. We'd nailed the two interviews we had to sit through with an agent questioning us to make sure we were a legitimate couple, and I liked to think we passed with flying colors. I remembered complaining over how I couldn't deport him anymore if he got on my nerves.

Aiden didn't say anything as he wrapped those massive arms around all three of us, ducking his head to kiss one dark head of hair after the other. Then he smiled at me and leaned forward to kiss me. To really kiss me, like we weren't surrounded by people cheering and yelling over the second-biggest possible win in the NFO.

I knew right then. *I knew* that he was fine, that everything was going to be more than okay regardless of whether he won the big championship or not. We would figure the future out. This guy who gave everything—his career, me, and now the boys—his all, didn't half-ass anything. He never would; it just wasn't in him.

"Are you happy?" I asked.

With his arms still around the three of us, he looked up at me through those incredibly long lashes and nodded almost distractedly. "Yes." Those massive hands went to the small spines of his mini-mes before detouring to gently touch the pudgy cheeks, his smile growing even wider as his gaze landed on mine once more. "But I can't remember anymore what it's like to not be happy."

As a thank you to the loyal readers of Mariana Zapata, please turn the page for exclusive, never before seen bonus content!

LOVE AT THE FINISH LINE

Sealed with a kiss! Aiden Graves was spotted demonstrating a surprising amount of affection on February 6. The couple were seen embracing on the other side of the finish line at the Dallas Ultra Marathon. Sources confirm that the woman is his once-assistant and new wife, Vanessa Mazur. "Aiden and Vanessa have known each other for years," spills a source. "It's been a surprise to everyone. Aiden hasn't dated anyone since he entered the NFO. We didn't even know they were together." Another source says otherwise. "It wasn't love at first sight, but they have always had chemistry. Once she quit working for him, he didn't know what to do with himself." The defensive end for the Dallas Three Hundreds, 30, and the graphic designer, 26, worked together for two years before secretly eloping. "Aiden is so focused on his career, he wouldn't be able to be attracted to someone who didn't understand his work ethic. But he and Vanessa are committed to each other and will make it work."

Aiden and Van in the distant future . . .

"Are you sure you don't want to just tell me where we're going?"

"I'm sure."

"How sure?"

Aiden's subtle, deep laugh was a gift and a blessing that hadn't lost its value in the years we'd been together. "You used to love surprises," he reminded me.

Squeezing my eyes closed tighter, I tried not to frown at how dark everything was through the blindfold he'd put on me what felt like an hour or two ago. When he'd told me to trust him, and said he had a surprise, I wasn't sure what to expect, but I'd been optimistic. Mostly thrilled. But when he'd doubled the layers over my eyes, making sure I couldn't peek at anything through the top or the bottom of the material . . . I'd gotten suspicious.

It was our kids' faults.

"You don't remember what happened the last two times the kids tried to 'surprise' me?" I muttered, positive I heard him choke from behind the wheel of the car he'd led me into after blindfolding me halfway through our charter flight. "Yeah, you 'member."

The fact that he couldn't *contain* his choke confirmed that yeah, he did.

How the hell could he forget?

The second to last surprise I'd gotten had been from Sammy, who had come into the house carrying a garden snake like it was . . . I don't know what. A jump rope or something. I'd screamed so loud Aiden had run down the stairs—making the house rattle in the process. Both of them had gotten a real kick out of me screaming, but how was I supposed to know what was venomous and what wasn't? How did *they* know?

The last surprise I'd been blessed with had been to find Fiona drawing on the brand-new couch with a red Sharpie. Bless her little heart, she was trying to "make it pretty like mommy does." Except my art went on my tablet. It wasn't the end of the world, but it had still killed me inside a little just thinking about how long it was going to take to clean it off.

Mostly clean it off, as I'd learned. It wasn't called a permanent marker for nothing.

I'd never been a terror when I was little, probably because of my relationship with my mom, so I was pretty sure all three of them had gotten this shit from their dad because it sure as hell hadn't been me.

"We're almost there, Van, *trust me*," he replied, amusement lacing his familiar, beloved voice. After his whole body, it was the thing that grounded me the most. That reminded me of love and safety and just happiness.

. . . even when he said or did something that had me remembering my days of flipping him off out of his view.

Skating my hand to the left, brushing over the console between us, I slowly touched his thigh and felt my way up until my fingers touched his warm forearm.

He knew how much I trusted him. How much I would always trust him.

But still.

"I do," I told him just to soften the "but hurry up, okay? I want to know what we're doing and why we aren't in Maui even though you told me that's where we're going."

He must have let go of the steering wheel because a big palm plucked my hand off his arm and gave it a gentle squeeze, swallowing mine up whole. "We're going there after this. Tomorrow."

"Tomorrow?"

"Yes."

Was he laughing again? I squeezed my eyes closed even tighter like that would make me hear the nuances in his voice better. "And the kids are still meeting us there?"

"Yes."

"Do they know where we are?"

"Yes."

I turned my head in his direction and squeezed his big, rough palm right back. Somehow, he hadn't lost any of the calluses even in the years since he'd retired. An NFO champion finally. He'd said it was in the top five moments of his life.

I knew what the other four were.

"Does Diana know where we are?" I kept going, sounding so much like Sammy when he was on a roll I was going to be thinking about that for a while.

He was big like his dad, and just as protective but he had been scheming since he was two and he noticed everything. He was my child. God, I loved that kid.

I brought my attention back to Aiden who *was* choking again. Laughing just loudly enough under his breath I couldn't help but smile. "Of course she does, Muffin."

"So you've all been in on it?"

He squeezed my hand. "Yeah."

"But they're still meeting us in Maui tomorrow too?"

Aiden wasn't even trying to hide it anymore, he chuckled just about as loudly as ever. "Yes. It's only us today."

Where could we be that he'd want to surprise me with? We had only left the kids at home one other time, and that had been for two days to go to Zac's wedding. When Gray had called us the first night then and told us he missed us, even the big guy had gotten teary.

We had moved from San Diego to Austin a year ago so I could be closer to the only other family I had—Diana and Oscar, who had somehow ended up in Austin by some sheer miracle right before Aiden retired. It had seemed like fate. As nice as the California weather was, we both wanted what we hadn't had growing up: an extended family. And since Diana's family was my family, her parents took our boys in like they were their own too. It filled my heart with something I couldn't describe to see them care for my children, to have grandparents like I never had, and the ones Aiden had adored. I was pretty sure it helped them too after everything they had been through. You could never have too much love in your life.

But that had nothing to do with me being blindfolded in a car in God knows where.

I really did used to love surprises.

I fidgeted. "Can I have a clue?"

His laugh did that same thing again. "We're going to be there in less than three minutes."

If I wasn't so curious or excited, I might have wanted to take a quick nap. I'd slept my way through the chartered flight we'd taken, opening my eyes only once to find Aiden asleep in the seat across from mine, just as dead to the world. We'd been up until three in the morning, trying to pack the kids' suitcases and laughing over the random shit we found in their drawers.

Gray had a rock collection that consisted of 90 percent gravel.

Sammy had sweet and sour packs from a fast food chain we literally never ate at. I'd been wondering what he'd been spending his allowance money on because there was no way that boy was trading his lunch.

Fiona had a lip balm obsession.

Even sweet Leo had a collection of old toys we'd discovered beneath our bed.

Right before we'd left Diana's, she had wrapped her arms around my neck, leaned into my ear and whispered, "I'm gonna marry Louie, ma."

Louie being Diana's youngest nephew slash son.

Aiden hadn't thought it was that funny but I did. Di was going to shit her pants when I told her Fiona was eyeing her little Lou. The thought made me smile.

How fucking lucky had I gotten? I asked myself then as Aiden turned the car to a sharp right just as he slowed down and seemed to park. Maybe the beginning of my life hadn't been the best, or anywhere near it, but now. . . .

I'd fight to death to keep what I had. To protect it.

I listened and waited, the sound of the driver side door opening and closing before mine did the same, a blast of heat instantly making me wince.

Where were we that it could be this . . . ?

The familiar scent and energy coming off Aiden radiated from him as he leaned across me, undoing my seat belt before slowly moving my legs and upper body around to position me to get out of the car. But before I stood, those big hands started touching around my face, at whatever he'd used as a blindfold that he gently removed before covering my eyes with his palms to block out the sun.

I blinked a few times, my heart warming at his gesture, and when I thought I could handle it, I tugged his hands away, down toward my lap, instantly taking his fingers in mine while I got used to the light.

And when I did, I blinked some more, sure, no, *positive*, I was imagining what the hell I was looking at.

There was no way. . . .

No way. . . .

I laughed as I met Aiden's eyes, taking in the small smile over his even-more handsome face. "Are you for real right now?"

He nodded, dead serious.

"Are we doing what I think we're doing?" I asked, my voice higher than it probably ever had been from the sheer shock.

He wrapped his free hand around both of ours. "Today's technically our real anniversary," he said like I could have forgotten. We celebrated the day that he'd said all those beautiful words to me years ago as our anniversary, instead of . . . well . . . the day we'd actually gotten married.

"I know," I said, looking around us, taking in the subtle differences. The building had been painted. The sign had been replaced by one that seemed more ecofriendly. But other than that . . . I smiled so hard my cheeks hurt and shook my head. "We're really doing this?"

"I thought about doing it in Hawaii, but then I figured we might as well come back to the place that started it all," he explained, gesturing behind him, or maybe around us.

Fucking Las Vegas.

The same chapel where we'd gotten married a decade ago.

I wasn't sure whether I wanted to laugh or whistle, so I laughed, then whistled. . . . So overwhelmed . . . so surprised. . . .

"Diana said you would rather get married again in your underwear than wear a white dress," he said. "So I figured, let's do it again, but better." He let go of our hands and fished in his pocket, pulling out a glittering band that he tipped toward me. "I'm ready this time."

My God. My ovaries. "Big guy . . ."

He petted my fingers. "If I could go back in time, I wouldn't have taken a nap and had to come find you. I would have had a ring for you. Would have kissed you when they told us to. Smiled in our picture."

I laughed and that made his beautiful, special smile bigger.

Aiden, my big guy, leaned forward and dropped his voice. "I'm sorry we didn't do it right the first time."

"The first time was just fine," I promised him.

He squeezed my fingers a little tighter, moving toward me even more so that we could press our foreheads together. "I thought we could do everything the same. I got us reservations for *Cirque du Lune* and the same restaurant." Aiden brushed his mouth against mine. "And maybe

ACKNOWLEDGMENTS

First and foremost, the greatest readers in the universe—I can't thank you enough for your love and support these last few years. Each and every email, message, post, and review means the world to me. You guys never cease to amaze me with your wittiness and kindness. I don't know what I did in another lifetime to deserve you all, but I'll be forever thankful.

A massive thank you to my Canadian friends who answered all of my annoying questions: Hope, Romancia, Julie, Stacey, Sandra, and Kathleen. Ashley and Naomi, my title wouldn't be what it is without your vast knowledge of prepositions 😊 Thank you! Letitia Hasser at RBA Designs, you know you're the (wo)man. Lauren Abramo and Jane Dystel at Dystel & Goderich for being the best agents.

To the two people who helped me so much with Winnie: Dell Wilson and Eva Marina. I'm so thankful for your patience, support, and friendship that my words would never be able to do my appreciation justice. Winnie wouldn't be Winnie without you two.

A great big thank you to the people who mean the world to me: Mom and Dad, Ale, Eddie, Raul, Isaac, Kaitlyn, Nana, Nico, my Letchford family, and the rest of my Zapata/Navarro family. And last but never least, my three guys: Chris, Dor, and Kai. Love you.

ABOUT THE AUTHOR

Mariana Zapata lives in a small town in Colorado with her husband and two oversized children—her beloved Great Danes, Dorian and Kaiser. When she's not writing, she's reading, spending time outside, forcing kisses on her boys, or pretending to write.